Mrs. Valerie Hill
37 Colenutts Road
Ryde
Isle Of Wight
PO33 3HT

CW01249476

Emma's War

BY THE SAME AUTHOR

The Shop on Coppins Bridge
The Family on Coppins Bridge
Out of the Dust
Ebbtide at Coppins Bridge

EMMA'S WAR

Elizabeth Daish

CENTURY
LONDON SYDNEY AUCKLAND JOHANNESBURG

Copyright © Elizabeth Daish 1989

All rights reserved

First published in Great Britain in 1989 by
Century Hutchinson Ltd
Brookmount House, 62-65 Chandos Place
London WC2N 4NW

Century Hutchinson South Africa (Pty) Ltd
PO Box 337, Bergvlei 2012, South Africa

Century Hutchinson Australia Pty Ltd
89-91 Albion Street, Surry Hills, New South Wales 2010
Australia

Century Hutchinson New Zealand Ltd
PO Box 40-086, Glenfield, Auckland 10
New Zealand

British Library Cataloguing in Publication Data
Daish, Elizabeth
Emma's war.
I. Title
823'.914 [F]

ISBN 0 7126 3476 2

Printed in Great Britain by Mackays of Chatham PLC,
Chatham, Kent

*To Derek, Simon and Sally
and in memory of Mary*

Contents

PART ONE   Peaches and Champagne   1

PART TWO   Beer and Buttercups   151

PART THREE Coffee and Syringa   297

PART ONE
Peaches and Champagne

1

The pin didn't go in very far, just enough to make Emma twist away from the woman who was tugging at the side seam of the dress.

'Sorry, Nurse,' the sewing-room assistant said, and Emma stood straight, holding her breath while the tape measure checked her bust and waist.

I feel like a plaster dummy in a shop window, having material draped round me to look like a garment, thought Emma. The woman had taken a cut-out nurse's uniform dress from a pile and was more or less moulding it to the girl's figure, breathing heavily and muttering instructions through a palisade of pins sticking out between clenched lips.

What if she swallows one? I'm not really a nurse. I have no idea what to do if she chokes. I don't know what I'd do if anything happened to anyone. Why did I come here? I'll never be any good. I must have been out of my mind. Emma let out her breath slowly, then gasped. It's funny how loud and awkward breathing is as soon as you begin to think about it.

'Can you hold your arm up, Nurse?' Emma obediently put up an arm, so violently that a shower of pins fell from the pale blue denim. The woman sighed and the pins between her lips were in danger of being inhaled.

'Sorry,' said Emma. She felt more humble than she'd been since she was in the fourth form in her old school. In the fifth and sixth, she had built up a sense of self-importance with the seniority and the relaxed discipline and it had been a good time; so good that she hadn't known it at the time and had thought this feeling would go on for ever.

'A big fish in a small pond,' said Aunt Emily, and now, two months after leaving school, she was a very small fish in a strange town, a strange house and a very different set of circumstances.

The sewing-room assistant eased off the dress, scratching Emma's neck as it was dragged over her head. 'Matron says you are coming in on Sunday. I'll have the first one made and in your room with the collars and aprons, and the others will be ready before you send it to the laundry. I'll make up the first cap to show you how it's done, but after, you'll have to get one of the others to help you.'

'Thank you, Miss . . .'

'They all call me Sarah,' said the woman, shaking the sleeve of the pinned dress as if it wasn't *her* choice of name. Emma put on her thick tweed skirt and jumper and pushed her fingers through her hair. She hadn't thought to bring a comb and she couldn't ask Sarah to lend her one, after staring down at the sprinkling of greasy dandruff on the woman's shoulders. She crammed her beanie hat on to the back of her head and hoped she didn't look as untidy as she felt.

She sensed Sarah's disapproval. Another flighty young girl with no idea what it would be like to nurse nearly a hundred disabled ladies.

Sarah smiled with the superiority of special knowledge. 'You start on Wing Six, with Sister Cary. She won't stand for nonsense,' she added accusingly, and dusted the ends of cotton from the polished work bench. Emma stood still, not knowing what was expected of her. 'That's the lot then, Nurse. I'll have it all ready for you.'

Emma pushed open the heavy mahogany doors of the sewing-room and her shoes squeaked on the wooden stairs, which were heavily polished with sticky Ronuk. She came out by the main doorway of the nurses' home where tall slender pillars supporting the arched porch cast long shadows over the driveway and the trees sent down a fine spiral of leaves in the sunshine.

She paused in the doorway, awed by the dignity and solidity of the buildings. There was an air of confidence and beauty about it all, as if only the very best quality had been used in the fabric and construction of the place, rather like Osborne House on the Isle of Wight where Queen Victoria had lived in style and sadness for so many years. Inside, one knew that the furnishings would be expensive, pleasing and made to last.

The main building was across the drive, beyond the central flower beds with a porch similar to but larger than the one under which she stood. A girl in blue uniform shrugged into a cloak as she came out, a gauzy butterfly cap poised on her tightly-coiled hair, the white wings catching the air. She walked over to the nurses' home and glanced curiously at Emma, then passed without a word. She looked sure of herself, superior, and had a pen and pencil poking out of her breast pocket and a pendant watch pinned to the pocket flap. She must be quite senior, thought Emma, and walked out between the intricate wrought-iron gates. She scuffed in the dry leaves, then remembering the high windows behind her she walked sedately, following the high stone wall and the Cotswold stone night nurses' cottage, along the lane to the main road. She ran for a bus that would take her even further out into the suburbs of Bristol and sat looking at her reflection in the grimy window.

'What happened?' Her mother poured tea and handed Emma a plate of fish-paste sandwiches, then settled down to get every bit of information she could from her only daughter.

'You know the building on the right?' said Emma. Her mother nodded, having viewed the outside of the buildings from every angle short of going into the grounds. 'That's the nurses' home, and down some wooden stairs at the side they have a big sewing-room and stores of linen for the whole place. That's where I went to be fitted. They showed me a nurse's room; not the one I'll have as it had someone's things in it, but it was very nice. Then I went to be fitted for my uniform.' Emma giggled. 'She had a mouth full of pins, just like old Miss Scovel who used to sew for Gran. I thought she'd swallow one, but she didn't.'

The BBC news came in disjointed spits from the wireless set, and Mrs Clare Dewar patted the set to cajole it into better service. 'It needs a new accumulator,' she said. 'Not that I want to hear news about another war. I had enough in the Great War, when all our best men went and got killed.'

Emma put on a thick jumper and combed her hair before she drank her tea. Mum had the idea that a coal fire wasn't necessary until Christmas. It saved fuel and there wasn't a grate to clean, but the one-bar electric fire wasn't much comfort when the sun went down and the dark evenings set in.

'You still want to go there? Don't you think, now you've been inside the place, that a nice little job at the BAC would be better? Bristol Aircraft are crying out for girls with good General Schools Certificates. You could do well with your maths and your matric. The pay's good and you wouldn't have to work too hard.'

Emma sipped her tea, half-listening. She'd heard it all before so many times that she let it slide over her as if it were two other people talking. She could make the right noises automatically. It had been like this ever since she'd begged to be allowed to stay on the Isle of Wight until she finished school, even when her parents had moved to Bristol, where work was plentiful and houses were springing up like rows of box-shaped mushrooms.

She'd held out for once, desperate to do as she wanted and to stay on the Island, and was surprised at her success with her mother in persuading her that it was better to stay on and take her exams without changing schools.

That last summer on the Island had been wonderful without her mother nagging and asking questions about everyone she met. Dear Aunt Emily. Emma thought back with a sense of tender nostalgia. She'd let her come and go as she pleased, trusting her to do nothing daft and taking a vicarious delight in all Emma's adventures, and so it had been morally impossible to do anything to make her upset. The pale, insignificant-looking unmarried aunt who had cared for her without any outward show of affection but with whom Emma had always had complete rapport, was more than a mother and much more than any of her school friends.

Emma had cycled all over the Island, going as far as Freshwater and back in one evening, twelve miles away from her home near Shide, where Aunt Emily now lived, having bought the house from Emma's parents when they left for Bristol. She could almost feel the swoop of the curving road by the Downs and longed to lie in the grass overlooking the cliffs, with the salt smell and the gulls and the small winding lanes. She bit her lip. She missed her friends.

'Not hungry? I cut them fresh just before you came in,' said Clare Dewar. Emma bit on a sandwich and chewed the rubbery bread. How were Don and Joan? And Peter, the boy with the nearly white blond hair and the lopsided smile. Why think of him? She'd never been out with him and never liked him much, but some said he had a crush on her.

'Well, if you've finished, I'll cover them with a plate and they'll do for your father.' Mrs Dewar went on talking but said nothing of interest and Emma helped herself to a piece of shop cake filled with jam and cream.

It had all been so good. Cowes Week, with fewer foreign ships than usual because of the threat of war in the summer of 1939, but plenty of visitors with whom to flirt and run from when the pace quickened – boys in camp and young men from the racing yachts. Nothing serious had happened but she was glad to get away from boys like Phillip and Ken who had suddenly grown up and started heavy breathing each time she went to the Medina cinema with either of them.

'What's so funny?' her mother asked. 'You'll laugh on the other side of your face if this war lasts for a long time.'

'I was just thinking about the woman in the sewing-room,' Emma lied. Phillip and she had sat for General Schools at the same time and been in the chapel choir. She wondered if she should write to him, just to say hello and to tell him that she had put her first foot on the very bottom rung of the ladder to a nursing career.

'I said, did you see the Matron again?'

Emma smiled. 'Sorry, I was miles away. No, I imagine I shan't see much of her, thank goodness. Much too toffy-nosed. "I hope you realise that it is a privilege to work here. You have seen our motto, Miss Dewar? *Love Serves*. We expect every pupil probationer who comes here to remember it. Nursing is a vocation and until you are old enough to be accepted for London Training, you will find here an invaluable lesson in hospital routine and professional etiquette." And all I did was to say yes, Matron, no, Matron, thank you, Matron.'

'Sauce, filling your head with ideas of going to

London. There are good hospitals in Bristol and then I can keep an eye on you and see something of you. That's if you stay in nursing. I can't think why you want to do it. A lot of hard work and no thanks at the end of it, and very poor pay.'

Emma shrugged. 'I want to give it a try. I can leave if I don't like it, or they don't like me.'

She took the cups and stacked them on the tray, putting it on the table in the bright new kitchen. She looked about her with distaste. It was all so bright and shining. 'Not a dark corner in the house,' her mother had said more than once with pride. 'I'd never have an old house again.'

The linoleum in the bathroom smelled strongly and still tried to roll up at the edges. 'Help me put the stool over it,' said Mrs Dewar. 'I nearly tripped up. Have to get your father to put a tack in it.' Emma looked at the pattern of orange and green circles and squares. The house was cheerful and aggressively clean, and she knew that if she lived there for twenty years, it would never be her home.

She ached for the faded red wall-paper in the Victorian house they had left, even with the damp smell in the drawing room that was hardly ever used, and for the graceful chairs and chiffoniers that had been thrown out as Clare Dewar refused to bring woodworm into a new house. The modern three piece suite and angular sideboard and dining room chairs gave Emma no pleasure, and the dressing table drawer in her room was inclined to stick.

'Well, I suppose it's nice to say I have a daughter who is a nurse,' said Mrs Dewar, smugly. 'With the war and all, people like to have something to talk about.' She watched Emma pack the leather suitcase. 'You don't need much. You'll be home in your off-duty,' she said. Emma put in a change of everything and plenty of stockings, her toilet bag and a few books. She hadn't liked to ask Matron when she could have time off to come home again, and when her mother told her to make sure to ask as soon as she got to the Home, she was uncertain who would tell her.

'I'll ask, but I don't think I'll be in for a while. There'll be things to do, I suppose.' What would she be doing? What work would they expect her to do? She'd seen wheelchairs and basket-work bathchairs filled with ladies being perambulated round the extensive and well-kept grounds of the Home. It was difficult to imagine what was wrong with them. She packed furiously, trying to think of other matters, but in the back of her mind was the suspicion that *The Haven of Comfort For Crippled Gentlefolk* was not what she wanted. It wouldn't be real nursing in a hospital where people got better, but until she was old enough to train, there were few alternatives other than fever nursing.

The next two days dragged away. The news was bad and Emma's parents seemed permanently glued to the wireless set whenever they had time to spare. Army lorries parked by the Artillery Hall, and the Territorial Centre hummed with self-importance. Men who had long outgrown the age for uniform, thronged the various offices in answer to calls for Air Raid Wardens, Red Cross and St John's Ambulance personnel and the newly-formed Local Defence Volunteers, and Emma felt that her family hardly noticed when she left for the huge mansion on the Downs.

The thick door swung to with a barely audible sigh and Emma reported for duty, wearing the first of the thin blue dresses and a cap pinned precariously to her loose hair. Sister Cary clicked her gold pen into the top pocket of her tailored silk dress and her lips formed a thin line.

'That won't do, Nurse.' She handed Emma a clean comb and a mirror. 'Do something with it before I come back.' She swept from the office, five foot nothing of latent displeasure, and Emma suspected that this was the usual greeting for all new nurses on Wing Six. She damped her hair with water from the tap and basin in the corner of the room, trying to recall how to make a roll of hair that wouldn't fall down, like one she had seen in a magazine with pictures of ATS girls, neatly dressed with immaculate hair. With the help of Kirby grips she had brought to reinforce the anchoring of the cap, she managed a reasonably scraped-back effect.

'Better, but not good. Come with me.' Meekly, Emma followed the tiny dynamo to the corridor. 'There are many things to remember from the beginning. The people here are *residents*, not patients, and live in the *wings* of the Home as we have no wards. There are seven wings, each with its own dining room and sitting room and sun loggia. All residents who are able, eat in the dining room and the rest have meals in their rooms.' She looked at her watch. 'There is time to take the menu round before chapel.'

'The menu?'

'Yes, the menu, and you will say Sister every time you address me, Nurse. I shall call you Nurse because it is better that the residents should look on you as such, but your contemporaries will call you Pro Dewar as you are only a pupil probationer. Now, I shall come with you while you take the menu and I can tell you about our ladies.' She knocked on the first door in the curving corridor and opened the door before anyone said, 'Come in.' Briskly, Sister told the emaciated woman in bed that this was the new nurse and here was the menu. No, she couldn't have just hot milk, she was to choose something from the menu and she could have hot milk before bedtime.

The woman closed her eyes as if the effort of

thinking was too great. Sister looked at her and said quietly, 'Put minced chicken and champagne for Mrs Otley.' Emma glanced at the menu. Neither of the items was shown there. Outside the room, Sister smiled bleakly. 'Mrs Otley is on special diet. Always offer her the menu even though she never chooses from it, then write special diet on the list.' She saw Emma's questioning eyes. 'She doesn't know she is dying. Everything must be done as usual, or she will think we have given her up. 'For the first time, Emma saw a trace of humanity in the pale blue eyes. 'I run an efficient wing. I stand no nonsense and Mrs Otley was very difficult at one time; very spoiled and disruptive to discipline when she came here first. If I relax too much now, and treat her too gently, then she will know she is dying, but we give her champagne for supper and she thinks she is favoured because she made a fuss.'

The other rooms were nearly all empty. The residents who occupied them were in the huge chapel which was the centre of the Home, and in the spacious four-bedded room at the end of the corridor, the beds were neatly covered with pretty floral quilts as if the residents were all walking cases and up all day, ambulant mild heart conditions and arthritic cases.

'Excuse me, Sister. Where do I take the menu?' Sister Cary hesitated in her progress back to the office. 'I don't know where to find the kitchen,' said Emma.

'The menu goes to Cook, down that turning and down the stairs. You ask Sister Ambrose in the dispensary for the champagne for Mrs Otley and the sherry for Mrs Delawear.' She walked away, each step filled with a kind of pent-up rage as if she was beset by fools.

The kitchen was bright with polished brass, warm and very large, and when cook glanced at the list she gave Emma a friendly smile. Another Pro was loading a trolley with baskets of fruit and bottles of mineral water. She stared at Emma and half-smiled, pityingly. 'New today?' Emma nodded. 'Where are you?' Emma told her and the girl laughed. 'Snap. See you in Green Alley.' She leaned against the trolley and sent it over towards the lift, and Emma went to find the dispensary.

She knocked softly and had no reply. She knocked again and thought she heard a hurried movement. A deep voice called 'Come in,' and Emma found herself in a long room lined with polished mahogany cupboards and shelves, ceramic jars and boxes. Sister Ambrose stood by the sink under the window, an array of bottles beside her. There was a strong smell of wine. On a tray were glasses of various sizes, each one labelled with the name of a resident. Emma saw that the bottles contained whisky, sherry, Sauterne, burgundy and brandy and there were several half-bottles of champagne of various vintages and dryness.

Sister Ambrose picked up a bottle of Sauterne and carefully poured exactly three ounces into a measuring jug and then into a cut glass with a name on it. She measured sherry into the glass for Mrs Delawear. 'Champagne for Mrs Otley? *More* champagne?' she enquired, accusingly.

Emma nodded and then hastily said, 'yes, Sister.' The clumsily-built woman went to a cupboard and unlocked the door. She brought out a half-bottle of champagne and handed it reluctantly to Emma.

'I suppose it has to be this one. It's the last of that batch. Very dry, very fine,' she said, as if she had sampled some from each batch. Emma could well believe that she sampled a lot of the wine, as the smell was greater each time Sister Ambrose pushed past in the confined space of the dispensary. 'Is she on peaches yet?'

'I don't know, Sister. I'm new today.' Emma picked up the glass and the bottle and made for the door.

'Tray, Nurse! Tray! Hasn't Sister Cary told you that you never carry anything unless you use a tray?' She gestured toward a pile of papier mâché trays and Emma put the glass and the bottle on one, steadying the bottle with one hand.

In the corridor, she nearly dropped the champagne, looked round guiltily and put the bottle under her arm until she reached the wing kitchen, where she then walked demurely, holding the tray properly.

'Where have you been?' The voice that Emma was learning to hate had a querulous note.

'I had to fetch the champagne, Sister.'

'No need to take all day.' The girl who had been in the kitchen before stood behind Sister, grinning. 'Go with Pro Evans and fetch the six wheelchair ladies from chapel. Hurry, it's nearly time for Green Alley and then dinner.'

'Where's Green Alley?' asked Emma as the two girls hurried along to the chapel.

'You don't know? You really don't know? Oh, let me savour this moment of innocence! Is it possible that anyone, but anyone, doesn't know about Green Alley?' Emma blushed at the mocking, cultured voice; the kind of voice used by superior sales staff in deeply-carpeted dress salons which had such a subduing effect on girls like her.

'Well, how am I to know if nobody tells me?' said Emma, defensively.

'Spirit? I'm glad to see a bit of spirit. I'd begun to think you were quite the little mouse.' Her voice was more friendly. 'You'll need it, and don't let *her* get you down. Come on, I'll show you.' She glanced back along the deserted corridor. 'We'll take a short cut. There's one Green Alley on each wing.' She gabbed Emma's hand. 'We're not supposed to use it as a cut-through but it saves ages and everyone does. There! What do you think?'

From the wing corridor to the main corridor was a linking passage lined from floor to ceiling with green tiles. Lavatories and washrooms, bathrooms and sluices were all covered with the same shining green. 'We have our little euphemisms, my dear.' Once more the voice was mocking. 'Must keep up the illusion that this is a home from home, where everyone will get better, everyone is happy and nobody ever dies.'

Her face had clouded but she laughed, her mirth sounding hollow in the dim place. 'So they don't go to the lavatory, they go down Green Alley, they never have bedpans, they retire with help. They never suffer, they have medicine, herbal tisanes and stimulants, not drink of course, but carefully prescribed spirits and wine if they ask for it or need it.' she shrugged. 'And if they are dying, they have hothouse peaches whatever season of the year it is, and champagne. They never die, they leave the Home. It's all done so bloody well,' she said with grudging approval. 'But it's all so bloody false.'

She saw the troubled expression on Emma's face. 'Take no notice of me. Nobody does. I'm a bitch. I talk like this and then do as I'm told. I disapprove of sham but I see the need, the kindness even. In its own macabre way, this is a wonderful place, and I can't wait to get out and back to London, back to civilisation and the nice clean smell of fog after *this*.'

A couple of butterfly caps hurried past them and the walking residents came slowly from the chapel. They wore dark veils. 'I thought this place was C of E,' said Emma.

Anglican. Very High Church and don't you forget it. If you take anyone into chapel, for goodness sake ask which side they want to be, or you'll be bobbing up and down each time you pass in front of the altar.' Emma stared up at the beautiful roof and the intricate screen. It was a bigger chapel than the Wesleyan which she attended at home, such an enormous place for a hundred people, and Evans told her that the resident priest had a lovely cottage of Cotswold stone within the grounds.

'It's another world,' she murmured. 'It's like a nunnery.'

'You'll think so when a man appears. They don't see a pair of trousers from one month's end to the next. The vicar is ancient and apart from visitors, the only men who come here are the doctors. There's a very handsome orthopaedic man who causes a few flutters, but no one else of interest, and they don't exactly encourage us to meet anyone! Have you seen the off-duty rota?'

Emma nodded. After the freedom of the Island with Aunt Emily, she could hardly believe her eyes. Two mornings off from ten until one o'clock, when she must be back in uniform for lunch, two afternoons from two to four, an evening before her day off never the same day, week by week, followed by the morning after it until eleven. If she stayed overnight in the nurses' home to sleep before her day off, she must report back at ten-thirty after going out for the evening, and sign the book. If she slept out, she had to hand in a note signed by her parents or guardian or the invitation to stay with friends.

I'm lucky, she thought. I can go home to my parents. I can stay out late for at least one night a week. She fetched another resident and put on her apron to help in Green Alley. She assisted at two bed baths and helped lift several of the bedridden arthritics, and when she had finished collecting dinner trays and tidying lockers, she was more tired than she cared to admit. She went down to supper and ate hungrily. The food was plentiful and good, with full dishes of cheese and butter on each table and a choice of dishes.

She thought of the meagre supper her mother would be preparing. Never much of a cook, Clare Dewar lacked the imagination to do a great deal with poor supplies. Well, I shan't starve here, thought Emma. She wondered what was happening in the world outside. At no time had she heard a wireless, although there was an impressive set in each sitting room. Nobody cares here. We are at war but it doesn't touch them. After only one day I am losing my grip on reality. She had almost forgotten what day of the week it was and it was quite a shock to realise that it was still only Sunday. Day off on Thursday, three days away; two if she thought she was going home on Wednesday night. Suddenly, it seemed a very long time. Her feet hurt, her bedroom was too warm with unaccustomed central heating and she was too scared to go down to the Common Room where the other Pros had gathered. Emma collected her sponge bag, had a deep hot bath and went to bed.

2

'I can't explain. I've told you about it, but you'd have to be there to see the place and the people. You don't understand.' It was impossible to make her mother feel anything but hostility towards the Home.

'All I know is that you seem to work until all hours, get ticked off for the slightest thing and have so little off-duty that you dash home and out again in five minutes. I wanted you to come with me when I went to tea with Mrs Hammond. She's heard all about you and it would be nice for me to have someone to show off for a change. She has a nephew in the army. I want you to have your photograph taken in uniform.' She sniffed. 'No use asking your father. I can't get him to go anywhere with me even if he had the time.' She looked out at the long piece of field grass which she fondly hoped one day would turn into a beautiful garden, ignoring the fact that all the neighbours grumbled about the wireworm-riddled clay soil underneath and the undeniable fact that there wasn't a born gardener in the Dewar family. 'When he'll start on the garden, I don't know,' she added, with a sigh.

'It's not as bad as you imagine, Mum. I work hard and get fed up sometimes but I've only been there a couple of weeks. I expect I'll get to know the other girls better soon.' She tried to look relaxed. The other girls! How could she explain the effect they had on her? The casual, expensive clothes, the easy laughter and conversation with the more intellectual residents, the 'In' jokes about people they knew or had met; important people, titled people, none of whom Emma had come closer to than on the cover of a magazine or a mention on the wireless.

'The less you have to do with them, the better. They don't sound our sort at all. A lot of stuck-up madams, if you ask me.' Mrs Dewar looked glumly into the larder. 'What would you like for supper? I forgot that you were coming in tonight. The sausages were for tomorrow.'

'Cheese on toast will do,' said Emma, trying not to think of the meal in progress at the Home, and wondering what she could do on a day off, in the middle of the week when most people were working. Her mother gave her the bread knife and left her to prepare her own supper.

'I said I'd go up to the Church Hall. They've started first aid classes,' said Mrs Dewar. 'I don't suppose you'd come?'

The evening to which Emma had looked forward with such eagerness stretched ahead empty. 'All right,' she said. 'It might be a laugh.'

The blacked-out street was still littered with builder's rubble and dark spaces showed where phase three of the estate had yet to be started. Emma held a torch, pointing downwards to show the uneven path until they came to the main road. It was cold, with the promise of fog later. Emma pulled her short coat closer and wished she'd worn a beret. The Church Hall was surrounded by sandbags, piled high in the first enthusiasm of war, looking as if the building would collapse without their support. A tarpaulin shielded the entrance and, inside, the lights were murky and the makeshift blackout gave a funereal gloom. An old tortoise stove sulked at one end of the long room and the small group of first-aiders stopped rolling bandages to stare at the newcomers.

The curate, directed as usual to the least exciting

evening programme, sat dejectedly on the edge of the stage and the local headmaster of the infants' school sat behind a trestle as if the desk gave him status and confidence.

Everyone talked of the news. Someone produced a portable wireless set and the nine o'clock news was received in silence. Emma's lips twitched. It was dreadful to laugh but the sight of Miss Harris, bandaged over her cardigan with a breast bandage that had taken Miss Johns all evening to do, still wearing her hat and rubber overboots, sitting with saintly patience until the programme was over and Miss Johns emerged from her trance to disentangle her; the sight of the curate with a tuft of hair poking out of the back of his mastoid bandage, and the headmaster with an arm turning a shade of navy blue under the too-tightly applied crêpe bandage – it was all just too much.

If enemy action destroyed breasts and mastoids, all would be well, but Miss Johns confessed that the breast bandage was satisfying and the only one she knew. Emma suspected that Doris, the girl bandaging the curate, wanted an excuse to press him to her developing bosom as she stood behind him to apply the bandage, and to be able to look into his eyes when she did the front bits. They must be hard up for men if that's the only one young enough for pretty little Doris, Emma thought.

She looked round the room. Of course, there would be no men, or very few of her type. Emma liked boys a few years older than herself and they would be going into the Forces. On the island, the war brought even more youth, to Albany Barracks, to the Navy ship installations and boatyards, but here, would there be any left after a while? She turned away and strolled to the other end of the room, absentmindedly folding a sling. She sat on a splintery chair and watched the others talking, packing up thermos flasks and putting away the bandage rollers. It was a night out for them, a social occasion when they could meet and get to know people who had lived in the district before the new houses came and to find friends among other newcomers.

Clare Dewar was flushed with pleasure as they walked home. 'Mrs Harris said you were very polite to her.' Emma couldn't recall talking to the woman but she smiled sweetly. 'And the curate wanted to know all about you. Such a nice man, and young for a busy parish like this one. He's not married.'

'Not my type,' said Emma. 'Really Mum, you think that everything in trousers is a possible husband for me! Remember? I'm going to be a nurse. Florence Nightingale and all that. I am going to marry my profession.'

Her mother fumbled for her front door key. 'What rubbish,' she said, comfortably. 'You won't last. I heard all about those boys you met when you stayed with Aunt Em. No, she didn't breathe a word, but Ida wrote and told me all the things you left out, and she doesn't miss much.' Triumphantly, as if opening the Houses of Parliament, she turned the key and flung open the front door, spoiling the effect by having to grope for the light switch. 'He's out again. Says it's LDV but they meet in the Bell. Lot of defence they do there – and he knows that beer goes acid on him.'

Emma fixed the blackout and made cocoa. The electric fire glowed with a dull red reluctance. The brand new open fireplace, as yet unused, gleamed behind it. 'When's the coal coming?' Emma asked.

'Oh, it's in the coalhouse but I'm not starting fires yet. Then I'd never get him out of the house in the evenings.' Emma filled a hot water bottle and made for the stairs. 'Quite a nice evening,' said her mother as she sat over the fire, warming her hands round a second mug of cocoa. 'I'll wait up. He never remembers to lock up.'

There must be more to life than that. Emma stared at the blanked window of her room and pulled the hot water bottle up to the chilly patch in her back. At home on the Island, she had noticed how little her parents had in common, and they had gone their own ways with a fairly cheerful acceptance that they were married and stuck with each other for life, but they didn't show their differences in public.

But this was now home, and with strangers they had turned to look at themselves and at their marriage, thrown together in suddenly discovered loneliness. Away from all that was familiar, they each knew that there was no comfort in the other.

Emma missed the central heating of the nurses' home and her feet were cold. She shifted the bottle down the bed and heard her father come in. Muffled voices and heavy footsteps came upstairs, her father explaining, her mother nagging softly as if to keep it between themselves.

If only I could have stayed on the Island, Emma thought. Dear Aunt Emily would have made sure she had a warm bed and a good fire in the wide hearth even when the weather was quite mild. Had she bought the house near Shide where Emma had lived all her life just to keep the continuity intact while Emma was busy studying for the General Schools exams?

She thought back, able to see more clearly now that she had left, and she felt almost guilty that her pale but energetic aunt should have quietly made sure that she could stay on the Island while her parents moved to Bristol.

'But you love the big house on the Mall!' Emma had said when her aunt revealed that she had sold it and would buy the house in which her sister Clare lived with her husband and Emma, their only child. 'You lived with Gran there until she died and you have made the garden beautiful.'

'It wasn't the same after Mother died,' said Emily firmly as if to make sure that no gratitude was necessary. 'Too big for me now that the rest of the family have scattered, and I can make something of the garden here when they've gone.' She smiled. 'Clare tried to copy everything we had on the Mall, even to the wall-paper, so it will be like home, and with you still here, I shall enjoy myself. I never see your Aunt Lizzie now and Janey is out East with Alex and her family. They adopted your cousin, Vikki, you know, when her mother didn't want her, and heaven knows when they'll see England again now that a war is likely. The others live on the mainland and we send a card at Christmas, so I'm really alone now or will be once your parents have left for Bristol to that nice new house your mother keeps on about.'

Emma looked fraught. 'You sold the big house and bought this one to make sure they had enough money for the new one, didn't you?'

For a moment, Emily looked startled and a pink flush coloured her cheeks. 'Don't you ever let me hear you say that again, Emma! What I do with my money is my own affair and your father does his best to provide even if he has to leave the Island to get work.' She spoke more softly. 'They aren't bad people, only misfits with each other, and they've kept you down more than I like. It was all right when your Gran was alive, as she had a knack of keeping us together, but now I can't say I miss many of them any more except Sidney in America.' Aunt Emily had a wicked twinkle in her eyes. 'My brother Edward had no sense of humour; nor has your mother, come to think of it. Don't know where you get that giggle from, my girl, not your father, that's for sure, and your Aunt Lizzie wasn't any better. I can't abide her boy one bit. He pulled the cat's tail something cruel the last time they were here and he's too big to slap. Almost a grown man and acts like a spoiled child, which he is.' She laughed. 'He's bigger than me, so I wouldn't dare spank him but Lizzie went off in a huff when I gave him a piece of my mind. Lizzie was always out for number one, even as a child, and thinks the sun shines out of his spotty face.'

She looked out of the window to see if Clare Dewar was coming back from the shops, but the road was empty, so she settled down in her chair again.

'It must have been nice to have so many brothers and sisters,' said Emma, wistfully. 'I hate being an only child. You must get fed up, with me running to you every time mother gets cross, but you are the only one I can talk to.'

'Rubbish,' said Emily but she looked pleased. 'You're only a child yet and don't know anything about life. You wait, my girl. There's more to come than school and hockey and silly giggling with the boys in the back seat of the Medina cinema.' She chuckled. 'You don't think I never hear, do you? Where's that nice Phillip these days – got too busy with his hands, did he?'

'Aunt Emily!' Emma went scarlet. 'Well, he is a bit intense, sometimes,' she admitted. 'Nice though, and I enjoy dancing with him and we like the same films. I hope I get more passes in General Schools than he did but he's brilliant at maths and I haven't a hope there.' She fiddled with her pile of textbooks and looked away. 'He doesn't do as much work as I do and wants me to go out this evening.'

'Well, you won't if you sit there talking to me. I'll knit and look out for your mother. I have to hand over some papers from the bank and they'll be off next week, so mind you're nice to them and say you look forward to joining them later, after the exams.'

Emma made a rude face. 'You'll make a rod for your own back and for mine if they think you don't want to live in Bristol,' Emily reminded her. 'They could still take you with them and make you change schools, and that would put you back. I know you want to be a nurse, but if you want to train in London as you so often say, then you'll have to get good results, and either stay on for another year or get something to do to fill in time before they'll take you in one of the big hospitals.'

'I know.' Emma shook her hair over her face as she did each time she hated a situation. 'I'll be very good, but not so good that they can't bear to leave me behind.' They giggled in a warm conspiracy of shared affection and humour. 'It will be fun, Aunt Emily. We can do all sorts of things that Mother doesn't like and I promise I'll work hard, too.'

'Meet who you like while you are with me, and have a good time, but don't do anything foolish, Emma. Young Phillip is a nice lad and fond of you. Bring him to tea the day after your mother goes and any time you want him here, but don't let him change your mind about nursing. He's the sort to cling and want a wife once's he's settled in a job and you won't be ready for that for a few years yet.'

'I'll make him play tennis and wear him out,' said Emma cheerfully, and Emily wondered just how long this girl with the soft green eyes and bouncy hair could remain unaware of her budding attractions. She was a child, about to learn of life and perhaps be hurt. Most certainly to be hurt and to see suffering. War. Would there ever be a time when it wasn't threatened? First the Boer War, when her father fought in Africa, then the Great

War to end all wars, they said, with its aftermath of misery for thousands who came back broken, and now, the shadow of Nazi Germany about to engulf Europe if that man was not stopped and that right soon.

She put away the knitting. 'You'll not get much work done now. Here comes a knight in shining armour. No, it's Phil all dressed up in tennis whites and looking as if he wants you for supper.'

She watched the two young people leave, with Emma laughing and teasing Phil, who looked down at her with a slight smile and an air of ownership.

'We ought to be swotting,' Emma said after two games. They were drinking lemonade in the pavilion.

Phillip rubbed his hair dry after a shower and laughed. 'For someone who hates studying and exams, you are plain silly to think of taking up nursing. Just think – more exams each year and a very hard life. You'd do better to get a job here and save up to get married.'

'I want to get away, Phil. I want to do something worth while before I settle down. My parents stifle me and I'm keen to live away from them once I'm over the exams and ready to work. Most hospitals make their nurses live in so I would be free.' Her eyes sparkled and her face was a pink and cream picture of vitality.

'You have a year to fill in before you can go to London,' Phil said, in a discouraging voice. 'You can't swan off and live alone in London in a bedsitter.'

'Oh, must you be so . . . *right*! Of course I can't but there are pre-nursing jobs in hospitals, and some places take nurses at seventeen for another kind of nursing before general training.'

'After nursing in isolation hospitals, or TB. nursing in a draughty sanatorium?' he said in a scathing voice. 'You'd hate that even more than exams.'

'I know.' Emma felt deflated, then brightened. 'When I went to Bristol with my mother to help measure up for curtains and to find out about shops and things there, someone said that a place on the Bristol Downs wanted girls to work with old ladies for a few months before they could start training, it's quite a posh place and very well thought of apparently, so I might ask about it when I get to Bristol. I shall ask if I can live in.'

The pavilion was empty except for the two of them and Phillip took her hand, drawing her towards him. 'Stay with me, Em. I don't ever want to lose you.' He kissed her gently and Emma felt warm and cherished but oddly unsatisfied as if he was nothing more than a kissing cousin with a glint in his eyes.

'I can't. They want me to join them once they are settled and I have to get a job, Phil, so it might as well be one that I want to do and one that will be useful.' A tattered newspaper drifted across the doorway with pictures of men in RAF uniform. 'What if there's a war? You said you'd join the RAF, so what would I do then? Just sit and knit and twiddle my thumbs until you came home? Not likely.' She ruffled his hair and he chased her out into the tennis court, laughing, and when he kissed her again, his lips were firmer and with a touch that did manage to give her a tiny thrill.

But now, the Island was far away, the bed in the new house was cold and Sister Cary briskly tidied up her dreams.

Bristol was showing no signs of war apart from the thinning displays of goods in the shops, and even that was hardly noticeable. Food was in good supply though sometimes monotonous. Emma stopped by a shop window and saw that there were bolts of cloth being sold before clothes rationing soon came into force. She bought some artificial silk for underwear in a colour that her mother might have chosen but which wouldn't be much fun to wear, but she felt lucky to get it after the tales she had heard about rationing. Would uniform be rationed? At least she had plenty of new dresses and aprons, enough to last for the entire time she would be at the Home.

She queued to see a film and waved to attract the attention of her mother who was joining her. 'I thought I'd never get here,' said Mrs Dewar. 'Such a day I've had. I didn't have time for anything to eat. Have you had any tea?' She produced a greasy paper bag and took out a sandwich. 'I thought if I didn't come now, I'd get held up again.' She munched contentedly, ignoring the looks of a woman in front of her in the queue. Emma refused a sandwich. How could she do it? Anyone would think she was sitting on a sea wall at Seaview, having a picnic tea. But why should it be different here? Emma felt uncomfortable. It mattered a lot, and much of what she'd seen of her parents in their new environment repelled her.

'I'll have an ice cream inside,' she said, as if to make up for being ashamed of her mother. The screen was already showing the Pathé News as the slowly-moving queue released them into the back seats of the stalls. Mrs Dewar folded her coat before sitting down and settling herself. Emma watched columns of young soldiers flow into aircraft, sailors give a cheery thumbs-up from docksides and the bland voice of the announcer reassured the dark warm cinema with promises that it would all be over soon.

A talk about the French Maginot Line which

would keep the Germans at bay if they dared to come that far over Belgium to the boundary of France, gave a safe feeling that this time, the war would be contained in another country far away and life would return to normal. A bright fashion show followed and the audience relaxed, rustled sweet wrappers to the sound of *Maytime* which followed, and tried not to cough in the sentimental bits. The girl on the swing, dressed in a lovely gauzy creation of tulle, reminded Emma of Evans, the blossom fell in soft clouds and she escaped into a world where every man sang like Nelson Eddy and the rain never fell.

As the main film ended, Emma nudged her mother. 'I'll have to go. Sister said I couldn't have a seven to eleven. I'm off ten to one.'

'But you won't see the beginning we missed of the News film. You should have got here earlier.'

'I waited in the queue for you!' said Emma. 'Must go. See you next week. You can get a bus right outside the cinema.'

A bus took Emma to the edge of the Downs and she braced herself to walk along the lonely main road that bordered the dark wide spaces. She clutched her keys in her hand ready to use them as a knuckle-duster and wished that her pencil slim skirt was wider or had slits in the sides to allow for bigger strides, but apart from two soldiers entwined round two giggling girls who Emma suspected were maids at the Home, she passed nobody until she came to the lane leading to the main gate.

Emma heard vague rustlings among the dried leaves and tried the postern gate, suddenly frightened. It was locked. She ran down the middle of the lane, past another courting couple, holding her skirt above her knees to give her space, and arrived breathless at the door of the nurses' home.

Inside, the pale lamp glowed on the far side of

the hall over the book that had to be signed if girls had a late pass, and in which names for late breakfast were written for days off and nurses having an early off-duty from seven to eleven.

Bea Shuter looked up from the book and raised a quizzical eyebrow. 'Someone after you?'

'My watch stopped,' lied Emma. 'I thought I'd be late.' Bea smiled. It was good to think that little Miss cool-as-a-cucumber could be frightened of the dark. She paused by the door to the Common Room. 'Coming in?' Emma shook her head, embarrassed by her needless panic. 'Please yourself,' said Bea and pointedly went in and closed the door behind her, shutting out the laughter that Emma heard briefly when the door opened.

Emma fled upstairs. Her room was a sanctuary, private and above all, warm! She thought guiltily of the cold house with the one-bar electric fire with her mother crouched over it wearing thick layers of woollen jumpers and cardigans. She brushed her hair and went down to sign for late breakfast, half-hoping that the door to the Common Room would open and someone would speak to her. She almost expected her mother to appear and find out that she had lied about her off-duty. I'll lie in and take my time over breakfast, she thought, then walk on the Downs and look in the windows of the smart local shops. She hung a clean uniform dress over the back of her chair and made up a fresh butterfly cap.

The hum of hot water pipes and the distant hoot of an owl were the only sounds until the Pros came from the Common Room, giggling and running up the stairs. Emma heard Evans' voice, with its rich Welsh lilt, and Bea Shuter's higher, clipped words. They called goodnight and banged doors, laughing.

Emma sat in bed, very still, until the noise died

away leaving just the hum of the hot water pipes. She pulled the bedclothes up over her ears to blot out the lonely sound and almost wished she had slept at home.

Bea Shuter was at breakfast with three assistant nurses, all middle-aged except for Vincent who was too lazy to apply to a hospital and take full SRN training, in spite of Sister Cary's efforts to shame her into it. Another Pro came in, starting a day off, and Emma was fascinated by her earrings and a ruby cluster brooch. It was unlikely that they were real, but Emma had never seen anything like them outside the window of an expensive jeweller, and they certainly looked genuine. The girl helped herself to scrambled eggs and bacon and looked bored.

'What are you doing today, Nadine?' asked Bea.

'I have to have lunch with my father. He's going away again and managed to come through Bristol.'

'Lucky you. Where does he take you? The Grand?' Emma smiled, thinking that this was a joke. Whoever heard of anyone going there for lunch? On the Island, she had never been inside anything more grand than a café when she was out in the West Wight and too far from home to go back to tea. She had seen the deep carpets beyond the revolving doors of the hotel and been impressed by the huge, uniformed commissionaire by the reception desk. Her mother had said it cost a fortune to step inside that place and some people had more money than sense.

'No, we didn't like it last time when Mummy came too, so this time he's meeting me in the foyer of the Royal.' Emma choked on her bacon and hastily drank some coffee. Nadine picked up a suede handbag and a short fur jacket of Persian lamb, glanced into a small mirror and strolled to the door.

'I wish my father would take me to the Royal,'

said Bea. 'When he comes, he says it isn't good for me to go there for meals, even when he's staying there. Thinks it makes me even more fed up with this damned morgue.'

Emma said nothing and Bea eyed her belligerently. 'It's all very well for you to sit there looking unconcerned. You can go home every week. I suppose you have a mother and father and friends, all cosy together, and good home-cooked food and plenty to do when you stay there. It must be good. You just can't wait to get away from us, can you?'

Emma looked aghast. 'But you have parents. You said that your father comes and takes you to smart restaurants and you know so many well-known people.'

Bea gave a cynical laugh. The others had gone and the maid was clearing the sideboard. 'Numerically correct. One mother, yes. She's in America, married to husband number three. A father, yes. Staying in hotels with popsies whenever he gets the chance. That's the reason for never taking me into any hotel where he is staying. If you only knew just how much we all envy you.' She gathered up her coat and bag and went from the room, her face tight and her back straight and forbidding.

Envy *her*? It was impossible. All these girls had so many advantages, like expensive educations. Emma considered. Perhaps not better, just more expensive. Her Matric results had been really good and she had enjoyed school. Rich parents, and important contacts, then. That had to be better, but would the Dewars still be together if they had the wealth of the families of these girls? Economics came into it. When work on the Island became harder to get, her father had moved to Bristol in lodgings and took a job in the Bristol Aircraft Factory at Filton, but keeping two homes was a strain and reluctantly, and only on condition that they could buy one of the brand new houses a mile or so from the factory, Clare Dewar had agreed to join him.

Emma walked across the Downs beneath the mist-wet trees. She liked the smell of the leaves but missed the scent of the sea. The more she thought of Aunt Emily, the more she wished that she could be with her, and realised just how generous she had been to Clare. Emma had stayed with her in the big house on the Mall while the couple tried to sell their house near Shide and were finding it difficult, with Clare becoming more annoyed and vindictive each day when no buyer came.

Old Bert Cooper, who had handled Gran's affairs up until her death, quietly in her sleep, as she deserved to go, four years back, suggested that Emily should sell the big house and buy the smaller one which took less to heat and had fewer stairs. He knew someone who wanted a house on the Mall. Clare never knew how generous Emily had been, paying over the odds to give them more funds for the new house in Bristol, but with her usual distrust, continued to believe that Bert had cheated her.

Emma began to enjoy the walk and looked up at the small clouds in a clear sky. People walked slowly as she did, until the sudden moan of the air raid siren made them hurry, run to seek shelter. Emma turned back, forcing her pace until her legs ached and she cursed her slender high-heeled court shoes that might make her legs look long and felt so good to wear off-duty, but now impeded her progress. The back of her throat was hot and her heart pounded. At the gates, she slowed down. The All Clear sounded and another practice warning was over. 'Damn!' she said, and went to change into uniform as it wasn't worth going out again.

3

The smell of wintergreen and Pears soap mingled with the steam as Emma swirled the warm water into the bath. Ethel sat in a wheelchair, a pathetic faded woman with grossly distorted limbs, unable to cross or uncross her legs without help, with calloused patches between her knees where the skin rubbed, and wasted muscles barely covering the thickened joints.

Emma tested the temperature of the water again, then rang the bell, unable to postpone the bath any longer. Ethel shivered nervously, even though the fuggy atmosphere of Green Alley was hot and oppressive. Sister Cary, who had been waiting for the bell to ring, bustled in, her eyes taking in everything; the nearly new tablet of soap lying on the side of the bath instead of draining on the soap dish, a jelly-like scum already forming on its underside, the dripping tap over the basin and the towel which had slipped from the heated towel rail.

Emma blushed and hurriedly tidied before the thin mouth could pour out more caustic disapproval. Why does she come in just when I've forgotten something, she thought. Ethel shook visibly and her big brown eyes looked at Sister Cary like a pleading animal, begging not to be hurt, but knowing that it is inevitable. Sister rolled up her sleeves and flicked starched cotton frills over the rolled edges. She put her pen and watch with the discarded cuffs on the cork table.

'Now then,' she said. 'Wheel the chair closer and do as I do, Nurse.' The voice was soft and deceptively mild. She slid the loose dressing gown from Ethel's shoulders leaving her naked, then put one hand under her thighs and the other behind Ethel's back where she clasped Emma's hand and they lifted the woman over the side of the bath and Sister pushed the chair away.

Slowly, Ethel was lowered on to the submerged stool, so slowly that the effort of holding her made Emma breathe quickly and her hand in Sister Cary's grip felt as if it might break, but as the warm water enveloped her, Ethel relaxed. Sister stood back, giving no sign that any effort and been involved, her crimped blue-grey hair neat and her apron unspotted by water. Emma could feel tendrils of hair falling from under her cap and the front of her apron was soaking.

Sister bent over and massaged the crippled legs. Her hands were firm, her movements positive, and gradually, Ethel made an effort to move her limbs under water. Emma soaped a large sponge and washed her while Sister Cary watched, making sensible, if slightly sarcastic suggestions, and the water was drained away so that Emma could dry the woman down to her thighs. To her surprise, Emma saw that the legs were in a different position, uncrossed during the underwater massage. Sister helped to hold Ethel so that her back could be dried, splashed and rubbed with surgical spirit and made completely dry and comfortable with scented talcum powder. They lifted her back into the wheelchair and Emma wheeled her to her room.

In the bedroom, Sister Cary pulled back the bedclothes and lifted Ethel bodily on to the bed. She stood back, pulled off her sleeve frills and replaced her cuffs. She gave a bleak nod in Emma's direction and told her to hurry up as dinner would be up in ten minutes. As the door closed, Ethel gave a sigh of contentment. She asked for a small pillow to take the pressure from her bent knee and Emma was amazed at the gratitude in the woman's eyes. 'I'm always so relieved when Sister Cary does me,' she said.

'I thought you were dreading it.'

'I heard that Nurse Vincent was to do my bath.' Emma visualised Vincent's round and laughing face, her generous bosom and her beefy arms. Ethel saw her face and added, hastily, 'Oh, she's very pleasant and I like her, but she can't lift and she's rough. She doesn't mean to be, but she just doesn't understand.' Ethel gave a sweet smile. 'I think you have the touch, Nurse.'

Emma walked back to the bathroom to collect the towels and soap and then went to the sluice room where she could tidy her hair. Vainly, she smoothed her wet apron and pushed the damp hair back under her cap.

'Finished Ethel?' asked Vincent, who was sluicing a soiled sheet. Emma nodded. 'I can't stand the woman. She's full of grumbles before I even touch her. I think she puts it on half the time. Anything for a bit of attention,' she said with a tolerant laugh. 'Poor old thing. It's not much of a life, is it? I'm glad I don't have to do her very often.' Vigorously, she scrubbed at the stained sheet before flinging it down the laundry shute. She dried her red hands and Emma couldn't help contrasting them with the dry, steely fingers that had so gently soothed the locked limbs.

'Where have you been, Nurse? Pros must learn to be on time. How would you like your food half-cold? Take this to Mrs Dawson and then help in the dining room, and no gossiping in the corridor.' Emma's face burned and the other Pros tittered. Cat! How could anyone like her? She took such a delight in humiliating her in front of the others. I'll leave! I'll go home! I'll get a job where I shan't have to put up with women like her!

'You don't look very happy, dear.' Emma started as the gentle voice interrupted her thoughts. Miss Styles sat waiting to be fed, her spotless table napkin tucked into her dress front, water in a feeding cup and a small glass of brandy on a pretty plate. She smiled. 'Has Sister been ticking you off? She's very good at that, isn't she?'

Emma held the spoon to the woman's lips and Miss Styles ate the Sole Véronique with evident enjoyment. 'Delicious,' she murmured, as Emma wiped her mouth and pushed the plate to the back of the tray. The once-clean napkin was covered with splashes of food when the last of the fruit and cream and cheese had disappeared. Miss Styles sipped the brandy, trying to control her spasms. 'You are so patient, my dear. I wish there were more like you.' She glanced at Emma slyly. 'Do you like it here? How do you get on with the other Pros? Do you find Sister Cary very trying?'

Emma smiled politely. If I was at screaming point I wouldn't say anything to you, she thought. Although it was less than a month since she started at the Home, Emma knew enough about Wing Six to realise that there were people in whom you did not confide. Miss Styles was one. Everything said to her went straight back to Sister Cary and the two of them had long chats during their weekly walks round the garden whenever it was fine enough, with Miss Styles dressed up in her best clothes as if she was going to a garden party or a hunting picnic, according to the temperature, and Sister in a flowing gaberdine cloak, pushing the ornate and antiquated bathchair that Miss Styles refused to change for a modern wheelchair.

It was a dignified procession but tongues wagged whenever the residents and nurses saw them disappear beyond the flowering shrubs on the first lawn. Miss Styles was so eager to tell every bit of gossip and scandal that she had heard during the past week that she dribbled and from time to time, Sister Cary wiped her mouth.

'Shall I tell Sister you enjoyed your dinner?' asked Emma. Miss Styles nodded and then tried to persuade Emma to stay and sit down for five minutes before taking her tray to the wing kitchen. She had managed it once, during Emma's first week and was profuse in her apologies when she heard that Emma had been nearly in tears after Sister Cary discovered her washing up the dishes from Miss Styles' tray, long after everything else had been cleared away.

'That's maid's work, Nurse Dewar. Pros don't wash up, but I suppose you think the maids should wait until you are ready with the dirty dishes.'

'I was doing it to save Peggy, Sister. Miss Styles asked me to stay and read some letters to her.'

'You do as I say, not what the residents tell you. You ask *me* if you can read letters and waste your time. If you want to do maid's work, why did you come here as a Pro? Perhaps maid's work is all you are fit for. Don't let me catch you washing up again, or I'll have to send you to Matron.'

The threat of Matron had less effect on the nurses than Sister realised. If she had threatened half an hour more with her, it would have caused much more consternation. Matron was mild and ladylike. A snob? Not consciously, but because she had been brought up, trained and worked with people of similar backgrounds, she had fixed ideas and patronised girls who came from any but County families.

Emma was gradually learning something about the backgrounds of the other Pros. Most of them were girls who would normally have gone to finishing schools in Germany or Switzerland, but the onset of war had made parents seek other safe places for their adolescent girls. It was a kind of extension of boarding school for children of Diplomatic Service parents, Army officers serving abroad and others like them. Day pupils from grammar schools were novel and rather suspect as unknown quantities, and Emma was quiet on the few occasions she ventured into the Common Room.

She hurried back to the kitchen and took the trolley back to the main kitchen, the dispensary basket to the dispensary and the stores list to the office. She folded her apron and rubbed at the damp patch that had seeped through to her dress, and hoped that Sister wouldn't see it if she kept her hands over the mark.

Sister's eyes flickered, ice blue. 'Nurse Dewar, your dress is a disgrace. Don't let me see you like that again. You couldn't have been wearing your apron.' Emma opened her mouth to protest then murmured, 'No, Sister.'

The glance of searching displeasure passed along the line of nurses. Sister Cary made two more sarcastic comments, told them to be quiet when they went by the end room and reluctantly dismissed the day staff.

'She's on peaches,' said Vincent cheerfully, as they went past the dying woman's door at the end of the corridor.

Evans caught up with Emma as they came to the front porch. 'Doing anything tomorrow evening?' Emma shook her head. 'It's your evening off and my day off. Let's do something very mad and quite illegal, like going to the cinema and eating fish and chips out of newspaper.'

Emma giggled. 'After a month here, that really does sound daring, but I was going home.'

Evans made a rude face. 'You are quite the most stuck-up prig I've ever met. Do you know, you haven't been out with anyone from here! They are beginning to talk.' She looked sideways. 'I'm not joking. Joan and Bea were tearing you to shreds last night. They think you no end of a snob.' She smiled, taking the edge off her words. 'I can't believe that, but you can't live here in splendid isolation for ever. Do we smell?'

Emma buried her face in her hands. 'Oh! I'd no idea.' She laughed with a hint of hysteria. '*Me*, a snob? It's because I'm so shy! How can you expect me to walk into that huge room with all those girls from wealthy homes and influential families? Girls who might be presented at Court and have been to all the smart events like Ascot and Henley and may have been on the big boats at Cowes when all I could do was to paddle around to look at them in a small dinghy! Don't you realise I go home to escape? I'd love to come out with you, if you are really sure you want me to come.'

Evans hooted with laughter. 'You silly old thing. We all thought you disapproved of us and that we were not on your spiritual plane. Promise me that you will come down tonight after supper and we'll arrange it.' She glanced up at the sky and the slight dampness in the air, then back to make sure that no sister or staff nurse could see them, and they ran across the cold courtyard to the other dimly-lit porch of the nurses' home. Emma followed closely, unaware that a pair of frosty blue eyes watched from an upper window in Matron's beautiful apartment where Sister Cary reported on the day in Wing Six and was told the latest news from the committee.

Supper was good, as usual. Tonight, it seemed even better. Evans sat at the end of the table and gave her impression of Sister Cary, and Emma, to her own surprise, joined in as Miss Styles, carrying tales in a sweet patient voice. She hurried through her bath and belted her dressing gown firmly before descending to the Common Room. She wore the new black velvet mules that Aunt

Emily had sent for her birthday and wondered again how her aunt always knew just the right present to give her. The frivolous mules were just right to give her confidence and to strike the right note of an independent spirit.

Evans was already there, wearing a camel hair dressing gown and battered slippers. She fished out some cigarettes. Two other girls joined them, pink-faced and smelling of sandalwood talcum powder and they sat by the fire, drinking coffee. Joan and Bea came in from their day off, signed the book and lingered by the fire, grumbling that they'd had to leave their friends too early as they had to be in by ten-thirty. Emma, warmed by the fire, warmed with the new rapport she was establishing and warmed by the thought of exploring Bristol with Evans with no querulous mother to go with her, decided that perhaps she would stay a bit longer at the Home.

'Something is up!' said Bea. She peeped through a crack in the curtains and then let the heavy velvet drop so that the blackout would be complete again. 'Our dear Sister came out of the front door with Matron, both in their cloaks, and they stood looking at the front door from the drive as if they were about to take it away and paint it.' She saw the disbelief in the other faces. 'Isn't that right, Joan? Matron was saying that there wasn't time to do a lot and she thought that a few rows of potted plants from the greenhouses would be enough.'

'At ten o'clock at night?' Evans laughed. 'Is the war over? Last week the porters were grumbling that they might have to build a wall of sandbags by the front of the building, and now you talk of potted plants.'

'Mother Cary was quite excited and so I expect she'll have to tell us all or burst,' predicted Bea, and when they arrived on duty the following morning, she was waiting by her office door. She lined up her staff as if to face an execution squad and although it was early, she looked at her fob watch pointedly.

'Must be important. She wears that watch only when she is feeling terribly self-important,' whispered Evans. Nurse Vincent strolled on duty and saw Sister. Vincent glanced at the kitchen clock visible through the open door and relaxed. Even Sister Cary couldn't accuse her of being late on duty as the hands had another two minutes to go.

Sister Cary turned the face of the watch to hide in the folds of the silk bodice of her dress and the gleaming and tooled back was on show. She looked along the line. 'Well,' she said in the curious rasping voice that showed that she was not necessarily being censorial. 'We are to have a great honour.' She smiled. 'Matron says that we are to entertain a *very* important person, here to tea, one week from today.' She folded her hands in front of her waist and the stiff linen cuffs rustled against the silver belt buckle. 'A *very* important visit,' she repeated, as no one ventured a remark or even a reaction. She paused and heard Evans shuffle uncomfortably. 'Did you speak, Nurse Evans?'

'No, Sister.'

'Oh, I was rather expecting you to complain. It is, I believe, your day off next Wednesday.'

'Yes, Sister.'

'I'm afraid you'll have to change it or take two half days if you can't be spared.'

Evans gazed at a point on the wall just beside the shadow of Sister's cap. 'Yes, Sister,' she said.

Seeing no further reaction from Evans, Sister turned back to her news, disappointed at the apathy shown so far to the announcement that had filled her with pride. 'I shall want everything spotless. You will all have extra work every day instead of every other day as you do now, and there will be no grumbling if you are asked to do jobs that you think are beneath you.'

'Cleaning drains?' murmured Bea.

'There will be a rota on the board in my office which you will follow and tick off each job as you complete it, so that I can inspect it. We must make sure that the linen room is tidy.' Evans gave a barely audible groan.

'Nurse Evans, I hope that on Wednesday next, you will manage to control your feelings. I am sure that our visitor would be shocked to hear of your behaviour.' Emma looked round at the other faces and found them as blank as her own. Who was this visitor? 'I shall also, as Matron suggested, post a Pro from this Wing as it is nearest to her flat to stand by the door on the Day, to take messages. There will be another Pro by the lift, and another at the foot of the lift, in case a message has to be passed to the kitchens. Matron wants no telephones to be in use and no residents' bells ringing and no noise or clatter.'

She consulted a typed list. 'Before you go on duty, I have a few announcements. We have word that butter is to be rationed. That will not affect us of course as we have many friends who will continue to supply the Home, but Matron asks that all economy must be observed. Eggs, too, are in short supply outside but fortunately we have a new batch ready for pickling. Nurse Dewar, you will go to Stores Sister to help her this morning.' She glanced at the list again. 'Milk is available freely but cream will not be sold commercially for the duration of the war.' She smiled as if it was strange that anyone could impose restrictions on the Home. She read more notices warning the girls about the impending arrival of soldiers to be billeted in the school next door, the fact that the blackout regulations were to be more severely enforced, and that there would be an air raid and fire drill once a week. She dismissed her staff with a curt nod and turned away, her highly polished shoes glinting with importance.

'Can anyone tell me who is coming?' asked Bea in a pained voice. 'Am I the only one in the dark?'

'She didn't say. She made it sound as if we all ought to know without being told. It must be the vicar of St Michael's. She goes into a tizz whenever he crosses the doorstep. He's the youngest man to come here – not a day over fifty-five,' grinned Evans.

'It's not the vicar. Don't you really know?' They turned to the Wing Six maid, Ivy, who had come in the kitchen behind them. Ivy knew everything. Bea said she was like the wise monkeys who hear all, see all and say nowt, but Ivy had forgotten the last attribute. She was another Miss Styles and Sister would take her word against that of a Pro any day.

'Come on, Ivy, tell us!' They clustered round her and she smirked. She carefully folded two tea towels before replying and Evans got impatient. 'Come on, Ivy, I've got to feed Miss Styles, and as I have to change my day off, I need to know if it's worth it.'

'It's Queen Mary!'

'And who else?' said Bea, rudely. 'Pull the other one, it's got bells on it.'

'It is, I tell you. It's the Queen Mother.' Ivy was aware that they were laughing at her. 'I *do* know. It *is* the Queen Mother, Sister told me. She said she was coming to tea with Matron and will inspect the whole place.' She dropped her voice to a hollow whisper. 'They say she looks everywhere.'

'Don't believe you, Ivy. Do you mean that the Queen Mother will come all the way down from London or wherever she lives, just to have a mouldy cup of tea with Matron?'

Ivy tossed her head. 'Well, all right, don't believe me, but it's true. Matron said that the Queen

Mother is staying at Badminton while the war is on and there is a danger from bombing, and she says she wants to come here.'

'Oh, yes, she must have heard how comfortable it is here. I expect she wants to be put on the waiting list for a room. How grand to have a Royal living here. I wonder if she'll like Green Alley?'

Ivy looked uncertain as she did whenever Bea Shuter teased her. 'You're having me on,' she said. She looked at Evans. 'You'll cop it if Sister finds you here. You should be with Miss Styles.' She spoke with the familiarity of someone who had worked with Sister Cary for years. 'You'd best be down that corridor, Pro Evans.'

Evans poked out her tongue, looking more like a naughty child than the smooth, assured young woman whom Emma saw. When they had gone to the Whiteladies cinema together, Emma had been very impressed by the easy way that Evans dealt with usherettes and with the waiters in the small restaurant attached to the pub down the road.

'I must have a civilised meal,' she'd said. 'We haven't time to go on down to Park Street, but this isn't bad.' Emma had been glad to settle for a simple licensed eatinghouse and wondered what her mother would say if she knew her daughter had gone to a place where they sold alcohol, and not to a safe cafe where women alone were supposed to go. She glanced at the table covered with wine bottles and blushed when Evans teased her, and drank a glass of cider after protesting that she couldn't.

'Where have you been all your life?' asked Evans, fitting a Sobranie cigarette into a short black holder. 'You don't drink, you don't smoke and you jump like a scared rabbit if a waiter looks at you.' But it had been a good evening and bit by bit, Evans was beginning to tell Emma about herself, and the years in boarding school in the depths of the country, her father's businesses in Swansea and London and how she wished she could see more of him; and the long holidays spent with her mother, divorced and now married to a naval officer.

Shyly, Emma told her of the Island, the freedom and the sea, the long cycle rides, the day school and the old house on the Mall where her grandmother had lived with Aunt Emily and where Emma had spent so much of her time, and her own home that was a miniature of the house on the Mall as Clare Dewar had copied the style and decor as much as she could. 'Not as warm, though,' she said. 'Gran had a fire winter and summer and my mother is mean with fires.'

Evans saw her eyes misting as she talked of Aunt Emily. 'You are so lucky,' she said. 'You have people you love and who love you and give you their time.' Her musical voice was suddenly harsh. 'That's why we resent you when you don't mix. You have so much while most of us are dumped here so that our parents can leave us without a backward look. They are damn pleased to get rid of us. Maybe my father cares, but he hasn't the time.'

'Don't you have brothers and sisters?'

'One brother in the Army. He's a regular soldier, and I have a half-sister whom I've seen once. She was sick all down my coat.' She smiled. 'I don't feel a thing for her and certainly have no desire to see her again.'

Emma stirred her coffee. 'At least you have a brother. It must be nice to have someone nearly the same age. Most of my cousins were older and even they moved away from the Island and I saw very little of them. Did you have fun growing up together?'

'Yes, Tony's nice. You'd like him. He makes me laugh. He used to shield me from family rows but he went into the Army as soon as possible, as he'd taken all he could and wanted to get out. I miss him,' she said, twisting her wine glass stem between her fingers.

Two soldiers moved to the next table and eyed the girls hopefully. Evans stared at them arrogantly without smiling and they turned away, embarrassed. 'Now at least they know we aren't cheap pick-ups,' said Evans. She signalled for the bill, then looked at Emma, sharply. 'You'll find that values are different in a city like this one. You left your innocent young past on the Island, Dewar. You're in the big bad world now. Be careful. I can look after myself but you are a babe in arms. Troops are taking over the school next door and the wall looks over the Home.'

They walked back across the Downs, secure in each other's company, but neither of them referred to the footsteps that followed them from the pub to the gates of the Home. When the door of the Common Room closed behind them, Evans said, 'They don't give up easily. I hate coming along the lane on my own and now, they know where we live.'

Emma remembered this as she walked across to the stores. A distant wolf whistle told her that the troops were arriving, and already were noticing the tantalising wisps of the butterfly caps in the grounds of the Home. She looked in through the half-open door of the stores, beyond the tree-hidden building that she had recently learned was the mortuary. The stores were built of the same thick Cotswold stone and roofed with the same warm red tiles as the rest of the buildings, and the huge room was lined with tiers of shelves and dry goods. Oak doors led to other rooms, also filled with stores.

She coughed as her timid knock had not caused Sister Ambrose to turn. Sister continued to stare in front of her and there was a hint of tension in her shoulders. She turned slowly, her mouth working and she swallowed hard. 'Pro Dewar reporting, Sister.' Sister Ambrose swallowed again and coughed. 'Sister Cary sent me,' said Emma. 'I'm to help with the eggs.' Sister Ambrose nodded and ambled into a side room. Emma stood tall to see what was on the end table that she had left, and saw the remains of a peach and some chocolate wrappings. No wonder she's so fat, she thought. Just the place for her, the dispensary and the stores. She followed into the room picking her way between rows of coloured bins to a space where Sister was mixing a solution of isinglass and water. Stacks of cardboard egg partitions lay on the table separating dozens and dozens of eggs.

Emma put on a rubber apron over her uniform and tested each egg for freshness, lowering it gently on to a folded towel in the base of a water-filled bowl. If the egg floated, it was discarded as bad, if it showed its end above water it was put aside for immediate use and if it sank, it was packed, point down into one of the zinc baskets lining the huge bins. To pack the first layer. Emma had to bend over double, nearly overbalancing. She grinned, not surprised that Sister Ambrose needed help. She might have done a good imitation of the Duke of Clarence, without the consolation of drowning in good Malmsey wine.

They worked in silence, Emma because she knew that a pupil probationer was the lowest form of life and must remain silent unless addressed by a senior, and Sister Ambrose because she seldom spoke to anyone, but lived from day to day in her own stone-walled world of food and cleaning materials, lists and dispensary. She left Emma for a while and returned, chewing. Emma's stomach rumbled. She glanced at the clock, and Sister nodded. 'You may go for elevenses,' she said. 'Take the stores to Wing One and Wing Five and make sure the ward maid checks the contents as I refuse to make up any deficit unless I am informed immediately. Some people are not entirely honest.' She lowered her voice. 'I think I could do with my coffee now,' she said as if she had fasted for days. She lifted the speaking tube that connected stores to kitchen and asked for her tray.

As Emma pushed the trolley to the lift, she saw a kitchen maid hurrying down the stairs to the back door of the store where it joined the main building. There was a large silver coffee pot, two toasted muffins and a plate of biscuits. Ah well, thought Emma. It would be a tragedy if I went back and found she'd died of starvation.

Bea Shuter was in the dining room, stuffing bread and cheese into her mouth. She still managed to look elegant. 'What's the rush?' asked Emma. For once, Bea had shed her air of calculated boredom and cynicism. 'You'll choke.'

'I'm having a half-day. I've one due and my father telephoned Matron, requesting my company. Sister was livid. He's taking me out to lunch and then to friends in Bath.' She glanced at Emma. 'I don't think he's brought a popsie this time as we're having lunch at the Royal where he's staying.' She sipped her coffee. 'I can't think why he made the effort; he's not that good at the loving pater bit.' She grinned. 'But a slap-up lunch, a drive in a decent car and the chance to have a civilised conversation that isn't about bedpans and back rubbings will be heaven. Not that you'd understand. You escape more than most so it's no novelty to you.' She finished her cheese. 'Must dash. Sister will have my skin if I don't finish polishing those bloody trunks before I go.'

'Trunks?'

'Oh, yes, didn't you know? She's gone barmy. You don't know what you're missing. Not only do we have to listen to Royal Visit for a week but Sister has a bee in her bonnet that the Queen Mother will want to look in all the linen cupboards. Immaculate as always, they are being turned out yet again. The Queen will look inside the ovens, and have an earnest desire to see the pig bins, then she'll go on to inspect the assorted luggage stored in the tiled store. I personally and at great sacrifice of personal freshness and energy, have been polishing each trunk, suitcase and piece of hand luggage belonging to every resident on Wing Six. It smells like a saddlery in there, and I shall smell like a groom when I meet my father, who really does prefer his women to smell of roses.' She danced out of the room and Emma thought how beautiful Bea was when she smiled.

The egg-packing took most of her on-duty time. Sister Ambrose stirred a little, made up more solution and retired at intervals to regain her strength with the help of some hand-made confectionary that she was making for the Royal Visit and had to test each of the many different sweets to see if bitter or sweet almonds were best, if the chocolate was dark enough and if the stuffed dates were not too dry.

It was peaceful in the stores and Sister Ambrose had a tea tray at three-thirty and went to the dining room a four-thirty to see another Sister and have a quick cup of tea. Emma finished the bins and sluiced the sink and mopped the floor, then she strolled round the stores inspecting the shelves while Sister was away. There were tinned meats and sardines, whole chickens canned with truffles, and tinned game. Rows of preserves and jars of bottled fruit that had been prepared in the kitchens of the Home sat in neat rows, with tins bearing foreign labels showing exotic contents. Whole sides of smoked bacon and hams hung in a cool larder over cheeses as big as car tyres. It was all stored as beautifully as in any of the famous stores in London, and would last for months.

In another section, foil-lined tea chests held Indian and China tea, huge metal containers were full of coffee beans and drinking chocolate and a glass-fronted cabinet was packed with bars of dessert chocolate and couverture.

Sister came back and said that Emma could go. It was too early to go off-duty. 'Is there anything more I can do, Sister?' Emma asked. 'It's hardly worth going back to the Wing.'

'Ah, yes, Wing Six.' Sister Ambrose smiled and it was like soft wax dripping down the sides of a round candle. 'Ah, yes, Sister Cary.' She glanced round the tidy store. 'You may take the stimulants to the dispensary for me and then go off-duty.'

In the corridor, Emma met Sister Cary and explained that she had just finished the eggs but Sister Ambrose still wanted her to take bottles to the dispensary, and Sister Cary nodded as if she had other matters on her mind. She had lists and rotas of duties to be finished, she had to have a last fitting for a new silk uniform dress and was trying to break in a pair of expensive duty shoes that still retained a slight squeak, so Emma slipped off-duty at twenty to six and missed the muted drama, when the resident in Room One couldn't wait for the doctor, for Sister or the Royal visit and slipped away peacefully before supper.

4

'Well, you might have told me she was coming!' Clare Dewar was annoyed. 'I'd have come up to see her. I could have waited outside with Mrs Hammond. She enjoys anything to do with the Royal family and likes to hear about all those we saw at Carisbrooke and at Cowes. I can remember Queen Victoria well – we saw her so often that nobody took much notice of her. If I'd been able to tell Mrs Hammond about this visit, she'd have been very impressed.'

'She came and went and I hardly saw her, and I couldn't have come out to see you as everyone was on duty with the outer gates locked until her visit ended.' Emma began to wish that she had made no mention of the Royal visit, but blessed the fact that at least she'd kept quiet until it was over.

Sitting on the new settee in front of the freshly-lit fire, she tried not to shiver. The fabric of the house had not had time to warm up, because her mother had lit the fire so late in the day, and although her knees were nearly singed, her back was frozen. The wireless grew faint and died, and Mrs Dewar gave a snort of annoyance. 'I asked your father to fetch another battery from the shop. They re-charge them overnight and give a good service but as usual, he forgot.' She didn't mention that her husband had been out for most of the night, firewatching after a full day at the factory where he was an inspector of aero-engines.

'Where is Dad now?' asked Emma.

'Up at the factory again. Always some excuse. I don't know what they get up to in that Nissen hut. They play cards and drink beer and a fat lot of firewatching they do. The AFS are as bad. They sit around because they're too lazy to join up.'

'They might be needed in a hurry, so they must be there,' suggested Emma.

'That's right, stand up for him.' Emma sighed. She had given up arguing with her mother. If she mentioned the girls at the Home, they were stuck-up snobs and why didn't Emma bring any of them home? If she mentioned work, it brought a tirade against the strict discipline and the fact that they paid so little, and it was a good thing that Emma had a comfortable home to which she could return and be looked after; but the remains of the supper on the trolley compared badly with the food to which Emma had become accustomed and even took for granted.

She's off again, Emma thought with a sinking feeling, as her mother told her where she had got the last half-pound of liver after waiting for her share in the queue for an hour. 'It isn't like when I was a girl. We could take what we wanted from our shop – fish, vegetables and fruit and never thought twice about it until your grandmother sold up and went to live on the Mall. I miss all that – I never thought I'd have to stand about in the rain waiting for a bit of liver or a few sausages, and as for those people at the furniture shop, I can't tell you how often I've been in to see when the rest of the furniture will arrive. I wish I'd kept some of the old stuff.' Clare Dewar looked round at the sparsely fitted room. 'At least it would have looked like home.'

Emma was tired after the Royal visit and needed a break. She wished her mother would read a book or knit or listen to the wireless and leave her alone as Aunt Emily had done when she was studying.

She had been quiet, or what was the word she wanted? Tranquil. It had been easy to study for exams in that house, even though her parents had lived there before Aunt Emily bought it. She had brought her own atmosphere with her and made the place homely and reassuring.

When the Queen Mother came, the Home had been in a ferment of activity, with Sister Cary as tense as a coiled spring, ready to notice anything awry and to reprimand at every turn. The room next to her office, where the death had occurred, had been cleaned and aired until the smell of decay had vanished under the pungency of Ronuk and disinfectant and furniture polish. The curtains had been changed and the bed made up invitingly with a new blue and white quilt to match the curtains and screen cover. The polished floor gleamed and the window sparkled, and Sister left the door ajar to show The Visitor a typical room when empty, but each time that Emma passed by, she wanted to close the door and blot out the memory of that parchment face, the brittle hair and the smell that she would remember all her life.

Her Majesty arrived on the dot of time. Her chauffeur was entertained by the kitchen staff and was impressed by their hospitality. The equerry was content to browse in Matron's study among her many books, while Matron, prettily pink of cheek, gushed platitudes and hovered at the side of Queen Mary, who refused to be hurried and had her own very decided views on what she wanted to see. Sister Cary lined up her staff and picked an invisible speck from Evans' shoulder. For the umpteenth time, she told them what to do after the Queen Mother had inspected them.

Evans was to stand to attention by the door of Matron's flat, ready to fling it wide after the Queen had inspected the other wings and was ready to take tea with Matron. She must be ready to take messages to Emma, who was at the head of the stairs by the lift, and Bea Shuter was to be ready to run from the bottom of the lift shaft to the kitchen if anything was wanted.

Three committee members came to join the small procession, and Queen Mary, dressed in a close-fitting coat of silver grey with a huge collar of fine grey squirrel, matching toque hat and soft leather shoes, walked with dignity down the first corridor and into Wing Six. The atmosphere was electric but silent, as all bells had been removed from the beds so that no resident could ring during The Visit. Internal telephones had been left off hooks and all staff wore rubber heels on their shoes. Even the trolley wheels and door hinges had been freshly oiled and the taps in Green Alley were checked twice for drips.

The only sound allowed was the faint, crematorial moan of the chapel organ played by a specially invited broadcaster from the newly-arrived BBC; the Corporation was installing broadcasting equipment in some of the fine old houses in Whiteladies Road, Bristol, in case of air raids on London.

The Queen Mother walked and looked and spoke to residents. Emma could have wept for them. In an effort to appear festive, they had decked themselves out in all their finery, in jewels and ornaments they had worn to operas long ago. Miss Styles, in a beautiful tiara, insisted on lipstick which spread and dripped as she salivated, confronting the unfortunate lady with a face that appeared to drip blood. Her Majesty didn't linger with her. Miss Forsyth drew back her lips in a resolute smile, trying to ignore the cramp that wracked her lower limbs. It was a bad day for her as the physiotherapist had cancelled her visits in honour of the occasion, just when Miss Forsyth needed her desperately. The Queen admired her books and was impressed when she saw the inscriptions on some of the fly leaves, written by the famous man to whom Miss Forsyth had once been governess and who sent her the first copy in print each time he had another book published.

She touched Miss Forsyth on the cheek with a gloved hand. 'How happy you must be; how fortunate to inspire such devotion.'

The rest of the Wing was inspected, approved and to Sister Cary's immense satisfaction and the incredulous joy of the Pros, who had taken bets on the subject, the Queen *did* look in the linen cupboards *and* in the tiled baggage store. She nodded her approval several times and said something to Sister that made her swell visibly. 'She'll never be the same again,' whispered Vincent. 'Just worse.'

The door closed behind the party and the Pros relaxed in their various stations, glad that Sister Cary had been invited to tea and couldn't be on their tails. There was deep silence as even the organist had given up and was enjoying tea with the equerry and the chaplain, but the door opened suddenly and Winnie, Matron's maid, hurried out, stiff in a new black uniform with dazzling white cap and trim fluted apron. 'She wants *cream* in her tea,' she said in a panic. 'We've got milk and lemon, Indian tea and China but she wants cream in it.'

Evans ran to the lift shaft where Emma waited. 'cream!'

'Sh!' said Emma. 'You mustn't shout!'

'*Cream*,' said Evans in a stage whisper. 'She wants cream in her tea. Tell Bea to tell Cook.'

Emma rattled the lift gates gently. 'Bea, *cream*! Bea, get some cream.'

'What?'

'Cream. She wants cream in her tea and there's none there.'

Bea ran to the kitchen where the chauffeur was giving an expansive account of his life at Badminton. Cook and her assistants were hanging on his words.

'Cream!' said Bea, breathlessly. 'No cream.'

'We haven't any,' stated Cook. 'Don't you know there's a war on?'

'Plenty where we come from,' the chauffeur said.

'Well, there shouldn't be,' Cook retorted. 'It's illegal.' But all the time she was talking, she skimmed thin cream from the surface of a jug of milk and went to the larder to skim more from a churn, and two minutes later, Evans handed in a small jug of impoverished cream, only to find that Her Majesty had graciously accepted milk in her tea.

Emma leaned against the wall and wondered when the tea party would end. There was so much work to be done, but the door to Matron's flat remained shut. The lack of noise and the absence of bells was almost sinister, as if everyone was dead behind the closed door. She wondered if anyone had been detailed to do a discreet bedpan round, as the poor souls must be bursting without a bedpan since lunch. The residents had eaten early and would have high tea instead of dinner tonight, as they did when a special service was arranged in chapel. She smiled. Someone couldn't wait; the flush in Green Alley sounded like a rushing river in the deadly quiet of the corridor.

As if the flush was a signal, the door to the flat opened and Evans stood to attention. Queen Mary nodded to her, glanced down the empty corridor and began to walk down the stairs, refusing to use the central lift. A ripple of movement greeted her as the majority of the staff waited in the main hall to see her. The big black limousine was outside the door, the down cushions dented with wear, but somehow enhancing the quiet luxury of the car. A pale grey glove waved and the toque inclined in a slight bow as the chauffeur took the Queen Mother back to Badminton, the countryside, the Beauforts and log fires.

With her went the false silence. Sister Cary came back, rolling up her sleeves and flicking on her work frills. Her voice barked orders, the wheels of trolleys and wheelchairs swished along the corridors and bells rang again. Emma and the other Pros were run off their feet as they answered agonised requests for bedpans and found that some of the weaker vessels had not been able to wait.

Miss Forsyth was in a savage temper and screamed like a stuck pig when her back was rubbed. Miss Styles, upset because the Queen Mother had stayed with her for half a minute less than the resident in the next wheelchair, was slow and uncooperative, trying to goad the nurses into being rude to her or into complaining that Sister had upset their work routine. Emma and Nurse Vincent went together doing bedpans and back rubs and came to Room Six where Mrs Devere waited to be put on the commode. She was a big-boned woman carrying excess weight because her appetite was good and she had no exercise. She suffered from syringomyelia, a degenerative disease of the nervous system which made her lower limbs lack sensation. She could have no hot water bottles near her as she might be burned, and could never walk alone as she had so little sensation in her feet that if she put weight down, she missed her footing.

Vincent usually helped Mrs Devere whenever she was on duty, partly because she was strong and partly because Mrs Devere gave her presents, a habit discouraged in the Home as it led to jealousy among the long-serving assistant nurses.

The Pros were forbidden to accept gifts of any kind.

Vincent threw open the door and stopped. She gasped and told Emma to fetch Sister Cary and then bent over the heap of bedclothes on the floor under which the still form of Mrs Devere lay. The commode was close to the bed; close enough for any fairly mobile patient to reach without help. Vincent called her by name and Mrs Devere moaned. Vincent tried to disentangle the clothes but the heavy woman lay on them and she couldn't be moved by one person alone.

Sister Cary came into the room and it was the only time that Emma had seen her run. She stood over the crumpled heap, taking in at a glance the way Mrs Devere was lying, the unnatural angle of her right leg and the fact that the commode was by the bed instead of being in its rightful place on the other side of the bedside rug, where Mrs Devere couldn't reach it, and would have to be helped on to it by two people.

'We need a stretcher,' Sister Cary snapped. 'Ring down for two porters.' Vincent fled and Sister bent to take the pulse in the flaccid wrist. She straightened. 'Look at the way her leg is lying, Nurse. What do you notice?' she asked calmly. Emma was shocked. How could she ask silly questions while the poor woman lay on the hard floor? Surely the first thing to do was to get her warm again. Her thick bedsocks had slipped off and Emma bent to pick them up, but Sister told her briskly to leave them alone and to answer the question.

'But Sister, she's cold,' said Emma.

'So would you be if you'd fallen out of bed trying to reach a commode that had no right to be where it is now. Well, Nurse, what do you think of that leg?'

'It doesn't look comfortable. It's at an odd angle

and it's going blue with the cold or lack of circulation. I thought she had to be kept warm,' she added with a hint of accusation.

'I'll ask you another question. Is it better to leave her foot cold until we get help or is it best to move her and make her condition much worse?'

'Worse, Sister?'

'Almost certainly. Don't you recognise a fractured femur when you see one?'

Emma went closer. Reading in a textbook that a foot adopts an unusual angle if there is a fracture was one thing, seeing the reality was quite different. It was impossible! How could this happen to an elderly lady, cared for in luxury with plenty of staff to run in answer to her bell? But of course, she couldn't ring, and being a fastidious person she would have been humiliated if she had soiled her bed. The seriousness of the situation came to Emma at last.

Sister nodded. 'Yes, Nurse, it's bad. It had no right to happen and I shall want to know who put the commode within her reach.'

'I don't know, Sister. I was doing Miss Styles after lunch, with Pro Evans, and then we were with Miss Forsyth.'

Sister almost smiled. 'Yes, you were putting all that ridiculous makeup on Miss Styles. It was quite grotesque, but important, as I think you are learning. She didn't know how she looked, and it was good for her to make the effort. That's why these visits matter; not because we need them but the residents feel that they are not completely forgotten. This accident is a pity, a great pity that it had to happen today, but on any other day with a full staff, it could never have happened.'

By now Sister was sitting on the floor, stroking the woman's hand and had dropped a light shawl over the exposed feet. Emma stood helplessly by until the trolley arrived and then she, the two porters, Sister and Vincent lifted Mrs Devere on to the stretcher on the floor, and transferred her on to the bed, taking care to leave the leg at the same angle.

Sister telephoned the hospital to ask the orthopaedic surgeon to call her urgently, and then went to see Matron, returning with a grim face. 'There will have to be an inquiry with the committee,' she said. Again, she took the pulse rate. Mrs Devere was breathing stertorously and her eyes were half-closed. Light, warm mohair shawls lay over each foot and a metal cradle was brought so that other bedclothes could be added without adding weight to her legs.

The Pros were sent to finish the bedpan round but when Vincent tried to follow them, she was curtly told to wait.

Outside the room, Evans came to take Vincent's place. 'What happens now?' asked Emma. 'Will she go to hospital?'

'The last time someone had an operation, she went into a nursing home until the stitches were out and then came back here, but Mrs Devere looks ill apart from the injury, so they may not move her,' said Evans. 'There'll be one hell of a row.' She shrugged. 'They'll keep it within the Home, though. What's the point of a fuss? If she dies, it means that she will have lived longer just by the care she had here. She couldn't be as well looked after at home. I know they pay here, but everything is done for them and they don't have to interview or pay staff. With just one patient, it would be terribly expensive to manage in a private house.'

'What if she dies? You don't think she will?'

Evans looked mysterious, and suddenly very Celtic. 'There is a saying that death comes in threes. Room One started it and there are two to go.'

'That's ridiculous.'

'Better shut up about it. We've got Miss Styles to do.' Evans knocked briskly on her door. 'She's had a bedpan and drink but she's due for a bath in Green Alley. We'll have to cover for Vincent as she expects her to do it.'

'Where is Nurse Vincent?' asked Miss Styles, her antennae twitching as she sensed drama.

'Everyone is yelling for attention and we've been given different jobs,' said Evans carelessly. 'Some of the residents won't get baths today, so you are lucky. Did you enjoy the visit, Miss Styles?'

'Oh, yes, it was pleasant enough but I'm used to meeting important people. It was not a strange feeling and I felt completely at home with the Queen Mother. She stayed and talked to me much longer than with any of the others, you know.'

Emma grinned at Evans over Miss Styles' head as they trundled her along the corridor. A man hurried from the lift and took a short cut through Green Alley just as they reached the bathroom. 'Who was that?' asked Miss Styles, trying to turn her head to see him, but her neck went into spasm and she had to concentrate on controlling it.

'I have no idea,' lied Evans as the young orthopaedic surgeon disappeared from view.

'He looked like that nice young man who comes to see Edith Parsons. Now what does he want here? He doesn't come often and he wouldn't come today if there wasn't something urgent happening.'

Evans turned on the taps and swished bath salts in the water while Emma spread the towels to warm. 'Maybe Queen Mary forgot her umbrella,' said Evans. 'Her equerry was quite young.'

'I feel that there has been an accident,' insisted Miss Styles. 'Something must have happened or he'd never be here at this time of day.'

'How interesting. Do you often have premonitions?' asked Evans. 'Do you tell fortunes? I adore having mine told me. My auntie in Wales has premonitions and she's never wrong. Perhaps something will happen tomorrow.' She launched into a long and boring account of her auntie's psychic powers and all the time, they got on with the bath, ignoring Miss Styles' protests that they were rushing her. They dressed her in a fresh nightgown of fine nun's veiling, and put a quilted bib round her neck. They wrapped her warmly in her camel hair dressing gown and fur-lined slippers and spread the rug carefully over her knees before venturing out into the corridor, but she stopped them taking her to her room. 'Fetch my black veil,' she said with as crafty smile. 'I'll say my prayers in chapel, tonight.'

'Sorry,' said Evans firmly. 'Supper is early and the bell's gone.'

'Then I'll have supper in the dining room, now I'm in a wheelchair.'

'You know why she didn't want to go to her room?' said Evans as they took soiled linen to the laundry chute. 'She wants to sit by the window and watch the drive to see if the man appears, the artful old soul. She'll know all about it by breakfast time.'

Sister was with the surgeon and old Dr Drake, partly retired, whose bedside manner far exceeded his medical skills but who satisfied the limited requirements of the residents, all of whom had been diagnosed years ago and depended on him for prescriptions for painkillers, vitamins and stimulants and loads of charm. When they reported off-duty, Sister waved them away, hardly looking at them. Evans raised her eyebrows at the night staff nurse who wanted to know what was happening. 'Blast!' she said. 'I'd hoped for a quiet night with everyone tired after the Royal visit, but it's a strange thing that when anything like this happens, they all get edgy and sit on their bells half the night.' She flung her cloak into the cupboard. 'Listen to that! It's started already. Two bells ringing and one of them Miss Styles.'

It had been quite a day, but Emma had no intention of telling her mother about Mrs Devere. There was a kind of loyalty in keeping the affairs of the Home private, so she said very little, in spite of her mother's evident curiosity. Emma leaned back, hoping it would make her back warmer. Mrs Dewar put more coal on the fire. 'Must cost a fortune to heat that place,' She remarked. 'Must be nice for you to come home to a proper fire.' She seemed to be in a good mood despite her disappointment about Queen Mary's visit, and Emma began to hear what she was saying.

'What telephone?' she asked.

'I might as well talk to the wall! I told you. A man came to see us from the Post Office and said our name was on the list for a telephone but even though they have laid all the wires, they can't link up until after the war or when the Government give permission. If your father becomes a Special Constable, as he says he might, that would give us priority, but the man said we would definitely have one if the RAF were allowed to use it.'

'The RAF? You must have it wrong, Mum. Why would they want to use our phone? We are nowhere near the airfield.'

'I don't know. I thought it was strange but they never really tell us anything. They just say there's a war on and careless talk costs lives and all that, but Mrs Hammond knows. She had an Army Sergeant staying with them as she does bed and breakfast sometimes.'

'Mrs Hammond can't possibly know.'

'She said they might want to build a shelter in our

garden to hide secret papers and have a telephone because they would want to know if the hospital was bombed as we are quite near.' She stopped, suddenly aware that either solution was unlikely. 'Well, she thinks she knows and I suppose they'll tell us what they want in their own good time. It would be nice to be on the phone – I could ring you up.'

'Not on duty, Mum,' said Emma quickly. 'Unless you want to get me into trouble.'

'That's mean. I suppose you could ring me when you are off-duty and not have to bother with those girls. We can meet in town.'

'I couldn't let you give up your afternoons at the clothes club,' said Emma hastily.

'No, there is that. I do enjoy going; not that we'll ever need clothes and blankets for bombed people here, but we have a handy collection to send if anyone else needs them. We've started giving out wool to old people to knit up into squares for blankets. They like to do something and it's a kind of war work.'

Emma tried to imagine the ladies in the Home knitting balaclavas from coarse blue wool and then wondered how Mrs Devere was progressing. Whenever she came away, her mind wandered back across the Downs and her parents' home was more and more unreal. 'I was given a card today,' she said. 'I shall never use it, of course. I don't think the Germans would bother to come here. They may drop a few bombs on their way back from raids on military targets, but they won't come here. I can't really see myself stopping a car or a lorry and commandeering it to get back on duty, can you?'

Her mother examined Emma's official card. 'They gave us fire drill and showed us how to put out fire bombs with sand and to take the bed cases down into the subway quickly,' continued Emma. She was suddenly serious. 'They taught us a lot and although it's not likely to affect us, they insisted that if an air raid warning went, we were to get back on duty to help the residents as quickly as possible, if we were within six miles of the Home or even if we were off-duty. It would be terrible to be trapped in a bedroom if you were disabled and bombs were falling.'

The front door chimes sounded, sickly sweet, and Mrs Dewar plumped up the cushion in her chair before going to the door. She switched off the hall light and then opened the front door. Emma heard a man's voice. The outer door closed and Emma looked up at the tall RAF Sergeant who came in with her mother. He nodded to Emma and stood before the fire, twisting his cap in his hands. 'You'll have to leave the form. My husband is out at the moment,' said Mrs Dewar.

'What is it?' asked Emma.

'It's a form giving us permission to use your telephone during air raids and alerts. We have a field telephone but until we have a permanent system, we need to be in contact with the public services in an emergency and also if our own permanent phone is struck and put out of action.'

'But the landing strip is a long way off, so why here?'

He smiled. 'Haven't you seen the changes they've made to the upper field where they stopped building?'

'I saw the huts and barbed wire,' put in Mrs Dewar.

'It's no secret,' the Sergeant said. 'By tomorrow, the whole district will know that we have a barrage balloon up there and two anti-aircraft crews. It will mean us having a door key, Mrs Dewar, to gain access at all times or if you are away, and a chair in the hall for the LAC on duty. He will bring messages to us and then return for more, or if it hots up, two men will be posted, one to take messages and one to be a runner.'

Emma smiled, thinking of the relay of messages for the cream. The Sergeant brightened. 'Do you live here, Miss?'

'Not really,' said Mrs Dewar. 'My daughter's a nurse, you know. We're new to Bristol and she hasn't any friends yet.'

'Of course I have, Mum. I know a lot of people at the Home.'

Mrs Dewar invited the Sergeant to stay for cocoa and went into the kitchen before he could refuse. Emma sighed, but answered questions pleasantly, and when her mother returned she had found out that their caller was twenty-four, his name was John and he had a wife and baby daughter at home in Essex. That should settle Mum, Emma thought.

He left an hour later, leaving Mrs Dewar in a state of excitement. 'We shall be quite important to the War Effort,' she said, 'and all the others in the road will have to wait ages for a telephone. Just wait until I tell Mrs Hammond.'

'A pity you can't telephone now,' said Emma dryly.

A telephone engineer came the next morning to link up the set and an airman borrowed a front door key to have more cut. Emma walked up to the field and saw the amorphous heap of silvery balloon fabric wallowing half-inflated on the ends of hausers. Pumps were throbbing and the clumsy whale rose and flopped, struggled and made for the air, rising more quickly as the wind took it. It was tethered just clear of the ground, with its hutments, Land Rovers and generators clustered below it like waiting handmaidens. A fresh platform of concrete was surrounded by sandbags from which peeped a camouflaged anti-aircraft gun and a searchlight.

We really are at war. We could be bombed. Emma felt no panic but knew now that the news was not just propaganda, it was real. She felt the wind in her hair as she gazed skywards. A lonely plane sidled down to the Bristol Aircraft landing strip, a trainer with ochre wings. Of course! The RAF had a base at Filton just beyond the factory. Bristol was vulnerable and would be a military target.

She walked back to the house slowly, avoiding the rough patches in the unmade road. This was the real world, not the cloistered insulated existence within the thick walls of Cotswold stone, where rumours of war lost all impact.

Emma went shopping for her mother and felt foolish when she didn't know about rationing, but accepted all the small wrapped portions that the girl handed her without asking if she wanted them. Customers took everything to which they were entitled as a matter of course, and knew that someone would use what they didn't require. She saw a queue forming and joined it, before she knew that they were selling liver. It was off-ration and so Emma bought what was offered, becoming almost as obsessional as the rest of the waiting women, but when she got back she was depressed. Was this how it would be? When would it end? Surely there was more to life than exclaiming with joy over half a pound of ox liver?

I'll go into town, she decided, and was glad that she was meeting Evans later. When Evans said, 'Penny for your thoughts,' Emma mused, 'I bought half a pound of liver today, off-ration.'

'So what? I hate liver,' said Evans. 'I'm glad they don't often serve it for supper.'

'Do you know that the RAF have taken over our

telephone in case of air raids? We now have a barrage balloon at the top of our road.'

'Have you been drinking? Come on, it's late. Let's get a snack in Berni's. I haven't tried it there and I'm running out of places to feed. Whoever heard of Vienna steaks? I've had them twice recently and all they are is mince made into a rissole but oval and not round. The last one was nearly all potato.'

'Don't you know there's a war on?' She plucked at Evans' sleeve and they listened. Above the city noise, far away over the docks came the first up-lurching wail of the air raid siren.

'Practice,' said Evans and calmly walked towards the café.

Emma thought of the LAC who would be hurrying down to the house on his bicycle to take over the telephone. She thought of the huge grey mass that would be rising to force enemy aircraft to fly high above and away from the aircraft factory if they got that far. 'It is a warning, so we must go back,' she said. They ran up the hill to the Downs and the Home lay rosy red in the evening sun. Traffic went by as if nothing was happening and the sky was empty.

'I shall spit if there is no need for us to go back, on my evening off,' panted Evans. 'We're going to look stupid, turning up as if the whole German army was after us.'

Emma said nothing but forced the pace and they arrived in the lane in time to see three army lorries leaving the school, with a strange-looking gun mounted and towed behind an armoured car. Evans stared. 'Come on! Something *is* up. That's a pom-pom. Tony told me about them. They're used in places where they need a mobile gun, and they're going towards the docks by the look of it!'

Inside, the Home was peaceful. Sister Cary looked at the hot, dishevelled girls with amused cynicism. 'We don't need you here. It's a false alarm.' She stood quite still as the first of the guns sounded like distant thunder, with an almost gentle sound. A loud bell shrilled inside the building and everyone move to their stations.

5

The rumble of bed wheels and the continual whine of the elevator were the only sounds in the usually quiet corridors that indicated anything out of the ordinary was happening. The Home lay solid and dignified on the green edge of the Downs and the gardeners continued to smoke in one of the sheds after work, in spite of the air raid siren and the distant gunfire.

'Trying out the guns, I reckon,' said the head cook as she stirred the béchamel sauce and wondered if the seasoning was right. Sister Ambrose, who happened to be passing through the kitchen, tasted the sauce and gravely gave her opinion. She absentmindedly helped herself to a jam tart and wandered down to the stores, quite forgetting the alert.

Emma and Evans were still in civilian clothes and many of the more vague residents from other wings thought that they were visitors who had come in to help with the emergency. They were unable to believe that any young girl not wearing the butterfly cap could be a Pro or a nurse. Emma tried to push a heavy wheelchair over a two-inch step into the lift. Evans had pressed the button too soon and the lift was temperamental. Together, they heaved it up and two chairs were safely side by side, but already, the iron shaft was being shaken impatiently by nurses on the top floor waiting with more of their charges.

Emma followed the covered way to the subway under the stores and left Miss Styles with Ethel, who was propped up uncomfortably in a chair, half asleep as her sedative was now taking effect. Miss Forsyth, who had shrieked so loudly that Sister Cary had helped push her bed to the lift before anyone else went down, complained that there was a draught.

'Nurse! Nurse?' said Miss Styles. 'Why aren't you in uniform? Has Sister seen you? What will she say?' Her eyes gleamed with anticipation of the row that might ensue.

'She can't say anything,' said Evans shortly. 'This, believe it or not, Miss Styles, is our off-duty, and a fat lot of thanks we're getting for saving all of you from the bombs. Is it worth it?' She ran after Emma. 'The old cow will tell Sister I've been rude to her again,' she said cheerfully.

'I can't hear any guns now,' Emma told her. 'I bet it was a false alarm. They have to try them out to keep everyone on their toes.' She wondered if her mother had hindered the war effort by interrupting the lad by the telephone, or had she gone to the new Anderson shelter next door?

Sister Cary looked up from writing a report as the girls hovered in her doorway. She regarded them with disapproval. 'I don't like to see my nurses here in mufti,' she said. 'Go to the nurses' home until the All Clear then come back properly dressed.'

'But we're off-duty, Sister. Can't we go now? The residents are all safe.'

'We are all on duty during air raids. Even you have to make a few sacrifices, Nurse Evans. You must learn to be unselfish. It's time you learned that nursing is a vocation and that the motto of the Home is to be obeyed.' She half-smiled. 'What is our motto, Nurse?'

'Love serves.'

'I'm glad you know it.' The thin ascending note of the All Clear sounded. Evans stared at the calm woman seated at the desk, her eyes hot with anger, but Sister Cary seemed not to notice. She raised an eyebrow. '*This* time, you may remain in mufti,' she said. 'Go down and bring them up again and settle them down. There will be warm milk in the Wing kitchen for those residents who need it. I'll help with Miss Forsyth and the walking cases.'

'Is Vincent here, Sister? We might need her to help lift.'

'Nurse Vincent is on duty but it appears that it was she who left the commode within reach and was responsible for Mrs Devere's accident, so she has been told to remain with her as it will be impossible to take her to the subway now that the fracture has been extended.' Emma glanced at Evans. 'You may tell Nurse Vincent that she may help downstairs now but she knows her place during any alert we may have; she stays with Mrs Devere whatever happens during a raid, even if bombs are falling.'

'The callous bitch!' said Evans as soon as they were away from the office. She shrugged. 'But as usual, she makes sense. She couldn't leave someone alone up there, with her leg strung up on a Balkan beam. She must have been glad of an excuse to nail Vincent for that job. The wily old thing. It's the perfect answer for her. If there was a case like that on one of the other wings, the Sister would have to choose someone to stay. If Vincent gets bombed, she can justify her choice.'

Vincent was very quiet and Emma sensed that she had been very scared, alone with the sick woman while the alert was on. Vincent wheeled residents back to their rooms but made none of her customary jokes, and it was clear that she was badly shaken by her interview with Sister Cary and the order to stay with Mrs Devere.

The mobile gun turned into the lane as Evans and Emma walked out to the main road. It was too good an evening to waste as Matron had given them both late passes so long as they stayed together and didn't remain in town in the blackout after the buses stopped running. They caught a bus to Queen's Road and bought a newspaper, but it had been printed before the alert and there was no fresh news, just engagements abroad, and yet more territories being eaten up by the German war machine. 'It's all so far away,' said Evans with relief. 'Come on, I'm sure this is the place.'

'Is it?' asked Emma with disbelief.

The tiny room in the side street was crammed with tables in varying degrees of decay, covered with oil-cloth. A bottle of bright red tomato sauce had spilled some of its contents over a particularly nasty pattern on one cover and the ancient wallpaper hung in shreds in one corner of the room.

'It's very busy, so we'll have to queue,' said Evans, 'but this is the place they mentioned. They said the surroundings weren't up to much but they were right about the food. I haven't seen such big portions in a café for months.' They waited for nearly half an hour and when they did get a table, they ordered fish and chips. 'We could have steak,' whispered Evans, 'but I can't afford it tonight.' Emma was relieved because she couldn't afford it either as she had only a few shillings to last her until the end of the month, but the fish was fresh and delicious. 'Steak?' said Evans. 'Who wants steak when you can have this.' They ate and paid and pushed through the queue that now filled the garden path.

'The steak must be on the black market,' said Emma. 'Oh, I've laddered my stockings on that awful old chair. I wish I knew someone who could get me more stockings. This is my last decent pair.'

'Let's walk back,' Evans suggested. 'It's not very late and there are masses of people about so we'll be all right. I've eaten far too much and need some exercise.' There were Home Guards on the

Downs, self-consciously carrying guns and wearing ill-fitting coarse uniforms. Army lorries crawled away in the dusk towards the docks and the balloons were still high. Along the lane, soldiers stood in small groups smoking and eyeing anyone who came or went through the wide gateway of the Home. Wolf whistles followed the girls and one or two men called after them, but they walked steadily on. Evans tossed her dark head with mingled amusement and annoyance. They were not followed, but Emma felt uneasy and wondered what it would be like when she had to walk back alone from the bus. It was almost dark, and further down the lane they heard giggles and one muffled laughing scream.

Vincent was in the lobby, dressed in her outdoor clothes. 'You aren't off-duty tonight,' said Evans.

'It's after supper and I *am* off, even if the rules say I must stay in. Don't sneak on me, Pro Evans. I'm fed up with this place. I'm going out.' She buttoned her jacket and tried to smile. 'You won't say anything, will you? Sister has been ... Oh, she's so awful. She went on and on and on.' Her voice broke.

'How will you get back in? It's getting late now. No use giving you our late passes as they'll check names against the signing-in book. If they think you are in, you could get locked out all night, unless you ring the night bell.' Evans was worried. 'You've had one big row, Vincent. Do you think you ought? Not tonight. They'd give you the sack if they caught you now.'

'They don't bother with us assistants as much as they do with you innocent ewe lambs of Pros. They think you know nothing of the big bad world but we can take our chances. I hope they do find out. I'm leaving as soon as I can. I just can't stand that woman any more.' She glanced up defiantly, but her eyes were hurt. 'I was scared up there with Mrs Devere snoring away and the ack-ack blazing. Go on, laugh! I know you all do. You think of me as big, thick-skinned Vincent who hasn't the guts or the intelligence to shift myself and do my training. I'm twenty-two and no nearer it than I was at eighteen. I've stuck here and I'm fed up and I never want to see that hard-faced bitch again.'

'You aren't running away?'

Vincent sighed. 'No, I haven't the courage for that. Not tonight, anyway. I'd never find Gloucester in the blackout. I'll go to a club I know, and when I come back, I'll climb in through the linen store window. It's easy but I'll have to hang around until the porter unlocks the nurses' home door to polish the hall floor. He's always early and I can slip past him and change.'

'But you hate the dark and you hate being alone,' said Evans.

Vincent laughed with a little more of her old spirit. She gave a knowing wink and outlined her mouth with scarlet lipstick. 'I might not be on my own all the time,' she said. She shook out her hair and let it fall to her shoulders from the French pleat she wore on duty, glanced in the mirror on the wall and picked up her handbag. She walked carefully on the very high heels and the tight skirt outlined her buttocks. The thin silk stockings showed off very good legs.

'Our Vinnie looks a real tart tonight,' said Evans. 'I wonder who gave her those stockings.'

'Where is she going?'

'I saw her in a club off Whiteladies Road one night when my brother took me there. She was with a crowd of local people, mostly men, but a few women. Businessmen mostly. I wonder if she's thought about it enough? She'll be scared stiff walking across the Downs in the blackout, but she's so mad that she hasn't considered that.' They heard a distant wolf whistle. 'She's run the first gauntlet,' said Evans dryly. 'Perhaps she needn't go any further.'

'What do you mean?'

'Hasn't Mummie ever told you, dear? When a woman has that look in her eyes, she's out to find a man, and Vinnie isn't all that fussy, from what I hear.' They signed the book and heated milk for Horlicks. Emma brought some biscuits down to the Common Room and they ate hungrily as if they'd touched no food for hours, then went thankfully to bed.

Emma was nearly asleep when the siren sounded. She saw that it was midnight, dressed quickly and flung her cloak round her shoulders. A senior nurse was unlocking the front door and Pros and nurses ran to their various wings.

Sister Cary was wide awake, on duty before anyone and immaculate. She gave orders and the beds and chairs began to roll again. 'If this is another false alarm, I shall spit!' said Bea Shuter. 'Where's Vincent?' The rest of the staff on Wing Six were busy except for two who had sleeping-out passes and were too far away to return for the alert.

'Wish she'd hurry up, Sister's getting waspish. She keeps calling for her to sit with Mrs Devere. She can't leave her alone strung up like that.'

'Nurse Vincent?' Sister was opening and shutting all the doors along the corridor. She glanced into the kitchen, the dining room and then searched Green Alley. 'Where's Nurse Vincent?'

'I haven't seen her since the siren,' said Emma.

'She's hiding, or she's gone down with the residents. Go down and tell her to report to me at once,' said Sister Cary. Emma hesitated. 'Do as I tell you, Nurse Dewar. Vincent knows where she must be during raids.'

'Perhaps she's frightened,' ventured Emma.

Sister sniffed. 'What nonsense. There's nothing to frighten anyone here. The Germans would not dare to bomb the Home. Vincent is lazy and careless and not fit to care for anyone but she knows what I expect from her.' Her pale eyes glinted and her voice rasped more than usual. She's enjoying this, thought Emma. Bea looked at Evans who turned down the corners of the mouth and drew her aside, and Emma went down to the busy subway, wondering where Vincent could be, alone in the city or on the dark and silent Downs.

'I can't find her, Sister. Perhaps she didn't hear the siren and is asleep,' she said, hoping that Sister would now give up and leave the row until morning. She backed away and fled, taking refuge with Bea who was struggling with a heavy bed that had uneven castors that were not intended for such heavy duty.

'What's up? Evans tried to say something but there were too many people about. Vincent run off, has she?'

'She's out without a pass,' Emma whispered.

'Crikey! She's for the high jump.' Miss Styles tried to stop them as they passed her chair and asked where Vincent had gone. 'Trust her to smell a rat,' murmured Bea. 'She's on special duty with Mrs Devere,' said Bea sweetly. 'Isn't Mrs Devere lucky to have a nurse all to herself? If you could break a leg, I'd stay with you, Miss Styles.' Miss Styles looked at her sharply, but Bea was smiling tenderly.

'I thought Nurse Dewar was looking for her down here,' said Miss Styles, suspiciously. 'While you are here, Nurse, would you go back to my room and fetch my brandy? I didn't take it after dinner; I saved it in case there was an air raid, as I get so nervous.'

'Good grief! Are we expected to give drinks

parties as well as losing our beauty sleep?' asked Bea. 'If I go up to your room, they'll all want something and I *must* do as Sister says, mustn't I? She said we have to stay down here until the All Clear.'

'Then what about Sister and what about Nurse Vincent?' Bea noticed that Sister had not come down, and she whispered the fact to Evans who shook her head and whispered her reply, making Miss Styles wild with curiosity. 'Nurse,' she said, but they pretended not to hear and moved to the other end of the subway.

Sister Cary stood by the bed of the woman with the fractured hip and listened to the bubbling harsh breathing. She saw the blue lips and smelled the faint odour of putrefaction. She felt for the pulse. Mrs Devere sank deeper into her pillows and nothing could be done to prop her up enough to make her water-logged lungs expand. With no feeling in her legs and one of them on traction, she was a helpless mass of chilled flesh. Sister wiped the crusts from the corners of her mouth, then sat on the bedside chair, hardly hearing the distant explosions. All was peace in the room, with the tranquility that death brings. Sister Cary held the hand of the dying woman with gentle strength, as if physically helping her to make an easy transition from life into the hidden spaces.

She moistened the puffy lips with champagne from a Sèvres feeding cup and wiped the mouth. The champagne trickled out again and a few drops bubbled in Mrs Devere's throat. Sister Cary re-corked the nearly-full bottle and put it on the dressing table with the bowl of hothouse grapes and fragrant peaches.

The sound of laboured breathing continued and Sister put out the light so that she could open the curtains without light escaping from the room.

Searchlights over Avonmouth caught the high barrage balloons in a filigree web and an aero engine droned, heavy with an unfamiliar beat. Ack-ack fire splintered the distance and the droning engine came closer.

On the edge of the Downs, Vincent glanced back to the main road and thought that someone was following her. The clientèle of the club had scattered into the night at the first wail of the siren, with no thought for a young woman out alone. The bank clerk who had hoped to see her home and perhaps have a cuddle on the Downs muttered an apology and said his mother would be worried. The barman shut the inner rooms and looked pointedly at the few remaining customers in the bar. Everyone left and Vincent walked to the top of the hill with two girls who lived in Durham Park. Suddenly, with the empty Downs ahead, she was alone.

Clutching her handbag in her left hand, she held her key ring over two fingers of her right, with the hazy idea of using her keys in self-defence. She took a few steps forward and stopped. Would it better to stay until the All Clear, when cars and people would be moving again? People from shelters would hurry home, respectable people intent on getting to their beds, not men on the loose looking for a cheap pick-up. The sky towards Avonmouth was lit by searchlights and the drone of a plane came nearer. She heard a crunch of something with untidy side effects and the anti-aircraft guns crackled as they followed the searchlights to pinpoint the target.

As the sound came closer, Vincent panicked and ran, thinking only of the safety of the solid walls of the Home and the quiet of her own room, or even the comparative safety of Mrs Devere's room. Why had she been so frightened to stay there? It must be safe within four solid walls of thick stone even if it was not on the ground floor.

Vincent stumbled, her calves ached and the seam of her stocking rubbed where her stocking met the heel of the shoe. She paused to slip a finger between shoe and stocking to ease the pressure on the blister and heard footsteps behind her, coming closer, quickly, with the sharp sound of metal Blakeys on the hard road. Army boots? She ran on, feeling worse now that she had stopped for a rest. The rapid tattoo of her heels, the steady beat of the metal boot-tips and the distant gunfire merged into an erratic pulse in her brain and she ran faster.

The footsteps behind her quickened with an alarming burst of speed. 'What's the hurry?' said the man. 'Can I come, too?'

Vincent ignored him, looking ahead into darkness. Oh, God she thought, why doesn't the moon come through? Why can't he see me and know I'm not like that? He was walking easily by her side, his strides smooth in contrast to her uneven stumblings. I mustn't let him see I'm afraid. I mustn't panic, she thought, stifling a shuddering moan that came to her lips. The dark tree shapes swayed and sighed and an early chestnut leaf drifted down to settle on her shoulder. There was the wall that marked the beginning of the grounds, but she knew that the small gate on the main road would be locked. There was menace at her side. He was very quiet. Why didn't he speak? She touched the wall as if the familiar stone would protect her and followed it to the end of the lane between the school and the building she had left and thought she hated, two hours ago.

'Where are you going? Where is this?' He sounded angry. 'There's nothing down here. It leads to a hospital, or something.'

'I'm a nurse,' she managed to say.

He gave a coarse laugh. 'So's my arse! Come off it, dearie. I saw you waiting for custom at the top of the Downs. One of the Sea Walls lot, are you? Too stuck up for me? Waiting for a nice car to do it in?'

'No, I really am a nurse,' she said desperately. 'I have to get back on duty while the alert is on. I have to stay with an old lady who can't be moved to the subway.'

The wrought-iron gates loomed up against the sky. Let them be unlocked, she prayed. Oh, God let them be unlocked. She tried to go faster but her legs refused to coordinate.

'Why didn't you say?' he asked, half-believing her. 'Why make me come all this way? No, you're no nurse! You don't fancy me, I suppose. Don't fancy Home Guard uniform, is that it? I can pay maybe better than most.'

'Please! Go home and leave me alone. I *am* a nurse and I have to be on duty.' The gates were near. Oh, God – let me touch them and scream and someone must hear me. Someone *must* hear me.

'You had me on.' The voice was cold. 'I went up the Downs, special. I wanted a tart and I'm bloody well having one.' He seized her shoulders and swung her towards him. She struck wildly at him with the keys but her hand did no more than fan his face and the keys fell on the ground. He shook her and slapped her face, a sullen fury in his hands, then forced his mouth on to hers. He smelled of onions and stale beer and sweat and she tried to turn away, revolted, but his hands tore at her blouse and the thin rayon satin ripped away from the buttonholes. Vincent swung her handbag and hit the side of his head. He ducked away, expecting another blow and relaxed his grip. Vincent kneed him in the groin and twisted away, leaving her jacket in his hands. She ran for the gate and tugged but nothing happened. She remembered that the gates opened inwards and pushed. She fell through into the drive and fled for the nurses' home. He shouted, leaving her in no doubt what he would do when he caught her, and she heard him running on the gravel, stopping to listen and then cautiously picking a way along the side of the flower bed.

Vincent crouched behind the pillar on the porch, now blessing the complete darkness. She thought the door was locked but she could ring the bell if he came any closer. Surely he wouldn't come right up to the door? She heard him swearing and the rip of her jacket as he deliberately tore it, then the sound of Blakeys on first gravel and then the tarmac of the lane, as his boots clicked away to the main road. She leaned against the door and it opened. Of course, there was an alert! She pushed back the heavy folds of blackout curtain inside the door and went up the dimly-lit deserted stairway. She sobbed as she clung to the mahogany banister rails, dragging herself to her room on the first landing. The water pipes made doleful murmurings and a floorboard creaked as she crossed the landing. She flung herself on the bed and wept, and the All Clear sounded.

The lights dipped and glowed in her room as the electricity load increased and the elevators worked overtime to take the residents back to their floors, but Vincent lay exhausted across her bed and heard nothing, letting the tears flow down unrestricted over her cheeks, smudging the mascara on her eyelashes and turning her pancake makeup into a bronze mud. She had forgotten the alert, Sister Cary and the residents and thought only of the rough hands as he slapped and tore at her clothes and tried to force her thighs closer to him to meet his lust. It was impossible to bring the torn edges of her blouse together over her big breasts, but she had no initiative to change or even to hide the damage under a dressing gown. Dimly, she heard the first of the nurses returning to their rooms, and for the first time, wondered if she had been missed.

The door opened softly and Vincent raised her head. Sister Cary stood in the wide open doorway, the light glinting on her silver belt buckle, the crisp lines of her cap undisturbed by air raids, sudden emergencies or recent death. She folded her hands as if waiting for a consultant to make a round of the Wing, and as she surveyed the bed, taking in the torn stockings, the ruined blouse and skirt and the obscenely exposed bosom, she noted with almost clinical curiosity how that particular type of makeup went darker when wet with tears and how repulsive it was on a swollen bruised face.

'Nurse Vincent,' she said in a quiet voice that could have cut steel. 'We have missed you. Your friends tried to cover for you and they tried to convince me that you were in bed and had overslept and not heard the alert, but I knew better.' She stepped closer and Vincent sat hypnotised, her lipstick smudged and her lips swelling where his teeth had caught them. She looks almost as bad as Miss Styles when she wears lipstick, thought Sister Cary. She looks quite as revolting.

'So as well as being a coward, a bad nurse and irresponsible member of staff, you are also a slut.' She paused as if to allow Vincent to reply, but the terrified girl only stared at her. 'You are a slut who goes with men and I don't have to put words to what that makes you.'

'I didn't,' ventured Vincent.

'It will be my duty to tell Matron what I have seen here tonight. She will agree that you are not fit to mix with young Pros and contaminate their minds.'

'Sister, you must believe me! I did nothing wrong except to go out after duty. I was coming across the Downs to get back on duty and I was attacked. He tried to rape me.'

'What were you doing out on the Downs alone late at night? You were on your own, without a pass. Why go walking if *that* was not on your mind? And made up to look like a prostitute!'

Vincent began to sob again and Sister Cary stood stiffly before her, seeming to fill the room with her dynamic personality. She smiled as if what she had to say would amuse Vincent. 'I'm not so concerned with your morals, Nurse. Not this time. I've really come to tell you some news.' She flicked off her working cuffs and rolled down her sleeves as if finishing a piece of work to her own satisfaction. She buttoned the cuffs of the dress with care. Vincent dared not speak.

'You've killed Mrs Devere,' said Sister Cary in a mild, conversational voice. 'She died an hour ago.' She heard the sound of wheels on the gravel, the sound coming clearly even through the thick curtains. 'Listen. That must be her now, on her way to the mortuary.'

Vincent turned on her face and buried it in the pillow, trying to shut out the sound, and Sister Cary swept out past the group of nurses who had listened to every word. They shrank back to let her through and she went down the stairs and out to the Sisters' Home, outwardly unaware of the wave of shock and dislike that followed her.

Bea bent over the shaking woman. 'Vincent, what happened? You poor thing. Oh, you poor thing.' She took the woman in her arms, ignoring the brown patches that rubbed off on her pale blue dressing gown. She stroked her head and Emma brought a glass of water. Evans fumed by the door, too furious to speak and the whole of the nurses' home hummed with the news that Vincent had only just escaped being raped and that all Sister Cary could do was to accuse her of murder.

They undressed her as if she was a helpless resident, washing her face free of the tears and makeup and they disposed of the torn blouse and stockings. One shoe was missing and the wardrobe was locked, which made it impossible to get out fresh clothes until they found the keys where Vincent had dropped them, but all she really needed was cleanliness and a nightie from a drawer.

Emma tossed in bed an hour later, recalling the ice in Sister's voice, the terrible things she'd said and tried to forget her gentleness with Ethel, her care with Miss Forsyth and the wonderful way she ran the Wing for the comfort of the residents.

She doesn't make sense. I wonder if she's mad?

6

'There's a letter for you,' said Clare Dewar. 'It's not from Emily. Not her writing.' She peered at the unfamiliar writing and the smudged postmark, reluctant to give it up until she knew the contents. 'Well, aren't you going to open it?'

Emma turned the envelope over. 'I think it's from one of the girls I knew at school. It looks familiar. I'll read it later and drop her a line. It's time I wrote a few letters but I keep putting it off.' The weeks had passed into months and the Island seemed as remote as a dream, but she could still conjure up places and people whenever she thought of them and the memory never failed to fill her with regret and nostalgia, but wartime Bristol made many demands on her time and she was often too weary to daydream about peaceful cliffs, the breaking waves and the soft air.

It would be good to lie on a beach today, she thought, glancing out at the badly-dug garden with its harvest of wireworm riddled potatoes. The sun was hot and the breeze in her hair as she cycled home from the Downs had been dusty and dry. Her mother snapped shut the clasp of her purse and examined the ration books. Emma remembered the Emergency Ration Card she had and produced it crumpled from her pocket. 'They give us these, now. One a month if we sleep out for days off.'

'How much meat is there?' Clare Dewar smiled. 'That's not bad. With ours, we can have a real joint of beef. When do you come in again?'

'Don't bother about me. I don't mind what I have. Use it for the weekend. I expect Dad and you can do with a bit extra. If I have a holiday, I shall have more cards to cover any time from the Home.' The food was still good at the Home and Emma felt guilty if she ate any rations from her parents' books.

'It's time you had leave. They work you all hours and make you push heavy beds. It shouldn't be allowed.'

Emma ignored this latest grumble. Once, she had let slip the fact that the residents were taken to the subway every time the siren sounded, and now, her mother pounced on this as if a crime had been committed. It made no difference to her that she was among the first to take shelter in her road. She had a bag packed with personal and household treasures ready to take to the Anderson shelter next door with a basket of food and Thermos flasks of coffee and hot soup whenever a raid was threatened.

She was very proud of the fact that the Dewars had an early warning of raids as the RAF still used the telephone and told her when raids were imminent. Emma had spent one night in the Anderson, her shoulder hard against the damp wall with a smell of musty earth everywhere. It was hot and crowded and claustrophobic and she had only stayed because she couldn't face the cycle ride back to the Home at two o'clock in the morning. The six-mile rule had been relaxed, to everyone's relief; it was understood that staff would return if possible, but only if it was safe to leave other shelter to do so. Extra muscle was provided for bed-pushing by soldiers from the batch next door, to the delight of the residents.

After the attack on Vincent, the committee had seen the danger of girls returning late in the blackout, and Vincent had escaped censure from them; they had concluded that her ordeal was punishment enough. Sister Cary was tight-lipped when her demand for Vincent's dismissal was refused but she still made snide comments when her work wasn't good enough. Vincent applied for work in the Land Army on a farm near her home in Gloucester, and the routine of the Home went on.

Mrs Devere was laid to rest in her family grave, a small announcement appeared in *The Times*, with brief details of her husband's career in the Foreign Office, the room was cleaned and garnished afresh with bright chintzes and it was as if she had never been in the Home. '*There were many touching floral tributes*,' said a local paper report, and Emma wondered who had sent them, as Mrs Devere had received no visitors for a very long time.

Emma cycled back to the Home and breathed deeply under the riot of late roses that climbed over the wall of the nurses' home. She opened her bedroom window wide to look across the central flower bed where two men were working, slowly and methodically. The young men had gone but there were still five gardeners who were over the age of military service, and it was as if nothing could touch the peace and gentle passage of time within the high walls.

She opened the letter and sat hard on the bed. It wasn't from Eileen, the girl with whom she had played tennis in the school team. It was from Phillip, who had asked Aunt Emily for her address. Emma felt her cheeks warming and was surprised to find how glad she was to hear from him. He was home on leave, he said, and was returning to duty at a camp, '*somewhere in England*'. An inspired guess told him it might to near to Bristol.

'*I joined up as an LAC and was chosen for a course right away.*' Emma recalled the bright boy who had come top in nearly every subject and had a Special in maths. '*I'm taking officer training and hope to fly.*' He gave an address which could reach him, and under the casual tone she detected an urgency, a need to contact her, or someone like her with a link with his home. She wrote a short note, telling him the dates of her next two days off, and the address of the Home. As an afterthought, she gave him the telephone number of her parents' house.

Evans burst in without knocking. 'Know what? Brother Tony is coming on leave. He's coming here to Bristol and I've asked Matron if I can have some of the extra time off they keep promising.'

'What did she say?'

'She agreed, reluctantly. Suspicious old so-and-so. Do you know, she wanted to read the letter! She thought I was off for a dirty weekend! After Vinnie she thinks we're all panting after carnal pleasures.'

'Did you show it to her?'

'No, I certainly did not! I said that if she doubted my word, then I'd bring him to see her and introduce him. She had the grace to apologise.'

'I wish I had your nerve, Evans. When does he come?'

'Not until Friday week. I'm going to stay at the Grand for two nights and have some fun. He'll stay there, too, and we can see some night life that hasn't hot water pipes running through it!'

'But that will cost the earth!'

Evans shrugged. 'Money is no problem. Never has been and I've nowhere to spend it and nowhere to go as a rule so I keep forgetting to go to the bank. I think I'll buy something new if I can find anything wearable. Come to Brights with me and help me choose.'

'I had a letter, too,' said Emma shyly.

'Dewar! You are blushing. A hidden lover? I do believe you've been holding out on us all. Just wait until Sister Cary hears. She'll label you a scarlet woman immediately. Who is he? Let these poor old starved ears hear about your romance, dear.'

'Oh, stow it, Evans,' said Emma, throwing a pillow at her. 'It's not like that.' She told Evans about Phillip and Evans suggested that she must ask for extra time off, too. 'I don't know. I think I'll leave it. I really don't know him very well apart from a few walks round Carisbrooke Castle and visits to the cinema. Suppose I don't like him after I've said I have plenty of time off. He might not like me after all this time.' She found it hard to recall what he looked like. Funny. Phillip who had taken her home from school, been to tea with Aunt Emily and played tennis with the crowd, was faceless, while she recalled every detail of Miss Forsyth and Miss Styles.

'Take your usual evening and day off,' Evans advised,' and take some time later if you do like him.'

'I'll do that,' said Emma, but when Evans had gone, she looked out her prettiest summer dress with cap sleeves and a wide belt and whitened her buckskin shoes, then hurried on duty for the evening, remembering that it was her turn to pull the blackout curtains in the maids' rooms.

The domestic staff had rooms on the top floor of the main building, each maid having a comfortable room with good solid furniture and thick curtains, but lights had been reported visible from the windows and it was now the duty of Sister Ambrose to arrange a rota of nurses to see that it was done properly. A very vulgar Air Raid Warden had threatened Matron with prosecution if the blackout didn't conform to regulations. According to Sister Cary, Matron had been saddened and affronted and said that it didn't do to give power to such people.

Emma reported to Sister Ambrose. She nodded vaguely when Emma told her that she was ready to go and pull the curtains. Sister Ambrose rummaged in a drawer and produced a large bar of chocolate. She gave it to Emma with the order not to tell the others. 'Come back after doing the blackout. I've asked Sister Cary to spare you to help me lay out the vestments in the sacristy. The Bishop is paying us a visit tomorrow,' she added, without enthusiasm. 'That means taking out his special cope.' She sighed at the thought that her routine would be upset.

Emma ran up the stairs to the maids' corridor, ignoring the lift and feeling lighthearted. It seemed a pity to draw the curtains on a warm night but she hurried from room to room, efficiently blotting out the sky, disgusted by the spilled face powder and cheap scent that stained the dressing tables. As each maid was responsible for cleaning her own room, the difference in personal habits was clear. Only in the rooms of Ivy, and Winnie, Matron's maid were any signs of care and their rooms were neat and disciplined and smelled of polish.

She needed air after the stuffy bedrooms and climbed the stairs she had noticed on a previous tour of the rooms. The flight of stairs led to the flat roof between the gables. She tried the door and it opened, stiffly. Emma stepped out and saw the sky tinged with rose and turquoise. She walked to the low parapet. Below, the gardens stretched and seemed to merge with the green Downs. The sinking sun glinted on the glass of the immense greenhouses and the vinery, and the well-weeded paths cut gently into the manicured turf. There was complete stillness in the gardens, and on the Downs beyond except for two distant figures walking a dog.

Emma traced the smile of a gargoyle at the edge of the leads. There were gargoyles guarding each projection, some benign and some obscene in their malevolence. They are seen only by people like me who come up here almost by accident, she thought, and yet the craftmanship was as good as anything on view day after day in the main buildings. They gazed at the dusky sky, and above the chimneys, small bats circled.

The door closed behind her and she stole back to the chapel. Sister Ambrose handed her a small pair of scissors and told her to unpick the stitches in the sheet shrouding the Bishop's robes. 'It will all have to be sewn up again after he goes,' she said glumly, and popped a sugared almond in her mouth to give her the energy to watch Emma working. Together, they inspected the gleaming altar silver and the priceless baroque lamp, straightened the candles in the long candle holders and made sure there was plenty of Altar wine and wafers in the tiny cupboard. It was almost too dark to see and they couldn't black out the high windows so they closed the door carefully as they left, to prevent the corridor lights from showing through the chapel windows.

As Emma walked across the garden after supper, the siren went and the heavy crump of bombs came clearly on the still air from the coast. It was a bad night, with many enemy planes trying to find the aircraft factory, using the river as a guide from Avonmouth. A dull glow came from the docks and Emma felt her mouth go dry as she heard the earth tremble away towards Filton.

The residents were surprisingly philosophical and Miss Forsyth persuaded nurses to read to her to pass the time, almost resenting the All Clear. At four o'clock, the weary nurses climbed into bed and the call bell shattered their deep sleep after what seemed like minutes.

'Have you heard?' The whole place was suddenly aware of life outside the Home as rumours spread that Avonmouth was flattened, the aircraft factory destroyed and the centre of the city had been hit.

'It's that Mr Goering,' said Miss Styles. 'He isn't a gentleman, you know. My brother, who is a very important official in the Foreign Office says he is very odd; very odd indeed. He uses scent, you know.'

'How can she know that when her brother comes only once a year to see her when he can't put off paying the bills any longer? It beats me how she knows,' chuckled Bea. 'She'd be good in charge of counter-espionage. The Germans wouldn't have a chance.' She glanced at Emma. 'You all right?'

'Do you think Matron would let me use the phone to ring my parents? I heard something heavy drop over in that direction.'

Bea took her arm, and marched her off to the porter's lodge and within minutes, Emma was speaking to her mother, who was in a bad temper as she had fallen asleep in the shelter and missed all the excitement, although she reluctantly admitted that there had been no damage near them. Emma rang off as quickly as possible. Now she knew there was no danger, she wanted to sever the link again between her two lives. She refused her mother's offer to ring the Home after raids. 'I'll ring you. It's easier for me,' said Emma.

The mobile guns rumbled back down the lane and firemen laid out long snaking hoses on the Downs in front of the Home to be checked and re-rolled. 'How untidy it makes it,' said Miss Styles later that day, from her shady, sheltered spot under a chestnut tree. 'It should be forbidden. I do believe I need a stimulant, Nurse. Will you fetch my brandy? It's all too exhausting.' She took a sip from the glass held by a white-faced Pro, then snuggled under her rug. 'I think I'll have a little nap,' she said. 'I need my sleep.'

'Don't we all?' said Evans.

'Ah, but you are young and strong, my dear.

You enjoy late nights, don't you? Where will you go when your brother comes to see you? Will he take you to a nightclub? Are there many open now that the sirens go so often? Are you allowed to go to such places? I can imagine Sister Cary's face if she heard that you frequented such places.'

'If I find one sufficiently shocking, I'll come and fetch you, Miss Styles,' said Evans. She told Emma about the conversation. 'How does she do it? I think she has a crystal ball. For goodness sake don't tell her that you have a boyfriend coming to see you or she'll make a meal of it.' She laughed. 'But it would be nice to make her really curious. Wouldn't it be good if we met *both* the boys. I'd love to walk out of here with two men.'

'It's a lovely idea but I doubt if we could do that,' said Emma ruefully. 'Isn't it a rule that officers and other ranks can't mix socially? I've known brothers who can't drink in the same bars. Phillip is only a cadet and you said that Tony has a commission.'

'What rubbish. Who is to know, if they are out of uniform? But I suppose they would wear uniform.' Evans made a face but didn't pursue the subject.

The raids continued, bad enough to send everyone to shelter but doing little damage inland. However, when Phillip arrived he told Emma of attacks on convoys off the south coast, with stray bombs landing on the Island and on south coast resorts, and Emma found it difficult to visualise the West Wight covered with barbed wire and camouflaged guns and searchlights. She wondered if she really wanted to go back if the high cliffs were so desecrated.

Phillip was more serious than she recalled, with a more stolid manner but it was a relief to have someone of her own age for company, away from the Home. He was obviously pleased to see her and the grey eyes under the carefully-angled Air Force cap with the white flash showing that he was taking officer training, held a warmth that was disturbing.

They ate a meal in the city and Mrs Dewar insisted that Phillip should spend the night with them so that Emma could show him over Bristol the next day. He hired a bicycle from the local shop and pumped up the tyres of Emma's cycle before they pedalled over the Suspension Bridge into the country, eating bread and cheese in a small pub and then walking along a stream under the beech trees. It was warm, with the sultry warmth of a fine late summer, the earth soaked in sunshine and the trees growing lazy, letting their leaves hang down now that the fruit was ripening

Emma bought apples to take home to her mother and the farmer's wife gave her a half pound of butter, saying that she often had some to spare if Emma was ever out that way again.

'Do we have to go back?' Phillip lounged on the bank of the stream, in his shirtsleeves. Without his cap, he was more like the boy she remembered on their walks round the Castle and over Mount Joy and Emma was more at ease with him. She picked up the cap and fingered the fine worsted cloth, so much better quality than the army uniforms she saw on the boys billeted in the school next door to the Home. He was smart and well-groomed and smelled of soap and hair cream. She teased him about being one of the RAF Brylcream Boys and he ruffled her hair and kissed her cheek. His hands were firm and his touch lingered, but as she saw the laughter die from his eyes and his mouth grow tender, she drew away, smoothing her crumpled dress and trying to rub the grass stains from her white shoes, while he watched, biting inches off a long blade of grass.

Emma sat aloof on a log while he slowly fixed his tie and uniform and put the cap at the regulation angle. He looked so good that Emma regretted evading his more ardent kiss, and they rode back quickly as it was downhill most of the way. They took the apples and butter back and went out again. Emma was glad that her mother was out at a Wardens' meeting and could make no suggestive comments, or make extravagant oohs and aahs about the butter for Phil's benefit. She scribbled a note, Phillip took the cycle back and they caught a bus into town. The sky was clear and Phillip looked up and frowned. 'Just the night for a raid,' he said. The city engulfed them in dusty dry air. They ate lumpy vegetables and Vienna steaks in a café and moved closer to the Downs for some coffee.

It was dark when Phillip escorted her to the gates of the Home, minutes before her late pass expired. The lane was deserted. It would be, she thought. If I was on my own there would be a group of soldiers, whistling after me and trying to make a date. Phillip drew her to him, awkwardly. The first kiss landed on her ear and she giggled. The next had more confidence and took far longer. 'You'll write?' he said.

'I'll answer any you send,' she said.

'I have no idea when I'll get another pass, but you will come out with me again when I do? I've missed you, Emma. I can't tell you how much this means.'

'Must go. I have to sign the book,' she said. 'Goodnight, Phil. Take care.'

'And you, and don't forget me. Be good.' His hand clung to hers for a moment longer and then she ran quickly into the driveway.

He was still at the gate when she opened the door of the nurses' home and when Bea came in a few minutes later, she said that there was a RAF type in the lane. 'Not bad, at least in the dark,' said Bea. Nadine made no comment, but as Bea said, she would notice no one under the rank of Squadron

Leader. Emma said that she had been out with him and had known him for years. Bea looked surprised but asked no questions and was far too interested in her own day off to want the confidences of a girl as green as Emma.

Emma wondered when she would see him again. He'd said nothing about his training but she could understand that as it was essential to keep quiet about such matters and when Clare Dewar had pressed for details, he had grinned and said he had no idea what the Air Ministry had in store for him but he would like another cup of tea if there was one going spare. The hoardings carried messages like '*Careless talk costs lives*', and '*Keep it to yourself; don't be a Fifth Columnist!*' The less she knew, the better, Emma decided. She could pass on nothing in conversation with anyone, and her mother could say nothing to that awful friend of hers, who gossiped about everyone.

She hoped to see Phillip again soon. I suppose he could be in danger when he finishes the course, she thought and found that it mattered. He was a link with her past and the Island, but that wasn't all. He was warm and human, and after months looking after flabby, querulous old ladies, he was blessedly young.

7

Miss Dingle arrived during lunch and Sister Cary clucked with annoyance as she wasn't expected until the Wing was quiet and the residents were taking afternoon naps. The uniformed chauffeur helped the head porter with the hand luggage and the two under-porters gazed dolefully at the heavy leather trunks that stood on each side of the hall. Each piece of luggage was sprinkled with labels hinting that any place Miss Amelia Dingle had not bothered to visit was unworthy of a label.

Sister sent Vincent down with a wheelchair and told Ivy to check the bedroom to make sure that everything was in order. She left the last of the lunch servings to Bea and Evans so that she could wait at the lift gates to receive her newest addition, and be a one-woman, immaculate reception committee.

All that morning, Miss Styles had been agog and the nurses grew tired of answering her bell. 'What is it now, Miss Styles?' asked Evans as it rang for the fifth time.

'I didn't ring, dear. It isn't working properly. I just touched it and it went off.' Her neck twitched with excitement. 'But as you are here, my handkerchief is on the floor. Has the new resident arrived?'

'I'll sound a bugle when she does and you'll be the first to know, as usual,' said Evans.

'I'll tell Sister you were rude to me, Nurse Evans.' She smiled with an assumed attempt at understanding. 'Or has she put you in a bad mood with all her tellings off and the hard work she makes you do?'

'We all love her dearly,' said Evans and slammed the door after her, cursing Miss Styles, Sister Cary, new residents and most of all, Hitler for disturbing her sleep for so long. Tony had gone back saying he'd ring as soon as he heard about his next leave, and for a while they had escaped the mundane when they stayed at a civilised hotel, saw a good play and rode into the country in a hired car, but the coming back had been traumatic and Evans dreaded Tony's next letter which he hinted would be to tell her he had embarkation leave.

Poor Tony, and poor me, she thought. When he goes, it will be my last close relative with whom I have any sense of belonging apart from my father. It had been good to have this time together and he had confided in her more than usual when she asked laughingly about his love life. Evans now knew that Tony was in love but could make no commitment in case he was killed in action.

She thought of her brother often and wondered if in his dark, Celtic way he had a death wish or some premonition of evil. She shrugged away the morbid thoughts and put her sadness down to lack of sleep.

The lift doors clanged discreetly and Sister stood erect, all smiles while Vincent wheeled Miss Dingle into the corridor. Sister's smile froze. She had heard about her new resident, amply supplied with references from eminent clergy and titled members of the acting profession, with plenty of money to fulfil her obligations to the Home, but until that moment, when the lift doors slid back, she had not seen her.

For wartime Britain, Miss Dingle was a sight for sore eyes. She emerged as a bird of paradise, her dyed hair red and flowing over her purple velvet cloak which was clasped on one shoulder by an immense pin, large enough as Evans remarked later, to pin back the curtain of the Theatre Royal. Her full, gypsy skirt and blouse were bright and shining patent leather shoes peeped out aggressively from under the many folds. Sister also noticed the painted nails and the mascara and decided in one second that Miss Dingle was *not* a lady.

Miss Dingle eyed Sister Cary coolly. 'Hello, sweetie,' she said. 'Do you think I could have a very dry Martini? I am simply parched.'

Vincent's eyes lit up with joy. She was glad she had stayed on at the Home. She was glad that the Government had seen fit to tell her that nursing was a reserved occupation and she couldn't change it for a life on the land. It was worth it to see the internal explosion being controlled under the crimped grey-blue hair of Sister Cary.

'First things first, Miss Dingle. You must be tired. Nurse Vincent, please take Miss Dingle to her room while I telephone Dr Drake.' She smiled. '*He* will prescribe such stimulants that he sees fit for you to have here. Our duty is to your health and well-being and you do have a heart murmur, I believe.'

'A dry Martini never hurt anyone and I'm thirsty.' The voice was lower and a trifle worried. 'Matron, I'm thirsty!'

'I am not Matron. I am Sister Cary in whose charge you will be while you are resident here. If Dr Drake says you can have Martinis, they will be prescribed as are all stimulants in the Home, and dispensed as medicaments. Until then, if you are thirsty, Nurse will prepare fresh orange juice or lemonade, barley water or fresh milk. Lunch will be sent to your room immediately.' Sister turned away and a hint of amused respect gleamed in Miss Dingle's eyes.

'She certainly knows how to exit,' she said. 'Quite, quite superb.'

Vincent led the little procession and Miss Dingle threw off her cloak as she entered the room, raising herself to her feet by means of a gold-topped walking stick. She went to the window and gazed out at the dull sky then turned back to the room with a slight shudder. 'This is my home,' she said, dramatically. 'After all I have had, all I have done and been, this tiny room is all I have left.' The porter dropped one of the cases and Vincent looked unimpressed so Miss Dingle dropped her pose. 'Was she really serious?' she asked. 'Is this place dry?' She rummaged in a huge bag and produced a flask. 'Just as well I took precautions.' She popped the flask into the bureau, locked the drawer and put the key in her bag.

Evans tapped on the door and brought in the lunch tray. Miss Dingle raised the silvery lid over the fricassée of veal and noted with satisfaction the silvers of lemon, the fresh vegetables and the *pommes duchesse*. Evans arranged the tray on the small table by the window and withdrew, exchanging delighted glances with Vincent who was smiling broadly for the first time since she heard that the Land Army wouldn't take her.

As they left, Sister met them with Dr Drake in tow. Firmly, she took him into the room and shut the door. The girls tried to listen but could hear only a murmur of voices. They fled as the door opened again and ran to answer Miss Styles' bell. 'I heard the lift. Was it the dispensary?' she asked. 'It isn't often as late as this.'

'But you have had your tablets, and your brandy. Was there anything more you wanted?' Evans asked politely. Miss Styles fussed and tried to keep her but Evans wouldn't say if the new resident had arrived. 'Why not stay up after Green Alley and have dinner in the dining room? You miss all the fun in here,' was all she would say. Half an hour later, Miss Styles rang again, asking to have her bath before going to the sitting room. 'Well, that's one off the bath list for tonight,' said Evans when Emma asked who was being done early.

Miss Dingle was a complete success from nearly every point of view. She brought a shock wave of colour and frankness to the Home, she waved aside petty rules and insisted on draping her bed with gaudy indian rugs and on the floor she had a tiger skin. 'Given to me by a very wealthy admirer, dear,' she said. Sister was quiet but watchful, and Emma wondered what went on under the neatly crimped hair, as apart from these small idiosyncrasies, Miss Dingle was very little trouble to anyone. She was the ideal resident, needing minimal nursing care and she arrived punctually in the dining room for meals. She moved slowly, as if afraid that her heart would give her pain or bring on some kind of attack. She rested every afternoon, with a Do Not Disturb notice on her door and seldom rang a bell. After her rests, she would emerge and make an erratic course to Green Alley and it became apparent that Miss Dingle used her siesta time for refreshment, not only of body and mind, but to ease her thirst.

Dr Drake was completely under her spell and prescribed two stiff whiskys a day and wine if and when she wanted it. Miss Dingle wanted it! She also paid visits to friends whom, she said, lived across the Downs and she made her visits by taxi with carrier bags that held something bulky but light, returning during off-licence hours with heavy carrier bags which she put away, unopened, in the wardrobe.

Her huge trunks remained unpacked in the baggage room as her wardrobe and drawers were already filled with her clothes, and sometimes when Sister was away for a weekend, she would ask one of the Pros to go with her to select clothes to replace the ones she sent to the cleaners. The girls vied with each other to have this job as the contents of the trunks were fascinating. The Pros liked to make her bed and to answer her bell on the rare occasions when she rang, as she was witty and appreciative. Sister tended to ignore her unless she had to speak to her about medicines or recreation, and the residents had mixed feelings about the newcomer.

Miss Styles was jealous. She met her on that first evening and tried to impress the actress with names of important people she knew or had met and by the fact that she knew everything about everyone in the Home and could tell the new resident anything she wanted to know about them. Miss Dingle countered with even more impressive name-dropping and the Pros took bets to see who would emerge victorious from each encounter.

Once, Miss Styles smelled beer on Miss Dingle's breath and asked sweetly if common ale was now being dispensed at the Home. 'I particularly enjoy a glass now and then,' said Miss Dingle. 'It reminds me of happy weekends I spent with a certain royal Duke who drank nothing but strong beer and made his guests do the same, to purify the blood, as he put it.' She smiled. 'But with all your connections, I thought you would have known that, dear Miss Styles.'

'I prefer Dukes who drink champagne. Beer makes the tapestries smell stale and it stays on the breath most unpleasantly, dear.'

Miss Dingle laughed, taking no offence. 'Well, I can't see us having champagne here, on tap.'

'Some do,' said Miss Styles, with a leer.

'Then I wish I knew how they did it. I love champagne. Confidentially, it *is* the only drink, the very greatest in the world.'

Miss Styles asked Evans to take her to her room, and Miss Dingle called after her, 'Do I ask Sister or Dr Drake?'

'Not necessary, dear. No need to ask. They'll give you all you can drink when they think it is the right time.' Her wheelchair had nearly reached the sitting room door, and she made a great effort to crane her neck to look round at Miss Dingle. 'All you have to do is die.' She chuckled. 'No need to ask. They give you as much as you can drink when you are dying.' Miss Styles chuckled all the way back to her room and the Pros had to concede her the victory that time, but on the day that Matron put up a notice to announce a concert in the small but beautiful theatre, Miss Styles was really upstaged.

'Due to the kindness of one of our newest residents, we are able to offer the residents and staff a concert given by . . .' and a list of very well-known names followed. Miss Dingle was mock-modest and waved aside the programme as if it was of little account.

'The dear things; they insisted. They are in the West Country, broadcasting you know, and offered to come here.' She basked in glory for a long time and even Sister Cary smiled at her, while Matron fluttered and arranged a dinner party to which the performers and Miss Dingle were invited.

For the concert, clothes were unpacked that hadn't seen the light of day for years, not even when Queen Mary came to the Home. These were more elaborate and suitable for soirées and the opera. Evans scrubbed away at a diamond tiara belonging to Ethel, who adored music and was very excited. 'I suppose it makes a change from scrubbing dentures,' she said, but she helped to dress her patient with care, seeing in the faded woman's face traces of the pastel prettiness she had once possessed. She made up her face delicately and with compassion, and could have wept when Ethel kissed her hand, wordlessly.

Miss Styles wore a satin cloak that got in the way of the wheels of her chair. She spoke of friendship with famous musicians and to hear her was to imagine that she was one of a large family in which Melba, Pavlova and Caruso were minor members.

The celebrities discovered that the acoustics were perfect as was everything in the Home, and a series of afternoon concerts was arranged, which would be dress rehearsals for broadcasts. The music lovers lived again and in spite of their first doubts, confessed their great debt to the gaudy star who had shot into their well-ordered but boring lives.

However on the day of the first concert, Miss Dingle was ill; really ill and was the one person who couldn't attend. Her heart began to fibrillate and a specialist was called. He wagged a finger at her and said she was drinking too much. She held his hand and smiled with all the considerable charm she could still muster. 'Don't tell on me, there's a darling,' she said. 'I don't mind dying. I'd rather die than vegetate. I came here to escape the sordid details of life. I'm a lazy slut at heart, Doctor dear, and I was tired of trying to do without staff and trying to beat the shortages. I didn't need to come here. I could have gone to a hotel, except for times like this.'

'You should take more care,' he said and smiled. 'I'm inclined to agree with you. I can't see you wrapped up in cottonwool just to prolong your life without enjoyment. I'd be the same, but not a word to my other patients!' He patted her hand and she reached up to kiss his cheek, then held his hand tightly.

'Keep in touch? In case I misbehave?' she said with a trace of fear. 'I promise to be good until this stops racing.' She smiled, wistfully. 'At least I'm in the right place, Doctor dear. They give you champagne when you're dying, and I'll take a long while to take my final curtain. It should cost them a fortune.'

In the days that followed, Miss Dingle kept to her room, weak and shivering, experiencing cramps and hallucinations as all alcohol was withdrawn from her schedule. Sister searched her wardrobe and took away several bottles of inferior black market Scotch and intercepted an order from a 'friend'. It was the opening that she had waited for and now, under the righteous guise of Sister of Mercy, she did good, despite the suffering in the closed room.

'Give me just one Scotch, Sister. My heart won't take cold turkey!' When she began to scream, even Sister was worried and relented enough to give her a certain amount to drink each day to keep her calm, and gradually, Miss Dingle recovered and returned to normal, except that she had been truly scared, both of her heart condition and of the fact that she really had seen pink pigs running round her bed.

Ethel sent her a present of expensive French perfume, now unobtainable in England and several of the others sent little gifts in short supply, convincing the sick woman of their gratitude and regard. The Pros hovered and gave her their best attention, and she leaned on their youth and high spirits until she could support herself on her gold-topped stick and her natural ebullience. Sister Cary was satisfied that she knew the woman's Achille's heel and that ultimately Miss Dingle would have to bow to her will.

Miss Styles sent a half-bottle of champagne and said that she hoped the gift was not misunderstood. 'I'll save it,' said Miss Dingle and asked Emma to put it high on top of her wardrobe as a reminder and grim warning.

Meanwhile, Emma had received two letters from Phillip. In one, he hinted that he might be moving on. He was doing well and would soon be commissioned, and after that it was anyone's guess what would happen to him. Emma welcomed his letters and replied to them at once, anxious that he should receive as many as possible before he moved away. There was talk of bombs that failed to reach their targets and the locals scoffed at the bad German aim, but others said with a wink, that they knew someone who knew that they had built fake airfields away from the military targets, to be lit at night and so mislead the bombers.

Autumn was near, ripe and doleful in rusty splendour on the Downs. Airfields were now being bombed in daylight and the sky was often alive with Spitfires darting among their more ponderous prey. More fighter-pilots were needed and there were rumours of Hitler's coming invasion. Mrs Dewar filled milk bottles with sand to throw at the tanks if they had the nerve to come as far as her home. Berlin was bombed as a reprisal for the daylight bombing of British cities, and everywhere, a variety of strange uniforms appeared as Free French, Poles, Dutch and Belgians joined the forces to help push back the German war machine.

'*They've hotted up our training, as they need all the pilots and navigators they can get,*' wrote Phillip, and added with regret that he would be a navigator and not a pilot. '*It's my blasted maths. I seem to be rather good at it and although they tried to keep me grounded, I've managed to be airborne.*' He no longer said he'd be in to see her soon, but asked her to call on his family if she chanced to visit the Island. '*I suppose you'll be leaving to begin your training soon. Let me know where you intend going so that if we lose touch and I go overseas, I shall know where you are and how to find you again.*'

He knows he's going away, Emma decided, but he can't say anything to me. She read the letter again and thought that she ought to do something about her future. It was only too easy to remain at the Home but she didn't want to end up like Vincent with long service but no real qualifications. If there was a waiting list for the bigger London voluntary hospitals, she must write off to them soon.

'We can write to several,' suggested Evans. 'You don't mind if I end up in the same hole as you?'

Emma was delighted. 'I didn't like to suggest it,' she said, and when the brochures arrived, Bea joined them in the Common Room and picked out the ones she preferred. 'Can't have you two let loose in London without me,' she drawled. 'You need me, my dears. That is, if you cut out St Thomas' and Guys as I have absolutely awful relatives who operate there.'

'Do you really mean you want to come with us?'

'I can stand it if you can,' said Bea, and smiled. 'Might be a giggle.' She opened another brochure. 'What about the Princess Beatrice? It has a wonderful reputation and I know a nice man in surgery there. Besides, if I am to have any immortality, I might as well pretend that the hospital was named after me. Some consolation for being christened Beatrice.' She flung the papers down to hide her real sincerity. 'That is, if there is anything left of London or the hospitals there. We may find there is nowhere left to train. The last time that London was bombed, two hospitals were hit. We seem to be out of it here, except for the odd raids on the docks and on the convoys in the Channel, but bombs or no bombs, I want to get to London. Any place will welcome us with eager hands after all this valuable experience. Imagine doing something *really* interesting and useful instead of rubbing backs and listening to Miss Styles bitching.'

At home, Emma didn't mention the fact that she had written to London. Clare Dewar was content to have her near so that she could discuss the Home with Mrs Hammond, although Emma told her less and less about her work there. Emma smiled when she thought of Miss Dingle and what her mother would think of her, and had a sneaking feeling that her mother imagined that she would stay on at the Home until the end of the war.

Three new Pros arrived, giving Emma a feeling of superiority. Even Sister Cary paid her a backhanded compliment by telling her off because the junior hadn't made beds as well as she did. 'See to it, Nurse. Show her and don't let me see corners like that again.'

'I need Nurse Dewar again, Sister,' came the request fairly often now as Sister Ambrose asked for more and more of her time and could take a nurse from the well-staffed Wing whenever she needed one to help with the stores and vestments, confident that her request would not be refused as she was senior to Sister Cary.

Emma liked working in the stores and handling the machine that now churned out discs of carefully measured pats of butter for the rations for staff in the Home. Rationing was at last catching up with the Home, although huge sides of bacon and baskets of eggs still found their way to the stores and there were no real shortages. Emma hated the sight of eggs and bins of isinglass but they meant a constant supply of feather-light sponges and soufflés for the residents. However, the chapel was her main concern.

The vaulted roof and sense of peace was soothing after a morning with Sister Cary and she was left alone to polish the silver and trim candles and arrange hassocks for services, trying to avoid passing the altar very often as she half-expected the minister of the Methodist chapel at home to come behind her and frown if she dipped in front of the altar in the way of the High-Church congregation. The silver was exquisite and a joy to handle and the vestments were embroidered and encrusted with gold thread. She learned which to put out for feast days and began to enjoy the ritual of the services.

Occasionally, a dark-veiled lady or two would come in to pray or like Emma, just to enjoy the peace. Miss Dingle came, with a turban instead of a scarf or veil. She sat like a painted figurehead, with one hand resting on her cane and the soft light from the stained glass windows echoing the gleam of her many rings. Emma was fascinated by her visits but Miss Dingle seemed unaware of the butterfly-capped figure who went softly from altar to sacristy and into the Lady Chapel.

Miss Forsyth learned to depend on the new resident for company and intellectual conversation. At first, she had taken no pains to hide her contempt for the painted huzzy but one day, when Miss Forsyth had been wheeled in the wicker garden bed to receive visitors in the sun loggia, Miss Dingle picked up a book from the bench on which the visitors had been sitting.

She sat down and opened the book, ignoring the stiffening and displeasure of Miss Forsyth's face. It was a new book of poetry, brought as a present. Miss Dingle began to read, in a voice that bore no resemblance to the affected drawl she usually assumed. She read with strength and tenderness and perfect control, instinctively becoming the actress who had held London in her spell so many years ago. Miss Forsyth wept and a strange friendship began that only death would end.

8

Emma put down the telephone. She sensed the inquisitive glances of the porters and smiled. 'Not bad news, then, Nurse?' asked Randolph. She shook her head.

'Going overseas, is he?' asked the under-porter.

'He didn't say.' Emma blushed. By suppertime, the entire Home would know that Pro Dewar had a boyfriend who was on embarkation leave. It was bad enough being called to Sister's office when she was on duty and being told icily that there was a telephone call for her in the porter's lodge. Sister managed to give the impression that a small phone call for one of the Pros would disrupt the whole working pattern of the Home, and Emma had fled, apologising as she went.

'Was it bad news?' enquired Sister Cary in the Ward kitchen, afterwards.

'No, Sister.'

'Then kindly tell your friend that it is against the rules for you to receive calls on duty. It is only because Matron is afraid there might be news of casualties that she has relaxed the rules at all. Please do not take advantage of her concern.'

'No, Sister,' said Emma and took Miss Styles' tray from the table. I won't tell her! I wouldn't tell her my private affairs for a week's leave, Emma vowed. She sensed curious eyes watching as she left the kitchen and Evans came after her, carrying a tray for Ethel.

'Phillip?' she asked.

'Yes, he's coming to Bristol and wants to see me. I think he's going away but keep it to yourself. I've no intention of Sister knowing.'

'Good luck in there, then.' Evans nodded towards Miss Styles' door. 'She'll have it out of you before she's eaten the first course.'

Emma laughed. 'I might tell her I'm eloping this weekend. That would make her eyes sparkle.'

'Perhaps you will.'

'Will what? Tell her or elope?'

'Elope, of course. Perhaps he'll whisk you off on a two-day honeymoon. Love you and leave you.'

'What rubbish!' Emma's face was crimson.

'Just be careful, Dewar. Emotions get a bit out of hand if a man's going away and doesn't know when he'll be back, or even *if* he'll be back. It brings out the animal in them. Mark my words.'

'Hark who's talking. Just how many lovers have you at this moment? But I forget. You are the authority on life, death, marriage and nursing' She dodged the other girl's foot and demurely tapped on the door.

'Who was that you were talking to, Nurse Dewar?'

'One of the nurses, Miss Styles. Nothing of interest,' said Emma as she unfolded the table napkin.

'I hope you didn't stay talking and let my dinner get cold. You know how fussy Sister can be and she likes us to have meals at the right temperature.'

Emma smiled and uncovered the cold meat and *salade niçoise*. 'Hot apple pie to follow, with cream. I left it to keep warm until you are ready,' she said. 'Remember? You chose salad because you don't like pork.' She cut the meat into dainty pieces and Miss Styles indicated when she wanted salad or meat and drank sips of white wine between mouthfuls.

All through the meal, Emma was only half-concentrating on Miss Styles and she was glad when the woman waved aside the last of the pie. 'I think that Cook has lost her touch with pastry. She made it featherlight at one time.' She tried to keep Emma with her, talking, but months at the Home had given her the facility to finish feeding a resident and to back out before it was realised she had gone, and Miss Styles was still talking peevishly as the door closed. Emma escaped to Green Alley and Miss Forsyth and wondered if Matron would let her have two days off together; when she reported off-duty that evening, she asked Sister to put in her request, ignoring the implied question when Sister Cary hoped it had nothing to do with the phone call.

Phillip would be staying at her home as Clare Dewar had given him a warm invitation to stay there whenever he was in Bristol and he'd be no trouble at all, and Emma couldn't do anything about it. She protested, but her mother was complacent. 'You could do a lot worse, Emma. You should snap him up and marry him. He's going to be an officer, and in the RAF, too. I'd be so proud if you married him. Some girls marry before their boys go abroad and they get quite a nice allowance. You could leave that place, take a nice job at the BAC and save for a house when he comes back.' She sighed and Emma knew what would come next. 'Don't make the same mistake that I made. I let my boy go to the war before I would marry him and he never came back.'

'*Mum*! Please! I have no intention of marrying him or any other man for years. I am a nurse and am going to do my training. I don't even know Phil all that well. I've been out with him a few times and we get on well but I'm sure he feels as I do. If you say anything to embarrass me when he comes, I'll walk out. I wish I'd never given him your phone number.' Uneasily, she wondered just what conversations they had and if he was serious, just what impression her mother had given him.

On Thursday night, Emma left her room until Sunday morning. Phillip was waiting for her at the gate and in spite of her previous thoughts, she liked what she saw. He stood briefly to attention and then grinned. 'I made it,' he said, and straightened the dark tie under the fine blue poplin shirt collar. In the uniform of a Pilot Officer, with the one-wing flash over his pocket to show that he was a navigator, Phillip was good to see. He took her hand and gently kissed her cheek.

'Congratulations,' Emma said, and introduced him to Evans who had come out with her.

Evans took in the uniform and smiled. 'No problems now,' she said. 'All officers together. Tony is coming tomorrow and I have the evening off and the next day. How will the Home survive without us? Could we meet tomorrow?' Phillip looked at Emma and smiled. 'We could meet at the Victoria Rooms, have a meal and then dance somewhere,' suggested Evans. 'From Clifton we can take taxis to wherever we are staying that night.'

'Air raids permitting,' said Emma. The raids were becoming a habit, a fact of life accepted as an inconvenience but not more than that. Even the stories of bombed houses and factories seemed remote as if the bombs could never come any closer, for Emma had no experience of friends or relatives being killed or maimed in the war. 'If the alert sounds, we can go to one of the shelters,' she said, and felt lighthearted, in spite of the news.

The autumn nights were lengthening and winter showed in the bareness of the trees on the Downs and the darkening of the sodden leaves. Incendiaries had fallen on Coventry, resulting in extensive fires and the destruction of the Cathedral. During ten hours of bombing, well over three hundred tons of high explosives had been dropped. Other cities had been bombed, too, but London had enjoyed some respite. The over-taxed Observer Corps worked round the clock on every high place surrounding the main cities, and Fighter Command had no breathing space. Dummy airfields led many bombers away from targets at night, but during the day, waves of enemy aircraft had to be diverted by Spitfires and Hurricanes and Defiants. The new Beaufighter planes, rushed into service as soon as they were ready, were fitted with more efficient guns and two-millimetre cannons. Rumours spread that night-fighter pilots were being fed on carrots to make them see in the dark. Some explanation, however stupid, had to be made to account for the dramatic increase in enemy aircraft spotted and brought down as the new secret radar equipment was installed in planes, and people in Bristol took comfort and believed that what had happened to Coventry could never happen there.

There was a chill wind blowing when the four met and they went into the café off Whiteladies Road that still managed to provide well-cooked and generous portions of food. As soon as the woman serving saw the uniforms, she smiled and brought out a half-bottle of whisky wrapped in a brown paper bag. Tony grinned and bought it and put it away in his pocket, and Emma wondered nervously if the police knew about this place. They ate and talked as if they had known each other for years. Tony was very much like his sister, but it was a shock to hear him call her by her first name. Even dressed in civilian clothes and with other people, the two girls found that they still called each other Dewar and Evans, and it was impossible to change.

The men got on well and were on first-name terms, but the curious formality of nursing could not be overcome even when they were in the dance hall. The huge ballroom on the Downs had revolving faceted glass balls in the ceiling that sent small squares of coloured light shimmering among the dancers, taking the harshness from uniforms and making faces relaxed and almost beautiful. Tony danced well, and sang softly as he moved. Emma liked his firm shoulders and dark brown Welsh eyes. He should be here with a girlfriend, she thought. Not his sister and two friends. There was sadness behind his smile and for no reason, Emma recalled what Evans had said when Mrs Devere died. 'There's bound to be three in a row to die.' There had been a third death when one of the women in another wing had died suddenly, two days afterwards. Emma shivered.

'Cold?' asked Phillip as they stood by the bar.

'A goose walked over my grave,' she said.

'Well, it isn't for me,' he said firmly. 'I've no intention of dying just yet.' He was relaxed and confident, obviously enjoying the evening. 'You don't get rid of me that easily.' He handed her a glass of lemonade. 'Don't get me wrong, but can we go somewhere alone tomorrow? I like your friends very much and hope we can repeat this evening some time when I come back, but tomorrow, I want you to myself.' Her eyes widened. It was his first reference to going away. 'Yes, I'm going on Monday,' he said. 'I can't tell you where, because we haven't been briefed, but at last we're on the move. Training was OK but getting a bit of a bore.'

He took her hand. 'If it wasn't for you, and knowing how much I'll miss you, I'd be glad to go.'

She blushed. 'You'll soon forget me.' She looked away. 'A girl in every town. They flock around the handsome Brylcream Boys.' She tried to sound slightly mocking, but her mouth was dry. He might go into danger now and her premonition could be for him.

'Tomorrow?' he repeated. Emma nodded.

Tony insisted that he wanted to buy a bottle of wine. 'There must be something under the counter,' but the barman could produce only warm beer and some mineral water. Tony fished in his wallet and looked at a card. 'Let's go there,' he said. 'It's a new club for officers and friends and open every night.' They walked the short distance through the dark Clifton Streets and found the cellar where the club had been set up.

'At least we can stay put if the siren goes,' said Phillip, eyeing the solid rock behind the bar. Tony waved a five-pound note under the barman's nose. 'Something special, is there? Something to cheer the departing warrior?' The man shrugged and brought out a small bottle of bad whisky and some ginger wine. Evans choked on hers and Emma sipped and left her share, not because it was so bad, but because she was increasingly aware of Tony's sadness and growing depression beneath his light manner. Under his determined conviviality lurked darkness, a darkness that Emma dimly recalled in her grandmother long ago, and one that she shared when she sensed danger or tragedy.

Tony became more sombre as he drank, and Phillip noticed that the girls were not drinking. He waited until the elderly comedian finished telling long-winded jokes then went to the bar and talked in a low voice to the barman. He came back and looked at his watch. 'He says they shut in an hour. Regulations. He also says that if we want taxis, there is only one rank working when the alert is on.'

'Alert?'

'Went an hour ago, while that woman played the sax. Of the two, I'd rather listen to the siren. Where do they dig up these acts?'

'The good ones entertain the forces,' said Tony. 'We'll laugh all the way to Hell.'

He's frightened, thought Emma. He's going away too, and he doesn't know where, but he thinks it will be bad. Evans knows how he feels, and she's as worried as I am.

'So, we're having a final celebration,' announced Phillip. 'Something really special is coming up. Something to remember us by when Tony is wherever he is going and I am zooming around somewhere up there.'

The waiter brought a bucket holding a thin layer of ice, but at least it was ice. He took the napkin-encased bottle and released the cork with a resounding and satisfying pop, and poured the pale champagne into glasses.

Emma took her glass and examined the bubbles. Tony swigged his in one gulp and held out his glass for more. Phillip sipped his, sensing that his gift was not a success, except with Tony, who drank again. Evans regarded her brother anxiously. She had not touched her glass. She saw Emma's full glass and smiled. 'You can't drink it either, can you bach?'

Emma gulped a little, bravely, and Evans sipped and said it was delicious. Tony finished his sister's drink and Emma pushed hers away, saying there were too many bubbles just yet. The barman jerked his head in the direction of the door where the cab driver waited, then corked the half-full bottle firmly and drank Emma's champagne, shaking his head over officers with more money than sense. Phillip and Emma dropped the others off at their hotel then the driver took them along the dark road out of the city towards Filton.

After a late breakfast, when Clare Dewar insisted on using up the last of the bacon ration and making far too much toast, Emma put on a thick coat and walking shoes and stuffed a woollen hat into one pocket. They refused a packed lunch and said they'd have bread and cheese in a pub, and managed to get away at last. Phillip grinned when they climbed to the top of the tram. 'I think your mother likes me more than you do.'

'She thinks that anyone over five feet nothing, wearing trousers and preferably uniform, and not mentally deficient is a suitable husband for me. Take no notice, I get this all the time.' Emma laughed. 'You should see the frightened looks I get from some of the boys sitting by the phone.'

'And do I fulfil some of those requirements? I'm over five feet – six foot one if you bother to notice and I do have all my marbles,' said Phillip dryly.

Emma wriggled uncomfortably. 'I didn't mean that.'

'Tell me I'm the most suitable yet and that you love me a little and I'll forgive you,' he said, tucking her hand into the pocket of his greatcoat.

She squeezed his hand. 'It *is* good to see you again, Phil.'

He looked into her face, his eyes grey and serious. 'Only good to see me? Emma, I haven't much time.'

'Sh!' she said. 'People are staring.'

'Let them stare!' he replied in a stage whisper that could be heard all over the top deck. An ATS girl giggled and wriggled her bottom as she went to the iron stairs at the back, giving the impression that some girls didn't know their luck.

The docks were windy and Emma was cold but unwilling to admit it, preferring to stay in the open in public view, beginning to distrust the odd tingling in her hand where it rested in Phillip's warm grasp. What did they call this? Attraction through propinquity? Just because he was male and young, and it would be the same with anyone as good-looking? She glanced at his profile, slightly pinched with the cold. It was a good face, handsome in a solid, British way. He was sincere and something told her that this was how she must be with him, but as yet she didn't know how she felt about him. She didn't want to put it to the test; not yet, when her life was opening out and she wanted to go away and train to be a nurse.

They lunched on dried egg omelettes in a café with steamed up windows, and neither of them said much. They drank half-cold coffee and the bread was tough and thick, and Emma wished that she could give Phillip one of the meals served at the Home. He pushed aside the remains of the soggy egg and lit a cigarette. 'I didn't know you smoked,' she said.

'You don't know much about me, do you? We are sitting here, eating rotten food and wasting precious time making polite conversation when all the time I want to kiss you.' She looked down at a stain on the tablecloth. 'I haven't much time,' he said. 'When I go away, it may be for months. I've been issued with tropical kit.'

'But where are we fighting in hot countries?'

'I thought I'd be operational at once, but they want us for further training in long-range bombers. I know very little and it's dangerous to speculate but I do know it will be a long way from England.' He paid the bill and led her out after consulting the entertainments page of the local paper. 'Come on, you've always wanted to see *Maytime*. Just right for a grey day.'

'I've seen it twice,' she protested, clutching her coat collar as they walked down the windy street.

'Then you can explain the plot to me,' he said. They were shown into the back row of the stalls. 'Like old times,' he whispered, as he put his arm round her in the dark. She giggled but sensed that this wasn't like the friendly hugs and shy kisses in the back row of the Medina cinema in Newport, and when the first pale petals fell on the girl on the swing, Phillip took Emma's face in his hands and kissed her so that the tingling spread, leaving her limp and passive and trying to convince herself that this was not love.

They had tea in an ornate café in Queen's Road, sipping from thin china and eating quite good cakes. The place was filled with servicemen and girls and from a lower room came music. They wandered down and found a tea dance in progress, to the strains of outdated songs played by three ladies of indeterminate age – one cellist, one pianist, one violinist. The cellist had red hair and her dress was cut low, showing what should have been well-hidden as she had neither the figure nor the allure to warrant such a display, but Emma smiled, thinking of Miss Dingle.

'She's a bit like one of our residents,' she said. 'But Miss Dingle is wonderful. We all love her.' Emma was surprised to find that it was true. Miss Dingle wasn't just liked, she was loved. She talked of the other residents, more than at any time to any person outside the Home, then saw Phillip's bemused expression. 'It must sound funny, but it isn't,' she said. 'I don't know how to express it but it is a wonderful place, in its own strange way.' Her voice faded. He didn't understand. His air of vague repugnance showed that he caught a picture, not of warmth and service and caring, but of degrading work, old age and death and no humour. She wanted to shake him and to shout *IT ISN'T LIKE THAT*! – but knew that he would never understand.

'I wish you weren't going to London,' he said. 'You've nothing settled, so why not do as your mother suggest – work at the BAC and have more free time and certainly more money?' Emma sighed. So she'd been hinting the same things to

Phillip, had she? He held her close and trod on her feet as he tried to dance a tango. 'Sorry, I can't do these outlandish dances; only fit for a lot of dagoes.' They sat and drank more tea and had some biscuits and a peculiar cake that was covered with green hundreds and thousands and had cream in it that had never seen a cow and tasted faintly of oil.

'Look, Phillip – I'm going to do my training,' Emma said for the third time. 'I've always wanted to train in one of the big London hospitals, and I'm going to do just that. My mother should mind her own business and leave me to get on with my life.'

'And me? Do I fit into your scheme anywhere?' He sat close to her and she felt his breath on her hair. 'In the cinema, you didn't hate me. I hoped you had changed your mind. I'm falling in love with you, Emma. Promise me you'll be here when I come back?'

'Phil . . .' There was pleading in her eyes. 'Phil, dear Phil – I just don't know. I shall miss you very much and I'll think of you so very often, but I just don't know anything any more.'

They danced again and sat under the rosy glow of pink shades, an illusion of warmth and intimacy. Phillip went to the cloakroom and Emma looked around the room at the various uniforms and faces of the different nationalities. She started as a soft voice asked her to dance and she looked up into the face of a Polish airman. She shook her head, smiling, as Phillip hurried back. He sat down and gave the Pole a stiff smile, leaving him in no doubt as to whom Emma was attached. England must be full of lonely men she thought, and wished she could have talked to him. 'Can't leave you alone for five minutes,' said Phillip. 'Promise me you won't get involved with them when I'm away?' He was laughing but Emma knew that he suffered. 'I'd like to lock you up in a high tower,' he said.

'And let me starve?' She took a biscuit and bit into it, not really wanting anything more to eat.

'I could put a ring through your nose, or on your finger. Please Emma, let's get engaged before I leave. I think I may be going to a place where diamonds are of the best. Say you'll marry me later and then I'll be sure that you will be safe from . . . unwelcome attentions.' His slightly contemptuous glance flickered over the Polish, French and Irish soldiers and airmen. Emma was annoyed but tried to hide it. He made marriage to him sound like prison. 'Please, Emma darling?'

'I'm not ready for that,' she said firmly. 'I'll write often and look forward to your letters. I hope you come back soon, but it isn't fair to either of us to tie ourselves down at this time. You might find someone on the other side of the world you could love better and I might be swept off my feet by a rich American.' She picked up her bag. 'We ought to get back. Buses are bad and we may have to queue.'

As they left the tram half a mile from her parents' house, and picked their way along an unlit street, the sirens sounded, and almost at once, the sky lit up with searchlights over the docks. The dull roar of heavy bombers filled the sky and Phillip seized her arm and almost dragged Emma into the big underground shelter by the shops. 'Come on, *run*!' he shouted. 'It sounds like a full-scale attack.'

'But we are only a few minutes from the house,' Emma protested.

'We stay here,' he insistd, and Emma collapsed breathless on the wooden bench inside the wall of the shelter. Soon it was full of people, some sitting on benches, some standing by the walls and some lying on blankets they had brought with them ready to stay the night if necessary. Phillip looked at Emma and grinned ruefully. 'What a way to spend our last few hours together.' She smiled as if in sympathy but was glad that they had no further chance to be alone.

Distant gunfire and heavy explosions became a continuous sound. The Warden by the door said that the city was hit badly and that a pall of red smoke hung over the centre. Once or twice, the earth shook; the roar of heavy engines droned on until Emma felt her eyelids drooping in the stale atmosphere. She jerked herself awake, guilty that she should feel sleepy while there were homes being destroyed. Phillip held her close and she snuggled into his coat. If it was like this all the time, this warm affection and security, I could love him, she thought, but tomorrow, he would go away and there was work to be done. How was the Home faring? Were there any soldiers spared to help with the beds? Was there anyone who couldn't be moved down to the subway? Suddenly she wanted to be back there more than she wanted the comfort of Phil's arms.

When the All Clear broke the tension of the night they walked home in silence, with Phillip knowing that he had only two hours before he must be ready to expect the jeep to take him back to the airfield.

Clare Dewar emerged from the Anderson shelter, hung about with carrier bags. 'I wondered where you were,' she said cheerfully. 'Mrs Hammond said you'd go into one of those surface shelters and get bombed like they did in Cardiff, but I said that Phil would have more sense. You're lucky to have a man to look after you, Emma. Your father is never home and what does he care if I'm blown up?' She grumbled about the gas pressure under the kettle, then buttered bread, talking all the time. Phillip stirred his tea and ate a piece of bread and Marmite, glancing sadly at Emma. He washed and Mrs Dewar brushed his uniform, clucking over the absence of knife edges to his trousers. A motor horn sounded and Phillip looked desperate, but Mrs Dewar thrust a bag of cakes into his hand and bustled him out to the jeep.

Emma stood aloof, embarrassed by her mother, and Phillip left with only a touching of hands and a chaste kiss. He turned to wave and Emma stood back, blowing kisses when her mother wasn't looking, and Phillip smiled before he turned the corner.

'He didn't have much to say for himself,' said Clare Dewar. 'You haven't been horrid to him, have you Emma?'

'He didn't get much chance to put a word in edgeways,' Emma pointed out.

'Well, someone had to talk. It's dull enough in this house. Your father is never here and when he is, he tells me nothing about what happens at the factory. If I'd stayed on the Island, at least I'd have had my sisters to visit.' She looked at the clock and poured another cup of tea, topping it up with boiling water. 'He takes his time. Said he'd be on duty all night. I suppose they played cards again. I've told him – I'm surprised he doesn't take his bed up there and stay for good.'

'Are you sure he's all right?'

'The chief Warden said the factory wasn't hit and he should be home soon. I'll put the kettle on again. It takes ages to heat up.'

Emma took her bicycle from the shed. 'I think I'd better get back,' she said. 'There might be work to do. I hope they're all OK.' She cycled through the dim morning, arriving in time to be let in by the porter cleaning the hall and stairs. The late-breakfast book was still there and she signed in as she was still off until eleven, then undressed and lay for a long time in a hot bath. She wondered where Phil would be now, and where he would be this time tomorrow. She wished she'd entered

Evans' name in the breakfast book as she might come back early too, but she heard nothing from her room.

The thick towel was warm and comforting, and Emma dried herself and rubbed the ends of her hair dry. She dressed quickly in uniform as she was cold now, having dreamed away all the hot water. She thought of Evans and Tony and hoped that their shelter had been more comfortable than the one in which she and Phil had spent the night. She glanced into the room again but it was undisturbed. At least Evans had the excuse of the raid if she was late this morning, as buses had been off the streets since the attack, according to the porter. Emma went back to her room until breakfast-time then strolled over to the dining room.

From the window, when she was halfway through her scrambled eggs, Emma saw the head porter hurrying from the lodge. Something urgent about his movements made her lose her appetite. Vincent saw him too and went to the window. 'Randolph looks a bit odd,' she said. 'Never knew he could move so fast.' They looked across the central flower bed and saw the black ambulance.

'Mrs Lisburne went to hospital in an ambulance like that,' said Emma.

The porter came back, his shoulders sagging. He waved the ambulance in, pointing to the path by the stores. He followed as if it was a funeral and he was the chief mourner. The van disappeared behind the trees.

'Someone has died,' whispered Vincent. 'It's going to the mortuary.'

Emma was cold. 'Whoever it was didn't die here. They are bringing someone back. Usually, they don't take them away until the day of the funeral. Vincent, it must be someone from here who was killed out there last night.' She jumped up, knocking over her chair and ran to the lodge. 'Who is it? Who was in that ambulance?' she gasped. The startled porter stepped back before the wild-eyed girl. '*Who is it?*' she cried.

'The little Welsh girl, Nurse. The officer with her is in hospital and isn't expected to make it.' Emma saw the lodge swing round as she hit the floor and dimly sensed Vincent catching her to break her fall.

9

Emma looked up from the pillow and saw the stiffly starched cap. The bow under Sister Cary's chin trembled and for once the cold eyes failed to meet Emma's. 'Come on now, Nurse Dewar, this will not do. It's time you got up and went on duty. Matron says . . .'

'I don't care what Matron says! I don't care what anyone says, I can't face anyone!' The words came in a series of uncontrollable shudders, the last hiccoughing remnants of her noisy grief. She was drained of all feeling except a deep depression and utter bitterness. Why Evans?

'You have your duty, Nurse.' The voice gained some of its normal chill. 'You have health and strength and there are all those helpless people waiting for your assistance. I know how you must feel, Nurse Dewar. I do understand, but we have to carry on whatever happens, when we are responsible for other people. Come now, wash and change and I'll wait for you down in the hall.'

Emma dragged herself from the bed and picked up her towel, so accustomed to obeying Sister Cary that she was dressed and neat in a very short time, the only traces of her weeping being a slight puffiness round her eyes and a nose that had a tendency to need blowing every few minutes. A last stifled sob and she was ready.

'Good girl, it's the only way,' said Sister Cary. 'Work and more work until you are exhausted. It's the best remedy for grief. I lost my fiancé in the last war and my brother too, so I know all about grief.' She turned away and opened the front door of the nurses' home. 'Now hurry up, Nurse. You have a lot to do if you want to get through the day. Pro Shuter will work with you later and the new junior will have to do her work.' She spoke sharply as if to erase any memory of weakness when she had taken a junior nurse into her confidence. Emma followed her, willing her legs to support her, dreading the fact that by now all the residents would be talking about Evans and her brother.

Was it only last night that the raid had destroyed the theatre and the main shopping centre in Bristol? Was it only two nights ago that she had sat with Evans and Tony and Phillip, while Phillip bought champagne? Tony had made sure of his champagne before dying. Was he dead? She began to think coherently. Tony had been taken to hospital, or so they said, but she knew that he was dead. It had been in his face while he joked and drank and in his last goodbye. She asked Randolph to telephone the hospital and he came to Wing Six bringing some mail as an excuse to see her. One look at his face told her the truth and she went into Miss Forsyth's room with an aching heart.

'I've been waiting for hours,' Miss Forsyth began. She looked at the girl's white face. 'I need turning and it's my day for a blanket bath.' She kept Emma busy for an hour, but talked softly of books and of the latest poetry reading planned by Miss Dingle. She knew the words flowed over Emma without her hearing what was said, but she talked on, noticing the gradual relaxation in the girl's manner as she concentrated on the work in hand. Miss Forsyth didn't grumble or complain once and Emma was oddly soothed by the quiet voice. She was also ashamed. It was true what Sister Cary had said. She had health and strength and so much to give; skill and gentleness – a kind of love. *Love Serves*, she thought without the usual Pro's derision, and it was right. Carefully, she tucked the small pillow in at the side of Miss Forsyth's face and turned towards the door. 'Comfortable?' she asked.

'Very nice. Have a sweet,' said Miss Forsyth and Emma took one of the special chocolates that had been sent from America by the famous writer who had been in Miss Forsyth's charge as a boy, and of whom she spoke with mixed pride and exasperation when she saw that he had ended yet another sentence with a preposition in one of his books.

The newspapers were full of the raid, with pictures of gaunt firemen and soldiers who had fought fires for two days without respite. There were heartrending accounts of children left without parents and parents losing children, with the inevitable story of the old man who had slept through it all and been rescued dusty but unscathed from a basement flat. Emma telephoned home and was told that her father had spent the night helping to dig out bodies from a surface air-raid shelter that had a direct hit. 'Nasty dangerous things,' her mother said, as if the fault was partly her husband's. 'I said they never should have built them. It put him off eating his breakfast as he found a leg still in a boot. Came home and was quite sick.'

Emma rang off unable to mention Evans. It was as well that she had never taken her home. She need never mention her again to her mother.

At the Home it was different. Matron was quickly in touch with Mr Evans who flew back from the north of England and came to Bristol for a memorial service in the Home Chapel after the double funeral in Wales. Emma dreaded it, but as one of Evans' closest friends, she knew she must be there. On the morning, the vestments were ready, the candles lit and wheelchair ladies in black veils sat in the chapel waiting. Miss Dingle was draped in her purple cloak and wore jet earrings and long black gloves. She sat by Miss Forsyth in her long wicker bed and wiped the tears from the helpless woman from time to time. Miss Styles licked her lips frequently and looked nervous. She couldn't keep away but hated this close contact with death, having avoided all funerals for years, but this was different, and was drama to be savoured. The death of a young girl wasn't the same as it didn't touch her own age or infirmity. It was sad and deeply satisfying.

Emma met Mr Evans and he hugged her, tears in his eyes. 'She spoke of you often and said you'd be going to London together.' He held her hand. 'I was so pleased. Not many friends had my Maeve, and Tony, too. You said you liked him?' Emma nodded, suddenly strong as the man's hands quivered and tears threatened. He has no one, she thought. He's divorced and has no other children, and she knew that she was lucky to be alive.

Sister Ambrose snuffed out the last candle as the wheelchairs left the chapel and Emma walked to the gate of the Home with Mr Evans. Impulsively, she kissed his cheek and he hugged her as he said goodbye, then she went back to help with the menu and Green Alley. Miss Dingle was slightly drunk again, overcome by the tragedy that touched the whole Home. Not only was she sorrowful over the death of a young girl of whom she had become very fond, but she waxed tearful over the destruction of the Princes Theatre, and that night, in the dining room, she insisted on recalling every performance in which she had appeared there. She walked the corridors, still wearing her cloak and black gloves and veil, slipping into her room for whatever stimulant that came to hand. As she visited other residents, to tell them of past triumphs at the Princes, she absentmindedly sipped from their stimulant glasses.

'You should have seen my Lady Macbeth, my dear,' she said as she drained Ethel's sherry. 'I think that was in Bristol,' she added vaguely. She wandered from room to room and settled with Miss Forsyth to whom she read *Lycidas* in a sepulchral whisper, and excerpts from *Paradise Lost*.

The alert sounded early and the residents made no fuss when taken down to the subway. Suddenly, they were aware that people got killed in raids; people they had met and liked. It could happen again, only closer as bombers aimed for the aircraft factory and the docks again and again. Emma went about her duties mechanically, unable to relax and unable to sleep as raid followed raid and off-duty became a joke. She telephoned home each day and fortunately, there were no casualties near the house, but the factory was hit again, not badly, but killing people in what were thought to be safe shelters.

Emma and many like her began to think that it was safer to be in the open during a raid rather than huddled in a building that could collapse. When she went home, she refused to go into the Anderson shelter and had her first good night for weeks, oblivious to bombs and gunfire.

Her mother objected but left her, saying that if she got killed, she had only herself to blame. She liked the company in the earth-smelling shelter. It was a club where one's friends and neighbours shared coffee and soup and news and local gossip. They listened spellbound to distant bombs, each recounting a tale of the blitz, lives lost or gruesome details of the clearing up that had to be tackled by the Auxiliary Fire Service.

'It's the AFS I feel sorry for,' said Clare Dewar, forgetting her earlier contempt for that service, when they sat about waiting for fires. 'They do a grand job. I've always thought them especially brave.' She dispensed wisdom and coffee and soup and thoroughly enjoyed telling Mrs Hammond that Phillip had a Commission in the RAF. She looked complacent. 'I think they'll be married as soon as he gets back. No, they haven't said, but I can tell. He's very keen.' She ignored Emma's previous denials, choosing to think her coy. 'Young girls are all the same,' she told her friend. 'Say one thing and mean another. Mark my words, they'll be brushing off the confetti when he comes back.' She had begun to save sugar, in glass jars, and in paper bags that made the sugar go to rock hard, against the time when she would make a wedding cake. 'I can't keep butter as it would go rancid. Oh, I do wish my sister Emily was here. She makes a lovely cake.'

Without Evans, the nurses' home was quiet. Emma missed her laughter and her company but gradually, Bea Shuter became, not as close, but better understood and liked as she sought Emma's company. It's strange that I can call her Bea yet never used Evans' first name, thought Emma, but it had been Evans who had called her Bea and everyone copied. Under her cynical pose, Bea was unhappy and vulnerable. 'I almost wish it had been me and not Evans,' she said one day. Emma was shocked. At no time had she wanted to change places with the dead girl.

'You want to do your training, don't you?'

Bea shrugged. 'I suppose so. I'm not what you might call dedicated, and I can take it or leave it. I should like . . .' She gave one of her sudden illuminating smiles.

'What?'

Bea clasped her hands behind her head and wiggled her hips. 'I should like a rich husband who would cover me with diamonds and furs and give me a villa in France after the war, another in Switzerland and a house on Long Island, and ...'

'Stop!' said Emma. 'He can't afford any more. He'll have to be a multi-millionaire.'

'Don't fuss. He will be. I'll have to find one. Perhaps when we go to London we may both find millionaires, sick and helpless in a private patients' ward and we'll work our evil ways with them and make them marry us.'

'If they are in that state, they'll be ninety!'

'All the better. No, what am I saying? I'd be back to bedpans and back rubs in a stately home. I couldn't bear it.'

'No millionaires?'

'No millionaires,' said Bea, turning down the corners of her mouth. 'Perhaps I'll marry a Greek fisherman. Have you seen them, Dewar? Wonderful bodies, dark hair and deep brown eyes.' She smiled. 'Perhaps I'll have both. I'll marry a millionaire and have a lover, a beautiful virile lover who will drive me out of my mind.'

'You can't have both. It isn't allowed. You wouldn't, would you? Not really?'

'You've gone pink, Dewar. You thought of someone, beautiful and virile! Tell Auntie – who is it?'

'There's nobody but Phillip, and he's not like that.' She smiled. 'I can't imagine anyone like that being interested in me, and I'd be embarrassed if there was.' She looked at the high cheekbones and straight nose and delicate ears of the other girl. Bea had a marvellous figure, too. She could really drive a man mad, Emma decided. Bea stood tall and preened, looking like a mischievous, well-groomed cat.

'Not much good looking for him here,' said Emma.

'I shall find him. I shall have lovers when I'm

ready,' promised Bea. 'I shall take lots of lovers because it runs in my family.'

'What if you find one man and fall in love? You'll marry him and never want lovers.'

Bea moved restlessly. 'I don't think I could settle to one man. My mother couldn't and I'm a bit like her.'

'Perhaps she made a mistake and didn't find the right man.'

'Oh, Dewar, spare me that! Spare me the sermon on waiting for Mr Right or the man on the white charger who will take me away into the desert.' She giggled. 'Maybe that's the answer. I'll be abducted by a sheik and have no choice. How wonderful to be taken by force.' Her eyes held a dull fire that Emma failed to understand. 'Violence and love are often close,' she said softly.

The winter was long and cold with power cuts and a lack of fuel. As more and more convoys were sunk and warehouses became empty or were destroyed, bread grew darker and tasteless and off-the-ration treats such as liver or tripe became rare. However, in the Home, Sister Ambrose chewed in the well-filled stores and the residents still had a limited but good choice of food. Bombers droned over the larger cities so regularly that a kind of insensitivity developed. Once, Emma went on the roof of the Home to watch the fires below in the city. In the red glare, spires of churches peeped through like toyland buildings. The gargoyles gazed blindly across the Downs, lit by spasmodic red fingers of ack-ack lightning in the sky. Emma was no longer afraid that she would die in enemy action and her mother had a fatalistic attitude, learned from Mrs Hammond. 'If the bomb's got your name on it, it will get you.' She knitted socks for her husband, and to Emma's horror, some thick ones for Phillip.

There had been one letter from Phillip, obviously posted just before he left England. News filtered through from the Island, but Aunt Emily wrote sparingly and only now bothered to mention a little matter called the Evacuation of Dunkirk and how it had affected the Island. '*Old Matthew down on the quay went,*' she wrote. '*They asked if they could take his barges and he told them if they took his barges, then he was going, too. They told him he was too old and he said that he wasn't too old "to kill a few bloody Germans", and so they let him go with them. He did well and brought back a string of boats towed by his old steam-engined barge.*'

Mrs Dewar repeated this to Mrs Hammond who was rather shocked. 'Well, Mr Churchill says it's all right,' asserted Emma's mother. 'He has said that if the Germans come here, we can all take one with us.' She said this with a kind of pious righteousness, as if she could give a sharp slap on the wrist if necessary.

Emma wrote to Phillip at a service address which forwarded mail and then an airmail letter-card arrived. '*By the time you get this, we shall have landed in South Africa. This mail is going ashore by launch and we still have a few hundred miles to go before I know which forwarding address to use. It's hot and we sleep on deck as much as possible. It's good to have the light kit as it really can be sweltering.*'

He had tried to tell more, but two lines were heavily covered with blue pencil and all place names were deleted. How unpleasant to think of someone reading one's letters before sending them on, she thought, and was carefully noncommittal when she wrote, hesitating even to put '*Love from Emma.*' I hope he doesn't get too sentimental, she thought, imagining a giggling person avidly censoring the letter. She grinned and signed, with her love. There would be far juicier things in some letters and there must be thousands to plough through. Phillip's were hardly likely to arouse interest.

It was pleasant to think of him as more than just a friend now that he was away. With him, she had been confused, feeling the pressures that he could exert, wanting her as his wife and the mother of his children. She frowned. She didn't know any small children and even her cousins were older or far away. I'll have to nurse children in hospital, she thought, but I don't want to be tied to a family of my own just yet. She was fully aware that her birth had not brought her parents any happiness, and sometimes, she wondered if her mother had always been as selfish and her father as silently sullen. She read the letter again and was glad that she had not become engaged before Phil left England.

Bea was mildly amused that Dewar had a steady boyfriend but eyed his photograph with grudging approval. 'Good shoulders,' she said, 'but a well-behaved mouth.' When Emma asked what she meant, she laughed. 'Don't you notice mouths? You really are the complete innocent. They're the perfect giveaway. Meet someone as nice as pie but his mouth will tell you what he's really like.'

'I've never noticed,' said Emma resentfully. 'And I disagree. Eyes are far more important.'

'Rubbish,' said Bea. 'Some of the worst blackguards there are can look you in the eye with the most sincere expression and then do something quite despicable. They actually practice the honest eye bit and the firm handshake.'

'If I listened to you, I'd end up trusting nobody,' reproached Emma.

Bea dropped the picture on the bed. 'Have no fear, little girl. You can trust that one to marry you, give you a house full of screaming children and to look after you, if that's what you crave.' She looked pensive. 'But he'll never make your knees turn to water or your heart do somersaults.' She smiled. 'I know the type I want but I haven't seen him yet. It's early and I'm not really looking but I'll find him one day and you should look further, too.'

They picked up their cloaks and went on duty. 'Do you see what I see?' whispered Bea. 'Matron has taken a fancy to a Corporal.' The soldier tried to walk on air as he left Matron's study, acutely aware of his nailed boots on the parquet floor, and the noise they made in the silence. The Wing Sisters followed him, carrying the small bundles of leaflets he had come to distribute. 'We'd better get to Sister's office ready to report on duty,' said Bea.

After their shift, when the night staff arrived and the day staff were ready to go off-duty, Sister Cary lined them all up to tell them what Matron had said. She put the leaflets on the desk as if they were beneath her notice, but read the main one aloud, as if it was her own composition.

'Now listen carefully, Nurses. The army has placed heaps of sand at intervals round the walls of the Home. There are buckets of sand in all the corridors and rakes with long handles hanging by them. On no account are you to pick up a fire bomb with your bare hands.' She glanced round as if ready to impose a heavy penalty on anyone she caught doing it. The culprit would almost certainly be sent straight to Matron.

'Why sand, Sister?' asked Bea. 'We have a lot of fire hoses.'

'You haven't been listening, Nurse,' said Sister Cary, ignoring the fact that Bea had slipped away to answer a bell and hadn't heard the rest of the talk. 'If water is put on a fire bomb, it will explode and spread the fragments and more fire. Also, some of the bombs now being dropped contain explosive charges as well as the incendiary devices.' She looked at each of the serious faces. 'If one of you finds an incendiary inside the building, scoop it up and put it in a bucket of sand and place it outside for the soldiers to deal with. Any fire caused by the fire bombs can be put out with water after the bomb is removed. The bombs must be completely covered with sand.'

'Why all the panic?' asked Bea when they left.

'Didn't you hear? The last raids have dropped more fire bombs than anything else. They say it's because the Germans want to start up fires that will lead them back at night-time for bombing raids with high explosive.'

'I wish I could firewatch on the roof,' said Bea.

'They already have them up there,' said Emma. 'Home Guard and cadets and AFS.'

'Exactly! I saw an absolute gem going up there last night when I did the maids' blackout. Can't think why he isn't in the Forces. Must be a boffin or a Conscientious Objector or something very vital to the War Effort. He was gorgeous.'

'I'd rather get some sleep,' said Emma. 'I hope they don't come tonight.' She yawned, and even Bea who was a night owl and thrived on late nights, looked pale. 'It's not fair,' Emma pointed out. 'Here we are, night after night and Phil who is supposed to be protecting us from the air is having a wonderful time, swanning about in the sun, with no rationing, no bombs and plenty of entertainment.' She fished in her pocket. 'I had a letter-card today saying he's just got back from a weekend with a family who invited him to their holiday cottage. Some cottage! Complete with swimming pool and outdoor kitchen. They had chicken grilled over charcoal and ate it under the stars.'

'Wonder who put on an apron and did the little woman bit and cooked it for him?' asked Bea. 'Was good little Phil a good little Phil?'

Emma made threatening gestures but laughed.

He had said he missed her and would rather be in England with all the shortages, sharing the danger with her and people he loved, than having to be polite to very nice people who hadn't a clue as to what was happening in the cities of England. He also wanted the measurement of her third finger, left hand, just in case.

'*I've seen some beautiful diamonds,*' he wrote. '*Apart from anything else, it would be a wonderful investment.*' He makes me feel like a Berber woman dressed in all her bridal gold to impress on the neighbours just how much he values his woman, Emma thought. Then she felt rather mean, knowing he wasn't like that, not really.

She treated it as a joke and asked if he wanted the morning or evening measurement after a day in Green Alley doing baths. She had described her hands as red and rough and swollen, but she looked at them complacently. Not true, she decided. Only one broken nail this week. She put away the good photograph of her in uniform and sent him a less flattering one, making her letter bright and humorous, noncommittal and giving no promises, and not mentioning the brochures that she had studied with Bea about entry to London hospitals.

'If I wanted to study economy I'd stay in Bristol and live at home when I'm off-duty,' Emma told Bea. 'But I want to go to London, that is – if there are any hospitals left to train in. I'm sure the poorer parts of a city would give us a better training as we shall meet a much more varied set of circumstances. Even Sister Cary says that is important.'

'So long as there's a bus to the West End,' said Bea. 'But if we are a little way out, we might escape being bombed.'

'Maybe they'll turn us down,' said Emma.

'From here? You haven't heard Sister Cary on

her hobby horse. They'll grab us with open arms, according to her. Hasn't she licked us into shape and taught us how to be respectful? All nicely broken-in slave labour, reacting to the whip with never a tremor? She insists that every girl who went from here in the past was a success. How can she know? Surely no one ever came back to tell her? Can you imagine us writing cosy letters to her once we escape?'

For several nights there had been peace and no raids. The city was tidied and heaps of rubble awaited removal from the main streets that were difficult to remember as they had been, with huge department stores and restaurants, now flattened. Strangely, the residents were restless and far more trouble when left in their rooms to sleep peacefully. The ladies needed little prolonged sleep and had built up an interesting pattern, meeting people from other wings whom they seldom saw away from the subway. Miss Dingle missed her nightly readings at two am and had to take sleeping pills. Miss Forsyth was claustrophobic if she woke up in her room as she expected a bomb to come through her window at any time, and Miss Styles and many like her missed the extra attention.

The mobile residents took to walking about and having illicit cups of tea in the Wing kitchen once the night sister had been on her rounds, and to them, night brought a feeling of relaxation instead of fear.

Emma picked up her cloak and went back on duty after eating toast and real farmhouse honey before the fire in the Common Room. She reported on duty and took trays to the bed cases. All was quiet as the ladies in the dining room ate slowly and with enjoyment. They sipped white wine which was a birthday present to Miss Briars, who sat at the head of the table and made sure that everyone shared her treat. Her brother had sent in a crate of fine wine and she was enjoying her moment of fame. 'Have the bed ladies had some?' she asked, and sent Emma with four large bottles to make sure they all had as much as they wanted.

'Go to the others first,' whispered Bea. 'If you go to Miss Dingle early on she'll have the lot!' Miss Dingle was having supper with Miss Forsyth, listening to a programme of music on the wireless. Emma poured some wine into a feeder by the bed and filled Miss Dingle's ready glass.

Miss Dingle drank and held out the glass for more. 'It's very fine,' she said, as if that made it as innocent as lemonade. Emma smiled. Miss Dingle had been sober for nearly a month with a few near-misses. She poured more and left the bottle which was two-thirds empty. 'You are a dear duck,' said Miss Dingle.

Vincent took the last full bottle and hid it behind a curtain in the corridor. She winked. 'Might as well wish her a happy birthday when we go off-duty,' she said. They tiptoed past the door of a dying woman and Emma hurried, imagining the thin figure breathing her last in the warm, luxurious room. Did it help to know that she was having the very best attention? Did she know she was dying? Did the flowers and fruit mean anything now? A small trolley was outside the door, carrying the usual assortment of cotton wool, lotions and bowls. Underneath was a bottle, a champagne bottle and it was unopened. 'She's probably gone,' said Vincent cheerfully. 'That came up this morning and it hasn't been opened.'

Sister served pudding and left to write her report. The atmosphere relaxed and Miss Briars insisted that each nurse should drink a glass of wine. The residents giggled like schoolgirls as they pictured Sister's face if she saw this happening. Miss Styles wasn't present as she resented all the fuss being made of Miss Briars who had been in the Home for only three years.

Emma felt suddenly exhilarated and independent. She was going on holiday soon and would be able to travel north to see relatives of her father, or if she could wangle a pass, spend some time on the Island. She recalled her outings with Phillip and decided that wherever she went, she would put a cycle in the guard's van.

A sound came that was half-expected and yet a shock as they had heard no siren for days. The usual drill started, bed cases having priority, followed by wheelchairs. Emma stood by the elevator ready to lift and ease the chair over the edge and went back for another chair. She looked in each room as Sister had instructed and made sure that every one was downstairs. The heavy planes were low and Emma went quickly into each room to check again. She closed curtains and shut doors, then glanced into the room where the trolley was by the door. On the bed was a shrouded figure covered with a sheet which was tucked in carefully as if to keep out draughts. The face was covered but from under the sheet peeped a large cardboard label, tied to the right foot with a piece of new bandage. The bow was a work of art. It seemed wrong to leave the old lady there alone, but she couldn't be hurt. It was too late for pain. Emma softly closed the door.

The other rooms were all empty. As Emma turned off a light in the four-bedded room, she heard a sound almost as if a child had flung a firecracker while someone else had simultaneously lit a Catharine Wheel. Another sound, like the first but nearer, made Emma check that no light appeared from the corridor before opening the curtains slightly to look across the Downs.

It was like a gypsy camp. She had once seen a film in which small fires dotted a plain and it was like that now. How pretty, she thought, and then realised that these were fire bombs. She saw five burning within the grounds of the Home, and as she watched another fell in front of the window, letting off a hissing white light. It was as bright as a marine flare, the magnesium igniting and spreading, showing up the outlines of the leafless trees. There were cries and running steps and more shouts: figures in khaki and dark blue with steel helmets and high gauntlet gloves converged on the fires.

'Dewar?'

Emma swung round, letting the curtains fall back, but nothing could hide the light from outside. Blackout was irrelevant. 'Bea?' she answered, dazzled.

'Come on. Sister's having kittens. She had a rocket from Matron because she didn't check that all staff were down. I said I'd make a round as Miss Styles was playing up and Sister couldn't leave her.'

'Look!' Emma drew back the curtain.

'Good grief! Fireworks. Almost as good as Cowes,' said Bea. A wide frond of light sprang from a new batch of incendiaries. 'There must be dozens,' said Bea. 'They aren't fooling!' She rushed to the internal telephone and rang the subway, saying that there was a danger of fire. 'I'm staying with Nurse Dewar,' she said firmly. 'Someone must watch from here. Tell Sister Cary we'll patrol the rooms until the All Clear.' She rang off before anyone could object and grinned happily. 'Come on, Dewar, we'll do a round and watch where they fall.'

The second wave had encircled the Home, and the

Downs were dotted with more. Some came close enough to threaten the structure of the building and there was a shout and a shower of sparks and sand. 'Those were on the roof,' said Emma nervously.

'The Army is dealing with them, but we must watch down here,' said Bea, and jumped away from a curtained window as the glass cracked. They felt a breeze tinged with burning and the curtains went up in flames. Emma dragged them down and away from the oak panelling, while Bea rushed for sand. She struggled back with two buckets, one of water and one of dry sand. Emma took the sand and a shovel and advanced warily towards the grey cylinder which spewed white light at her. Bea doused the curtains with water.

'Open the French doors along there by the loggia,' said Emma. 'I need a clear run. I'd never get it over that high sill.' Bea ran and stood ready by the door, waiting to fling it wide when Emma came near, but avoiding making a draught until the last moment. Emma bit her lip. 'Here goes,' she said, and scooped the bomb into the bucket. The light died a little but the heat was intense. It travelled along the metal handle of the bucket and it was as if she carried a lighted blow-torch that hadn't made up its mind which way to blow flames.

She ran but the heat was intolerable so she slowed and it became bearable. I mustn't drop it. I must get it out, she repeated but the door seemed a long way off. 'Come on!' shouted Bea. She ran to meet her and held one side of the bucket handle so that they could lean away from the heat, but their hands were blistering. They reached the doors and pushed them open, almost falling into the garden, gasping as the fumes hit their lungs. The bomb flared and they dropped the bucket on to a mound of sand. Soldiers quickly shovelled sand over it and it died.

'All right in there? Any more?'

'We'll let you know,' said Bea. They went in, closing the door again. Emma's hand was stiff but she ignored the pain. 'Ouch!' said Bea. 'We'll check the rooms and then get something on our hands. Bang goes my lifetime ambition to be a concert pianist.' They found one more incendiary on a window ledge and shouted to the soldiers below before brushing it off the sill. Everything else was safe and the planes had moved away. 'Let's go,' said Bea and headed for the dispensary. The door was unlocked and the light was on. Sister Ambrose turned from the sink and eyed them with mild curiosity.

'You've burned your hands, you silly girls,' she said.

'We were making toast, Sister,' whispered Bea as Sister Ambrose opened a cabinet. She treated the burns and bandaged them neatly with surprising skill and care and already they were less painful.

'We've one good left hand and one right between us,' said Emma. She looked at Bea and laughed. Bea chuckled and Sister Ambrose gave a throaty gurgle. 'Your hair,' spluttered Emma.

'Your eyebrows!' said Bea. They looked in the mirror at two white faces, with eyebrows covered with spent magnesium.

'I've lost my eyelashes,' said Emma.

'So have I,' said Bea triumphantly. 'Now, they'll grow like mad. They'll grow thick – they always do after singeing.'

Sister Ambrose poured brandy into glasses. She added water. 'Shock, you know. Better be on the safe side.' She handed round the glasses, taking care to take the largest helping.

'Thank you, Sister. We'd better get back and see that everything is all right,' said Bea and they left Sister Ambrose contemplating the brandy bottle.

Everywhere was safe and quiet now and Emma

felt completely limp. 'It really is shock,' said Bea. 'Brandy makes me thirsty and we've earned a rest.' She put a hand behind the curtain and brought out the big bottle of wine that Vincent had hidden. They went into Miss Dingle's ground-floor room to borrow two cut-glass beakers, sat on her bed and drank the smooth white wine. They toasted friends, relatives, all those they loved and hated and when the bottle was nearly empty, they even toasted Sister Cary.

'Oh, how lovely! A party!' said Miss Dingle. 'Can anyone join?' She had a strange lump under her cloak and her eyes sparkled.

'Why aren't you downstairs in safety?' Bea asked with dignity.

'Didn't you hear the All Clear?'

Emma shook her head and stared at her, owlishly. It was jolly good wine. She'd never drunk so much in her life. It had been a lovely big bottle. Bea looked serene, like a warm Siamese cat with one white paw. 'Come in! Come in, dear Miss Dingle.' She waved an all-embracing arm. 'Do join us, but I'm afraid the wine's all gone.'

Miss Dingle laughed. 'I found something outside a room. It was so lonely,' she said sadly. 'I couldn't bear to leave it there in case it got bombed.' She put the bottle of champagne on the table and went for another glass, then saw the bandaged hands. She heard voices outside the window where soldiers were making sure that the heaps of sand held no further danger. She opened the curtains slightly and called. 'Would you mind helping me?' she asked politely. 'Yes, do come in through the window.'

Two soldiers appeared from the gloom, their faces as white as the girls' and their eyes red with exhaustion. 'Come in and close the curtains. We don't want them back, do we?' said Miss Dingle.

'Would one of you be an absolute dear and open this.' She fetched two more glasses, some biscuits and another bottle of wine.' I said I'd help her with the leftovers. Miss Briars isn't what I call a wine drinker,' she said. 'Whoops!' The froth took the Sergeant by surprise. Miss Dingle poured the champagne with care, handing a glass to each of the soldiers and making little speeches that got longer as the champagne grew less. She kept most of the champagne for herself, relieved when the men said they preferred the wine, and when Emma said she hated the bubbles.

When the last of the red wine that Miss Dingle brought from her wardrobe was finished, and she was slightly incoherent, she sank back on her bed. 'I want to thank you all,' she said. 'Thank you, gentlemen. If I don't wake up in the morning, this is the best way to die.' Emma and Bea propped themselves up, back to back on the tiger skin rug and the curtains closed behind the two unsteady soldiers.

Sister Cary flung the door open and saw the two girls. She took one look at the white faces and limp bodies and left to find the porter and wheelchairs. Randolph and the under-porter came running and Sister Cary watched from the door as they helped the girls into the chairs. Randolph sniffed and hid a grin. 'It's all right, Sister. Just exhausted and shocked, I reckon. You get on. You've got a lot on your plate tonight. We'll get them to their rooms and ask some of the nurses to clean them up and undress them.'

Sister Cary nodded and set off down the corridor to check the patients back to their rooms. 'Good thing the place stinks of burning,' said Randolph. 'It smells like a taproom in here. Come on, my brave lovelies. We'll get you away before she twigs what really happened.'

The next morning, Emma awoke with a headache and groaned. Bea staggered into her room and said, 'Move over.' They lay side by side and then sipped the tea that Matron had ordered for them. Sister Ambrose had told her of the burned hands, glad of an excuse to be found in the dispensary when she should have been in the subway, and by now, everyone was talking of the heroic behaviour of the two Pros, convinced that they had saved the entire Home from burning to the ground.

'Do you remember getting here?' croaked Bea. Emma shook her head and then wished she hadn't. 'I remember Nadine undressing me,' Bea went on. 'It was a very good party.' She giggled, and said, 'Come in.' The maid from Matron's apartment brought a tray of breakfast, newspapers and their mail.

Emma pushed aside the blue airmail letter and picked up the stiff white envelope.

'Snap!' said Bea, waving an identical one. They tore open the envelopes and a long whistle escaped from Bea's lips. 'You too?'

Emma smiled with tears in her eyes. 'Me too.' The message was the same. They could begin their training at the Princess Beatrice Hospital in southeast London in April.

'We can give in our notice now, while we are still in their good books, take a holiday and pack for The Smoke!' said Bea exultantly. 'London, we are on our way!'

PART TWO
Beer and Buttercups

1

Paddington Station was crowded. The overall colour was sludge brown with occasional bursts of blue where a contingent of sailors waited for their transport, leaning on badly-stacked kitbags. Emma tugged at her heavy case and half-wished she'd accepted the help of a soldier who had travelled all the way from Bristol in the same carriage, but he had his own lot to carry and she had no intention of making his two days' leave more interesting.

One or two half-hearted wolf whistles followed her. They do that as a matter of course, she thought. Out of uniform, they'd be far too inhibited. She smiled. Uniforms had much to recommend them. They were a disguise that hid natural shyness, lack of clothes sense and in many cases, the superficial gloss acquired from education and background. Uniform was a mask behind which she could hide and be the person she wanted to be, away from home and family.

She glanced at the piece of paper on which she had scribbled the instructions. The first bus stop was outside the station: she could go as far as Victoria before changing for another bus to take her south of the river, then a third one would take her nearly all the way to the hospital.

After that came a long walk, even if it was less than the one from the Underground, as she had discovered when she came to London for her interview. Emma hesitated and put her case down for a minute while she made up her mind. The thought of venturing down to the Underground again was daunting. She remembered the acrid smell of the tunnels and the added aroma of bodies and bedding that didn't disperse even during the day, as more and more people staked a claim to a patch of platform where they could spend the night away from the bombs.

There were shelters and bombing in Bristol but the passive acceptance of people in the Underground had been chilling. She knew that many had been bombed out and had no other place to feel safe, but she hated the thought of the windy tunnels and the dry air and the crowds.

She carried her case to the bus stop and the bus conductress pointed to the luggage gap by the stairs. 'Leave it there, ducks. It'll be quite safe. Nobody pinches anything on my bus.'

'Don't you believe it!' said a tall Sergeant. He leaned across and pinched the clippie's bottom. His mates roared with laughter as she tossed her head and tried to look annoyed. Emma smiled faintly, and looked out at the grey world that was London. Not a lot of bomb damage to the casual observer but sometimes the light that shone through empty windows showed that there was just a facade left and the buildings were open to the sky. Heaps of rubble were piled away from the roads to allow the passage of traffic and some landmarks that Emma had seen in magazines were still recognisable and reassuring, as if London was not as badly damaged as she'd imagined it would be.

Masses of uniforms everywhere made her think of Phillip, the boy she had known from childhood on the Isle of Wight, and who was still in South Africa doing more training in the RAF. She wondered if he really would like to be back, for all his letters tried to make her jealous, telling her of parties and pretty girls he met and the lavish hospitality of the South African rich who tried to do something for Britain by looking after her sons, but under his lightness, she knew that he wanted to get back and take an active part in the war.

The bus stopped and Emma alighted and stood on the pavement, the slip of paper in her hand. She wasn't even sure at which exit from Victoria Station the bus south would be. On an impulse, she went to the taxi rank and put her case at her feet, sighing with relief. The heavy leather trunk had gone ahead and would be at the hospital waiting for her, she hoped, but even one medium-sized suitcase, also of leather, was heavy before it was packed and seemed to weigh a ton now, as the number of last-minute things had grown each time she thought of being away from home for six months and needing clothes for each season.

The line of people dwindled and she was next in line expect for two men, one in the uniform of the AFS and the other in civilian clothes. She glanced at the man in the blue suit and wondered what he did for a living to keep him out of uniform. He was young and looked fit and intelligent but her subconscious registered the fact of his civilian clothes rather than his physical appearance.

He turned and looked at her with penetrating grey eyes. 'Where are you going?'

Emma hesitated, then saw a taxi slowing down ready to join the rank. 'South of the river.'

'I'm as far as the Elephant,' said the AFS man.

'Where, south of the river?' asked the man in the suit. His smile was mocking as if he sensed her distrust.

'You want to watch him, Miss!' the AFS man winked. 'No careless talk, mind, and don't get picked up, is what I say to my girl.'

'I'm going the same way as you but further on,' she said.

'Right.' The man in the suit took her bag and lifted it easily into the front of the cab. 'Start for the Elephant and Castle and then on towards Camberwell,' he said to the driver.

The driver looked at the civilian clothes. 'Is your journey really necessary?' he said. Emma smiled. The whole country had begun to talk in clichés taken from the spartan advertisements put out by the various ministries. In the queue someone had said, 'Pass along the bus says Billy, To block the entrance is so silly.' Oh, that Billy Brown of London Town had a lot to answer for! The driver grinned. 'A bit out of my way, Guv, but if the lady has to get back to the 'Orspital, that's different. Any more for Camberwell Green? This is your last chance!'

Another man pushed into a seat with a suitcase at his feet. 'Brixton,' he said.

'I don't go that far. Only as far as the 'Orspital and the Green. You'll have to get out at Coldharbour,' said the driver. The man nodded.

The pull-down seats were full now as they crossed the bridge and entered the rubble-littered streets south of the Thames. Gaps and half-demolished houses, boarded-up shop windows and barricades round holes in the road made the same picture that Emma had seen every day in Bristol but here there had been more effort put into clearing the roads. Only once did the taxi have to follow a detour.

She rubbed a patch of window clear and peered out. The taxi was emptying and one street looked like another. She stretched her legs as the man in the blue suit folded up the seats and settled in his corner. She was conscious of his eyes, not staring in any way to which she could take exception but noticing everything about her. She opened her handbag to take out a handkerchief. 'Cigarette?' he asked.

'No, thank you. I don't smoke.'

He held a silver cigarette case. 'Do you mind if I

do?' She shook her head and he selected a cigarette and lit it. The flame from the matching lighter was short and efficient, and she couldn't imagine it not working for him. She glanced at the strong fingers and wondered again why he wasn't in uniform. His hands were too clean and well-kept to be those of a manual worker or a soldier. A civilian in a plush reserved occupation? In some prosperous racket? London was full of such people and the taxi driver had certainly had reservations about him.

'Well, have you decided?'

'I beg your pardon?'

He looked at her through the thin blue smoke. 'You can't place me, can you?' She looked at him, coldly. 'You were staring,' he said.

'I wasn't. I was far away,' she retorted.

'Was the driver right? You are going to the Princess Beatrice Hospital?'

'You seem to be the inquisitive one,' she answered.

'Better own up,' he mocked. 'We're nearly at the Green and from the way you looked out of the window every two minutes from Victoria, I imagine you aren't sure of the way there. If he stops now, you've a half-mile walk away from the main road.'

She sighed. 'I didn't know I had the address written on my face.' The taxi stopped by a block of apartments called Peabody Buildings to let off the man who wanted to go to Brixton, He tried to persuade the driver to go on there.

'Sorry mate. I'm going to take this young lady to Beatties and then try to get a fare back from Dulwich. I'll go back that way as I doubt if I'll get a fare from around here.' He eyed the man in the suit. 'You getting out here, too, Guv?'

'No, I'm going to the hospital too,' he said. The driver gave him a searching look and turned to Emma.

'Do you know the nurses' entrance?' she asked.

'Never wrong,' said the driver. 'Just beginning, are you? You'll like it there, Miss. My brother lives just over the park. All his lot's been in there. Lovely place. You, coming all this way from the station could be going to only one of two places and after we left Tommies behind, I knew it was either Kings or Beatties. You couldn't be a local. I know them all.'

He started the engine and in a few minutes Emma recognised the entrance to the hospital.

'Thank you. How much do I owe you?'

'I thought you were together.' He gave the other passenger a look that hinted that he'd better watch his step. He accepted payment from Emma but refused a tip. 'With this lot coming over every night, I might need you, Miss. Good luck.' He took the offered money from the man and the very generous tip with only a grunt of acceptance. 'I'll take your bag in, Miss. See you safely in, like. You never know!'

He lugged the case out and almost ran between the open gates to the entrance with it. Emma followed and glanced back but the man had gone. 'Best be careful here, Miss. Plenty of wide boys about these days. Follow you, did he? If you get any trouble like that, just tell the porter at the gate. He's a cousin of my brother's wife.'

'I don't think he was following me, but thank you for your help. You are very kind. In any case, I shan't be here for long as we have to go into the country to the preliminary training school now that the one here was destroyed by a fire bomb.' She smiled. 'If he was following me, he'll be very disappointed as I don't think he'll find me in darkest Surrey where we are going.'

'They say they might try to get the bus route going again from down the hill. That will be better for you when you want to go up West and have to come home late. It should be running when you come back to Beatties,' the taxi driver said. 'Safe as houses, here. It isn't the locals you want to worry about, it's them spivs up West.'

Safe as houses? Emma thought. How can anyone say that now? She rang the bell in the lodge. The smell was almost the same as the smell of the Home on the Downs in Bristol where shoes squeaked on the sticky floor-polish applied too lavishly by the porter. A wave of nostalgia akin to homesickness threatened to make her eyes smart. It wasn't her parents or the very new house on the freshly-carved estate that she missed, but the gentle light on grey stone walls, wide corridors and solid serenity, the scent of flowers and the sight of residents cared for and intelligent. Miss Dingle had given her a brooch and even Miss Styles had insisted on giving her a small packet of sweets before she left.

Don't be stupid, she told herself. You couldn't wait to get away from Green Alley and the snide remarks of Sister Cary. I've dreamed of this, coming to London to start on my real career in a leading London hospital. I can be myself and live my own life, she insisted. I can be a personality in my own right and not be bullied by that awful Sister on Wing Six. Her spirits lifted. I'm free! I needn't go back for at least three months and my mother can't nag at me here.

Even the porter was like the one at the Home. All the young men had gone into the Forces and such jobs now fell to older men. He checked her name against a list and told her to go to the dining room for lunch, saying that the coach would collect all the nurses outside the entrance at two o'clock precisely. Emma followed his directions and found the dining room. She glanced up at the vaulted ceiling and the oak panelling, high up to the narrow windows. Long poles fitted with hooks stood by each window ready to ease the heavy blackout curtains over the windows. Almost as difficult to curtain as the chapel, she thought, then made a determined effort not to compare everything with the Home.

A table at one end of the room was empty and she saw the note saying it was reserved for the new Preliminary Training School intake. She sat and watched the nurses come and go, listened to the chatter and wondered if they liked it here, working in a busy acute hospital. Was it as exciting as she hoped? Would she fit in and be a success? Two girls joined her and she smiled timidly. 'I'm Emma Dewar. Is this your first day, too?'

'Margaret Turpin and Annie Force,' one said. 'We met on the train from Yorkshire.'

'Have you done any nursing?'

'I've done Red Cross Cadets and first-aid classes,' said Margaret, but Annie shook her head. 'It's all a bit big, isn't it? We couldn't find the dining room and wandered into some very funny places,' the girl called Margaret added.

'I suppose we'll get used to it after we've finished PTS. I must say I like the idea of being let down gently at first and not going directly to the wards.' Emma saw that Annie was very nervous. 'Imagine being shunted into a full ward and having to cope from day one! I think I must be mad to come here.'

Others came, and soon there were eleven girls chattering as if they had known each for years. Most of them were about the same age but two of the girls were older and Emma wondered if they had done nursing as auxiliaries, like Vincent at the Home. Anxiously, she looked towards the door and wondered if Bea was coming or had decided to give the Princess Beatrice a miss. At half-past one, there was still no sign of her. It was fairly typical of Bea to do unpredictable things but usually she managed to keep to appointed times.

Still no sign of her, and a Sister with a crisp white bow under her chin came to gather them for the coach. She showed them a cloakroom they could use before the journey and waited for them, clipboard in hand. 'One of us hasn't come yet, Sister,' said Emma.

'Oh, you will be Nurse Dewar.' Sister smiled. 'Nurse Shuter said you might worry. She's already in the coach.'

'Did you get lost?' asked Emma as she slid into the seat that Bea had kept for her. Bea looked marvellous. Her bright red suit and pure silk blouse shouted *haute couture* and her handbag was soft suede and expensive.

'Lost? Don't be silly, duckie. What did you have for lunch?'

'Fish of some sort and potatoes. Baked pudding, I think.'

'Well, there you are! You took your last meal of freedom in a perfectly awful dining room, eating perfectly awful food while I had a very nice little meal at the Dorchester, with a glass of quite acceptable wine.'

'You didn't go there alone?'

'No.' Bea looked disappointed. 'No, I have to admit I wasn't alone. My father turned up to wish me well and insisted on taking me out.' She chuckled. 'It would have been more fun alone. There was the most divine man sitting all alone two tables away. He did nothing but stare at me and if only my father hadn't been there, well – who knows? I might have rung the hospital and said I had the flu and would come on later.'

'You wouldn't! Bea, you're teasing.'

'I suppose so, but I still had a very good meal and an exhilarating eye contact if nothing more.

Delicious sensation, flirting. And he had a *very* wicked mouth.' She looked sideways at Emma's clear profile. 'I suppose you have no idea of what I mean. Do you know what a physical thrill is, Dewar? Why didn't you settle for a nunnery and go the whole hog for chastity? I suppose all this beautiful scenery will be lost on you.' She looked out at a group of white-coated figures who strolled across in front of the parked coach. 'And to think, we have to go into the wilderness for three whole months before we can see them again, let alone touch!'

'You are impossible, Bea,' said Emma comfortably. 'I believe about half of what you say.'

'I'm not staying out in the Styx if it's too deadly. I assume we have some off-duty when our shackles will be unlocked for exercise and then we can fly away to the West End. We'll have a wonderful time, Dewar. We'll book in for a night at the Cumberland and go to a theatre.'

'It's all very well for you, Bea. You've never been short of money.' She mentally counted her resources. What money she had must last until she was paid at the end of the three months trial in PTS. I'm lucky that they have just said that we needn't pay for our first uniforms, and this is the first year when all dresses and aprons are provided free, she thought, but the first three months had to be covered at her own expense. She blessed Aunt Emily who had sent her a cheque to help her get started, when Clare Dewar had tried to make her give up the idea of going to London by saying they couldn't afford to keep her while she worked for nothing.

The outlay on uniform would have been heavy as the minimum included four dresses, fourteen aprons, six pairs of stiff cuffs, and six pairs of false sleeves to be put over rolled-up uniform sleeves on duty, when doing dirty jobs. The caps were made specially by one firm and had pretty frills that had to be starched and made up in a manner that Emma had yet to learn. Duty shoes of a rather old-fashioned but expensive style were to be bought from a West End store and had made a great gap in Emma's cash.

'Did you buy those awful shoes?' asked Bea.

'Of course. They were on the list of things we had to get.'

Bea snorted. 'You didn't! I wouldn't be seen dead in them.'

'But they said . . .' began Emma.

'I wrote to Matron and said I had very narrow feet and could I have ward shoes made to fit?' She smiled. 'They are neat and plain but in no way do they resemble the Mother Gamp things they suggested. I suppose you did exactly as you were told, down to the last collar stud?'

'Well, if they are anything like Sister Cary, they'll check up on what we bring and wear.' A feeling of horror that she might be the only one to conform, struck Emma. 'What about dresses? They said fourteen inches from the ground.'

'Oh, did they?' said Bea airily. 'I thought they seemed a bit long when I measured that. Who is going to look at my very sheer black silk stockings if I have skirts down past my calves?'

'That's why,' said Emma dryly. 'The sight of the backs of our knees is supposed to upset the male patients and raise temperatures.'

'Is that so? And little Dewar actually knows the symptoms?' Bea giggled and took out a packet of chocolate. 'Have some. My father gets it from Switzerland. It's very good. Go on, I've masses more. He brought me a dozen pairs of silk stockings, too, so at least I shall not have ladders for the next few weeks.' Emma took two squares of milk chocolate and saw that it was the very best Swiss make. 'You know, Dewar, you worry me.' Bea put more chocolate in her mouth. 'Are you really as cool as you make out? We are away from the Home now and in the big outside world. No, don't look like that. How many men have you kissed?'

'Several,' said Emma.

'Apart from kissing cousins!'

'I haven't any who lived near enough for that,' said Emma, 'except for a little toad at Cowes that I wouldn't touch with a barge pole.'

'Is Phillip a prime example?'

'It's no concern of yours, but he is the one I'm most fond of.'

'Good grief! Fond! So you haven't been swept off your feet in a frenzy of passion with him raining kisses on your bare bosom?'

'Bea! Stop it! Sometime you have the oddest ideas. I like Phil very much and he has asked me to marry him.'

'And do you mean to waste the rest of the war waiting with a candle in the window for your hero to return?'

'No candle – remember the blackout. In any case, what opportunity have I had of meeting someone more exciting? We've been shut up with old ladies for so long that even the vicar was a thrill.'

The coach sped through damp lanes and side roads. 'We'll soon be there,' said Bea. 'I know the Old Coach House. My parents took me there before the owners went to America at the beginning of the war. They've upped and ratted but the house is very pleasant. It had a swimming pool, too, so we shall be all right if it's still there.' The coach slowed and went through a wide archway into a cobbled yard. The woman who sat in front with the driver called to the girls to identify their own luggage and to ask her for room numbers.

'There are three large rooms used as small dormitories.'

'Like being back at school,' said Bea later, heaving one case on to her bed. She had the place by the window and the other three beds were well-spaced in the corners of the room. Pale green panels of velvet under twinned wall lamps carried the pale green and gold scheme from the thick curtains and paintwork. The floor was covered with a more utilitarian covering and Emma assumed that the good carpets were in store.

Bea absentmindedly slapped a mosquito against the pale wall. 'Heck! They're everywhere. Must ask for some insect repellent. The pool must be full, and stagnant.'

The tall windows that opened all the way down to the floor were stiff to open, but Bea managed it at last. She stepped outside and Emma followed closely. It was hardly the weather yet for swimming, but a pool would be lovely. The owners of the house must have had a wonderful time, stepping out of the drawing room on to a terrace and into the pool.

They stood in shocked silence by the empty pool. Weeds pushed through the sides and in one corner was a dead hedgehog. To Emma's horror, Bea burst into tears. 'Everything has changed! Nothing is the same and it never will be again. It's all gone for ever, all the things that made life worthwhile, and I wish it was me who died and not Evans.'

'But, Bea, it's only an old swimming pool, and it's not warm enough for swimming even if it *was* full and clean.'

'Oh, YOU! It's all very well for you, Dewar. You, with your smug acceptance of everything, your good little boyfriend and a family at home sitting there thinking of you and missing you.'

Emma put an arm round her shoulder. 'I wish it was like that. I thought you were the happy one,

Bea. I've always envied the way you dress, the way you talk and all your self-confidence. The casual way you take over and have fun and everyone jumps to serve you in cafes. When I listen to you, I feel like a lump of lead. I have no money to dress really well apart from a little my grandmother left me, I haven't the courage to do half the things you take for granted and as for my parents, I find I really don't like either of them.'

Bea dashed away the tears and emerged like a slightly damp dragonfly. 'If that's true, I have a new mission in life! I shall lead you into all sorts of mischief and make you a thoroughly bad lot like me.'

They laughed and went back inside to unpack and to change into uniform, which they were told would be checked in detail by the Sister Tutor in charge of the school. Gradually, their room lost its neat unfriendly look and absorbed the four girls who were to live there for the duration of the course.

Emma sat on her bed, writing to Phil. She glanced across at Bea and smiled. Bea bent over one of her dresses, unpicking the hem to let the dresses down to the regulation length. 'It is forbidden to show your popliteal spaces behind your knees when working and bedmaking,' Bea said in a good imitation of Sister Roper. 'God, if I'd known that, I'd never have come. I have beautiful popliteal spaces and I want to flaunt them.'

'At least you haven't time to lead me down the primrose path. How many have you left to do?' Emma dodged a pillow. *Dear Phil,* she wrote. Would 'dear Phil' be enough or would 'my dear Phil' be better? And did she want him as her dear Phil? It sounded a bit condescending. His last airmail letter-card had said 'Dearest'. Dear, dearer, dearest – were these degrees of loving? Or degrees of conventional greeting that meant very little? She scribbled '*Darling*' on a scrap of paper and hastily crumpled it. Not that. '*Dear Phil, I have just arrived in PTS somewhere in England. I suppose that's right in case the censor thinks we are bombworthy . . .*' She bit the end of her pen. Why not '*Darling*'? He'd said he loved her and when she thought hard enough, she felt a faint thrill at the memory of her face against his uniform jacket and the insignia of the half-wing. The uniform and not the kiss? Did she love the window dressing and not the real goods?

'One more and I've done. Good thing I only tacked them up and didn't cut the hems, so I've no sewing to do. You must have written reams while I've been slaving. Give him my love and tell him not to be too good, but with that mouth he couldn't be anything but angelic. Nice face, though, and a change from the wandering hand brigade.' Bea sat forward on her bed, her face in her hands and an expression of inane interest on her face. 'Do tell me, has he ever ventured below the waist? All right! Don't be cross. I was teasing, but has he?'

Emma turned her back and scribbled furiously for five minutes, slipping the letter into the envelope and sealing it before she could change her mind. Not that it was much warmer than ten other letters but she had said '*Love, Emma.*' She searched in her handbag for the field post office address. 'I met a man today,' she said, almost to herself.

'Tell me more.'

'I'm not saying another word, Bea Shuter.' Emma smiled. 'I was just wondering what you would have said about his mouth.'

2

'Well, how do you feel about the weekend?' Bea sat on the bed and regarded Emma with anxiety she tried to hide. 'Not going home, are you?'

'I don't know. I ought to, I suppose. I keep getting rather touchy letters from my mother who thinks that we are out in the country, doing nothing.'

'Nothing? My godfathers! She calls this nothing? It's worse than Green Alley. Bathing old ladies had nothing on scrubbing out the damned basement and polishing furniture. That's maid's work. Look at my hands! I feel ashamed to go anywhere.'

'What are you planning to do? Is your father in town?'

Bea shook her head. 'I'm virtually an orphan. I shall be all alone in the big bad city unless you come up and stay with me.'

'You know I can't afford it, Bea. My legacy money comes every three months and the cheque from Aunt Emily is all gone. I can only just afford the ticket to Bristol.'

'Money! What a lot of fuss about nothing.'

'Can't do much without it,' said Emma, dryly.

'Well, this time you can. You come with me and you needn't spend a thing. No, don't put on that proud, stubborn look again. Just shut up and listen. The parent is away and has sent me the key to his pied-à-terre. I didn't know he had one, the artful old devil. I suppose he kept it a dark secret while he wanted a place for his dirty weekends. Since the divorce, he's had several women.'

'How do you know? It may be just a convenient

place to sleep when he's passing through on business.'

'You are so trusting, it isn't true. My parents have gone their own ways for years. My mother takes lovers like you take toasted tea cakes, and over the years, he's done the same to pay her back. I shall follow the tradition.'

'Don't be daft. I never know what to believe about you, Bea. We've been here for two months and I thought I knew you, but I still want to shake you when you say awful things like that. I thought in Bristol it was just a pose, but now, I think you almost believe it. What you are really saying is that your kind father has given you the keys to his flat in London so that you can go there and take your friends.'

'Haven't I been saying that for hours?'

'No, you haven't.' Emma smiled. 'I'd like to come, Bea. It could be fun. I can save my fare money and we can go to the National Gallery and perhaps see a play. Do you like ballet? I've never been to the real ballet in London.'

'Hey, steady on. If we go to town, we don't go anywhere near an art gallery. That's my only veto. Ballet, yes if you like. We can queue for gallery seats at the Angel if you want to save money. Now, that should be fun. I've never sat in the Gods. The other night we can go somewhere really wicked, like a dance hall. Have you ever been in one of those places where they have those sparkly bits on the ceiling that revolve and send shadows and coloured lights on the people dancing? It looked very decadent when I saw it on the news reels.' She laughed. 'We can tell our families we went to Covent Garden to absorb culture.' She saw Emma's blank expression. 'Didn't you know? They've turned the Opera House into a dance hall for the duration of the war. It will be oozing with men of every size shape and rank,' she added with relish.

'Oh, I don't know if I ought,' said Emma.

'You are coming. Now I know you aren't going home, you have no excuse, and honestly, I would be lost without you, Dewar,' Bea said with a sweet smile that was only half-mocking.

The house was spotless as usual, the last bandage rolled and put away in the practice room and Bea poked out her tongue at the plaster model used for bedmaking and bed baths. 'What do they think we did all that time in Bristol?' she said.

'At least it came easily for us. Some of the others were so clumsy,' said Emma. 'And it's so easy on the model.'

Bea shut the model in the cupboard and turned the key. 'I'll try to find a boyfriend for you if you'll take that stupid grin off your face,' she promised.

Sister Roper went through the list of addresses to which the twelve girls were going for their weekend off. What might seem over-zealous curiosity made good sense. 'I'm responsible to your parents for your safety,' she explained. 'None of you is over twenty-one and most are barely eighteen. If enemy action, illness or accident made it necessary to contact you, we have to know where to find you. Nurse Shuter?'

'I am staying in my father's apartment in London and taking Nurse Dewar with me, Sister,' said Bea demurely, and Emma wondered if Sister would have smiled so approvingly if she had known that they would be there alone in a flat in St James'.

'I hope that Jerry leaves us alone,' said Bea. 'We don't want to waste time in the Underground.' The air was cool but dry as they waited for a bus, clutching small overnight bags and smiling with anticipation. 'They clear the theatres during alerts.' London had a light mist shrouding the river and Emma said it would keep the bombers away. 'So long as it doesn't turn to fog. Have you ever been in a real peasouper? That isn't funny,' said Bea.

They emerged from the Underground in Oxford Circus. 'Let's dump our bags and freshen up and find a meal somewhere,' said Bea. She led the way down a side street and they came to a solid-looking building in a quiet, elegant cul-de-sac. No enemy action had marked this place and Emma felt the slight awe she had when entering anywhere very smart, impressive or grand. Bea had no such reservations but whistled as she opened the front door. 'Well, I have to hand it to him. He does his floosies proud.' She slammed the door and put down her bag. 'Now, where's the kitchen? We'll have coffee here if you don't mind evaporated milk. I brought a small tin as I knew there'd be none here. Coffee, yes; tea? Ah, there it is, two kinds, China or Indian, and I do believe a tin of Swiss biscuits and he hasn't eaten all the chocolate ones. Help yourself.'

'Are you sure?'

'Plenty more where those came from. Tuck in,' said Bea. She lit the gas stove and opened the door to the refrigerator. 'Eggs and cheese and plain biscuits in the other tin, so we'll exist. What's this? A tin of chicken. We're in luck tomorrow for lunch, so we can eat out this evening and go to Covent Garden to dance, queue for the ballet in the morning and look at clothes in shop windows, and eat here when we feel hungry.'

London after dark was a blur of dark blues under muted street lighting, and shadows flickered as hotel doors opened and shut on dimly-lit foyers. Emma blinked in the sudden glare of the Quality Inn in Leicester Square. 'Why here? It isn't like an ordinary café.' Menus printed in vivid colours hung on the walls, listing many choices of food and more menus were on each table. 'Choose a number against what you want to eat,' said Bea. 'It's an American idea but quick, cheap and very good. You have everything on one plate and for once, I approve.'

'Do you like Americans? I haven't met more than a couple who came to work at the BAC where my father works. They were boring and just like him except for the accent.'

'If we don't get on with this war, I suppose we shall see them here in droves,' Bea replied. 'My father says the Isolationist movement is still strong there, but losing steam. They have enough sense to know that if we go under they'll be next or their precious economy will go for a Burton.'

'Don't look now, Bea, but do you know that man two tables back by the wall?'

'In uniform?'

'No.'

'Then I'm not interested. If I get picked up, I shall insist on nobody under the rank of Flying Officer.'

'Don't be funny, Bea, he's coming over.' Emma bent over her food and tried to ignore the approaching man. She thought of all the tales she had heard of girls being molested by strange men, abducted, even raped, then she smiled slightly. This was a public restaurant, with Bea who could look after herself anywhere. How could Bea sit there calmly, picking at a chicken bone as if there was nothing going on!

'Well, well,' said a slightly drawling voice. 'Slumming, are you, Bea?' The tall fair-haired man rested a hand lightly on Bea's shoulder and smiled across at Emma.

'Eddie ... darling,' said Bea casually, and shrugged away from his hand. 'Surprise. What are you doing in town?'

'What are you? Didn't I hear that you were nursing the nation's wounded, somewhere in England?'

He continued to look at Emma, who couldn't decide if she should go on eating, smile as if she was with Bea, or pretend to be just another customer sitting at the same table.

Bea glanced at her with an amused expression. 'Oh, this is my horrid cousin, Eddie Ripley. This is Emma Dewar who is a far better nurse than I'll ever be and so dedicated that she'll do it all her life.'

'One of the Buckingham Dewars, or the Scottish lot?' he asked.

'Neither,' said Bea briskly. 'Emma is one alone, so there's no need to start name dropping, Eddie.' Her tone was acid and slightly protective. 'Emma and I are in London on a cultural mission, or to put it plainly, we have escaped from darkest Surrey to dance and mingle with the proles, so that rather lets you out. Goodbye . . . Eddie, darling.'

Eddie sat on the one vacant chair by the table. 'But you are in no hurry. You haven't finished eating. Don't let me disturb you. Nothing worth drinking here, but we can go on to a little place I know.'

'We have our plans for this evening,' said Bea.

He continued to stare at Emma, a half-smile making his face seem benign. 'What lovely hair,' he said. 'And Emma is such beautiful name. So fresh and unspoiled and quite different from your usual friends, Bea.' Emma looked down at her plate and tried to eat but her mouth was dry. She was acutely conscious of an unfamiliar but pleasurable tension forming between them but she ignored his comments. He laughed and asked Bea if her father had been in touch.

'Not for ages,' she said. 'I really will have to write to him again.' Emma sensed that Bea disliked her cousin very much and had no intention of telling him their plans.

Emma glanced up when at last she put her knife and fork neatly together and could no longer avoid looking at him. His eyes were light blue and his smile didn't quite melt the ice but left the impression of a latent force lurking, that could erupt into something passionate or violent.

'And what does Emma think of your plans, Bea? I take it they are *your* plans?'

'We pooled ideas,' said Emma, resenting his tone as quickly as she had been attracted.

He raised his eyebrows. 'My, my, there must be more to you than a serene face and good figure.' His eyes took in every detail of her face and hair, her clothes and the soft line of her breast. She wanted to button her coat high under her chin. I've never felt like this with Phillip, she thought. But Phillip never looks at me in this way.

'A lot more,' said Bea, pleased that Emma showed a little spirit.' My dear cousin thinks he's the answer to a maiden's prayer. He even thought I was fair game at one time.' Her voice was hard but she smiled. 'Darling Eddie, don't waste your time. Emma is taken. She has a dashing RAF officer just lusting after her'

'I have the distinct impression that I am not welcome. Where shall I go now? I know a little club in Greek Street that would amuse you. They have black market hooch and if you're very good, I might buy you some genuine American nylon stockings.'

'I've heard of them. They wear a lot better than silk, don't they?' Bea sounded more friendly. 'But I really must use up the dozens of silk stockings that Daddy sends me from time to time. I don't need American gifts, and it's no use tempting Emma. She is incorruptible and wears only cotton lisle stockings on duty and hand-knitted woollen ones off-duty. Push off, Eddie. Get yourself a nice little tart in that awful club. We're going dancing and you would keep all the talent away. We came to town to enjoy ourselves.'

'How are you getting back tonight?'

'All arranged,' said Bea quickly. 'We are being driven back by the kind uncle of one of our set at PTS.'

Eddie looked annoyed. He stood by the table like a predatory bird, his narrow face and ascetic hands adding to the impression. 'Au revoir, mes enfants,' he said finally. 'I promise I'll see you soon.' He left without another word and Emma breathed deeply as if someone had opened a window. Bea found her cigarette case and took out a Sobranie. She offered them to Emma who took one for the first time, needing something to hold in her hands, something to control and to stop her fingers from picking at the bread roll she had left half-eaten.

'My cousin is evil,' said Bea slowly. 'I don't trust him and neither should you. When I see him, I believe in the devil.'

'Me trust him? I've only just met him and by the way you treated him, it's unlikely that I shall see him again.' In spite of her relief at his going, she was slightly resentful. The tension had gone with him but the admiration in the pale eyes had been real.

'Any girl who gets mixed up with Eddie is playing with fire. Come on, let's get along to this den of iniquity. I was serious when I said that Eddie would spoil it for us. He can freeze out anyone with just a look. Uncanny, somehow. We'll find ourselves a couple of partners and stay as late as we want. It's not far to walk back to St James', and we can tell anyone who is a bit too persistent that we are being collected by my father.'

'Not the nice uncle from Surrey?'

'I couldn't let Eddie know we were staying in town.'

The short queue grew quickly behind them as the doors to Covent Garden dance hall opened for the evening. 'Popular,' said Emma. 'Where shall we sit?'

Bea was delighted. 'We have come at the right time. Plenty of room so far and we can sit there and look over the newcomers as they arrive and then decide who we want to dance with.'

'Doesn't the man do the asking?' said Emma dryly. 'Suppose nobody brothers. They may all bring their own partners.' She recalled the hops at home when men propped up the bar at one end of the room and the women waited hopefully at the other.

'That's the silliest thing you've said tonight. You just pick your man and fix him with an unwinking stare as if you can't believe it. You know you've seen him somewhere before. Just as he begins to wonder who you are, you turn away, light a cigarette and you do *not* look at him again until he arrives two minutes later to ask you to dance. Then you stub out your cigarette as if you can't bear to be parted from it, give him a faint smile as if it's all too boring and dance.'

'You've been watching too many films,' giggled Emma. They walked into the vast hall and looked up at the tiered galleries and boxes still festooned with the crimson and gilt of more cultural days. The dance floor was well sprung and surfaced and the small tables surrounding the dancing area were gradually being taken. There were many men and some girls in parties or in couples, and uniforms were in the majority. Bea ordered orange squash which arrived looking unhealthily synthetic in thick glasses, but served to show that their table was occupied. The band was good; a famous big band with a heavy leaning towards tenor saxophones and drums.

A slow foxtrot began and several couples were dancing, but to Emma's amusement no man had as yet riveted Bea's attention. 'Come on, come on,' muttered Bea with a teeth-clenching smile.

'Not all men can do a slow foxtrot,' said Emma. 'So, if they've never been taught, be thankful that you haven't beetle crushers all over your dainty feet.'

The music changed to a faster beat and the floor filled with erratically bobbing couples. Two RAF Sergeants battled through the dancers towards them and stood, grinning. 'Care to take a turn, ladies?' said a Scottish voice and Emma found herself clutched to a hard chest with tunic buttons digging into her breasts. Her face was on a level with a brawny shoulder and as she was firmly gyrated, it was as if her face was being rubbed gently with sandpaper.

'D'ye come here often? This is our first time. We thought we'd give it a try as we shan't be here for much longer.' There was no need for Emma to do more than smile and try to avoid his feet. He might be a Scot but not an inarticulate one. In five minutes she heard that he was a primary school teacher in civilian life, but unmarried. This was accompanied by a quick squeeze of the hand as if to hint that if she played her cards right she might fill that gap. He told her that he was stationed in Gloucester and had two days leave before being sent on somewhere overseas, and Emma wondered just how much information was given innocently to pretty girls with coloured lights glinting in their hair.

He still hadn't asked anything about her when they returned to the table. Bea was already there with her partner, a much smoother version of the

Scot. Bea looked amused at the gingery eyebrows and solid body and glanced at Emma's feet where dusty marks now marred her white high heeled shoes. 'Did you say you were in the Tank Corps?' she said sweetly. Emma's partner looked puzzled but Emma giggled. She sipped her drink and tried to stop laughing. The music began again and she said she wanted to powder her nose.

Bea followed her to the ladies room. 'It's easy to get a partner but how do we lose them? Look! They've sat themselves at our table as if they've taken root.' As they came out of the rest room, two sailors grabbed them and whirled them off into a waltz. Emma's was short and smelled strongly of beer, and this time it was difficult to dance without looking him in the eye or staring over his shoulder.

He released her as a soldier tapped his back. 'It's an Excuse Me,' he said. Emma changed partners several times, each one more breathless and silent than the last as the music kept up a fast pace. The two Sergeants had gone and Bea was being whirled by, laughing up at a very good-looking man in army uniform who took her skilfully through the steps of the tango. Many couples left the floor as the music changed to rumbas and tangos and everything with a South American beat, and Emma's latest partner hesitated as soon as he knew he was required to do more than march along one side of the room, turn and march along the next. He looked relieved when someone tapped him on the shoulder and Emma found herself looking into a pair of pale blue eyes that glinted with humour and triumph.

'Surprise, surprise.' Eddie placed a hand on her waist and propelled her skilfully across the dance floor. Emma had loved dancing ever since the local tennis club had held winter sessions helped by local volunteers who tutored a little, but left the evenings as mainly social events. True, most of the partners were uninspiring, like Mr Almore the husband of the tennis coach, who had a burgeoning paunch against which small girls bounced during the quickstep, but she had learned the basics and adored the tango and Latin American steps whenever she found a partner who could do them.

Eddie danced superbly and she forgot that he had followed them after Bea had told him plainly that his company was not wanted. She forgot the ice behind the smile and the mouth that was not like Phillip's strong firm lips, and not like the generous mouth of the man she had met briefly on her way to Beatties, but sensual, with a full bottom lip that belied the asceticism of his slim hands and rather long face.

Spaces appeared as if by magic as they slipped into an inspired rendering of '*Jealousy*'. A woman in a spangled dress that clung to her body like a fishtail, clutched the microphone and sang huskily, '*Jealousy . . . it was all over my jealousy.*' Eddie didn't talk and Emma enjoyed the effortless way he steered her, checked and took her through all the correct positions. Slightly out of breath, she looked at him with laughing eyes as the music stopped, and he released her immediately. He took her back to the table where Bea was still talking to her soldier. Bea froze, then solemnly introduced the two men.

'We're from the same outfit, I believe,' said Eddie. The man looked blank as if shutting off everything that might be used against him or against his country and Emma noticed for the first time that a cap lay on the table. It wasn't a peaked cap or a forage cap, but a red beret. 'Parachute Regiment with special commando training,' said Eddie softly. The man grinned but said nothing.

Emma had heard of the Parachutists who were dropped behind enemy lines on mysterious missions and she had vaguely heard of Commando

Units, but cloistered as she has been in the solid building on the Downs, war news drifted by as unreal ghosts. The Evacuation of Dunkirk had been a sensational story in which she had no part, the bombing of Bristol was much more relevant and far too close for comfort, but she knew very little of any other activity. She stared at Eddie. Was he fooling? He was in civilian clothes and had made no mention of the war or if he was in any of the Services.

'Back to barracks, tomorrow?' Still the man avoided comment but took time to light a cigarette. 'Good man,' said Eddie. 'But you can give your CO a message. Tell him that Major Ripley will be with him at eighteen hundred hours.' The orchestra played '*The Green Cockatoo*' and Eddie dragged Emma to her feet. 'Let's see how we manage the other Latin American dances,' he said.

'Is he what he says?' asked the soldier when Eddie was out of earshot.

'Major Eddie Ripley, and my cousin,' said Bea.

'If you are in the Forces, why aren't you in uniform?' asked Emma. 'Don't you find it embarrassing? Every man who is well-dressed and looks leisured is taken for someone in a reserved occupation or a spiv.'

'And you suspected I was a spiv? Selling nylon stockings and illicit drink?'

'Of course not.'

He laughed. 'That's a relief. I can go to far more places in civvies than I can in uniform. Here, I can mingle with other ranks and have a good time, but I couldn't come here showing my rank unless I stuck with my own party.' He looked across at Bea, who was still talking to the soldier. 'I don't think Bea is very pleased with me. I'm really quite scared of my vitriolic little cousin, so why don't we leave them to that frightful orange confection and find somewhere cosy with real ice in the drinks?'

'No, I'm here with Bea and we are staying together,' Emma said firmly. He twirled her round at the end of the dance and held her close for a second, then kissed the top of her head, lightly.

'Pity,' he drawled. He held her in a tight embrace until the music started again and Emma thought it might be worse to struggle than to pretend that she thought he was only keeping her with him for another dance.

The lights went low and the spangled stars of the revolving globes of faceted glass wove patterns among the dancers, but this was nothing like the time when she had danced with Phillip and Tony under similar lights in Bristol. Eddie held her so close she could hardly breathe and she felt his heart beating under the fine worsted jacket. No sandpaper rub this time, and he smelled of cleanliness and fresh cologne. He bent to kiss her cheek and then her mouth, gently and teasingly and she felt hypnotised, drifting, not dancing as saxophones oozed their sentimental question '*Who's taking you home tonight*?'

The dancers thinned out as the times of last buses and trains were checked, and as a hint that the dance hall would be locked up very soon, lights were doused in the far corners and there were patches of darkness behind the broad pillars and behind the empty banquettes. Bea was still clamped firmly in the embrace of the parachute soldier and Eddie tried to manoeuvre Emma towards the exit.

'No, I must wait for Bea,' she said, resisting him.

'She's busy,' he said.

'We came together and must stay together,' she insisted.

'We'll make up a four,' he suggested.

'You can't do that, *Major* Ripley. Bad for discipline,' she said, laughing to hide her growing unease.

He gripped her wrist. 'I must have you to myself,' he said harshly. 'Are you such an innocent? You've driven me crazy all evening and now I have to kiss you properly.' He dragged her back and into the shadow of a pillar and Emma found herself helpless with her back against the mock marble coldness, with the syrupy music still being played and the band leafing through the music for the National Anthem that would finish the evening's programme.

'Leave me alone!' Her words were stifled as he pressed his mouth down hard on hers in a kiss that had nothing of tenderness. His hands tore at her blouse and she felt the tiny buttons opening. His body was hard against hers and his mouth clung, forcing her lips apart with his tongue. She could see the glitter of his eyes and an almost mad desire, and knew that he could kill if anything came in his way. He forced a way to the bare skin of her breast and she could feel a response that shamed and aroused her. Never had she known a man with such strength. The narrow hands were like steel, and she felt powerless to get free, but the heel of one shoe snapped and she fell sideways, and away from him for a moment. He grabbed at her, all pretence of caring gone and she was very scared. She clutched her blouse together and ran, limping on one high heel, but into a blessed pool of light. Bea was looking anxiously round the nearly-deserted dance hall.

She took one look at Emma and threw her jacket round her. The boy in the red beret had not dared wait for his superior officer and had gone as soon as the National Anthem began. 'Let's get out of this,' said Bea. 'Break the other heel. It's the only way you can run.' She seized the good shoe and wrenched off the heel. 'Come on, he doesn't know about Daddy's flat and he'll think we're making for the station. No, better still, the carpark, where we are to wait for that dear old borrowed uncle to take us back to Surrey.' She glanced back. 'That's why he didn't bother to wait by one of the exits. He thinks we have to go there to find the car.' Bea didn't slacken her pace. 'We'll get a move on,' she said. 'He might just twig we aren't going there.'

They ran until their breath came in harsh sobs and the sight of the front of the austere apartments in St James' was wonderful and looked like home. 'Tea or coffee?' asked Bea as if they had just come in from a stroll. 'We'll get ready for bed and then have something while we listen to the late news.' Bea changed into her father's dressing gown and had the kettle boiling when Emma came into the sitting room with her face washed and wearing a light kimono. 'I made tea. We've had enough stimulant for one night,' said Bea. Emma looked ashamed, and took the offered cup without more than a murmur of thanks.

Bea regarded her thoughtfully. 'My cousin is a swine,' she said clearly. 'I knew what he was like years ago. He's several years older than me and he was always a bit odd when I was a child, fondling me and my friends. At first it was a joke but as I grew older it wasn't so funny and he took a bit of explaining to visitors who brought nice little curly-haired children with them and he played with us. You are in no way to blame for what happened. At least get that into your thick head. If girls don't come up to scratch, as he says, he tries anything – charm, bribery or violence, and he loves anything sweet and innocent, like you, duckie.' She glanced at Emma. 'I really do hate him, but did you feel it? He has a certain macabre fascination for me.'

Emma sipped her tea and blessed Bea for being so matter of fact. 'Yes,' she said. 'I was very scared but a part of me ... wanted him.' She was crimson with embarrassment. 'Bea, he made me feel like Vincent. Do you remember the night she was nearly raped on the Downs? I knew how she felt before she went out, thinking the evening would be fun, and how she felt when it all went wrong. I think this has put me off men for a very long time.'

'Too late, duckie. He's not the man I'd choose for any girl's awakening, but he's made the first crack in your shining armour and you can't ever go back now.'

3

'You have all missed a lot of the London bombing by being here in Surrey, although it's good to know that it's quieter now and those who went to London for the weekend were safe and able to enjoy their off-duty,' said Sister Roper. Bea looked at Emma as if to say that Sister Roper had no idea of the dangers in the city apart from the bombs.

'Do we get our results before we go to Beatties?' asked Margaret Turpin, who was aware that her Red Cross experience had been very small and she had nightmares that she might have to leave her training before it really began. She sat next to Annie Force, who had arrived at the same time from Yorkshire and who shared her fears.

'Yes, I have them here. I'm pleased to tell you that you have all passed except for one who will go to Beatties with you and have a month on the wards to see if she grasps the work better when it is in a more practical form. All results are confidential, so the girl who is not certain to stay at Beatties need not say anything. I have already talked to her, and you all go up to the hospital on equal terms.'

She looked from face to face, smiling slightly at the change in some of the girls who had never worn uniform before but who now looked well-brushed and smart and wore their uniform with ease. Their work had gained a competence that she hoped would see them safely through the coming months.

'Sister?'

'Yes, Nurse Shuter?'

'Do you know which wards we are on?'

She nodded and produced a list. 'Of course, none of you will work together again for a time, as one from each batch goes to a different ward for experience as junior.' She read out the names of the girls and paired them with wards and departments. 'Now have coffee and be at the door in half an hour. You'll need cloaks as it looks like rain, so don't pack them.'

Emma sipped her coffee and read the letter from home. Her mother had heard of London bombings and seemed almost accusing that Emma had escaped them, living in the peace of the Surrey countryside. '*Mrs Hammond says that Hitler is going to invade soon, so I expect you'll be glad to be safely out of the Isle of Wight. I asked Em to come up for a while just in case he does. She could stay as a paying guest if she doesn't want to put on us. Mrs Hammond says that Hitler will get a shock if he tries and it will be all over in a day or so and they'll be driven back.*'

'Clever Mrs Hammond,' murmured Emma. She skimmed over the next page and more that the dreadful woman had said. There was no mention of her father and he sent no message to her, nor did he ever write. 'Invasion! That's all that my mother thinks about,' she said to Bea. 'Do you think they will come here?'

'Could be,' said Bea. 'But can you imagine us letting them walk all over us as the French did? Can you see us watching them goose-stepping along Whitehall as they did through the Arc de Triomphe? That monument was sacred to the French and yet it happened. I'd die trying to stop them.'

'Die is the operative word,' said Emma. 'I don't think anyone can know what they'd do in the same situation.' She looked out at the dull day. 'Perhaps Hitler is giving us a rest or has run out of bombs.' She offered Margaret and Annie a boiled sweet each from a bag that was fast becoming too sticky to give up its contents and Annie sucked away the paper from her sweet before settling down to eat it.

'I don't know why I buy them,' Emma said. 'I forget to eat sweets and I never bought them before rationing, unless I could afford chocolate.'

'We take what we are allowed even if we aren't terribly keen,' said Margaret. 'Back home on our farm, people come and try to cadge extra butter and it's difficult as we do have some to spare but daren't sell it under the counter in case we get fined, so my mother makes lovely cakes and sells them and the Government thinks she is using margarine or nut oil. People give her their sugar ration and she does the rest. She made a lovely wedding cake the last time I was home.'

'Imagine thinking that a slice of cake would be a luxury,' mused Bea. 'And as for those people sleeping in the Underground, it seems impossible to believe that they really have lost everything but their bedding and a few belongings.'

Later, the coach passed streets with rows of boarded windows and one road was flooded where a water main had ruptured weeks after the bombing had weakened it; the once-sparkling windows of offices and shops were dusty and untended. 'Hold your nose when we cross the river,' one of the girls warned. 'They say it stinks, as a sewer burst and slopped into the Thames after a raid and they thought we'd all die of cholera or something. They had to pour in chemicals to neutralise it, and all the fish died and the smell was awful.'

To Emma, the city looked very much as the centre of Bristol Centre had done after the big raids but to girls from country districts who had never suffered bombing, it was new and frightening to see the devastation, even during this respite when no sirens had sounded for several weeks. She wondered if the barrage balloon was still tugging at its hausers at the top of the road near her parents' house and if her mother would grumble less or more if the RAF decided not to use her telephone.

An army lorry overtook the coach and the open back was filled with young men wearing red berets. 'Eddie's lot, most likely,' said Bea, and Emma sat well back as if he was actually there and could see her. She tried to think of the future and the new beginning that had at last opened up for her. She would be doing real nursing and not just helping old ladies to prolong a painful and unexciting life.

'It's very quiet,' said Bea. 'No petrol is a good traffic controller. I hope the war doesn't end just yet, before we get a chance to do something useful.' She laughed. 'No, I'm not getting an attack of the Florence Nightingales, duckie, but have you thought of all those gorgeous men we might meet who are wounded and helpless and in our power?'

'No chance of that,' said Emma. 'Beatties is an acute general hospital, not a military one. The Army have their own base hospital, with SRNs dressed in those attractive caps and tiny shoulder cloaks, all grey and scarlet and very nice.'

'*And* they don't have dresses fourteen inches off the ground,' said Bea.

'Maybe they have ugly popliteal spaces,' Emma suggested. 'So it doesn't matter.'

The nurses' home was spartan but adequate. 'No wonder we had to bring our own bath mats,' said Bea. 'I'll have to get some more towelling slippers too, or my feet will drop off when they touch that icy tiled floor.' The beds were harder than the ones in PTS and when they went down for the first meal, it consisted of baked beans with bread and a stodgy pudding. Emma thought nostalgically of the food at the Home and even envied the store with the hated preserved eggs. They were shown their wards and the Common rooms and then told to take the rest of the day off to unpack and to make their rooms tidy. 'No leaving the hospital until you are really straight,' said the Sister in charge of the nurses' home. 'And you'd all better go to second supper.'

'That effectively rules out the flicks,' said Bea. 'I saw a cinema down the road but who knows when I can go there? Never mind, we may need our beauty sleep, after a stimulating cup of cocoa.'

They all went down to the lodge to see if any mail had arrived. To Emma's surprise, two letters for her were in the pigeonhole marked D. One was the familiar airmail letter-card from Phil. It seemed strange to see his neat writing miniaturised on such a small piece of stiff paper, but every ounce counted when tons of mail had to be flown home from military bases abroad. She put it in her pocket and turned the other envelope over. It was addressed to: *Nurse Dewar, (New nurse at The Princess Beatrice Hospital), London.* Well, it had found her! But who could have sent it? She didn't recognise the writing.

She slit the envelope and froze. It was a short note of apology from Eddie Ripley, begging her pardon and asking her to meet him. She looked at the date on the letter heading. He had written it the day after the dance at Covent Garden and it must have been awaiting collection for nearly two weeks. I couldn't possibly meet him again! she thought. I detest the man. How on earth can he expect me to meet him again even if I was prepared to forgive what he tried to do?

She read the dates he gave for possible meetings, suggesting that he might come to the place in Surrey if she would send the address. The last date was the day before the PTS left for London. She sighed with relief. Even if she'd wanted to go, it was too late. She thought of the lorry load of red berets and knew that it had indeed been his lot.

Bea took the note and read it. 'You wouldn't have gone? Eddie is a snake and would try it again. He doesn't give up that easily. I saw the way he looked at you, Emma. I can tell when he is really attracted. He prefers his women unsullied until he gets to them! He can charm the birds out of the trees when he wants anything badly enough and he's very, very cruel. Promise me you'll never go near him, Emma?'

Bea was pale and when she used Emma's first name it meant that her pose had gone and she was sincere. 'I promise,' said Emma. 'But it looks as if he won't be around for a while. They seemed to be on the move. I wonder where?'

'Well, don't get weak and send him a pair of hand-knitted socks,' said Bea.

'No chance of that. I shall have my own bodyguard. Phil is coming home.' That letter too had been waiting for collection. 'He's in England now,' she said in a flat voice.

Home Sister inspected the rooms and the trunks and cases were stowed in a large room at the end of the corridor. Emma kept one small case for when she went home and miraculously, all her clothes fitted into the roomy wardrobe and chest of drawers.

'Nurse Turpin, you may not stick drawing pins into the picture rail for any purpose. Nurse Foster, you may have no more than four photographs in frames on display, and Nurse Force, you do not leave the blankets showing during the day. Use the bed cover and make your bed neater. I know it is because you want to sit on the bed, but there is a chair in each room and bed covers are there to be used.'

'At least we were licked into submission by Sister Cary,' Bea muttered in Emma's ear. 'I take it for granted now that they *do* check on the rules they give us, and my *dear*, I was shocked at some of the things these young girls do now.'

'She hasn't finished,' whispered Emma.

'The bell will wake you at six-thirty and you must be in the dining room by seven. Half an hour for breakfast and on the wards by seven-thirty. Is that clear?' Bea didn't even groan. 'And remember, Nurses, if you are late, it means the hard-worked night nurses will be delayed and rightly blame you for going off-duty late. You all know your wards?' A murmur of assent and she dismissed them after telling them for the third time that it was strictly forbidden for any member of staff to go outside the gates of the hospital wearing uniform. 'Any nurse discovered wearing any article of uniform including stockings worn on duty, will go straight to Matron and possibly be sent home for good.'

'Shades of Sister Cary,' said Emma.

'Are they all like her?' Margaret looked worried. 'I can't stand being told off.'

'It's as well to know what we can or can't do,' said Annie, trying to smile. 'But it seems a bit hard.'

'So far we've been told what we can't do,' said Bea, 'except that we are allowed to get up at some unearthly hour and work. I am too depressed to stay up and talk. I shall go to bed and dream I'm nursing a handsome Wing Commander who falls desperately in love with me.'

The night sky was clear and the balloons were low. Late trams whined up the hill over towards New Cross Gate and an ambulance crunched the gravel by the nurses' home. Emma dreamed of parachutists dropping into a ward and pushing all the screens over.

The bell was a thing straight out of Hell. Its

strength and duration must have woken every living thing within range, and yet when Emma hurried down to breakfast, trying to do up her collar stud as she went, she saw a notice on a door, saying Do Not Disturb. Someone with a day off, she thought. But who could sleep with that racket going on? Breakfast was much better than she'd expected. Fortified by drinkable coffee and good scrambled eggs made by someone who had found a way to make dried eggs palatable, toast and a preserve that alleged it was marmalade, Emma waved goodbye to the others and walked quickly along to Ward 4, Womens' Surgical and Gynaecological.

The outer doors swung silently inwards, and Emma found herself in a stone corridor from which four doors opened into two side-wards, a nurses' cloakroom and a utility room which she later learned to call the flower room. Beyond this was another double door leading to the clinical room and the nurses' duty room. The ward stretched away beyond with a solid desk halfway down the room and two large square blocks with fireplaces on all four sides. Coal fires burned in two opposite fireplaces in each square and the others were laid ready to take over when they needed cleaning. The tops of the squares were shining and vases of flowers sat there, left over from the vases allowed on each locker.

A ward maid in a bright pink dress was cleaning out a fireplace and scrubbing the surround. Some of the beds were surrounded by tall screens on wheels and more portable screens were stacked at each end of the ward and some in an alcove near the middle.

A staff nurse sat at the desk, and one by one, each nurse reported to her and was told her immediate duties. Only then did they retire to the duty room to take off their stiff cuffs and roll uniform sleeves high, covering them with the false sleeves that buttoned on to the shoulders. Emma smoothed down her stiff apron and walked down the ward, feeling that everyone was watching her. This was so different from the Home where most of the residents had individual rooms.

She collected a wash basin and a tray containing talc and surgical spirit and swabs and some coarse fibrous material, for use after bedpans instead of paper, called tow, made from flax. This routine at least was familiar and the four bed baths that followed were easy as the new nurses were given semi-ambulant patients to supervise.

At eight o'clock the day sister took report from the night staff and went to the long bed trolley laid up with report book, pens and notebooks, charts and special reports on all patients. The ward work continued as she went from bed to bed, checking information added by house surgeons during the night rounds and the observations made by the Night Superintendent. In this way, each ward sister was fully conversant with every treatment, temperature, pulse and respiration in the ward, spoke personally to each patient and listened to grumbles, or heard about reaction to treatment, pain and the inevitable anxiety about family and future. She made notes if she thought a visit from the Almoner would help with problems of clothes and home conditions and if a rest in a convalescent home would be of use when home conditions were bad.

'Read the night report as soon as you can, Nurse,' the night staff nurse said to Emma. 'You must have read it by the time Sister says we may serve breakfasts.' She smiled. 'It's difficult at first, but you must learn to memorise all the names and know what is wrong with each patient.'

Emma looked down the length of the ward with

a sense of hopelessness. How could she remember each name? They were all mounds in beds and there was no time to fit diseases or conditions to individuals. She tried to think of the women she had helped with their bed baths. The woman with the intravenous drip had been operated on for an obstruction of the gut a week ago and still needed help, with the drip still in place. Names, she thought. Oh, how can I remember the names of anonymous faces?

'You are Nurse Dewar?' Emma found herself standing by the centre desk looking down at a pretty woman with frilly cuffs rather like the ones that Sister Cary used to keep her rolled-up sleeves neat and clean. Her dark green uniform was well fitting and her hospital badge shone on her apron top. Instinctively, Emma smiled. 'Go with Staff Nurse Mason to make beds after the bedpan round. I believe you have experience of back care? That is good as we are going to be very busy and I need to know that I can rely on you without my having to check all the time.'

'Yes, Sister. I know all about bed patients.'

'Well, we'll see. Patients for surgery are a little different from bedridden old ladies. We have an operation list tomorrow. You are Number One until next week. Each day look at the off-duty list in the duty room. As Number One, you are responsible for all bedpans on that side of the ward, Number Two is on the other side, Number Three helps Junior Staff Nurse with dressings and does simple treatments like enemas, and Number Four relieves the off-duty of these three. If we have an extra, she helps with heavy cases and I am on duty with Junior Staff Nurse when Staff Nurse Mason is off-duty. Is that clear?'

'It sounds very straightforward, Sister.'

'It's very hard work but you do have the advantage of working to a routine, and I hope you get into the swing of things here. I think you'll like it. This is a very happy ward and you'll find that most surgical wards are good as there is the satisfaction of knowing that the majority of your patients are going to get better.' She looked at her fob watch. 'Put screens at the door to show that the ward is closed and no one is allowed in until the bedpan round is over.'

'No one, Sister?'

'Not without my permission. Off you go. If you need help to lift someone, ask Number Three.'

After a hectic half hour in the sluice and rushing about with bedpans, Emma was hot and sticky. She had spilled a little from one of the enamel pans and knew that her apron smelled. She asked if she could change her apron and Sister nodded. In PTS they had been told that this was the routine after the morning round. How right they are, she thought and hurried to her room to change her apron and wash her hands more thoroughly. She combed her hair under the unfamiliar cap that didn't hide as much hair as the butterfly caps of the Home. The coffee that filled a huge urn in the dining room was hot and good and she was allowed two biscuits from a large dish by its side but there was no one from her set in the room and she felt out of it.

She hurried back to the ward and found Sister talking to a tall man in a white coat. 'Yes, Nurse? Ah, you've been to change. Good. Come with me while Dr Coombs does a round of the gynae patients.'

She told Emma to load a trolley with the piles of charts and X-rays on the desk and to follow them, bringing screens when a patient had to be examined and tidying beds after the examination. It wasn't a full consultant's round but the house surgeon had to make a round if his chief was busy, to ensure that the right treatments had been ordered and given. All gynae patients were in one section of the ward so it was easy to pull screens from bed to bed and return them to the alcove when the round was over.

Two women were written up for blood tests and premedication was ordered for the next day's list. One woman was told she could go home and another was examined thoroughly. Sister brought a covered tray from the clinical room at the end of the ward. Emma saw instruments she had seen only in textbooks and recognised the vaginal speculum and long swab holders. A gallipot of antiseptic, swabs and pads made up the rest of the tray and when the old pad was removed, it was greenish with discharge and smelled badly. The house surgeon took a swab and put it in a test tube which Sister corked firmly and labelled with the name and age of the patient, and the date and ward. The woman seemed apathetic when she was examined and not in the least embarrassed by the intimate examination.

'I'll write her up for an appointment in A-Block,' said the house surgeon.

'I'll move her into a side-ward until the path lab send a report,' said Sister. They washed their hands very thoroughly at the sink halfway down the ward and Dr Coombs obviously took a boyish pleasure in using the immaculate fan of huckaback towelling that was really there for show, as the Junior Staff Nurse explained to Emma later when she found it in a crumpled ball. 'Only consultants have the cheek to use them. What's wrong with the ordinary towels?' she grumbled. 'Takes ages to make up.'

The next patient looked as if she was nine months pregnant, but when the bedclothes were neatly turned back, Sister said that it was an ovarian cyst. 'You've had this far too long, haven't you Mrs Bright,' she said. She smiled and the woman beamed at her. 'I've promised Mrs Bright a nice slim waist for Christmas and she's having her operation tomorrow. Is there anything more you want to tell the doctor?'

'No, Sister. I've told you everything and you know what to do.' She ignored the HS and held out her hand to Sister. Emma grinned. He looked as if he was only visiting.

'Doctor Coombs will be helping the surgeon tomorrow,' Sister said rather pointedly. 'When you come back here, he will know far more than I do.'

'Fancy that!' Mrs Bright smiled at him but as he left, she winked at Emma. 'You'll be on duty after my op, won't you dear?' she whispered to Sister.

'What happens during an alert?' asked Emma when she checked the soiled linen into bags and the Junior Staff Nurse ticked off numbers on a list.

'You've had experience of raids in Bristol, haven't you? I imagine it's the same routine. Beds are pushed down into the basement. We moved the orthopaedic ward to the ground floor as those on traction can't be moved in a hurry. The ENT who are mostly ambulant, now live upstairs at the top.' She grinned. 'The Private Patients are unlucky. They have the best views over the park but it's a bit high for comfort.'

'Do we have to go down if we are off-duty in the nurses' home?'

'Definitely. They check each room to make sure you are out.'

Emma sighed. 'They did with us, too, and yet I feel safer without the thought of tons of masonry falling on me. Incidentally, there don't seem to be many patients who have been here for very long after operations. Why's that?'

'We send them off after two days if possible to one of the sector hospitals. You know, the EMS places.' She saw that Emma didn't understand. 'The main London hospitals, the big voluntary hospitals like St Thomas', Guys, the Middlesex, Kings and Barts and Beatties, have joined in staffing hospitals outside of London where they can send post-ops as soon as possible after surgery. They call them Emergency Medical Service hospitals and we send ours to two places in Surrey. One was a home for the blind and one a mental hospital. It's a huge place near Epsom and can hold more than a thousand patients.'

'If it's that big how do they staff it?'

'It's shared. We have our wards and the other hospitals have theirs. They have a lot of nursing auxiliaries and Red Cross for some duties but we tend to keep to our own training school routine. There are hospitals like it all over the country ready to take hundreds of casualties. That's another thing. We keep a lot of wards empty there but ready for use at a moment's notice. Some places nurse soldiers but we seem to be filled up with casualties from the London bombing.'

'You seem to know all about it,' said Emma.

Nurse Paget smiled. 'I've just come back from three months down there. It's quite hectic at times and quite macabre, but wonderful.'

'What did they do with the mental patients? Surely they didn't send them home?'

'They were absorbed into other huge mental hospitals. There are several in the same area. Some of the staff insisted on staying to look after the interests of the hospital and so there is one wing where treatment still goes on, done by mental nurses; shock therapy and malaria therapy, which is the treatment for tertiary syphilis.' She sensed the questions that Emma wanted to ask and looked at her watch. 'Can't waste time here. I have dressings to do. When are you off-duty?'

'This afternoon, Nurse.'

'Well, finish this place and ask Sister if she wants you during the drug round.' She glanced out into the ward. 'Oh yes, Mike Coombs has gone and you'll catch her before the physio people arrive. Most of the physio crowd are good but one leaves the beds very untidy and if this happens on your side, you are responsible.'

Emma watched Sister measure out medicines and wondered how it was that here, everything was immaculate, the patients happy and the staff bright and eager to help and the general efficiency was quite as good as the Wing Six ruled over by fear and Sister Cary. Sister Marion Nickolas was attractive and obviously loved her work. She had a smile for each patient, a word of humour or comfort where it was needed and an instinctive reaction to a patient's needs. Emma watched the slim strong arms hold a woman forward while she coughed, bracing her hands over the barely healed and still sore line of sutures, and the look of gratitude that followed her, as she left the bedside, adjusting her cuffs neatly.

'Mrs Morris had a pan-hysterectomy done ten days ago but was too ill to be transferred to Heath Cross. We left some sutures in after the buttons were removed in case the wound broke down but she's fine now and will go down to Surrey tomorrow after the rest are out.' She looked along the row of patients. 'We are busy as the lists come in all the time, but the casualty wards here are nearly empty. If this goes on, the staff may be able to come back from the sector hospitals to make the spare wards into what they were, more surgical and medical for civilian patients.' She laughed. 'That wouldn't be popular. Heath Cross has a certain fascination, and by all accounts, the nurses have a good time there.'

She asked Emma when she was off-duty and promised to take her over the notes of the patients due for operation the next day, when she came back on duty for the evening. 'Go to second lunch and stay off-duty until five and report to Nurse Mason who will be on until six when I come back on duty.' She smiled. 'And you might look up panhysterectomy before I see you again.'

The rest of the morning flew by and Emma sank into a seat in the refectory with sigh of relief. She ate hungrily, hardly noticing that the food was unappetising and like the kind of meal her mother provided out of war-time rations. There were two others from her set in the room but neither were off-duty for the afternoon and there was no sign of Bea in her room. What was there to do in three hours off-duty? Would there be time to go on a tram to the West End? What was there of interest near the hospital?

She changed and walked down to the lodge, although the air was damp and the road outside uninviting, but Home Sister had said they must have some fresh air every day and she had a feeling they might check. The lodge was empty and there was a slip of paper with her name on it in her pigeonhole. She unfolded it. *'Message for Nurse Dewar. Will call again after nine tonight.'* No name, no further message, but the hint that nurses did not receive calls while on duty. She stuffed the message into her pocket and went out into the mist, wondering if her mother had had a sudden unlikely desire to waste money on a trunk call to London. She bought a paper to see if the West Country had suffered more bombings, but the reports from the big cities were of quiet nights. She wandered down to the ABC café on the corner and ordered tea and a sticky bun. It was good and fresh and she ate two before going back to the hospital, then felt over-stuffed with carbohydrate.

Was this all there would be? Bedpans and sticky buns, grey streets and hard work? It was as bad as Bristol but the food was worse and even Sister Cary was blurred at the edges and seemed less of a menace from a distance. I'll have a hot bath and write to my mother, Emma decided. She smiled. I must be at a low ebb. The letter from Eddie Ripley bothered her. She wondered what would happen if she met him again, and fear mingled with an unwilling sense of adventure. She envied his ability to take what he wanted, and knew that she could never do that.

If only there was someone, not like Eddie, but with strength of will and determination. The telephone call might be from Phil. Why had she forgotten that he was in England and would be in touch? Why had his quiet, reliable face dimmed, forced out by a face that haunted her, gently? Not Phil and not Eddie, but someone in between, with a mouth that held all the promise of passion with gentleness. Why think of him? He belonged to the category, as Aunt Emily would say with a shrug, of 'Ships that pass in the night'. She had seen a man in a blue suit who had come as far as the hospital and then disappeared. Did he live close to it? She knew nothing of his life, whether he worked or manipulated the black market, or was in a reserved occupation, and she was unlikely to see him ever again.

She caught up with Bea as she reached the steps of the nurses' home. 'Were you off? I couldn't find you.'

'I didn't stay to second lunch. I changed and was in Leicester Square by two-thirty. I managed to get some mascara and some quite good talcum powder. They had heavy lace by the yard. I wish I could sew. It makes heavenly blouses and is off-ration as it doesn't fit into any category of woven material.' She sat on her bed and slipped out of her high heels. 'What did you do?'

'Nothing. I wish I'd seen the lace. I have a very good blouse pattern. I could hand sew it.'

Bea tossed a package on to the bed. 'They said this was enough. You don't owe me for it, but I thought you might like some.' Emma protested that she must pay but Bea laughed. 'You needn't think you're having it for nothing. You make me one, too, but we must never wear them together.'

There were more sticky buns for tea and Bea ate hers and Emma's as well as bread and margarine and jam, as she had missed lunch. 'See you later,' said Emma. 'If you hear there's a call for me tonight, give me a shout.'

Sister gave out drugs and the ward lights were dimmed. The evening treatments were done, the ward tidied and the patients made comfortable. There were seven empty beds and the side-wards were empty except for the suspected VD patient, who sat miserably alone in the four-bedded room.

'Come along,' Sister Nickolas said to Emma. 'I can give you report now. Sit in front of the desk.' She went through each chart referring to the patients by name and never by bed number, and Emma recalled being taught this by the Sister in PTS. It made everything more personal and the patients appreciated being treated with courtesy, and not feeling like just case histories. She wished she could make notes but this was not allowed. The woman with the pan-hysterectomy was fortunate. She was not a cancer case but had so many fibroids and so much infection that her uterus and fallopian tubes and ovaries had been removed. The surgeon had left just enough of one ovary to make sure the patient had a certain amount of hormones available.

The operation list for the following day was put on the board and the nurses were told what to expect when the patients returned from the theatre. A special nurse would come to sit with the unconscious patients until they recovered from anaesthetic.

Emma tried to remember what was said but there were so many different conditions and routines that she knew it would take time to absorb it all. It was bewildering but exciting.

The telephone rang at five past nine while Emma waited in the hall of the nurses' home. 'Remember me?' said Phillip.

'It's been a long time,' said Emma. 'Where are you and how long have you been in England?'

'It's too long a story. I'm in London now. When are you off-duty tomorrow?'

'Off at six but I have to be back by ten-thirty.'

'I'll be outside by six. It's wonderful to hear your voice.'

'Yes, it's wonderful to hear you, too,' she said politely. 'I'll be off-duty as soon as I can.' There seemed nothing more to say and she went upstairs wondering what they would find in common after all this time.

'Heard the news?' asked Bea. 'There's been a terrible raid over Coventry and the Cathedral's been hit and hundreds are dead.'

But over London, the balloons were low that night.

4

One hand was still damp as she ran down the stairs at ten past six. Stupid thing to do, she fumed, to spill face powder just as she was leaving. She brushed traces of peach-coloured powder from her skirt with the damp hand and hoped it wouldn't cling. She pressed her lips together to spread the lavishly-applied magenta lipstick over the whole lip surface and knew that it was a mistake, but Bea had insisted that it was right with the pale blue blouse and dark red skirt. 'Devastating!' she said, and now, Emma felt devastated at the idea of anyone seeing it. At least it's dark outside, she thought. He'll see an outline but no colour.

'Emma!' The voice was the same but deeper, the smile the same but more ecstatic and the arms that folded her in a bear hug of blue greatcoat and hard muscle were strong and confident. His lips were warm and she experienced a pleasant frisson of elation when he kissed her. It's going to be all right, she decided with relief. He tucked her hand in his and then both deep into a vast pocket. 'You're cold . . . and wet,' he said.

'I had to hurry so much that I didn't dry my hands thoroughly,' she said. 'I get them so wet all the time that I hardly notice.'

'Well, you aren't in the sluice now. Where do you want to go?' He laughed and the sound was warm and friendly. That's what I've missed, she thought. Not love, not the need for a man to want me; I've just missed friends.

'I know as little of London as you do. You might even know more as you had a leave here before you left the country.'

'Well, I'm starving. I got off the train at four from my debriefing outside London and took my bag to my club and rushed over here by taxi. By the way, your mother sends her love.'

'You've been to Bristol?'

'We were brought in to Filton so I stayed the night with your family, then I had to come nearer to London to debriefing and now I'm free for a while. Your mother seemed put-out. I gather you haven't been to see her for ages.'

'No, I've been far too involved here and I've had only one full weekend since I left Bristol. I've had days off and one half day and day off, but not enough to make it worth that journey.'

'Pity. I look on your mother as my staunchest ally.' He laughed. 'Not to worry, we'll have plenty of time for visiting some day. Now, what shall we do? Go dancing? I know you enjoy it and there are a lot of places now where the bands are good and they have decent floors. What about the one in the West End – the Astoria? Or the one in Covent Garden seems the favourite from what I hear.'

'Not there. You wouldn't like it. It's mostly other ranks and I know how awkward it is for you as you can't fraternise in uniform.'

'You seem to know all about it. Do you go there often?' Emma giggled, and Phil looked along the street. 'Come on, it has to be a bus. Not many cabs in this neck of the woods.' He grabbed her arm and they ran to the bus stop. 'We'll take this one. It's bound to get us up West eventually.' They climbed to the top deck and found seats at the front. The dull blue light made everyone look grey and Emma wondered if her magenta lipstick made her appear in the last stages of cyanosis and heart failure. 'Well, you haven't told me how a girl who knows nothing about London knows all about the dance halls. I suppose there are dozens of handsome doctors all clamouring for dates with the nurses?'

'I've been there once, just for a giggle,' she said lightly. 'Another girl in my set wanted to go. Remember Bea Shuter who was with me in Bristol?'

'The good-looking blonde with the haughty eyes?'

'Yes, I suppose you could say that, but she's great fun and I don't know what I'd have done without her, stuck for three months in PTS.' Why am I making excuses and being defensive? Bea is my friend and my free time is my own. 'She was there after Evans was killed.'

'I remember that,' said Phillip. 'Poor Maeve. Bad luck on her and her brother but that's war. If your number's up, you'll catch it.' His profile was stern and Emma wondered how he felt about death. He seemed to share the fatalistic attitude of so many who had experienced bombings, although he had seen less action than she had, in spite of the impressive uniform. She looked more closely. 'Thought you'd never notice,' he said and grinned.

'Flight Lieutenant?' She pointed to the rings on his uniform sleeve. 'That was rapid. I didn't know they promoted officers so quickly.'

'Only the best,' he said. His voice was teasing, but he couldn't hide his pride. 'It does mean I don't have much leave.'

'Oh, Phil, you aren't going away again?'

'Nice to know you care,' he said and put an arm round her shoulder. 'I have to go away in bombers. Not Europe, or not unless the orders are changed, but away in Wellington bombers. I've been training for weeks before we came back to England, and now I have a week's leave. After that, who knows?'

They walked down Regent Street and tried to look into windows but most of them were in darkness or boarded up. All round them a buzz of activity made the darkness alive, and at Piccadilly, crowds of servicemen and women flocked together, searching for friends, lovers or new adventure. Eros had disappeared, protected by a barrier of stout planking which boxed in the god of love but left his minions on the streets.

Prostitutes accosted young boys in uniforms that still had the packing creases in them. Many looked quite scared, some blushed and turned away, then paused to look back at the face of temptation. Phil kept Emma close to him and pushed open the door to the Auberge de France. 'We can't eat here! It's terribly expensive,' protested Emma.

'One thing I've learned; a tip from a guy on the desk at the Wings Club. No restaurant may charge more than five shillings for a meal whatever they served. They may add an extra shilling for a cover charge, but that'll all, and even a cover charge is frowned on by the Ministry of Food. It does mean you get good value in decent surroundings without paying more than you would in a British Restaurant, whatever that may be.'

'They aren't so bad. Mostly a large Nissen hut or two, rather like canteens where anyone can get a cheap meal. Aunt Emily supervises one on the Island. She gets very tired but she enjoys feeding people, and she is good at costing the meals. She was always a good cook and interested in food, unlike my mother.'

'And are you a good cook?'

'I don't really know. I haven't had a lot of practice. Food at home was never very interesting and if I tried to make anything, my mother accused me of criticising her cooking, so I gave up trying. I did do some when I stayed with Aunt Emily. She let me mess about even if I ruined it. She's a very special person.' Her voice became husky, and she hugged

Phil's arm closer. Aunt Emily and he belonged to a period when she was truly happy, when there was a warm wind from the sea and the fragrant downland and she could lie on the cliffs listening to the gulls and thinking of romance that had no hint of violence or fear.

They were waited on by an elderly waiter who looked as if he had been unwrapped from retirement but had failed to be issued with new feet. The food was quite good and for pudding they had ice cream with real wafer biscuits and slivers of chocolate. They drank coffee and the rest of the evening lay ahead, empty and suddenly embarrassing.

'I want to kiss you,' said Phillip. He took her hand across the small table. 'This huge city . . . and nowhere to be alone.' He brightened. 'I'll take you along to the Wings Club. We can have a drink there and then I'll take you back and we can walk in the park by the hospital. It's a fine night.' He looked up at the sky as they walked along the pavement. 'A night for Jerry,' he said.

'I think he's given up. We haven't had a raid on London for ages.'

They walked into the foyer of the Wings Club for RAF officers and their guests. Emma stared fascinated at the beautiful ceiling and the wide staircase curving away and up to the broad landing. Pictures hung on the walls, glowing in the muted light of chandeliers that seemed to be hung with diamonds. Phillip pointed out a picture that he had been told was an original Titian. The bar was thronged with dashing-looking officers of every rank. A group in one corner slumped lazily on leather chairs. They were in uniform, but in these august surroundings they still wore mufflers over roll neck sweaters, no neckties and some had high boots. Sheepskin bomber jackets were draped over the table and the peaked caps were bent to assume angles never intended for the uniform of RAF officers.

Some of the faces were young, some ingenuous, and all looked tired behind the fragile brilliance, humour and bravado. 'Fighter-pilots, bomber-pilots,' said Phillip bitterly. 'If it hadn't been for my damned maths, I'd have been with them.'

'But navigators have much more responsibility,' protested Emma. 'They'd never get to their targets without you.'

'In my saner moments I call them bus drivers, but this too-smart uniform speaks for itself. It will never have the passport to fame that those guys have.'

He ordered beer as the only alternative to bad gin. 'Shorts are difficult in England. We could have bathed in gin or whisky out there in South Africa. Anything we liked we had. Orchids and whisky and a good life.'

'Peaches and champagne,' whispered Emma, thinking of Evans and Tony killed in the Bristol Blitz. 'It isn't all the good life, Phil. Never buy me champagne: not ever.'

He took her hand and kissed the tips of her fingers. 'Never, I promise. No champagne, no peaches.' So he did remember. 'Nothing from me but beer . . . and buttercups, not orchids.'

'I like buttercups,' she said. There was warmth between them and the old affection, but he had changed a lot. 'What were the girls like – the ones you mentioned.'

'Pretty, smartly-dressed and rich. Good company,' he said.

'Was there one special one?'

'It depends.'

'On what? Surely you know?'

'You avoided giving me a measurement for a ring Emma, and I began to wonder if you had someone here. I was attracted to one girl but when it came to the crunch I knew it was no good. I want you, Emma. I want you soon and I want you for keeps.' She trembled as she tried to sip the sour drink. 'I love you. I've loved you all the time I was away and now there isn't much time, Emma. None of us knows what is in store for us.'

She hid her eyes, looking down at the table cloth. Such expensive linen in wartime? But it was so good it was made to last a lifetime, unlike most of the men in the room. A girl laughed and clung to the arm of the man who had brought her to the club. He put an arm around her waist, fondling the line of her breast and the tension between them heightened Emma's conviction that the feelings she had for Phil were not like that. She recalled the lust in Eddie's eyes. Not that, either. Not for me. Phil squeezed her hand. 'At least we can see each other this week,' she said.

'That's not what I mean.' She looked up, startled. Bea must be wrong. Phil might not be too good to be true. The look in his eyes was unmistakeable and he was going away again. She glanced towards the group in the corner. There were two left and they were joined by a man in uniform. He wore the same correct uniform as Phillip but the flash on his arm was different. He was talking to a young pilot and they were laughing. He had his back to her and she saw only the unfamiliar flash and his well-shaped dark head. 'Stop eyeing the opposition,' Phil said with a hint of real irritation. 'Or do you know him? I suppose you might. He's a medic.'

Emma stared at the man, willing him to turn to face her but she shook her head to show that she didn't know him. Sirens began to wail and a half-groan of annoyance swept the room. The man picked up his cap and a small briefcase. He turned and looked straight at Emma, his smile left over from his laughter. Phil tugged at her arm. The man raised his eyebrows quizzically. He remembers me, she thought. The man in the blue suit remembers me.

'Come on, we'd better get down to the shelters. Damn, this is the story of my life where you are concerned. This way. I hope we can find somewhere comfortable.'

The sound of aircraft was faint and the ack-ack even fainter, and after half an hour, the All Clear sounded. Emma sighed with relief. 'I must get back, Phil. It might start again.'

'We can sit in the park until it's time for you to go in, even if the siren goes again.' Miraculously, a taxi driver was climbing back into his cab. 'Can you take us to the Princess Beatrice, south of the river?' asked Phil.

'For you, Guv, anything. I'm going that way and I'm not coming back tonight. They'll be over again, sure as sure. Did you hear about Coventry? Pasted it flat last night. Just let us get used to a bit of peace and they come back again. You give 'em hell, Guv! Go to it!' Emma suspected that he'd taken a little Dutch courage in the shelter but he drove well, talking incessantly about the war, the fighter-pilots and the heroes of the bombers while Phil pulled Emma towards him and turned her face to meet his kiss. It was warm and good and cherishing. Marriage to Phil would be that, she thought and responded with more enthusiasm than she had ever shown. He kissed her again and again without forcing the pace.

She remembered another mouth, hard and brutal on hers and her fascinated revulsion. It seemed a long way to the hospital and these kisses were all the same. Could kissing, and making love become a bore? Or was there something wrong with her? The trauma of Eddie's onslaught may have built up a resistance to love. That must be the reason for this lack of response. She moved away, forcing a laugh. 'I need to use that arm again. I've got pins and needles.' She rubbed her arm as if it was numb but it wasn't her arm that was devoid of feeling.

The hospital barely glowed. The blackout was complete and only tiny blue lights shone in the entrance to the ambulance bay shed. Four vehicles lined the driveway, ready to leave at a moment's notice. 'I wonder if I'd better go in,' she said. 'If there's another raid, I'll have to help push the beds.'

'How are they to know where you are? You're off-duty and not due back quite yet. You might have been held up in Town by the alert.' He led her into the dark and silent park. The earthy smell came sharply as they walked the rough, pebbled pathways under the weeping birch and bare magnolia trees. The shadow of the hospital wards stuck out like the spokes of a giant half-wheel and the moon rose, a bombers' moon.

'Damn!' said Phil. 'The river will glint like silver under this sky. It's just too easy.' They stood on the one patch of high ground in the park, backed by a wall and stone seats. Dull silver barrage balloons began to rise away towards Whitehall and the siren wailed its warning.

Emma thought of the bundles of bedding in the Underground stations. It was said that Mr Churchill wanted some of the actual tracks to be made habitable for shelters, but the London County Council vetoed the suggestion and tried to persuade Londoners to keep out of the Underground altogether and use other shelters, but no one could stop the silent, purposeful flow of humanity that took over the stations at night. 'I'll have to go,' said Emma, her voice muffled by his greatcoat.

'Hell!' he said. 'Tomorrow?'

'I'm not off tomorrow night. I have a morning off from ten to two.'

He took out a cigarette case. 'Surely you can do better than that?'

'I've only just come here. I have to take what off-duty I'm given. We're all the same and we have no choice.' She snuggled closer, aware of his acute disappointment. 'I have a day off in two days' time.'

'With a sleeping-out pass?'

'I'm not going home. It's too far for just a day.'

'I didn't mean that.' He kissed her firmly as if to imprint his will on her lips. 'You do love me a little, Emma? I can never tell with you. You have never once said you love me.'

'What did you mean about sleeping-out passes?'

He grinned and she saw the glint of white teeth and the slightly incredulous smile. 'What do you think? What every serviceman home from the wars thinks about.' She pushed him away. 'Oh, grow up, Emma!'

'I am quite grown up, thank you! And it doesn't mean that because you wear uniform that I have to become some kind of . . . camp follower.'

His smile died and she saw the boy she had known on the Island. 'I'm sorry, Em. I thought . . .'

'You thought I was like all those women in South Africa that you've been boasting about. I suppose they take one look at the Brylcream boys and fall flat on their backs. Well, no doubt you've had lots of fun but this is England at war and some of us haven't had it so easy. Excuse me, I have a job to do.' She broke away and ran towards the park gateway. The wrought-iron gates and palings had gone to help the war effort, they said, but she hardly noticed anything but the great building towards which she ran.

He came pounding after her, catching up easily

as she stumbled on high heels. 'I'm sorry, Emma. Please understand. I came home hoping we could be married quickly and then I wondered if there was someone else. In the taxi I knew it was all right, and so I pushed my luck.' He took her by the shoulders and held her gently. 'I'd never hurt you, Emma. You know that. I love you and I want to marry you. Remember Maeve Evans? There may not be time for anything worthwhile again. I may not come back once I am on active duties and you could go up in this.'

They stood side by side as the searchlights stabbed the sky and anti-aircraft guns sprayed tracer bullets into the night. A pall of smoke blurred the glowing lights and hid the eastern side of the city, the western side and the river.

'It's a full-scale attack,' said Phillip. 'We'd better make for shelter.'

'It isn't close enough to us for that,' said Emma calmly, 'It's no nearer than the Elephant and Castle. It's a bit like it was in Bristol. We are on the fringe.' An ambulance put on shrouded sidelights and disappeared, followed closely by the other three. 'But it doesn't mean that we shall have no casualties brought in here.' Men opened the doors of a Nissen hut wide and the emergency fire engine stood ready in case the hospital was hit. A sports car squealed to a halt at the main entrance and three men were silhouetted against the open doorway for a second. 'Everyone who can, is going back and so must I, Phil. I know what it's like.' She put up her face for his kiss. Her voice was calm and impersonal and he sensed her withdrawal to other things more important than his love.

'Will it always be like this?' he asked. 'Is there never going to be a time when we can get together?' He hugged her with a kind of desperate hunger.

'See you the day after tomorrow at ten in the morning.'

'If this lot's clear,' she said. 'Goodnight, Phil.'

He watched her go, knowing that he had been erased from her present thoughts as someone who could wait until the serious business was over. 'Hell, don't you know how serious I am?' he murmured. He walked slowly away from the hospital, thinking about the time in South Africa. It was so silly. He could have had his pick of half a dozen girls, all rich and spoiled and very willing. There was Monica, the society girl who had hinted that she was what he needed. She could supply all his needs, with a father in the background holding out the promise of a job after the war, eager to see his daughter married to a hero.

And I come back to a girl with mid-brown hair, a straight nose and good figure, whose no-nonsense attitude reduces me to helpless acquiescence. He lit a cigarette and quickened his steps. At least when the time comes, I know she'll be a virgin, he thought.

A shelter now seemed undignified. How could he spend the night skulking in a safe place knowing that she was working with no thought for her own safety? He ran and jumped on to the step of a bus going towards the city. 'Only trying for the depot, Mate. Don't know if we'll even make that.' Phil nodded and offered the conductor a cigarette. The crash of burning buildings came from the left. A church lit up as for a son et lumière erupted flames through the stained glass windows and Phil almost expected to hear organ music. There were more flames, like blood escaping from tight scars, and in front of the bus a wall swayed and collapsed.

'We'll never get past that lot,' said the conductor cheerfully and rang the bell. 'All change,' he said to the empty bus. 'We'll leave this lot to the demolition and see what's under there.' The driver joined them and they picked their way over the smoking rubble that had once been a neat terrace of houses. The wallpaper on a bedroom wall still showed its red cabbage roses and the bright dado of gilt and blue. A bed hung crazily over the broken edge of the floor and a moan came from the pile of bricks and dust. 'Shocking,' said the driver. 'My missus wanted paper like that but I put my foot down. Never get a wink with all that abart, would you, Mate?'

Phil looked about him for a telephone. Where could he ring for help? Oh, how stupid can I get, he thought. The lines were all down – but the wounded needed an ambulance now. He spoke with authority and the other two men seemed relieved to have any decisions made for them. 'Can you back up?' he asked the driver. 'We'll have to turn round and make for the nearest hospital or ambulance station.'

He left his greatcoat and jacket in the cab and rigged up a lamp from the bus batteries to light the dark hole under the rubble. The conductor mumbled about the blackout but the driver just looked up at the fires burning everywhere and shrugged. A full moon hung over the city, cynically bright on the stricken churches and the fire barges on the river that spewed water in a fruitless effort to stem the flames. 'Hello,' said the driver gently to a figure trapped beneath a pile of bricks. 'Hang on, Mate. We'll have you out in no time.'

But at dawn, the count was four dead and seventeen injured. The dusty bus drove them carefully to the nearest casualty station. 'Sit there,' said a busty little Red Cross nurse. Phil grinned through the dust and pallor of the night. 'Casualties who can walk, sit there,' she ordered.

'I'm not a casualty. We dug them out,' said Phil wearily.

The bus driver came over. 'We'd better give them the address of the street where we found them so that they can identify the dead.' He jotted down the particulars and handed the note to the nurse.

'We could do with a drink,' said Phil.

'Over there by the urn,' said the nurse. 'Help yourself.' She then rushed away to find a doctor who had less than five patients to see at the same time.

'Good cuppa char,' said the conductor, sipping the hot muddy liquid. 'Nothing like it after something like this. They give it for shock, like.' He rummaged in his pocket and winked. 'Needs a bit of help, though. Good for shock,' he repeated as he poured a generous tot into Phil's cup from the flask. 'Here's to the Raff, Gawd bless'em.'

Phil forced a smile. Shall I ever be able to fly over a city now, telling a crew where to drop bombs? I've seen the damage from this side, smelled death in foetid cellars and seen the suffering. He shut his eyes for a moment. The spirit of those who survived was even more terrible, and the admiration and trust of the bus crew put a burden of responsibility on him that he found impossible to bear. It was all very well for the comfortable, generous people in South Africa to entertain him lavishly and say, 'Go back and give the bastards hell! Bomb them out of existence. Give them one for us. Put Hitler's name on it!'

It wasn't like that. There would be men, women and children. Old women like the one trembling and mumbling on the bench over there, unable to give her name or the address of her next of kin.

'You look as if you've been on ops,' said the bus conductor. 'That nice uniform is a bit the worse for wear. Ever get any parachute silk?' he asked hopefully. 'My missus made bloomers out of some. It's khaki but all silk feels the same in the dark!'

'Give me your address and I'll try to send you some,' said Phil. He brushed the dust from the front of his trousers. 'You're right. This will never be the same again,' he said with satisfaction.

'Don't forget. Give them one for us,' said the driver. 'They may have my name on one so make sure you get there, Guv.'

'I don't drop the bombs,' said Phil, 'but I'll give the crew the message.' He banged his cap on the edge of the table and watched the brickdust fly out of it. 'I'd better try to get back and brush up. What are you two doing?'

'Well, I shan't get home tonight. Look at the time. Nearly five in the morning. My old woman will think I've bought it, or I've gone with a tart.' He laughed. 'If I go home now, nothing will convince her that I haven't been with a woman all night.'

'Aren't you worried about her?'

'Na, she's all right. She's down the Underground. Goes there every night, raid or no raid. I can tell you, Guv, it ain't much fun being married these days. Do you wonder I get myself a nice bint sometimes?'

'I know how you feel.'

'You? You married?' Phil shook his head. 'Well, you've nothing to worry abart. They start taking them off as soon as they see the uniform, don't they?'

'Don't you believe it! I only wish they did. Come on, I'm hungry. Where can we eat? If the market's still there, they serve food for porters, don't they? I'll stand you breakfast. It's the least I can do.'

They looked round the crowded café in Covent Garden market. The cloth caps and the hard flat porters' hats for stacking high loads of baskets were everywhere. Men talked of the bombing, of supplies diverted and delayed and others destroyed or polluted by dust and broken glass. They accepted the three men as just more tired and grimy helpers in the Blitz and Phil ate hot pies and cabbage and drank curiously warm dark beer. He smiled. Other ranks and officers must not fraternise in uniform or eat and drink together. He looked at the torn and dishevelled bus uniforms. It just didn't matter.

'I must find a telephone,' he said. 'I'll settle up as I go and then be off.' He put his cap on at a rakish angle because it was now bent naturally in one direction and there was little he could do about it. He carried his greatcoat and buttoned his jacket, brushing dried mud from the cuffs. He shook hands with the two men and stepped back. They grinned and raised their beer mugs to him. Phil saluted smartly and it was more to him than when he had saluted the top brass as he marched in the passing out ceremony.

It took more than an hour to pick his way over the tangle of hoses, the wrecked cars and the piles of masonry, but at last he was safely inside his club. Unharmed, it had the same sanctimonious hush that he recalled. The porter eyed his uniform with distaste. 'You'll want a valet, sir.' It was a statement, almost an order. No reference to bombs, no mention of the dead, but deep concern over a soiled uniform. Phil laughed. So Hitler expected Britain to lie palpitating with fear this morning, after Coventry and now London again had been viciously ravaged.

With men like Joe, the bus conductor, who stolidly ate pies and cabbage among the ruins and hoped to cadge a bit of parachute silk for his missus, and the porter who carried on as if nothing had happened, how could the German war machine ever hope to shatter the country's morale?

Meekly, he handed over his uniform to skilled and disapproving hands, had a long hot bath in far too much water to please the regulations of five inches in the bottom of the tub, dressed in civilian clothes and went to telephone.

'The Princess Beatrice Hospital?'

'No, I'm afraid you can't speak to one of the nurses. We have to keep the lines clear for emergencies.'

'But this line is to the nurses' home.'

'As the nurse you want is on day duty, she will be working on the ward now. We can't connect you to the wards. Are you a relative?'

'No, but I was worried. I thought she might be wondering if I was . . . oh, it doesn't matter.'

'Ring after nine tonight or during her off-duty.' The voice was neither warm, nor unfriendly, just impersonal.

His uniform came back cleaned and pressed and almost as new. He felt deflated. There was so little to show for the night in any area of operations. He had been firmly slapped down by the girl he loved, had spent hours digging out bodies and he didn't even look tired now. They had even managed to steam out the bend in his cap. I might not look tired, but I am completely drained, he thought. He undressed and slipped between the cool sheets, then shot out of bed again. As he closed his eyes, the shock of the night hit him for the first time and he saw again the child's arm that had come away as he tried to lift the body. He made it to the bathroom and vomited lost pride, disappointment and horror with the pies and beer.

5

'You all deserve a day off,' said Sister Marion Nickolas. She slipped off her stiff cuffs and rolled up her sleeves. The ward was quiet and the freshly made-up beds lay white and empty along one side of the ward. 'I've never seen the place so empty but we may be very busy again at any time so we can't slack off. I think everything has been done and there might be time to teach you all something about emergency procedures.'

Staff Nurse Mason came into the ward. 'That's the last ambulance on its way, Sister. There were a few tears from Iris Downs but I told her that she could be home again in about two weeks. I explained that we are sending them away to be safe from the bombing but she was more concerned that her mother couldn't visit her up North.'

'Her family come to Beatties with everything from ringworm to cancer,' said Sister. 'They love it and Iris was very upset at the thought of going to another hospital until her stitches are out. Compared to life in Peabody Buildings, this is luxury and the family can visit easily.'

'Does this mean we are to take only bomb casualties now, Sister?' asked Emma.

'No, Nurse Dewar. Ward Four is still surgical and we shall have gynae lists twice a week to fill the beds on this side of the ward and cope with acute cases that can't be taken down to Surrey or further north, but most of the non-acute surgery will be done there now until we are sure the raids have stopped.' She sighed. 'We have to gear ourselves to changing conditions, Nurse. The Ministry of Health now gives a subsidy to all voluntary hospitals for every geriatric patient they take in, and for keeping ten beds empty in each surgical ward, for emergency use. As we are dependent on public subscriptions and private insurances, we can't afford to refuse and it will be made law soon, I've no doubt.' She smiled. 'In any case, we must do what we can to help the biggest number of people, whatever their needs.'

'I think Nurse Dewar isn't all that keen, Sister.' Staff Nurse Mason chuckled. 'She nursed geriatrics for too long to look on this as a novelty. Cheer up, Nurse. It's one way to help the war effort, even if it doesn't include nursing handsome heroes.'

Geriatrics? Emma thought of the ladies in the elegant rooms at the Home in Bristol. Nobody called them anything but residents and it seemed wrong to put old people in such a demeaning category, whatever their background.

'Poor old dears,' Nurse Mason went on, as they walked down the ward to the four end beds. 'They don't care where they are so long as they are warm and fed. One is blind and completely disorientated and the others are mildly senile and none of them realise that they were bombed out of the old people's home.' She looked round the spotless ward. 'Amazing what we've done in the past twenty-four hours to make the change-over.'

'Well, Nurse Dewar will miss the next lot of back rubs and drawsheets,' said Sister. 'Off you go and have a good time, Nurse.' She was serious for a moment. 'Be very careful and if there's a raid stay put unless you can get back safely, and telephone when it is all over so that we know you are safe. We have to relax a lot of rules but Matron trusts you to be sensible.'

'Yes, Sister.' An evening off followed by a day off seemed a wonderfully long time. Sister had been very understanding, letting her have the morning after the day off as well and adding on an extra hour, to make up for some of the time she had worked, changing the ward round, long after the day staff should have been off-duty.

'Do you want sleeping-out passes for the two nights?' Sister had asked, but Emma had refused, asking instead for a theatre pass, until midnight on the first evening.

'I was given theatre tickets for the musical where Miss Joiner works,' said Emma. 'I hear it's quite good.'

'You may find half of Beatties' staff there, filling the expensive seats they can't sell while the raids persist,' said Sister. 'She gave them out like free leaflets to anyone able to go, as they like the theatre to look full at each performance. Even the night staff do quite well as we have tickets for most of the trade shows of films that are shown before noon for the press and critics.'

When Phil telephoned, Emma lied and said she couldn't have a sleeping-out pass as all had been stopped, but he seemed pleased that she had managed to get extra time off. 'You could use the apartment,' Bea said. 'I'm not off until the weekend when I have two days off together to meet my mother.' She wrinkled her nose. 'Can't say I'm very keen on her latest. Why she doesn't stay in America or the south of Ireland beats me. He's younger than her, of course, and not averse to pinching my bum in passing.' She laughed at Emma's horrified expression. 'Don't worry, duckie, he doesn't get anywhere. He's a bit wet, really. I suppose Mama has to take what she can get these days. Shame, all her lot are far away or dead.' Bea danced round Emma's bedroom hugging a pillow. 'They're either too young or too old . . . Either too old or too grassy green: the pickings are poor and the crop is lean,' she sang. 'But the food will be good,' she added. 'I'll come back stocked with tins. He's something in the black market, I suspect. I shall drown my conscience in good white wine and eat all I'm given. I still think you're an idiot not to use the place. My father is away and I shall be in Bucks.'

'For the last time, Bea, thank you but *no*! I'm not the kind who sleeps with her boyfriend. You ought to know that by now.'

Bea looked sly. 'Don't tell me you suspect he might venture into your bedroom when you are chastely tucked up for the night? Not good little Phillip?'

'Good little Phillip isn't as good as you said he'd be. He's already suggested it.' She turned her back and concentrated on plucking one hair from an already pruned eyebrow. Her lips were well-defined and inviting, coloured with pretty red lipstick that matched the checks in her jacket. Her hair glowed and had auburn lights from the suspicion of henna hair oil and her skin, as usual, was good.

'You are a tease, Emma. Girls who don't think they are can be the worst as they look so good and have that innocent air of Don't Touch Me. No, don't look so affronted. That's what drove Eddie mad, and if you go out looking like that, can you wonder that any man with red blood in his veins doesn't want you? You even have straight seams! I can never manage that for more than half an hour.' She looked at the misty stockings and the plain high-heeled court shoes. 'Did he give you the stockings?'

'Yes, four pairs. He brought them back with him.'

'The least you can do is to wear them for him,' said Bea. 'It does put a girl under a certain obligation, I suppose.'

'Not always,' said Emma dryly. She spilled a cascade of silk on to the bed from its tissue paper wrapping. 'He's not seeing me in that lot!'

Bea picked up the thin black silk cami-knickers and nightdress. 'I can't wear them,' said Emma flatly. 'I'm not the type, and I wonder what gave him the idea?'

'Rubbish! They're heavenly,' Bea chuckled. 'That young man has learned more than geography during his travels and all those long journeys to Africa. He'll expect to see if they fit. Do wear them and take the key to the flat. I'd adore to see you as a fallen woman!'

'Oh, you're impossible. I wish I'd never shown them to you. How could I wear them? If my mother saw them, she'd label me a scarlet woman at once, as soon as she glimpsed black lace. I can't wear them with Phil even if he couldn't see them. I'd know and it would embarrass me. Just suppose we had an air raid. Can you imagine what people would say if they saw me in those cami-knicks?'

'It would brighten the life of the ambulance men,' said Bea. 'The doctors would queue up to give you priority treatment. Go on, Emma, wear the cami-knicks. They give a lovely line to a skirt and I can see the line of the elastic under the one you are wearing. It shows through.'

'They would be good for that,' Emma conceded.

'If you really want to keep him off the grass, they are fine for that, too. They are first-rate passion bafflers. No decent man is likely to know about the tiny buttons, just there.'

'The voice of experience, *again*?' sighed Emma.

'Oh, yes. For really hot dates, I wear my old ballet dancing leotard under a sweater. It means undressing every time I go to the lavatory, but the fumblers are held at bay a treat.'

Emma slipped out of her skirt and changed into

the smooth silk. The skirt band sat snugly at her waist and she felt good. 'You're right; they feel fine. I must fly. I said I'd be no later than half-past and it's nearly that now.' She grabbed her purse and a winter coat. 'I wish I had the money and coupons for a new coat but as I have neither, I shall have to look shabby. At least there aren't many people with new coats this year. And if the theatre is warm, I can take the coat off.'

She ran to the stairs and down to the lodge. A figure appeared in the doorway and Phillip smiled at her.

'Hello,' she said. 'Am I late?'

'Come on, I managed to get a taxi and it's ticking away alarmingly, so run, girl.'

'What luxury,' she said as she tried to run gracefully in a tight, pencil slim skirt and very high heels. 'I daren't run faster or I'll ladder my new stockings.'

He guided her to the taxi. 'They look good,' he said, glancing appreciatively at the slim ankles. 'Are you by any chance wearing my other gifts?'

'A black silk nightie to the theatre? Don't be silly.' His arm hovered over her shoulders. 'No, Phil, you'll make my hair in a mess. How can I go to the theatre looking as if I've been dragged through a hedge backwards?'

He sat away, looking tall and aloof and lit a cigarette. 'We needn't go. We could go to a club and sit in a nice little alcove and have a drink and talk.'

'We can't waste the tickets. They are very expensive seats.' She sensed his coolness. 'It should be very good. They say the costumes came from America and are magnificent, for wartime.' She put a hand over his. 'Don't spoil a perfectly good evening by sulking just because I am not . . . I can't . . .' His arms were about her and his kiss hard on her lips.

'Don't you understand, Emma? I love you. That isn't just holding hands in the back of a taxi, and kissing in dark corners. I want you, and sometimes I feel as if we haven't much time left. None of us can afford to waste time when it comes to love.'

'That's not fair. It's a kind of blackmail. It's like going to the shops and everyone saying "Don't you know there's a war on?" to hide shortages and to make war the excuse for inefficiency. If this was peacetime, you'd never ask me to do anything I thought was wrong.'

'That's the whole point. We *are* at war. This isn't peacetime when you could say you'd marry me in a year's time after you'd filled a bottom drawer and we'd put down for a house. This *is* war, Emma, and you know the saying "All's fair in love and war"? I have no idea when I'll have leave again. I can't say where I'm going but it will be far away again, overseas. I might be killed and you might be bombed and neither of us will be the same people after it's all over.'

'That's my argument. It's life and if we aren't the same people it would be stupid to find we were tied to a partner we didn't love or with whom we had nothing left in common.'

'What if we do change? I love you now and I want you more than anything.'

Where were the dreams of romance, she wondered. Where was the dream of quiet wooing, with rose petals strewing the path to the altar? The taxi smelled of stale tobacco and spent passion. The driver had a hacking cough and Emma suspected he could hear everything said in the back of his cab.

'We're nearly there,' she said. She pushed Phil away and smoothed her hair. She smiled, to make her rejection less cold. 'Dear Phil, I do love you very much, but I just don't know if I'm *in* love with you. I don't think I've ever been in love.'

'I can make you love me. You were on the brink the last time we were in a taxi and you let me kiss and fondle you. You liked it then.' He straightened his tie. 'Well, let's see what a little treacly romance can do for you. What are we seeing?'

'*Lilac Time*,' said Emma. They stepped out into the grey dusk. Lilacs like the ones that bloomed along the terrace by Watergate Lane ... In early summer there were lilacs, with bright yellow laburnum and copper beech hanging down to the road. She glanced at the good face. Phillip was a part of that life, a life she had loved and now missed painfully, but how did she know if he was a part of the future? I am changing, she decided. None of us will be the same. 'I wrote and asked for a pass to the Island,' she said aloud. 'Aunt Emily said I'd have to apply if I wanted one, now that I'm not a resident there. It's a blow, Phil. It's my home! I've lived there all my life and they make me feel like an enemy alien. I know they are building boats and things and something very hush-hush but I went to school there! Aunt Emily is there and I want to visit her.'

'If you married me, you could have a pass. My address is still the same as ever, as my parents live there.'

'I wonder?'

'You mean you'd marry me just to get back there?'

'No, of course not. Don't be silly, Phil. I'd just remembered that we went to shool with a boy called George whose father is the deputy chief of police now. The father knew both my grandmother and Aunt Emily, and his son came to parties we had as children. I'll write directly to him.'

'I'd rather you used me, even if it meant you were ... using me.'

They handed in their tickets and sat in the faded

plush seats of the expensive stalls. A few older women with officers in uniform wore good expensive clothes, and one or two looked out of place in pre-war evening dresses, but most of the audience were dressed neatly in their best everyday clothes. There were a few fur coats of an old-fashioned cut, probably borrowed from mothers and aunts, and Emma saw many coats almost as shabby as hers. She folded her coat and hoped the theatre would warm up as more people arrived, as her lace blouse was chilly.

The lights dimmed and the modified orchestra struck up the overture. Several of the singers were stars who had made several last performances but were now working harder than ever to fill the gaps left by young actors and actresses, singers and instrumentalists who had gone into the Forces or to join ENSA. The leading man was very elderly to be the romantic lead and from where she sat, Emma said she could hear his corsets creaking, but the voice was still good and when she closed her eyes, the lilacs did bloom again in spring.

But it wasn't Phil who walked beside her down an English lane. The figure by her side was indistinct and when she opened her eyes, Phil was real as the lights went up for the interval and a babble of voices took over. In front was a row of RAF officers wearing the insignia of Aesculapius, the god of medicine, the staff with the snake.

'Just how many free seats were given away in your hospital?' asked Phil. 'The medics and nurses have cornered the market tonight. I wonder if they sold any for real money?' He stared almost resentfully at the row of shining heads. The man at the end of the row turned to see if ice cream was being sold and walked to the back of the theatre. He came back with four tubs and wooden spoons. 'Want an ice?' asked Phil. 'I didn't know you could get them in theatres any more.' He went to join a small line of people waiting for the girl to serve them and came back as the music began for the second act. 'Only one kind,' he whispered. 'Better than nothing.'

Emma dug her spoon into the dense white pack. It had little flavour other than a strong synthetic vanilla, but it was cold and refreshing. One kind, better than nothing: was life always to consist of making do with whatever turned up, and counting one's not very interesting blessings? Marrying Phil because he'd asked her and she had no idea if she was capable of falling deeply in love? Vaguely ashamed, she wanted him to go away and leave her alone to get on with her work at Beatties. She saw the colours on the stage change as the lights turned pink and blue and soft gold and she regained her sense of euphoria. The war would end one day, and everything would be normal again.

It was raining when they left the theatre and a flurry of wet stung her ankles. Phil told her to stay where she was and ran to find a taxi. They climbed in and sat damply side by side all the way to the hospital and heard the siren wail just as they turned off from Camberwell Green. The driver said, 'Going back up West, sir? I'd leave the lady now and get back. I can take you but you won't find another cab here tonight.' They reached the hospital and Emma persuaded Phil to leave her. 'See you tomorrow. We have the whole day together,' she said. 'If it's fine we can go down to Surrey by the river.'

He didn't insist on staying as the memory of his last encounter with bombed London had been enough, so Emma went to her room and found that most of the nurses had already gone to the shelter of the subway. The rest were shuffling along the corridor in slippers and dressing gowns, looking half-asleep, most of them clutching magazines and books. 'Come on,' said one girl, her face shining with precious cold cream that she had put on for the night and had no intention of removing. 'I tried to stay up here one night and got into the most awful row. Take your dress off if the skirt is tight and put on a dressing gown. She comes round to check.'

Emma closed her door and began to undress, intending to get ready for bed. At least here was plenty of muscle to do the bed-pushing with the help of the night staff, and people off-duty and on days were left to sleep or read in the shelter. She took off her blouse and hung it up, then shook out the slightly crumpled skirt. A loud knocking on the door made her grab her dressing gown. 'I had a theatre pass, Sister. I've just come back,' she said.

'There's no time to get undressed. You are all right as you are. Put on your gown and slippers and get down with the rest. It's always far too hot and you'll be glad you aren't overdressed.'

She waited while Emma put on her dressing gown and the black velvet mules that Aunt Emily had given her a long time ago. Emma smiled. It was strange to be wandering about the hospital in a pair of black silk cami-knickers and velvet mules and a thick dressing gown.

It was hot and airless, lying on the top bunk of the long rank of three-tiered metal beds that were now a permanent feature of the subways, leaving enough space for trolleys to pass by but having enough resting space for most of the nursing and medical staff who needed it. After half an hour, the All Clear sounded and some sleepy nurses groaned, having resigned themselves to being there all night and trying to get some rest. Emma went on reading for a few more minutes. I've got to this chapter three times, she thought. I must get on with it. She half-expected the siren to go again, but the bunks were quickly emptying and she realised that she was one of the last to leave. Two doctors in white coats went by, oblivious to the girl on the top bunk and she looked around for the steps that had been there earlier. She closed the book and put it into her holdall. There was no alternative to climbing down without steps. She looked over the edge and decided that she could put a foot down on the next tier, climb down and jump from there.

'If you try to climb down with those ridiculous slippers on, you'll break a leg,' said a calm voice. 'Drop them down to me first and then I'll catch you.' The man she had first met in a taxi smiled up at her.

She dropped the mules and clutched her gown more firmly round her, conscious that she had let it fall open in the dry heat of the subway. 'I can manage,' she said. She ignored the humour in his eyes and put her bare foot on the side of the next rail. It was lower than she had imagined and she slipped. 'Told you,' he said and she was grabbed round the waist by two strong arms. He lowered her to the bottom bunk and held out a mule. 'Allow me, Cinderella,' he said. 'Past midnight but still no rags?' His gaze had shifted from her face and she drew her gown closer, making up her mind that she needed buttons and not just a tie at the waist. He had seen what she had denied Phillip, the thin black silk and the filigree of lace on her bare thighs. He slipped the mule on to her foot with firm warm hands, then handed her the other as if he had no desire to put that one on as well.

'Thank you,' she said. 'It was silly to wear them here but I was sent down in a hurry by Home Sister and didn't have a chance to sort out my clothes. I had a theatre pass,' she continued, as if she needed to explain.

'I know. Did you enjoy it? The leading man was

hardly an ingénu. A bit long in the tooth but it made a pleasant evening.'

'You were there?'

'Just in front of you. In fact your escort pinched our cab.' They were walking towards the door that led to the nurses' home, beyond which no man was allowed. He stopped with his hand on the door, but didn't open it at once. 'I was surprised to see you here,' he said.

'Why surprised? You don't even know me.' Who are you? she wanted to ask. I've seen you three times but I have no idea who you are.

'But I do know. You are Nurse Dewar, new to Beatties, fresh out of PTS and panting to do good works.' His eyes were mocking. 'Nurse Dewar, all dressed up and ... nowhere to go.' His glance slid over the tightly-closed gown. 'What a waste. But air raids have a lot to answer for, haven't they?' He opened the door and stood back. Emma fled to her room and slammed the door. She tore off the black underwear and threw it into the linen basket. *If I dress like a tart, he has every reason to think what he likes – that I am just that.*

Unfairly, she blamed Phillip for giving her the clothes and putting her in a false position, then grew calmer. What did it matter what he thought? He was just a doctor who happened to be in the RAF, too. She was ashamed of blaming Phillip and when she was told at breakfast that there was a message for her to ring a certain number urgently, she rushed to the telephone as if her bad feelings towards Phil had done something terrible to him.

'Hello, is Flight Lieutenant Scantal there, please?' she asked. There were many voices in the background and she had to listen carefully to make out the words.

'Emma? Listen, darling. I'm sorry, I can't make it today. I've had a call from the Air Ministry.

They've put our posting forward. I have to leave at two this afternoon. I have to be briefed and collect my kit and we leave Victoria at two sharp. Can you be there?'

'Of course!' The warmth in her voice was due more to a feeling of relief than of any great outflowing of love.

'Bless you.' His voice was husky. 'Oh Em, I can't talk here with all this racket going. 'Bye. See you at the station. Promise you'll come?'

'Yes, I'll be there early. Take care.' She put down the phone and wandered back to the dining room to have some more coffee. If I'd gone with him last night I would have slept with him and nothing would have been the same again between us. For me it would have been a total commitment even if we drifted apart after the war. She wondered if her mother might have been happier and less bitter if she had married the man who died in the First World War, but she knew in her heart and from what Aunt Emily had said, that Clare Dewar had always been the same but grew worse as she got older. For me it's not the same, Emma thought. I haven't met anyone I could love for ever – and she was conscious of a sense of reprieve.

When she saw Phillip striding towards her across the station, his dear sad face tense with emotion, she felt an almost sisterly compassion. He put his greatcoat and a bulky parcel down on a bench and held her close. She let her body mould against his and gave kiss for kiss to send him away content.

'I'll love you until Hell freezes.' he said in an effort to be flippant. 'Be good and wait for me, please, Emma.' He picked up the parcel. 'Could you send this off for me? Open it and take what you want and then send the rest to Joe Acton and his mate Fred, the bus conductor and driver who helped me in the raid. I promised to get Joe some parachute silk. Some is white and some a nasty gold khaki, but he will be pleased. Here is the address.' He seemed at a loss for words now and glanced at the group waiting for the train that now steamed slowly into the station. 'Got to go,' he said and kissed her again with a hunger that made her weep. 'Tears, for me? I shall treasure them,' he said, never guessing that they were for the passion she couldn't return.

She waved until the face at the window became a blur and the train curved round and hid him from her sight. 'Forget me,' she murmured. 'Please, dear, dear Phil, forget me.'

She watched the different uniforms of men passing through the station or boarding crowded trains. The news had been bad again, with more losses in France and North Africa and convoys torpedoed in the Channel with a serious loss of men and ships, and on the station the piles of kitbags showed more troop movements. An Army doctor read a newspaper while his batman tried to get a taxi and Emma wondered if all units of the RAF as well as the Army carried their own doctors with them. Why should a doctor in RAF uniform be working at a civilian hospital, and for how long?

She walked slowly to the bus stop and wondered what to do with a perfectly good day off alone, and decided on the National Gallery in Trafalgar Square. It was good to do as she wished and even the thought of work was comforting as it was her choice of career. There was a lot of studying to do and people to meet and the excitement of being in London. I'll write to him often, she thought, but Phil's face was fading as she looked up at Nelson's Column and walked round the Landseer lions in the huge square.

6

'I can't believe it. So much has happened over the past four months that we seem to have been here for ever. I hated it when we changed wards after three months, only one month on a fresh ward and they want us to go down to the sector hospital,' said Annie Force.

'Stick-in-the-mud,' teased Bea. 'I've been dying to get down there after all they say about the place. Have you noticed, everyone coming back from Heath Cross has a smug look about them as if they have had a wonderful experience?'

Annie Force looked at the notice again and sighed. 'It's all very well for the pretty girls. They always attract boyfriends, and Heath Cross is seething with doctors from all kinds of hospitals.' She looked impressed. 'I heard that there were some from Holland and France and Austria who had escaped when their countries were overrun. My father had a Jewish doctor once and said he was very clever. I can't think how Germany can want to be rid of brilliant men, can you?'

'All the more reason for you going there. With a lot of spare men, we shall all be pursued. Isn't that lovely? In a country where men are almost nonexistent in the normal way, we shall have lots to date us and follow us around with tongues hanging out for a kind word or something a little more, especially if they are fed up and far from home.' Bea winked at the others grouped round the noticeboard. 'We'll fit you up with dates, Annie. Just leave off your glasses when they have dances, and smile.'

'I can't see without my glasses.'

'No need. You want to be seen, not see. You can take pot-luck at first until you know who you are smiling at and then get choosy. Short-sighted people look as if they have terrific eye contact as they can't be made shy by men staring at them, and you have big blue eyes under those awful frames.'

'We are going there to work,' said Margaret Turpin reprovingly. 'I shall be sorry to leave orthopaedics but maybe we shall have a ward like it there.' She looked sad. 'Pity that Beryl Foster didn't make the grade. She confided in me when we came to Beatties after PTS that she had failed her three months there and the Sister on men's medical told her quite kindly but firmly that she would never make a nurse and so she went home to join the Land Army.'

'What's the matter?' Emma joined them and stared at the notice.

'Heath Cross finds that it can't do without our set. We report to Matron's office tomorrow morning and have all our stuff packed, ready to leave by the afternoon,' said Bea. 'I suppose that means a few choice words about discipline and how to keep the good name of the Princess Beatrice high and pure.'

'She may also give us a pep talk if our Ward Sister assessments haven't come up to scratch,' said Emma. 'Talking of scratching! I shall be so glad to get out of skins! My hands are permanently grey after all that gentian violet and triple dye we use there. The bed linen is terrible. They have to keep it separate in the laundry as the dyes tint everything, and so we have sludge-coloured sheets, grey bath towels and graveyard brown dressing towels. I hated leaving gynae, and I was disappointed not to be sent to casualty as I think I might want to do a lot of theatre work when I am experienced enough.

I was sent there for two days when skins were not busy, and it's exciting and very busy in Cas.'

'You need a change,' said Bea as they walked back to their wards. 'You look quite pale. I shall enjoy being away from the bombs for a while but I can't think why they want to send us away now when we are getting casualties and Surrey is quiet. Do you think they will tie labels on us like they did on all those poor little kids to get them out of London away from the Blitz?'

'We aren't evacuees,' said Emma. 'Some settled but many went home again as they were too miserable. The Queen set a good example and refused to go to Canada with her children so a lot of people said that what was good enough for her was good enough for them, and now that a part of Buckingham Palace has been hit, they feel even more close to the Royal Family.'

'I need a change, too,' said Bea airily. She looked at Emma sideways. 'I love men's surgical but it can be a bit fraught. Still, I'd like to be there when Paul has his operation.' She smiled to show that she was fooling. 'He's a pet. He tries to kiss me when the screens are drawn, and writes little poems for me.'

'It's against the rules to get involved with a patient, Bea.'

Bea tossed her head. 'How can one *not* get involved? It's the stuffiest rule I've ever heard!'

'Be careful. I think I agree with it. Sister Nickolas was very convinced it was a bad idea, even on a women's ward, and she said it was terribly easy when nursing men to get into a tangle, emotionally.'

'She should know. That woman is as pretty as paint. No wonder they didn't give her a men's ward, but she might be a typical hospital sister at heart and not likely to fall for anyone.'

'She has her own following among the medics,'

said Emma. 'It's rumoured that the surgical registrar is mad about her.' She looked severe. 'But that doesn't excuse you getting dewy-eyed over a patient, Bea.'

'Unfortunately, you are right,' said Bea with a dismissive laugh. 'I could easily be an idiot over him but as my Irish grandmother would say, he looks as if he is too good for this world and the angels might take him at any time.'

'We're late,' said Emma. 'See you after duty. We'll have to pack up some things tonight or I shall be left with a few extra paper bags that will split in the trunk of the coach.'

There was even less time for packing. Early that night the sirens sent everyone not involved with patients and bed-pushing down to the subway, and from the Air Raid Warden who came down for the hot drinks prepared for his men by the kitchen staff, they heard that the East End and the Docks had copped it badly again. Emma sat on a lower bunk and tried to sew. The mattress was too hard for rest and the air was stale and lifeless. She thought of the lecture she should write up and then wondered if it would be wanted at Heath Cross and who would be their Sister Tutor there.

She had not seen the man again who had helped her with her slipper with such mocking courtesy. She knew nothing about him except that even in uniform he was familar with Beatties and free to wander about the subway as if he belonged. If I knew his name, I could find out where he worked and what he was doing in uniform. She thought of him again and needed to make him know that she wasn't the type of girl he obviously thought her to be, a girl dressed for a good time but who had backed out of a date because of an air raid. She tried to forget his dispassionate grey eyes. Maybe he didn't have that opinion of her, but she knew that black silk underwear usually meant more than holding hands, and his good opinion, for no reason that she could pinpoint, mattered to her.

After rushing to get packed, and feeling half-asleep after a bad night, the girls lined up in Matron's office. She smoothed her dark blue dress and stood by the window, looking at the nurses, her eyes missing nothing and her tone brisk. 'You will, at all times, be aware of your responsibility to your parent hospital. Beatties is one of the most famous hospitals and her doctors and nurses go to all parts of the world taking skill and comfort to thousands of people of every race and colour.' She paused for effect.

'Neither the Dean of the Medical School nor I approve of sending you or the medical students away, even though while in the sector hospitals you will continue your training and use the same methods in the wards as we do here. We have our own wards in two hospitals. The Middlesex have some and so does St Thomas' and some of the other voluntary hospitals, and a few of the LCC hospitals have nurses there, so that you may mix off-duty if you wish, but your training will be exclusively Beatties', in wards and theatres.'

She looked at the row of serious fresh young faces, 'The fact that we trust you to deport yourselves well and to bring no disgrace to your uniform or training school shows that we pick only the best to train here. There will be many times when you are unhappy and wish you were back here, and there are many temptations for girls away from home for the first time, but you must give me your word that you will seek the advice of your seniors if any personal crises emerges.' She coughed slightly. 'As yet we do not know, but you may be called on to nurse members of the armed forces. Please remember that you are nurses with a fine vocation, to serve and heal. You are women – but only second to your calling, and must *never* become involved emotionally with a patient. However much you think you suffer at the time, please believe that these feelings pass, on both sides, and you can give no real service with a mind clouded with subjective feelings.'

The girls stood stiffly and tried to avoid her penetrating gaze, and she gestured to Sister Tutor to take over. 'I hope you enjoy Health Cross,' Sister smiled and Emma thought she looked quite human. 'I have yet to meet a nurse who didn't dislike Heath Cross at first but when it comes to leaving it, most girls wish to stay. I believe the social life is good and you have weekly dances and many recreational facilities. I have your reports from your Ward Sisters and I'm pleased with them. Three nurses have shown very great promise. I will mention no names but I think their Ward Sisters have given them some indication of their progress. Please go on as you are. We may need you as Sisters here one day. Many of our best loved staff have trained here and stayed on.' She smiled and stood back and Matron nodded to show that the interview was over.

'Phew! I'm glad we weren't on the carpet. She hides an iron first under that graceful exterior,' said Bea. 'But she's fair and so is Tute.' Bea smiled and Emma knew that she and Emma and Margaret had been singled out for an extra smile to show that they were the best of the students.

'Come on, refugees this way,' said the driver of the coach waiting by the door of the nurses' home.

'God bless Beatties and all who serve in her and please send us lots of lovely soldiers to nurse at Heath Cross,' intoned Bea.

'Amen,' chorused the girls.

They followed the emergency detours through

the outskirts of the city to avoid the worst of the unsafe buildings awaiting demolition gangs to level them or to shore up the crumbling walls with scaffolding. Smoke hung like a cloud of depression, and gritty fog swirled over the river. 'I shall be glad to leave London,' Margaret stated.

'I shan't,' retorted Bea. 'What is there to do in the country in winter? It was bad enough in PTS, but at least that was in a fairly nice house. They gave us a good Christmas at Beatties. In fact they did it rather well.' She laughed. 'I didn't know I liked anything to do with it as my memories of Christmas are mixed, but they stuck to all the traditional things and it was quite moving, didn't you find, especially when we all sang carols and walked round the wards on Christmas Eve.' She saw that Emma was smiling as if she didn't believe her. 'Well, the patients thought it was good,' Bea said defensively 'And we had decent food for once.'

'I love the country,' said Margaret. 'I shall read a lot. I brought a few books with me that I found in a bomb damage sale and after I'd dried out the water that caused more damage than the bombs, I discovered I'd got some real bargains.'

'I shall miss the theatres. I know there aren't many still open and soon we shall be reduced to the Windmill where they have nude revues, but there are a few left where they show light amusing things, like the Whitehall Theatre, and the ballet still soldiers on out at The Angel at Islington.' Bea sighed. 'Just to walk along Whitehall or any part that isn't badly affected, gives me a lift. St James' where my father has an apartment is so peaceful and solid as if nothing can shake it. I love it.'

'You'll have us all weeping in a minute,' said Emma dryly. 'Does your father know you are going down to Heath Cross?'

Bea giggled. 'He wanted to take me out this

weekend to lunch with some top brass he knows. Believe it or not, I am now my father's claim to respectability and he likes to show off my good manners. The little popsies cannot be introduced to important people and so my expensive education is paying off as far as he is concerned, even if he is on edge when I hint at what I am doing at Beatties. Never could stand the sight or sound of blood, so I told him that duty called and I was being sent to tend the sick in a mental asylum.'

'You did say that it is now an acute emergency hospital?' suggested Emma.

'I quite forgot, duckie,' drawled Bea. 'I've never seen my pater so shocked. I think he'd rather I joined a high-class brothel.' She frowned. 'He's one of those people who would like to see all deformed and mentally sick people swept out of sight and mind. He just doesn't want to know about insanity or mental abnormality.'

'Hitler was doing that for years before the war,' said Emma. 'I hate to think what has happened now in the countries overrun by the Nazis. Surely your father wouldn't want them singled out and killed?'

'He'd rather not know, just as most of the German people would rather remain in ignorance. Out of sight, out of mind, but he does have the same cruel streak that dear Eddie has. I told him he might need a place like it one day, and I thought he could easily have hit me. He went all shades of purple.'

'My mother is afraid of mental illness,' said Emma. 'She told me once that one of her best friends went mad after having a baby, and she hated visiting her, as if it might be infectious or that the stigma might rub off on her.'

'I'm sorry for people who think like that, but have you heard about Heath Cross? It does sound weird. The first of the Beatties' mob who went there with some other hospitals to take over and get it started as an acute hospital, said the whole place stank of urine and disinfectant. The baths had thick wooden edges to prevent the patients from doing themselves harm on metal sides and there were three baths in each bathroom. There were protective metal columns encasing all lavatory chains so that only the handles were visible and the chains couldn't be used as offensive weapons or for suicide.'

'It can't be like that now,' said Emma. 'The patients have gone and they have no need of such things.'

'Don't you know there's a war on? They can't afford money or manpower or time to make changes. It will be well-scrubbed and clean but not all that different.' She gazed out at the leafless trees and the dismal hedges along the country road. 'I think this must be it.' The coach stopped outside high wrought-iron gates flanked by tall spiked metal fences. The gates swung back slowly as the porter came to open up for the coach and he closed the gates behind them. The driveway up to the main blocks of the hospital was more like another country lane than a drive. Trees of all kinds lined grassy walks leading away beyond flower beds that must have been beautiful when there were enough gardeners to tend them, but now lay choked with weeds, dank under last year's growth. Small villas, built of warm red brick and stone could be glimpsed between the trees, and the main block sat grey and forbidding against an avenue of poplars.

'It's huge!' said Emma. 'It's bigger than the Home ... the gardens, I mean.'

'I can't see any hothouses for grapes and peaches,' objected Bea. 'And I doubt if the poor things ever tasted champagne.'

'Thank goodness,' said Emma. 'If it's foul here,

I'll send Sister Cary a card, saying "Wish you were here".'

Bea shivered. 'I think I'm going to hate it,' she said. 'I'm homesick for Beatties.'

'You aren't thinking about Paul, the kidney boy?'

Bea nodded. 'I never really thought about death before, except when Evans was killed. That was war and could happen to anyone and it's usually quick, but Paul is different. He hasn't the choice of joining up and fighting, or opting to stay in a safe place. His death is with him, just waiting, unless there is a miracle and the one kidney they leave holds up to the pressure.' Her voice was low and she brushed her eyes angrily.

'He may come down here after his op,' Emma told her quietly. 'They do sometimes, as the main urological team is here.' She eyed Bea with apprehension. Paul was the first man for whom Bea had admitted any affection and Emma knew that she cared deeply about him, even if most of it was pity and because he was very good-looking and desperate for attention.

'Well, I can't do anything about it so I'll have to practice that cold objectivity they go on about. I just wish they'd stop ramming it down my throat.'

'It isn't cold,' said Emma. 'It's teaching us a kind of love that doesn't care who it's for. I have disliked some patients but I knew they needed just as much care amd warmth as the ones I really liked, and haven't you noticed, that several patients blend into one after a while, and once they leave, you can't recall details about many individuals? It's a shock when they appear all dressed up in their own clothes ready to go home. They become strangers.'

'My, my, the child can think!' said Bea with her normal acidity. She lifted one carefully-plucked eyebrow. 'You are of course, quite right, but don't right *all* the time, duckie. It gets boring. Men like us to be wrong sometimes; don't they just!'

The dining room was vast, with a vaulted ceiling higher than the chapel at the Home in Bristol. Maids in pink dresses pushed heavy trolleys from table to table, serving food quickly and clearing away dirty dishes. A stack of thick white plates was renewed from time to time on each table which meant a constant supply of clean ones but never a hot one. Bea ate her stew quickly before it was cold and took more potatoes. 'Just to keep up my strength,' she said. She prodded a dish of spinach that had a hard dry crust over it. 'The vegetables could be good if they hadn't cooked all the life out of them,' she said. 'Oh, good! Sponge jelly and custard. Reminds me of school.'

But the sponge jelly, which consisted of a slice of swiss roll set in red jelly and covered with a thick glutinous mass of yellow paste was not a one-day treat. It seemed to be the staple pudding and appeared at least three times a week, just as fish cakes that had only glimpsed a fish bone and had more than an intimate knowledge of potatoes, appeared with the same regularity for breakfast and sometimes supper.

'They said we'd learn to love it here,' said Emma. She cast her eyes heavenwards and gasped. 'Look, Bea! Do you see what I see?' On the sweeping archway ledge high above the stage at one end of the room, what looked like tattered pieces of blackout material stirred gently. One piece flew up and out of a ventilator. 'BATS!'

'Well, one hears of bats in the belfry but this is too macabre,' said Bea, laughing. 'I must write to my mother and invite her here. She loathes them. If the boyfriend is scared of them, he could come with her. So this is a batty place even without the patients. Do you think we'll all go slowly mad, too?'

She saw that Emma was trembling. 'What's wrong? You aren't scared, are you?'

'I hate them. When I was little, one got into my bedroom and I hid under the bedclothes and screamed. I'd heard of them getting into people's hair and as I had a mop of fuzzy curls, I was terrified. I never slept with the window open for years after that.'

'Nice to see you suffer,' said Bea. 'You are usually so cool that I could slap you.'

'Not true. I hide my fears under a calm exterior.'

'I bet Phil would love to see you now. Does he know that you have phobias too, like the rest of the human race? Poor lad, he must have quite a bad time trying to find the cracks.'

'I wouldn't know, I haven't heard from him since he left. Security is getting tighter all the time to prevent the enemy knowing what our men are doing. I write to a number in Whitehall and have no idea where he is, but on the Pathé News, we see troops so it can't all be a big secret.'

'Daddy said that the paratroopers landed behind enemy lines last month and brought out valuable intelligence,' said Bea. 'He is in cahoots with a lot of top brass now and hears more than I want to know. I suppose he was interested because of Eddie.'

'He isn't back in England, is he?'

'Back briefly after the marine commando drop but he went away again, almost at once.' Bea frowned. 'Men like Eddie would land up in prison or get themselves hanged in peacetime. He's completely ruthless and very strong. In wartime, they'll make a hero of him. It just doesn't make sense.'

Emma nodded. 'I know what you mean.' She thought of the decadent face, furious with frustration. 'I think he could kill,' she said and shivered. Would Phil have to kill? If he did, at least it wouldn't be hand to hand, seeing the man he attacked. With the remoteness of air attacks, there could be no personal hate.

Wards radiated from the main circular corridor and were divided by gardens which at one time had been cultivated by the patients. The linking main corridor was roofed, but above the low stone walls it was open to the gardens, and no permanent blackout was possible without main structural changes, so at night, small blue lights showed a murky path round the hospital.

An electrically-driven trolley, loaded with dispensary baskets and stores, hummed along the corridor as Emma and Bea explored. 'There must be miles of corridors,' said Emma, 'but it's easy to find each ward from the central hub and the admin buildings.' Nurses wearing the flimsy caps of another hospital walked by and looked at the newcomers with curiosity.

'I suppose we'll get to know them off-duty,' said Bea. 'I wouldn't like to mix with them at work as we shall have to go back to Beatties and the set routine there and we might get confused by other people's methods of teaching.'

'You sound like Tute,' said Emma, laughing. 'They'll have you with a bow under your chin yet!'

'I'm not Sister material,' declared Bea. 'Well, this is yours and I am further along the corridor. Good luck.'

'Men's medical! I'll need luck. Will it be like the Home in Bristol, only with men this time?' She went to report on duty and was given a brief account of what cases were in Ward Ten. Not all chronic sick as she'd imagined but a variety that promised to be more interesting. Even the few skin patients were absorbed into Ward Ten and didn't make for a dismal atmosphere as the other patients jollied them along and told them they looked better even when they didn't.

Emma tried not to stare when she was bathing a man covered with tattoos. It was impossible not to notice the more lurid designs. There were several names of girls on his arms, more covered by the entwined swirls of leaves and hearts and he insisted on showing Emma how the girl on his abdomen belly-danced when he flexed his muscles.

'I can't stay any longer, Mr Coles,' she insisted. 'Sister wants me to do another bed bath.'

He winked. 'Do me tomorrow and I'll tell you where I got these.'

'What is he?' Emma asked the Staff Nurse. 'He seems partly paralysed but otherwise healthy.'

'Mr Coles? Query VD.'

'What! And I've been bathing him without gloves?'

'Don't panic. He's in the tertiary stage, and not contagious, when the infection could be carried on from the primary sore. It's in the blood still, but there is no discharge and the House Physician took a Wassermann test. If he has a positive spirocaete he may go to B-Block. Judging by his tattoos and the highly-coloured accounts of his past life, we have no doubts of the diagnosis and he may have to have malaria therapy.'

'Isn't B-Block where the mental nurses still have a unit?'

'That's right. It's also attached to Professor Shute's unit. He found that syphilis can be killed by raising the body temperature by means of fever. Many of the dangerous fevers can't be used, nor of course the infectious ones, so he gives his patients malaria.' She laughed. 'No, I'm not mad. He breeds mosquitoes which carry the bug and lets them bite the patients to give them malaria. We have had two or three in side-wards here. It's very interesting and the psychiatric nurses do all the treatment. I have followed one or two as I find it fascinating.'

'It sounds like black magic.'

'No, it's all scientific. The mosquito they use is the female anopheles mosquito which is put in a gauze-fronted box and strapped to the arm of the patient until she bites. As soon as the fever mounts, the temperature is allowed to reach one hundred and four degrees – or more if the patient can stand it. Then it is brought down by careful gradual means like tepid sponging. Quinine is used to control the fever between treatments and the spirocaete is killed.'

'Will his paralysis get better?' Emma asked.

'Any permanent damage is there for keeps but if they get them early, they can arrest further loss of function or brain damage.'

'Is this the usual treatment for VD?' asked Emma.

'Only for the neuro-syphilis cases where the disease has attacked the brain and the meninges covering the spinal cord.' She smiled. 'Just bath him and take three quarters of what he tells you with a sack of salt! The other quarter is bad enough and possibly true!'

Emma had a fascinated audience that night in the Common Room. 'He told me the dragon on his chest was done in Hong Kong in a brothel! The coach and horses on his back were done in Germany and the trees on his shoulders were mostly Scandinavian. His one regret was that the girls in Norway were made to behave themselves, whatever that means! I was blushing with embarrassment but to him it was as if he turned the pages of a picture book.' She gulped. 'I turned him over to do his back and there was a hunting scene, with hounds in full cry chasing a fox that had . . . almost disappeared into . . . a hole!'

Bea fell back in her chair, enchanted, but Margaret and two others who had listened wide-eyed were shocked. 'I'd refuse to bath him,' said one nurse.

'Where's all this professional love?' asked Bea. 'You do as Dewar did, powder his bum and ignore the rest.'

At Heath Cross, the rules were easier to bend and at night, the nurses often slipped into the studies attached to wards, where students worked but took time to drink coffee and to put the world to rights. It helped them to make friends and find partners for the weekly dances and companions for tennis and walks on the heath outside the hospital. Paul didn't appear and Emma wondered if Bea had forgotten him as she didn't mention him again.

Phil wrote from India where he was training in Wellington Bombers. He hinted again of marriage as soon as he had home leave and painted a picture of a life that Emma found impossible, but she read his letters carefully and put them away in a cardboard shoe box. Her mother wrote more about her awful friend and pricked Emma's conscience enough to make her spend a precious weekend off in Bristol. She was miserable and longed to go back, even to sorting the soiled linen in the antiquated sluice room on Ward Ten. Her father was even less of a real person to her, spending most of his time fire-watching or drinking beer at the club. She walked across the Downs and saw the Home but that also seemed unreal and she didn't visit it, and when she stepped on to the train back to Heath Cross, she sighed with relief.

Spring came and went, and the emergency hospital was full of operation cases from Beatties and other London hospitals. The evenings were light and Emma no longer feared the empty dark corridors where the silent shapes flitted low and almost touched her cap, and life became predictable and even boring.

'Come on,' said Bea, bursting into her room one day. 'Put that book down and come for a walk. It's time we blew away a few cobwebs. It's a wonderful day and it's dry for a change. Dress up and come on the Heath. We can walk into Epsom and have tea at Fuller's.' Emma fished inside her wardrobe for a skirt and thick stockings that didn't have more than two darns and they walked along the main road and turned off through sodden swathes of last year's bracken through which sprang new shoots of fresh curling green.

'This was a good idea. If only the sea was over there, I'd believe that this was really spring.' Emma laughed. 'From the Heath, I can see life more clearly. I really am getting fond of that shocking old ruin back there.' She flung her scarf ends back into the wind. 'People outside would never believe it, would they? Remember the first time we had baths together? Those terrible rickety screens between the baths fell down and we decided to risk the sight of each other's bodies. I wonder what Sister Cary would say if she knew that three girls shared a bathroom with the baths edged with anti-suicide wooden edges, three in a room?'

'She'd label us raving lesbians and send us to Matron.'

'My mother would be shocked too. But lesbians, no. We all have menfriends. I think we look rather like a Rubens' painting.'

'Maybe Margaret does but we aren't as fat as that,' objected Bea. 'Do you know, I shall hate going back to London now. They were right. This place grows on one.'

So it had to be on that day, after tea and lemon meringue pie at Fuller's in Epsom, that the news came for them to go back to Beatties.

And it had to be on that day that Emma had a letter from her mother. . . . *so Phillip's mother told*

Aunt Emily and asked her to let you know.' Emma fingered the other letter, the one from the Island and wished she'd opened it first. It had been held up in the post and Emma could well imagine her mother rushing to the post office with hers to get the news in first.

Emma read both letters. Aunt Emily said little except to stress that the Air Ministry had reported Phil missing but had made no mention of his being killed or that he was presumed dead. Clare Dewar persisted in saying he was dead and that Emma had been very silly girl. '*If you'd married him, when I said, you'd be a war widow with a good pension by now. An officer's pension isn't to be sneezed at. Mrs Hammond says that those bombers should never have been built. They aren't safe, not like the Beaufighters.*'

Emma tore the letter into small pieces. Life had been drifting along pleasantly. She worked and enjoyed her off-duty, made do with shortages like everyone else, even to buying off-ration blankets to make a new, warm winter coat but where was the drama of nursing? Where was any romance in life?

Why am I so calm, she thought. Why can't I cry? I have no feelings except for a deep regret that a dear friend is gone, maybe for a while, but more likely for ever. If we had made love, would it have been different? I must be frigid by nature, like my mother, she thought with sadness. She sat down to compose a letter to his parents. '*I don't believe that he is dead,*' she wrote. '*I can't believe it and nor must you.*' Reading it they would believe that she was in love with their son, but it might help.

Only then did she weep scalding tears of loneliness that were not only for Phil because she had not loved him as he deserved to be loved.

7

'I'm sick to death of shortages but I'm even sicker of Yanks.'

'You shouldn't go out with so many Bea,' said Emma. 'And think of all those lovely food parcels they've been sending for the past year or so. My aunt on the Island says that some of the tinned meat is very good and they use it in her British Restaurant. Spam is the best and it makes good fritters. She uses canned sausages too, and says that they are encased in fat which she uses to make really good pastry for sausage and egg pies.' She laughed. 'Don't look so disgusted. I know it's awful to find a tin of Spam more precious than something really valuable, like stockings.'

'They needn't make a song and dance over what they do,' muttered Bea.

'Someone *has* upset you, but since the Americans came into the war after Pearl Harbour, you must expect them here in droves. Where else can they have bases for those huge Flying Fortresses? They are very friendly and eager to be liked but they still don't have the edge on many of our men, and you are never short of a date with whatever nationality you choose.' Emma regarded Bea with detachment. 'That's a nice pair of gloves. I haven't seen anything like that since before the war.'

Bea peeled off the fine leather from one hand and tossed it over to the matching handbag. 'Father is doing very well and gets a lot through Switzerland and from the Yanks but he's becoming a bore. He expects me to give up most of my off-duty to help him entertain at the apartment. I sometimes wish the bloody place had been bombed.'

'You have a better time than most, Bea. He's very generous and you eat in all the best places. Where was it last night?'

'The Bagatelle,' said Bea curtly. 'He brought a Wing Commander, two top brass Yanks and a female from the ATS, who looked as if she'd be more at home driving a tank than sitting on one of those dainty velvet chairs by a delicate coffee-coloured table. I told him that if he couldn't bring someone a bit brighter, I'd refuse to go there again. I had heavy men walking all over my feet for *hours*. I said I had to get back before my pass expired and guess what?' Emma shook her head. 'A *jeep*! An American *jeep* arrived complete with driver. Can you imagine me, sandwiched between a puce-faced Colonel with a wandering hand and such a big bum that I had no room to move, and a rather slim and precious Major of marines.' She paused. 'Come to think of it, he couldn't have been all that wet. They're a real tough bunch.'

'You begin to speak their language.'

'Oh, sure thing, baby! Did you ever hear such a misuse of the English language?' She opened her handbag and took out a letter. 'He must be tough. He met up with my cousin and thought him a great guy.'

'What's Eddie doing now?'

'Apart from asking about you, not a great deal in this country. He was in hospital in Kent after being wounded in a raid, but is back now with his unit.' She glanced at Emma's stony face. 'He still wants to meet you again. You must have made a lasting impression. Eddie was always more intrigued by the ones who resisted and as for the ones who got away, *wow*!'

'It's been years. He can't have written that now.'

'Why else would he bother to write to me? I've given you the message but I hope you never set eyes on him again. I can imagine him not wanting to contact you when he was immobile. Pride and all that masculine rubbish, and he had a month all strung up in hospital when he could think of you and plan his campaign. Now when he comes back, all battle-scarred and heroic, he thinks you might change your mind about him and allow a little rape and violence.'

'Don't, Bea. It sends cold shivers up my spine.'

'Any more news of Phil?' asked Bea. 'Maybe I should get you two married after all to save you from a fate worse than death with Eddie.'

'I had a letter from his mother. After he was picked up from the rubber dinghy he was very ill. He'd been drifting for twelve days in the Bay of Bengal and they thought he would die of dysentery. One man in the boat did die and the others have all lost a lot of weight and need hospital treatment.' She moved restlessly. 'What am I to do, Bea? I enjoy my work, I love it here at Beatties and I've a better social life than I thought possible. It's hard, but Phil just doesn't come into my reckoning any more. I cried with relief when I heard he was safe, but mostly because I could imagine his mother's face and I was happy for her. I want to see him again, as a friend, but I couldn't marry him: at least, I think I'm sure.'

'Are you sure you don't want him, Emma? I know you were sure before he went away, and long before that, for about a year, I thought you were waiting for something to happen or someone to come to you. If there is someone else who hasn't materialised, you could easily weave a sort of fantasy over Phil after all he's been through.'

'I'm not in love with Phil even now,' said Emma.

'Then who? There is someone. You're such a

dark horse. I thought I knew you better than most but this is something I can't even guess about. You date a few students and dance and play badminton and have a good time generally, with the occasional cuddle behind the tennis courts, but I haven't seen stars in your eyes after a chaste set of tennis or even after the heavy breathing on the dance floor. Have you been heavy dating one of our transatlantic friends or someone from here?'

'It's nobody. I don't know why you think there is. I did meet someone; well, not really meet him. I suppose encounter would be more true, for a few minutes on three occasions. I don't know his name and I know nothing about him except that he is a doctor in the RAF, but there was something about him.'

'Oh, come on, Emma! You aren't trying to tell me you've fallen for a dream? You can't waste your life lusting after a man you don't know, who has a wife and six kids, more than likely. He must be terribly handsome if he's made all that impression on you.'

'Not really. He has nice eyes and he's tall and slim and you'd approve of his mouth, Bea. I don't even know if I really liked him.'

'*Aha*! Now if you'd said he was wonderful I would have boxed your ears with one of those poetry books you carry everywhere, and told you not to be silly, but I hear that you are attracted to a man whom you don't know enough about to sense if you'd like him, well – that's different. Stupid, but different. You must come out with me more. I have to meet some pals of Pater's tomorrow for lunch. There's a car coming to fetch me and bring me back on the dot, but he has a box in the theatre at the weekend when you and I are both off. He can't use it and wants me to make up a party with two RAF types. If Phil arrives in London, he can come too and you can meet him in a group, where the other people will make it difficult for you to be alone with him.'

'He isn't arriving until Monday, so I can come. Thank you, Bea. I feel a bit down as if I need cheering up and yet I'm not unhappy.'

'Good. You'll like Frankie. He's a medic with the RAF. He used to be at Beatties and may be again after the war. There are several like him. They qualify, join the Forces and then come back after a couple of years to take Fellowship if they can. Frankie's fun, not my type, but fun.'

'You mean that anyone who comes to Beatties in uniform may have trained here or had a house job? Before we went down to Heath Cross, I saw someone like that.'

'Oh, there are several buzzing around. Eddie met one or two of Beatties' men and my father knows several of them, but his friends are the older variety with wives and families. That's so annoying. I have to be nice to all the middle-aged men and none of the young and devastating ones. I can't wait for them to come back from the wars. Don't you find the average student a bit wet after meeting the RAF types and people like one marvellous strong and silent Naval Commander I was allowed to talk to for just half an hour?'

'The students fill in the time for dances and the flicks.'

'Take what's on offer until you find something better, Emma. It's no use dreaming of a man on a white charger or a Chieftain Tank to drag you off to wherever they drag their women these days, now that we seem to have lost most of the Arabian desert to the Germans. The sooner Montgomery sorts them out the better – and he will. My father says his impact on the British Army is almost hypnotic. The average soldier adores him and would follow Monty anywhere as they know he cares about lives and never throws them into battles that will lose lives needlessly.'

'I am quite happy,' Emma protested. 'I shall probably take one look at Phil and decide to marry him and have six horrible children.'

'I can't see it happening. One day you'll fall so hard that you won't know what hit you. I shall be there to see it, I hope and I shall laugh like a drain! I only hope it happens to me too, but I doubt it, so I make life as bright as I can without going too far. It will serve you right to be putty in the hands of a man. Serve you right for being so bloody perfect – the perfect nurse, the perfect saint . . .'

'But not the perfect daughter according to my mother, who does nothing but moan about everything and complains she is lonely as my father keeps out of the house as long as possible and she hardly ever sees him. She spends all her time with a horrible woman who fills her with a lot of half-truths and goads her to be nasty to my father. Do you wonder I hardly ever go home? I wish I could get down to the Island, though. I have a pass now but no time until my holiday.'

'Keep away and never take sides. That's what I do and then they can't use you as a kind of sounding board. Before the divorce, life with them was Hell. They tore me to pieces.' Bea's face seemed to be thinner, her eyes darker. 'I hate them both and yet I'm fond of them separately. Can you understand that? Do you wonder I lap up any praise I can get and any affection offered me? I even like a routine that I can understand, with no drama lurking behind every phrase uttered. I'm flattered by every presentable male and then I hate myself for falling for something that might be false.'

'You never give them a chance to show they are sincere,' said Emma gently. 'How many men have you brushed off during the past few months? Some of the Americans are rather nice, once you've got used to them being larger than life to make up for not coming into the war earlier.'

'I might marry one. That would please my father and send my mother clean round the bend. I rather fancy a tall Marine. He has the same edge of violence that Eddie has but he's more stable and has bags of charm.'

'I hate men who aren't kind.'

'Duckie! When you really fall, you'll take anything, from having your hand kissed to being dragged into a cave by the hair.'

'What does your Marine do in civvy street?'

'I've no idea, but my other beau, Dwight . . . isn't that pure Tennessee Williams? . . . is something in beef.' Emma smiled her disbelief. 'Not a butcher, dear. He has a ranch in Texas, or so he says, but I've been warned to check up on everything they tell me, as even the Privates boast of oil-wells and ranches when some are no more than bellboys. It's all a part of the great American dream that anyone can be President or rich, or both if luck comes his way. At least they do have a dream.'

'Don't we all?'

'Oh, you, Emma! You dream too much and let life slip by. In ten years' time, you'll be a Sister at Beatties with feet that hurt and no love life.'

'Nothing wrong with my feet,' said Emma complacently. 'One minute you're marrying me off to Phil and then putting me into a ward as my hair turns slowly grey. What's wrong with being a Sister? It's been my ambition ever since I came here.'

'Well, before you go into a nunnery, concentrate on what you want to wear tomorrow. We have a box and are being picked up from St James' so we can arrive all elegant and svelte.'

'What are you wearing? I haven't a thing that will look good in a theatre box.'

'Wear that black skirt and the silk blouse. I haven't seen you in it and it's unusual and very pretty. I shall blossom out in a little number that my father brought from Switzerland.'

'I think the blouse is a bit much. Phil sent it from India before he was posted missing and I couldn't bear to wear it while I believed he might be dead.'

'All the more reason to wear it now before you see him and you can say truthfully that it was admired when you wore it. It will be if I know my lecherous old father. He might not be a cradle-snatcher now but he still loves a pretty face.'

Emma pressed the blouse before dressing for the theatre. It was soft and beautifully draped, the colours of the peacock mingling with such tiny gold threads that it was impossible to say that there was gold in it. There was just a sheen of brightness that was discreet and glowing, showing nothing of the more usual gaudy Indian designs.

Bea gave a coarse wolf-whistle. 'I'm not wearing it if it gives that impression,' said Emma. 'It's bad enough walking across Leicester Square in a dark coat and low heels. The last time I went up for a press show at the cinema in the middle of the morning, I was accosted three times by American soldiers, all chewing gum and looking at women as if they were cattle there for the prodding.'

'That's one end of the scale. We have them in our Forces, too. They can't be choosy as to who enlists or is conscripted and we have men from every background. They take anyone who can walk straight and see a tree at five yards. The Yanks have much more money than our men and think they can buy anything, but some are fun and they do know how a woman likes to be treated. I like their lack of inhibitions.'

'Like having fat Colonels grope you in a Jeep?' said Emma. 'I thought you'd gone off Yanks.'

'Not them. I can handle that easily. Dwight isn't like that. He's so big he could crush a bear but he's gentle.' Her eyes were dreamy.

'Bea, I do think you are falling for him. I thought you were set on the Marine with the charming violence,' Emma teased.

'It's funny, but I know that Dwight wouldn't stand for my usual nonsense. Under that beautiful calm façade he's strong and any woman married to him would have to play fair.' She was serious. 'I couldn't fool around. I'd have to behave and I think I might want to. He's the only one who hasn't made a serious pass at me.'

'Married? Maybe he has a girl?'

'He looks at me sweetly and opens doors. He's a good man and I shall louse it up and be left with someone like the Marine.'

'Is he coming tonight?'

'No, it's just the four of us. Should be fun having men we can control instead of ones with just one thing on their minds. They are my father's guests and know that this is a duty date for me. In any case, I prefer our own lot for blind dates. I can relax and know I shan't be expected to look at their etchings.'

Emma examined her stocking seams in the triple mirror of the apartment in St James'. Her skirt was well-fitting, showing how much necessity had taught her to make her own clothes in a professional manner. She shook back her hair, unused to the light feeling it had now that it was released from the French pleat that held it on duty. It made a lot of difference to her appearance and she felt slightly reckless. She dabbed perfume behind her ears and thought it appropriate for the RAF. It was Bea's perfume, of course. Who else obtained it in wartime?

'*Skyhigh,* and not at all bad, if one had never

known Chanel and Worth,' Bea said. 'Could you answer that before people think it's an alert?' she added as a prolonged shrill on the bell told her that their escorts had arrived.

Two immaculate men in uniform stood there, smiling. Emma called Bea and was puzzled by her own disappointment. They were good-looking and from the glances she received were very pleased with what they saw. What had she expected? A face she remembered? How stupid. Of all the RAF medics, why should it be him?

'I thought Frankie was coming,' said Bea.

'Your father said there was room for six and invited along a Yank whom Frankie is meeting first. Bad show! I hoped we'd have you two all to ourselves.' He smiled and Emma warmed to him. He was like Phil or rather like Phil used to be before he had asked her to sleep with him, and she knew that if she hinted that she had a boyfriend, he would respect this.

'Who's the Yank?' asked Bea. 'I've had enough of them for a while.'

'Good. That's what we like to hear,' said David, who had the badge of a medic on his uniform. 'Shall we walk? It's a fine night. I can fetch the car later to bring you back if you like.'

'If you have a car, then we use it,' said Bea firmly. 'I have no intention of ruining my hair and arriving like a scarecrow.' She smoothed her shining blonde hair and shrugged into a dark beaver lamb coat, sending a cascade of gold over the soft fur, fully aware of the effect. Emma picked up her coat, knowing it couldn't compare with Bea's throw-away elegance, but not displeased with her own work. Two soft beige blankets had made a very expensive-looking coat and she had trimmed the collar with ocelot-printed rabbit fur and covered an old clutch bag with the same fur.

The theatre still managed to generate the atmosphere of London at night. Bea's father met them for a drink in the bar before rushing off to a waiting car that would take him to yet another ministerial meeting 'somewhere in England'. The blouse was perfect and Emma was treated to a kiss on the cheek and a squeeze of the hand as he whispered, 'If I was only twenty years younger.'

It was pleasant to sit in the dimly-lit box and enjoy the well-upholstered chairs redolent of past luxury. Emma looked down at the uniforms and simple clothes that were so different from the view of the auditorium years ago when bejewelled women in silks and velvets must have thronged a much more fashionable and brilliantly-lit theatre. The dark olive, well-tailored jackets of American officers mingled with the drab khaki and navy blue and lighter Air Force blues, and splashes of colour were rare. As the orchestra began the overture, and the theatre lights dimmed even more, Emma heard the door at the back of the box open and close and sensed that two men slipped into the seat behind her. She noticed that the American was very tall and the other man was RAF and then turned her attention to the stage.

The play was a riotous farce by Phillip King, who worked on the principle that people laughed at funny vicars. He had so many that they seemed to pop out of every door and into every cupboard. *See How They Run* was the perfect antidote to shortages and aching hearts. From the back seats of the box, Emma was aware of deep and satisfying laughter, a good sound that hinted at a pleasant voice. She wondered if the man's face would match his voice but when she looked round at the interval when the lights brightened, he had gone.

'Frankie went to get drinks,' said David. 'If you don't get to the bar early, it's murder. The best thing about a box is that you can slip away without disturbing anyone.' The door opened and David took the tray and put it down on a seat. 'No shorts? Sorry,' he said. 'Oh, by the way, have you met Dwight, this great hunk of America, and Frankie.' He grinned. 'Not much good at getting decent drinks but a useful guy.' He seemed to think he'd made a joke.

'We have met,' said Frankie.

'Briefly,' said Emma stiffly.

'Well, grab a beer if you can drink it. Might warm you up.' David gave an exaggerated shiver and a look of mock alarm. 'It's chilly all of a sudden.'

Emma forced a smile. 'Thanks, I'd love some beer. I've got used to it, but when I first tasted it I thought it was awful.' Beer and buttercups, Phil had said, but he was just a part of the dream she had of the Island. He belonged to the past.

'Emma Dewar, I believe,' said Frankie. 'I did manage to get some crisps but avoided the sandwiches which were pretty foul-looking paste. Crisps are at least a little more aseptic.' He was talking but saying nothing, and his eyes were without expression as if he was undertaking a civil duty.

I wish someone would tell me his full name, Emma thought. Frankie doesn't really suit him. Maybe it was Francis or a nickname or Frank was a surname. She sipped the warm beer and laughed at Dwight's disgust. 'Doesn't any place have ice over here?' he asked plaintively.

Bea sat elegantly on the edge of a chair, nibbling potato crisps after dipping each one daintily into the tiny blue packet of salt that each envelope contained. She could be eating caviar, thought Emma, suddenly amused. Bea would rather die than drink beer with men, even if she was very thirsty after eating all that salt.

Dwight sat awkwardly as if his hands were too

large to manage the popcorn he produced. Bea condescended to try one and helped herself to more and he looked delighted. Emma knew that under Bea's downcast eyelids lurked a malicious and completely aware triumph of the havoc she was causing, but when she looked up, she was ingenuous and fragile. She could wind him round her little finger, Emma decided, and hoped she was serious about him.

The lights went down again and any tension in the box subsided and Emma heard the low laugh again that made her own lips twitch even when her full attention wasn't on the play. He had a good face but his eyes had told her that he had no intention of sharing his thoughts with her.

The curtains came down for the last time, the rush out of the theatre began and the party in the box waited until the exists were no longer jammed. Emma turned to pick up her coat and found it held ready for her. 'Thank you,' she said quietly. Firm fingers settled the garment over her shoulders and touched her hair. Hair has no feeling. Hair is dead tissue, so how could it conduct such tension between two people who had no mutual feelings of liking or disliking? She buttoned the collar and they were the last to leave the box. There were scraps of sweet papers in the grubby corridor that led to the side exit and a smell of cats and dirty blackout curtains followed them into the outer air. Above them hung a nearly full moon.

'Bombers's moon,' she said, almost to herself.

'They won't send him on ops yet,' he said.

'Who?'

'Your boyfriend, or are you married by now?' He took her left hand in his lightly, to inspect the ring finger. 'Not even an engagement ring? Surely South Africa was the place to find more diamonds than a girl could dream of.'

'I'm not interested in diamonds, and marriage in wartime is a mistake,' Emma said, firmly.

'If you were in love, it wouldn't matter if the sky fell, but I suppose you are right. It's not much of a bargain for a girl if the man was killed or came back maimed and helpless. He might be taken prisoner and be away for years and no man could expect a girl wait to for ever.' He sounded sad as if he knew all about it. He still held her hand as if he had forgotten he held it and Emma didn't draw away. He might not like her but his touch was warm and comfortable as if he had known her for a long time.

'Prisoners of war have every right to expect their girls to be faithful,' said Emma.

'From a sense of duty? Because she felt guilty? No Emma, that's not a good reason, but if she was truly in love, she would wait until he came back or died.'

'And if she wasn't in love or wanted to forget him?'

'She should have the guts to tell him before he went away or wait until he was safely back and could handle it. Men cling to anything that reminds them of home. It's easier to forget if he knows that he hasn't a chance, but if he has letters and photographs saying "I love you", then he has every right to dream and to find her waiting.' He checked on the edge of the pavement. 'It looks as if we are walking back. David and Sean wanted to go on to a club. Do you mind putting up with my company? I think that Dwight wants Bea all to himself for a while.'

Emma walked more slowly to let Bea and Dwight get ahead. 'Why are you talking to me as if I have a boyfriend in a Stalag? You don't know me.' Her resentment sharpened her voice. 'You sound as if you are accusing me of something.'

'Rubbish! You're right, I don't know you, but I

do have friends in 99 squadron who are posted in India waiting for the Japs to hot up the war.'

'And they know Phil?'

Frankie nodded. 'I assume that he was the man with you the first time I saw you?'

'The second time,' said Emma.

He laughed. 'I wasn't counting the taxi but I'm glad you haven't forgotten that.'

'Do go on,' she said coldly. 'I assume you know a lot more about my friend Phillip Scantal than I do.'

'Ouch! You make me sound as if I've been spying on you. But have you noticed, you meet someone or see a name in a newspaper that you have never seen anywhere and then you hear the name several times?' She nodded. 'A friend of mine was engaged to a girl – there was a ring, promises and everything. He went down over Germany and is now in a prison camp. He writes to her when he can, but she is having a ball with every American she can use to get nylons, chocolates and canned meats. She wears his ring as a kind of protection if she doesn't want to go all the way.'

'What has this to do with me and Phil? We aren't engaged, and I'm not like that!'

'He knew Phil, and his closest friend George was with Phil in that open boat. Phil was one of two who had someone waiting, or so he thought. George said that after that ordeal they had few secrets from each other and he hoped that Phil would fare better than his friend. I went down to the base hospital to see George and in fact saw all four of them. I could go in uniform which made it official even when civilians including relatives had no access to the survivors until they had been treated and de-briefed.'

'Only four? How many were there? Were they killed on the plane?'

'Six got out. Phil nearly went when he tried to

free a man caught by a Kriss knife he carried as a souvenir. When the plane came down, it floated for a few minutes but the doors were submerged. Two died of heat stroke on the inflatable and the others were in a very bad way.'

'I had no idea,' Emma whispered. 'Have you seen any of them lately?'

'No. You haven't seen any wounded yet, have you?'

'I've seen some from the Blitz who were brought to the wards.'

'All tidied up or have you been in casualty?'

'I'm due for theatre soon. But Phil wasn't wounded. He had dysentery and exhaustion and they say he has lost a lot of weight.'

Fankie gave a short laugh. 'The understatement of the year. As I said, I haven't really met Phil, but I saw him with the others and he knows I'm from Beatties.' He glanced at her under the sombre blue light of the shaded lamp-post. 'He's suffered, Emma, so if you love him, tell him. He needs comfort.' He sounded distant as if saying what he knew was right, but having no real inclination to say it. It was doctor talking to patient, not friend to friend.

'I've said I am not engaged to him. I've given him no promises and in spite of all you are hinting, with that fictitious talk of a girl going around with Yanks for what she could get out of them, I am *not* on the make!'

He stopped and lit a cigarette. 'I'm sorry. You are very angry and that isn't what I intended. I just wanted to warn you that he might not be as you remember him and if you don't love him then for God's sake let him down lightly. I'd give the same advice to any relative of any patient of mine. They wanted to avoid making them see psychiatrists at this stage as it might have done more harm than good. Some of them are a bit heavy-handed and to suspect that the powers-that-be think you are a nut as well as a physical wreck can't be very reassuring.'

He held her arm as they crossed the road but his touch was no longer warm and companionable. He rang the bell and turned to her. 'I'm a blundering idiot and I hate to see you look at me like that, Emma. I hate to see anyone hurt when it can be avoided – even me,' he added as Bea flung open the door.

'Come on, you two. Where have you been? Dwight was getting worried about you, weren't you, darling?' I hope the poor fool knows that she calls every good-looking man Darling, thought Emma, and tried to shake off the guilt and depression that Frankie had loaded on to her so efficiently.

No, I wasn't worried,' said Dwight and grinned. 'But as you're here, you can share the champagne.'

'Isn't it wonderful, Emma? Dwight brought two bottles, really for Daddy but what the eye doesn't see!' Her eyelashes fluttered and she was a little girl stealing a jam tart. Dwight looked adoring and Bea produced tulip glasses from a cabinet while he skilfully realeased the cork with a satisfying report and poured.

Bea's eyes were overbright and held a challenge. 'I adore Champers. It's the only really civilised drink, isn't it, Emma?' There was a question and a warning in the laughter, and Emma sensed her relief when she picked up her glass and gazed at the bubbles. Champagne, in fine crystal this time and not the thick glasses in the restaurant in Bristol the night that Evans and her brother drank with her; not the fine dry half-bottles that the dying were given at the Home.

'It's the one drink I find different,' said Emma and drank. The bubbles teased her nose, the cool perfection took away the taste of beer and the salty roughness of the crisps. Tomorrow when she met

Phil she must face the past. Tomorrow, she must tell Phil that they had no future together, but tonight she was drinking champagne with a man who had done no more than take her hand casually, and had upset her and made her feel sad and guilty. I may never see him again. 'Where do you go from here?' she asked.

He lounged in the deep armchair and looked at her. 'Who knows?'

Emma sat on a bar stool uncomfortably aware of her tight skirt and exposed knees, but unable to sit in the low chairs with any dignity, as she had discovered on previous visits. She slid back and slumped into the cushions if she tried to sit on the edge, erect. Bea too, avoided the chairs, calling them necking chairs for heavy petting and not for sitting in, a relic of her father's former conquests.

The carved semi-circle of mahogany that concealed the drinks cabinet had mirrors behind it reflecting the delicate porcelain and flowers on the early French escritoire. 'I'm sorry I asked,' said Emma. 'Nobody in the Forces ever admits to going anywhere.' The champagne warmed her and she smiled. 'Sometimes I wish I could be mysterious. I could ask Bea's cousin to drop me behind enemy lines and if I came back, I could tap the side of my nose and impress people, too.'

'You'd make a beautiful spy,' said Frankie. 'I go home first and then out of the Service and on to the Reserve if they can spare me. I haven't been told where I am to report after that.'

'But surely, they need you in the RAF even more than they did at the begining of the war?'

'Not in the field so much, but if we are to fight back and win, we shall have most of the wounded here in Britain. I shall be busier as a civilian surgeon than signing forms in Whitehall.'

'I didn't know you were a surgeon.'

He smiled with real humour. 'Emma Dewar, you don't know everything. Even if, as I hear, you are one of the best half-dozen nurses in training at this time.' He went to the bar and filled her glass, topping up his own. Giggles came from the kitchen where Dwight was helping Bea to make sandwiches. Frankie looked at his watch. 'If you want some more to drink, you'd better hurry before we finish it,' he called.

He's bored with me and vaguely disapproving. He can't wait for the others to come back and break up what he considers a dead date. 'I know nothing about you,' Emma said, as if it wasn't really important.

'And you'd rather keep it that way?' He raised his glass. 'Do *you* know where you're going? Don't leave it too late, Emma. Don't waste your potential.'

'You said you'd heard I'm a good nurse, so I'm not wasting my time.'

'That's not what I mean,' he said.

8

'How did it go?' Bea plastered oily margarine on to the thick grey bread that a hopeful Government had decreed was good for the nation. Emma pushed the last piece of potato to the side of her plate and took a slice of bread, covering it with her own supply of chocolate spread, a gift from Aunt Emily who managed to get such luxuries as a perquisite when working as supervisor of the British Restaurant on the island. 'May I?' said Bea, already helping herself. 'You seem to have been away for ages but if you bring this back, you can go away again.'

'He's ill,' said Emma. 'Much worse than I had imagined, even after Frankie hinting at what I ought to expect. He sat as if about to take flight and hardly ate a thing.' She filled her mouth with glutinous bread, to give her time to think. It had been terrible. To begin with, she hadn't even recognised him until he touched her arm and called her name.

'Phil!' she'd said as if she had just seen him and not been pitying the side view of the thin, nervy-looking Squadron Leader who kept looking at his watch as he waited at the entrance to the National Gallery.

'Hello, Emma.' Even his voice was different. He's completely changed, she thought, horrified. He can't be the same man – not Phillip Scantal, the solid and calm man I've known for years. She was all too aware of her own resilient health, her clear skin and firm hands. He held her hand and seemed uncertain if he was to kiss her. Impulsively, she reached up and offered her lips and he brushed them with cold lips before kissing her cheek, almost formally.

'Let's sit down. I've rushed and I'm tired,' she lied. He obeyed with a thankful sigh, and she saw the quick respirations and the pulse beating in his thin neck. The collar of his uniform shirt was far too large and the once well-fitting jacket hung as if made for a man many stones heavier.

'Let me look at you.' That was more like his voice. 'I've waited for this for such a long time. You look wonderful. You've changed but you are even more wonderful.' He took her left hand. 'Not engaged, or anything, while I was missing?'

God! He isn't wasting time!

'You suggested meeting here,' he went on. 'Do you want to look round or have something to eat?'

'There's an exhibition of war artists,' she said. Bea had mentioned it and said that Dwight was so fascinated that he wanted to buy some pictures to send home, believing that a picture of the London Underground at night might be salutary for his insular and ignorant friends. The gallery made a good excuse for Emma to meet Phillip in public while they both got their bearings. Emma had talked about the exhibition with the two men and she had mentioned some of the new poets emerging as well as new artists. Frankie, or Mr Guy Franklin, as Emma now knew him to be, had listened silently as Bea teased her about her love of the Romantic poets, but he quietly told her not to miss the exhibition. 'It shows the reality of war,' he said. 'Everyone should see it.'

'I hear it's good and worth a glance,' she said now to Phil. 'We can leave if it's boring.'

'How civilised! A picture gallery and tea at Lyons before you have to get back.' The irony was hardly apparent. They walked up the broad stairway and followed the arrows. A long dust-coloured mural confronted them. It seemed a blur of indistinct shapes that emerged as recognisable figures only when your eyes became used to the dusk in the picture. Sleeping bodies in every posture of exhaustion, despair and innocent rest were a part of the rough-cast background, the vague advertisements and the empty tunnel mouth of a London Underground station.

They walked past pictures of the Battle of Britain, with Hurricanes and Spitfires against a scarred blue sky. Emma wished she had never mentioned the exhibition. She tried to deflect Phil's attention from a Lysander aircraft on Air Sea Rescue, over a drifting dinghy to which a launch was speeding, with the aircraft showing the position of the inflatable, but Phil stood before it, oblivious to her or anything but the picture. She went on, hoping he would follow but the next picture was of a pilot, blindfolded, in limbo over the Dover coast, his bandaged hands holding a rose towards wrecked France. It was all horrifying when seen with Phil and not what she had expected.

They should have warned me, she thought bitterly, but they didn't know she meant to bring Phil here. Frankie had said with a twist to his smile, 'It's the reality of war, Emma. It exists and overflows with pain and suffering and misery and ... heroism. You should see it. It gives a glimpse of what happens and in its own way it *is* poetry. It makes the Romantics seem trite and faded.'

She had countered by saying that the old poets spoke of beauty and suffering. They had a message just as valid as modern war poetry with its message of the futility of killing, but he had shaken his head as if she was shallow and had no experience or understanding. This goaded her into asking, 'What do you know about it? Have you ever been wounded? Have you been on active service, dropped from a plane or trapped in a burning tank?'

'I've dropped twice,' he said. 'And suffered nothing more than a broken ankle.'

'Then how can you know?'

'You forget I am a doctor. I've been in a casualty station at Dunkirk and I saw enough then to know what happens. I've also been to East Grinstead to the burns unit and seen the miracles that Macindoe and his team are doing rebuilding limbs and faces and courage. See the exhibition – for it tells you about the war you may never see.'

And now, she had this pale drawn face beside her, with gaunt eyes devouring the pictures as if to see his own reflection. 'I haven't much time,' she said gently. 'Let's get some tea.' She wanted to ask if he could manage the walk to the Coventry Street Lyon's Corner House, but sensed his dread of dependence. 'Look, it says there is a tea-room here. It will save time and I can get a bus outside when I have to leave.'

'Your mother told me that you are going home for a week. I rang to let them know I was back.' His eyes seemed to bore into her soul. 'When is it, Emma? I'm on long leave and we could get married. That week could be our honeymoon.'

'I haven't said I'll go home. Nothing has been settled although I do have some leave due.'

'You have the time, your mother is more than willing to put me up and I love you. It seems simple to me.' He crumpled the empty cigarette packet and Emma noticed that he had smoked all ten since they had sat there in the tea-room, lighting one from the stub of the other.

'I was hoping to go to the Island.'

'I thought you were refused a pass,' he said sharply.

'Aunt Emily managed to get me one after talking

to the policeman I told you about. It's ages since I've seen Aunt Emily and I long to walk on the cliffs and smell the sea.'

'I've seen water . . . a lot of water.'

'What about your family? You must see more of them. What can they think of you staying in London now, when they have missed you so much?' She leaned forward. 'It isn't that I don't want to be with you Phil, for a holiday, but I can't stand it at home any more. It's never been a home to me. I've felt like a tolerated lodger each time I'm there unless there is another person about, when my mother is all sweetness and even speaks to my father. They are pure Hell together.'

He seized her hand. 'If I go to my parents and rest, will you promise to come to the Island for your leave?'

'I'll come and stay with Aunt Emily and we'll see each other, Phil, but be fair, I've never said I'll marry you.'

'Emma, I've dreamed of you, thought of you and wanted you . . . God, how I've wanted you. Once on the raft, when I was hallucinating, you were there with me, holding me. I can *make* you love me.' He crushed out his cigarette end. 'But I will give you time. I know I'm a wreck now, but each day I feel better and then after a while, we'll see.' His hand felt firmer and his smile held more spirit. 'You do know when you have leave, don't you?'

Reluctantly, she nodded. 'I go in three weeks' time,' she said.

'That gives me time to recoup. You will see the old Phillip when you step off the ferry. Perhaps you will find him more attractive?'

Emma had to run for her bus, after Phil said he thought he'd go home at once, as he couldn't face London even for Emma, and she sighed now as Bea took a huge heap of more chocolate spread.

'It was impossible. I just couldn't get it across to him that it wasn't his weakness and appearance that made me unwilling to marry him. He thinks that once he has regained his strength I shall fall into his arms. I haven't changed, Bea. I never said I loved him, not once! I know now that I never could marry him even out of pity.'

Bea wiped her knife blade on a dainty finger and licked off the chocolate. 'Don't be so sure. Who knows what will happen one fine evening when you get back to all that awful fresh air and birds you drivel on about. It could make you feel romantic and give you the odd urge for something more than hand-holding and a quick fumble.'

'I do know. I can't love Phil and I have a feeling that I might even be unlucky like him and never love anyone who can return my love.'

Emma thought of Bea as the train took her slowly to Southampton, stopping at every small halt. It was easy for her to hide her feelings under a flippant manner. Bea was clever and could manipulate people. Look how Dwight dissolved into jelly every time she gave him a kind word. If I wasn't so honest it would be easy. I could soon convince Phil that I had queues of men lining up after me and I just wanted a good time with no strings attached. If there was another man who really wanted me, I could make him the excuse for not loving Phil, but I'm not going to use Eddie's name or he might suddenly materialise through some kind of mental telepathy!

She watched the countryside but saw little and wasn't curious. Each time that Phil had asked if there was someone, she had been forced to say no, and he was convinced that it was only a matter of time before she gave in to him. In all their telephone calls, he harped on this one subject and she dreaded meeting him again.

The windows were grimy and the upholstery held pre-war dust. Dog-ends and sweet wrappings littered the carriage floor and although the coach was officially a non-smoker, four hefty soldiers smoked a powerful brand of cigarettes and offered them to her. She smiled and shook her head, but was soon talking freely with them. The contact with all kinds of men in the ward had made this simple and she listened to their tales with the same easy humour that she found so much a routine at Beatties. In a way they were her patients, telling her, a stranger, of their hopes and fears in a way that was often difficult with friends and relatives.

'Where can we go when we have time off?' asked one who knew nothing of the Island or of the huge barracks at Albany and Parkhurst. She told them of good places, and when they hinted that they'd like her to show them around, she smiled and said her boyfriend wouldn't like it. It seemed unfair to hide behind Phil in this manner but it did mean that stray men accepted that she was taken and didn't often press for more.

The soldiers insisted on helping her on to the ferry with her case even though they were loaded up with their own equipment, and when she was settled, brought her a beer. Emma bought stodgy sausage rolls for everyone and they sat in the bow on coils of rope, munching and watching Southampton Water. Where were all the small craft that sailed with sparkling paint and white sails? Where were the big liners with farewell streamers breaking against the sides of the dock and the ship as bands played '*Will Ye No Come Back Again*'? Where was anything of lightness and beauty? The soldiers sank into a kind of dumb apathy like the figures in the pictures of the Underground. The salt smell was the same, the gulls shrieked a welcome but the shore of the Isle of Wight was hidden behind a high barrier of corrugated iron and lumps of concrete as far as she could see along the coast, once they reached the open sea from Southampton Water.

'Strewth! I heard there was something hush-hush going on here, but they don't mean anyone to take photographs of whatever it is,' said one of the soldiers.

Emma joined the long queue of passengers who had to show passes and give details of where they were staying and why they were on the Island. To her surprise, she was asked only to fill in her address on a form and was waved on. The power of school friends and one quiet woman was not to be underrated.

Phil was waiting on the quay at Cowes. He was wearing a pair of grey flannel trousers and an open-necked shirt. His eyes were brighter and he had put on a little weight, although he was still painfully thin. He showed her his car with pride – a secondhand MG with more noise than speed, but as the wind blew through her hair, Emma laughed and felt the old sense of homecoming.

'It's so good to be back,' she shouted. He changed gears noisily. 'I want to see it all again before I go back to London. Is it really yours? What about petrol? Can you use it when you like?'

'At last I've found a way to her heart! Yes, if you behave, you shall go to Freshwater tomorrow. I have plenty of petrol coupons because I am off sick and on special leave.' He laughed and a little colour showed in his cheeks. 'They'd have supplied a driver and an official car if I'd wanted one. Crazy, isn't it?'

'No, I think you deserve all they can give you, Phil.'

'Of course, my mother and I suspect yours too, think I should be given a gong and be made Air Marshal, when all I did was to survive after falling in the water.' There was an elation he'd lacked at their first meeting, as if the role of returning hero wasn't unpleasant. Emma sniffed the air and watched the unkempt hedgerows flash past and the apples ripening in the orchards. Some of his vitality had returned and it was good to feel a warm and human male by her side.

After leaving her case at Aunt Emily's house, they drove on to Ryde and walked along the sea wall as far as the military restrictions allowed and followed the tide as it went out across the shallow sands. It was warm and the water ran in tiny rivers back to the sea, teeming with tiny shrimps and small fry. Emma took off her shoes and stockings and paddled, chasing the shrimps and letting the sand run between her toes. Phil took out a cigarette case then put it back in his pocket and peeled off his socks and joined her in the shallow pools.

They followed the tide out for nearly half a mile and they were alone with the Island, the past and the uneasy present. It was no time to think of the future and Emma hoped that Phil would give it a rest. There had been little bombing since the operation called 'Starfish', in which enemy bombs were attracted to places away from vital targets, or since the time when sticks of bombs unused inland had to be jettisoned by German bombers before returning to bases in France, and fell on the Island. The sky was empty and the sand was unsullied, smooth and shining and innocent. Emma scraped the sand and came up with two cockles. Phil laughed and helped her dig for more, filling his handkerchief and her scarf.

'We'll leave them to shed sand in a bucket of water tonight and can cook them tomorrow,' said Emma. 'Aunt Emily loves cockles but I doubt if she's had time or energy to gather them for ages.' She brushed sand from her feet as they sat on the sea wall. 'I feel that I'm really here,' she said. Phil put an arm round her shoulder and kissed her lips. She smiled. He was a part of it, her Island, her youth and her innocent friendships and his kiss had made no demands. 'Come on, let's surprise Aunt Emily and collect her in your MG,' she said. 'It's quite a long walk home for her after a day at the British Restaurant.'

'What a treat,' exclaimed Emily Darwen later. 'My feet are a bit bad today. No, I don't think I want to eat anywhere but in my own home tonight, if you don't mind.' She laughed. 'They got me to inspect some of the hotel kitchens and I know what goes on in there so I'd be wondering if they washed their hands before putting out the cold meats.'

She sat back in the car with relief and Emma felt a moment of panic. She looked old and tired and not as bright as her manner indicated. She couldn't change, could she? She must not change. In a world that killed and altered and soiled, Aunt Emily must stay for ever, to be there. She insisted on being left while they went for a meal in a hotel. 'Now have something more than a cup of tea and a biscuit,' Emma said, scolding her.

'We'll see. You have a nice meal and then send him home. That young man isn't fit yet,' she said. 'And I want to talk to you.'

The hotel that Aunt Emily scorned was as Emma remembered it, with fresh local fish on the menu and fruit from local farmers. Butter appeared in unrationed quantities, and there was real cream with the apple pie. Phil ate quite well and smoked only one cigarette while they drank mediocre coffee in the lounge before he left Emma and went home to his parents.

'Well,' said Aunt Emily. 'You don't look as if you need a holiday.'

'You do. Can't you take any time off while I'm

here and have breakfast in bed for a change? Or you could go to Bristol. Mother mentioned it once or twice.'

'I'm all right here. I like to sleep in my own bed and your mother keeps a cold house.' Emma made more tea and split the sticky binding round a tin of Swiss biscuits that Bea had sent with her love, although she had never met Emily Darwen. Aunt Emily sat with her swollen feet on a stool and took her time in choosing a rich chocolate concoction. 'If you brought these each time, I could do with you more often,' she told her niece. 'All that good coffee, too. I won't ask where it came from but I hope you didn't make any sacrifices for me.' It was her way of saying, 'I love you and have missed you more than I can say,' and Emma knew exactly what she meant.

'Well, I didn't sell my virtue to the Yanks,' said Emma, laughing. 'Not even for the nylons. I've brought some emergency ration cards, too, and a tin of sugar as I never take it in tea and you like everything sweet.'

'What about Clare?'

'Mother has plenty. I gave her the last ones and the RAF boys get her some extras. They still use her telephone and bring tins of Spam and dried eggs and powdered milk.' She refilled her aunt's cup and pushed the biscuit tin closer. 'Tomorrow, I'll do any housework you need doing and see to the shopping,' she said firmly.

'Are you telling me, or asking me?' The old snapping humour was there. 'That young man has other ideas, I'll be bound. He looks as if he's got the wind in his tail today. Didn't like his looks when he came down first but you seem to have done something to him. Hope you haven't, though.'

'Why do you hope that?'

'He's too sober for you. He's good and kind and

will make someone a fine husband one day, but a uniform isn't everything. It doesn't alter a man, not deep down, and wars end some day, even this one. Uniform only colours him for a while and then he'll be exactly like his father.' Her dark eyes had a glint of malicious humour. 'Yes, he's a good man, but not for you any more than his father was for me.'

'Aunt Em, you old fraud! You never told me.'

'Why should I? I was never one for talking about people, not like your mother.' She sipped her tea with maddening pauses.

'Well?' prompted Emma.

'He was sweet on me once, after the last war when I had decided that marriage wasn't for me and I was comfortable with your Gran in the big house on the Mall. Don't torment yourself if Phillip seems upset when you send him away.'

'You think I will send him away?'

'You are too like me. He isn't for you, Emma, and when he gets over it, he'll think it was his decision. Don't be blackmailed into marrying him because he looks like something the tide left behind. I wasn't, and I've never regretted it. You just remember, my girl! It was *me* refused his father, not the other way round, but now you'd think he'd never come after me, all hot breath and damp hands.'

'Phil has nice hands.'

'That's as maybe.'

'Did you ever regret it?' Emma sat by the small fire that Emily Dewar liked to see burning even in summer, and hugged her knees looking like the child that Emily had loved since birth. 'No regrets, honestly? I know you stayed to look after Gran, but you could have married.'

'I do regret tying myself during the First War. We had the shop but they could have managed without me even when the others left, but after the war it didn't matter and I was content. I should have done the other thing.'

'What other thing?' Emma persisted.

'If I thought it would help you, I'd tell you.' She shook the tin until a long chocolate biscuit surfaced, her eyes gleaming with pleasure. 'This is nice. You know I like a good biscuit better than a steak.'

'What other thing, Aunt Emily?'

'There was a man once and I wanted him but I didn't take what I wanted until it was too late, and then he died. He was good and kind too, but different. For me, anyway. You'll never know who it was, so don't be nosy, but when you meet someone like that, grab him while you can and turn a deaf ear to everyone if they don't like it.' Her fingers shook and she took two biscuits instead of one.

'Was he killed?'

'He died in the last lot and I had waited too long.'

Emma made even more strong black tea into which her aunt put a least four spoonsful of sugar and a splash of whisky. She seemed to have recovered and was in the mood for talking.

'And if I find him and he doesn't want me?' Emma asked.

'Make him.' Emma shook her head, remembering Guy Franklin watching her and not smiling.

'Looked in the mirror, lately? You've blossomed, Emma. No need to sell yourself cheap. You can have anything you want if you want it enough. You get anything if you are prepared to fight. Your Gran was a fighter and I am a bit like her but not as strong.' She chuckled. 'I saw some of those books you brought here. You fill your mind with romantic nonsense, while men think of the flesh.' She laughed when Emma blushed. 'Didn't think I knew about the flesh, did you? Aging spinster aunt who shouldn't know about sex?' She put down the heavy crochet lace on which she was working. 'It isn't all soft lights and sweet music, and if you don't want the rest, you lose everything. Not that you must give yourself just to test your own reactions. That's sinful!' She smoothed out the last two feet of the intricate lace and Emma picked up a handful and examined it.

'It's lovely. I haven't seen this before and it must have taken ages.'

'I started it for your mother during the last war but I knew she wouldn't use it. It's for you now and when it's done it will edge a double bedspread with ten inches of lace.'

'I'd better get married,' said Emma.

'I shall do the last few inches when I know who he is and not before, and it won't be for Philip. You look tired, and I think I'll sleep tonight.'

'How do I know?' begged Emma.

'You don't need me to tell you. When he comes, you'll know. At least, when he touches you and kisses you and wants more and more and you want to give, it'll be like all the angels in Heaven pouring warm treacle down your back, or so my mother said,' she added, with twinkle.

'I'm not sure that I like treacle,' said Emma. 'You go up and I'll wash these things.' She laid the table for breakfast and dried the dishes in the drainer, emptied the faded flowers from a vase and washed the stale smell of dead stems out of the sink. I'll get up and tidy around in the morning, she resolved. It was easy to gear her brain to thinking she was on duty at six-thirty.

There was dew on the grass as she picked roses from the bush she remembered as a child, ox-eye daisies and spikes of phlox. She filled two vases and laid a tray for Emily, cutting thin bread and butter and poaching two eggs that Phil had left for her. As she watched her aunt sip the first cup of tea, propped up in bed with a shawl round her shoulders, she thought again how frail she looked and wanted to scoop her up and carry her away to somewhere safe and restful, but she knew that this was where her aunt wanted to be and she was doing what needed to be done. No one had a right to interfere.

'What a rest!' Emily said. 'I hope this isn't a flash in the pan! I shall expect this every morning, now.' She was smiling and teasing but Emma knew just how thrilled she was to be pampered.

'I thought it time that *someone* stirred, and I seemed to be the one,' said Emma. 'More tea?'

'I can manage. You get your own. There's plenty of milk if you want cornflakes. Mind you have an egg, too. I don't need all those Philip brought, but it was kind.'

'Perhaps his father sent them,' said Emma wickedly.

She dusted and ran the carpet-sweeper over the sitting room, washed out tea towels and peeled potatoes for the evening meal, leaving them in cold water under a plate. She closed her mind to the fact that all the vitamins would be gone by the time that her aunt cooked them but followed Emily's routine. She knew, too, that the cabbage would appear at table very fresh and green but without a vestige of Vitamin C after being cooked with a piece of washing soda to keep the colour bright. For someone who had been brought up over a fruit and fish shop, Emily ate very little fresh fruit.

Emma recalled the barges laden with bananas, coming up the Medina River to the warehouses at Newport. She hadn't seen a banana for two years and oranges were a real luxury. She wondered if she could order some apples from the country to be sent to Emily when they were ripe and imported fruit was scarce.

Emily stood in the doorway with her tray, unable

to hide her pleasure. 'That phlox will drop all over the place. The roses are nice, though.' She glanced at the clock. 'Well, I must be off. We have supplies coming in today and if I'm not there to check them, they'll dwindle.'

Emma brushed her hair and made her bed. It was warm and there was no sign of cloud. She put on a summer dress of blue cotton with white buttons and belt and whitened her shoes, hoping they'd be dry when Phil called for her at eleven. The wireless crackled and spilled out the same old news of convoys sunk, of supplies getting through, of successful bombing raids and the numbers of aircraft lost. Cabinet ministers were mentioned, visiting areas of devastation, and Royalty was reported as seeing British Restaurants and emergency hostels and inspecting the arrival of more American troops, Polish pilots and Australians and Free French.

The klaxon made sure that everyone in the area knew that Phillip Scantal was waiting for Emma Dewar and Emma picked up her cardigan and bag, and a paper carrier of food and a flask of coffee. Phil looked rested and less gaunt. He stood easily without the tense twitch she had noticed at the National Gallery and when he smiled, he was the warm, friendly soul she loved.

'Come on, it's a lovely day,' he said.

'It was a lovely dawn, too,' she said, and laughed. 'I was up early. Aunt Emily is so tired. She does far too much but she'll never give up if she's needed. I shall have to help her as much as I can while I'm here, Phil.'

He frowned. 'I hope that doesn't mean you can't come out with me every day?'

'Of course not. I shall get breakfast for her and tidy up and do her shopping. You don't begrudge her that, surely?'

'That's not what I mean. I like her, but we haven't a lot of time and I want you all to myself.'

'Well, here I am,' she said lightly. 'I thought you were going to take me to Freshwater. Why waste time sulking? Let's go!'

He slammed her door and swung over the side of the car into the driver's seat. The exhaust was blue-black and noisy but the car took the hills well with a few extra snorts and groans. 'I bought her cheap,' he shouted over the noise. 'Chap was sent overseas and pranged badly and is in a Stalag now, so it was lying in a barn, doing nothing but make a roost for chickens,' He crashed the gears. 'Must look it over sometime and make a few repairs if I can get the spares, but it goes well. Hope it doesn't rain as the hood isn't a hundred percent.'

'What about the brakes?'

'Best part of the car. That I did check, but the exhaust needs repairing.' They went through Newport, up the High Street and past Carisbrooke Castle, taking the top road and coasting down past the late harvest and the fields of burning stubble. 'They burn the fields early now to avoid it showing at night,' he said. 'I met an old friend who is stuck on the family farm and can't get into the Services. He's lied about his occupation twice and nearly made it into the Navy and Fleet Air Arm, but they caught up with him. He's fed up to the back teeth. I said that if I'm here for long enough, I'll help him with the fruit harvest.'

The Military Road snaked round the edge of the rabbit-cropped Downs, and the seas pounded the shingle in Freshwater Bay, sending plumes of pure white spray over the rocks. Emma clambered down and picked her way painfully over the stony beach. 'Colder here than at Ryde,' she said. 'Aren't you coming? I might even have a swim later.'

'Every time you see water, you have to paddle.

Will you never grow up, Emma?' He lit a cigarette. 'I've had enough sea to last a lifetime. I shall never swim again if I can avoid it.'

She ran back, wincing over the sharp stones, and sat beside him. 'I'm sorry, Phil. What a fool I am! I should have known.' Her face was troubled, her eyes overbright and her mouth trembled. He kissed her and held her close, and she snuggled up to him as if she was the one to be comforted, and they sat with her head on his shoulder. Two boys passed, skimming stones across the water.

'It's too crowded here,' Phil said. He pulled her to her feet. 'That rock was killing me. Let's walk on the cliff.'

They toiled up the path to Tennyson Down and found a sheltered dip near the cliff edge. The sea sounds were muted and the sun shone warmly and there was no wind. 'We can picnic here,' said Emma. Contentedly, she unpacked the food and stood the vaccuum flask upright against a clump of gorse. Phil took a bottle of wine from his pack and some chocolate. 'It's a feast!' exclaimed Emma. 'But we'll never finish all that wine with one meal. It's a huge bottle.'

'We have all day,' Phil said quietly. 'And we have things to decide.'

'Just enjoy the day,' Emma begged. Her open palms embraced the view, then she offered him a sandwich and he poured the red wine into cups. 'It's strong,' she said, 'but very good. I haven't drunk much wine but I like it. It's so much better than beer.'

'I once thought that all I could offer you was beer,' he said. 'I'm glad that I've progressed since then.' He smiled conscious that his rank and future were good collateral, and Emma had an absurd picture of a man solemnly spelling out his assets as he asked a father for his daughter's hand in marriage.

'You aren't going to propose again, are you Phil? Not before lunch?' she laughed and he forced a smile. They ate and drank in silence, watching two gulls slicing the air, bright-eyed and thick-feathered and confident. Emma refused a third cup of wine, saying it did nothing to quench her thirst. She reached for the coffee and was worried that it did nothing to affect her light-headedness. Phil was very close to her, lying on his side on the bent rye grass. She picked a grass stalk and plucked off each spike in turn.

Phil leaned on his elbow, looking at her. 'He loves me, he loves me not, he loves me, he loves me not,' he chanted as they had done years ago, and Emma felt a remembered tenderness for the boy who had run with her over the grassy cliffs. He was dear and good. Even Aunt Emily admitted that and if she picked spikes of grass, who was it for? There was no other man in her life who felt as Phil did about her. Was any man likely to be as faithful, as loving and was she waiting for a dream?

He took away the grass, gently. 'You know there is no need for grass or daisy petals,' he said. 'I love you.' He picked up the wine bottle. 'We'd better finish it or it will be too warm in the sun,' he said, and filled her cup. His face was flushed, with hectic triangles of colour over the cheekbones and he seemed to be under great tension.

'What is this wine?' she asked. 'It's very good.' She giggled. 'Now I know what Keats means in his *Ode to a Nightingale*. "*My heart aches and a drowsy numbness pains My sense, as though of hemlock I had drunk . . .*" or something like that. I can't remember it all.'

'You aren't the only one who reads poetry,' he said. His face was above hers as she lay on the grass.

> *"Ah, my beloved, fill the cup that clears
> Today of past regrets and future fears.
> Tomorrow? Why tomorrow I may be
> Myself with Yesterday's ten thousand years."*

He kissed her brow and cheeks and then her lips. His hand caressed her breast through the thin cotton and he kissed the hollow of her throat but the cotton dress was modestly high in the front. Emma felt all resistance slipping but she had the thought that the zip to her dress was at the back and he couldn't reach it. This was no more than could happen after a dance when both parties knew when to stop. She gave kiss for kiss and reflected muzzily that he was much more practised than before he went away to South Africa. His hands slipped down her thighs and under her skirt, exploring, caressing and stimulating her. The wide legs of the French knickers made no barrier and she felt his fingers inside her warmth. It was good but only as a pleasant sensation mixed with a delicious fear.

He would stop before anything more happened. It was part of the code and Phil would never hurt her. This was what the Americans called heavy petting and was harmless, and one or two had almost reached this stage when saying goodnight in the shadow of the gateway by the hospital.

Phil took her hand and she felt his erection forming and heard his laboured breathing.

'No, Phil! You mustn't!' She struggled and half-turned away.

'It's all right, darling. I won't hurt you. I've come prepared.' She saw the rubber sheath in his hand as he tried to fit in on to the now limp organ. He was sweating and his eyes were feverish. The strength of his passion and of his body faded. '*Damn*!' he said. Emma saw his anguish and humiliation but could do no more than draw away, her expression showing him quite clearly that he had no further hope of thinking she could love him or understand his need.

The wine gave her the careful speech of the slightly drunk. 'You swine, Phil. You brought a French letter with you, thinking I was *that* kind of girl! How could you? I trusted you,' she added with sad dignity.

'I love you, Em. Christ! What did you expect? You let a fellow kiss you and lead him on and then act as if it's all my fault. You need to grow up!' She made as if to interrupt. He glared. 'If I wasn't like this, so bloody weak, I'd force you, to show you you can't mess around and then back out.'

'I've never said I loved you in that way, Phil. You know that. You have always been the boy I loved while we grew up. You have clung to memories just as I have and we felt safe together. It's you who needs to grow up and get away from the past.'

'What about you? You read poetry and cling to this Island as if it's the only place on earth, and you think that all decent men don't go below the waist.' He fastened the last button of his files and threw the rejected condom into the gorse bush. Emma hoped it looked like a discarded finger-stall.

He was calmer now and sat forward with no anger. Emma pushed the hair away from her face. 'I do love you Phil, but only as I've always loved you. Not like this, when you're trying it on.' The phrase seemed ill-chosen and they both smiled, relunctantly. 'You know what I mean. We both need this place to come back to when we need rest and reassurance, but we no longer need it together.' He tried to take her hand. 'No, I'm not saying this because of what nearly happened. I came to the Island to tell you that I can't see you again, ever, and I shall not write to you again. I shall love you in one way as long as I live, but I could never marry you.'

'After today, I doubt if you have enough normal feeling to marry anyone.'

'If that's true then I shall be a good career woman.'

'What am I saying? It's not true. You have such love and passion locked away in there somewhere, I know, but it seems that I'm not the guy to unleash it. There is someone else, isn't there? There must be. You've been different ever since I came back from South Africa.'

'There is nobody, no other . . . guy, as you said.'

'So, I'm not even better than nobody.' His dejection and hurt pride was complete and she saw danger to his mind and confidence.

'That isn't true, Phil. I can't say if there is anyone because I don't know. I did meet someone who made an impression on me but as far as he's concerned, he doesn't know I exist.'

Phil seized her hand. 'I knew it!' His eyes brightened. 'Oh, Emma darling, if you feel for him what I feel for you, I pity you.'

'It isn't like that.' But it was too late to convince him and she recalled Aunt Emily saying, 'He'll come to think it was his decision, like his father', so she smiled. 'I'm glad you understand,' she said. It was all so easy. He began to talk of old times, sensibly and with humour, and it was almost like those times again.

'Where do you go next?' she asked.

'It's back to SA, I think. They want instructors and I shan't be fit for anything but a desk job for ages. They hinted that a post in Port Elizabeth might suit me, and I don't want to do anything rash. I'm not cut out for heroism.'

'And without me in the back of your thoughts, you might concentrate on your rich attractive

South African women.' He blushed and half-smiled. Emma laughed aloud.

'You really don't care, do you?' he asked, slightly angry again.

'I care about you being happy,' she said. 'I wasn't laughing at that.' How could she explain that he was doing everything that her wily old aunt had said he would?

She got up and brushed the dried grass from her skirt and shoes. 'Come on, let's see what terrible things they did when they built the Radar station above the Needles. Can you manage it?'

'If we take it slowly.' He gathered up his gasmask and raincoat and the light haversack and they climbed the slope.

The grass was flattened where they had been and a clump of buttercups lay deflowered and scattered, already fading.

PART THREE
Coffee and Syringa

1

'In a way, I think I was almost fond of him,' said Bea Shuter. 'We fought every time we met when we were children and then of course he thought play could include sex and he had a complete disregard for one's feelings, but he did have a certain respect for me when he saw I wasn't going to cooperate with his nasty little games. To be honest,' she said with a rueful shrug, 'we had things in common. I can be ruthless if I want my own way, and let's face it, my family is one bad lot. Eddie was the worst and quite over the edge and I'm glad he's dead. If peace came, he'd be a misfit and might end up in real trouble, instead of dying a hero.'

'Does it say what happened?' Emma glanced at the unfolded letter on the bed.

'My father says that Eddie died while trying to get two wounded man back into a dinghy. They'd been on a raid and were bringing back an important refugee. Two men were shot as they tried to delay the enemy; Eddie saw his man safely into the boat and went back to try to drag the wounded out to it. One got in but Eddie and the other man bought it.'

'So the citation is a posthumous Military Cross? He was very brave,' said Emma.

'Brave but utterly bad,' Bea stated. 'He adored violence for its own sake, and sex. It was about even, I'd say. He didn't mind danger, so does that make him brave? Or was he just a sado-masochist who was good at war?'

'Don't!' Emma shuddered.

'Well, you should know, unless you have forgotten how my dear cousin tried to rape you?'

'I haven't forgotten, but when we met again in your father's apartment he seemed to have changed. He didn't try to date me, let alone make a pass.'

'He was at a low ebb, duckie. That was after his second time in hospital and he wasn't up to it.' Bea gave a coarse laugh. 'Must have been a shock. A bit lower and he'd have lost his balls. That would have made a difference to his performance.' She folded the letter. 'He did seem subdued though, didn't he? I saw him twice after that and he certainly wasn't quite the old cynic I knew. He might have mellowed, but I think he was in greater pain than he'd admit.'

Bea regarded her friend as if looking at her afresh. The crisp uniform suited her and the frilled cap of a Junior Staff Nurse was perfect on her piled-up shiny hair. 'You know, Eddie really did have a thing about you. I can't think why. You aren't his type at all.'

'I thought all women were his type.'

'Evidently not.' She produced a small package from the stiff manilla envelope in which the letter had come. 'It's odd to imagine Eddie thinking about his own death, but he left a note before that raid, telling my father to make sure I got his gold cigarette case and a rather nice dressing case he found and 'liberated' in France, and he wanted you to have this.'

'*Me*?' Emma took the small heavy object and opened the wrapping. In it lay a cap badge. 'I don't know what to say.'

'Maybe it takes a devil to love a saint,' said Bea. She smiled. 'It should have been the other way round. I collect badges and you could do with the dressing case, but we can't swop.'

'You couldn't add Eddie's badge to your collection. He's not one of your scalps.'

Bea spread the wide leather army belt along the bedcover. The leather gleamed softly where it showed, but most of it was hidden beneath badges of many regiments of many nationalities and Services. 'It's almost too heavy to wear,' said Bea complacently. 'I think I'll start another one.'

'If Dwight comes back and sees it, he'll think you slept with them. No man gives up his badge easily.'

'It's all right, duckie. I've told him I collect badges as a war souvenir and asked him to find me any interesting ones that *my father* can't get for me. In a way that's true. Most of them gave them up without a murmur as my father is a bit influential these days.' She laughed. 'I'm not tempting Fate. I know that if I want Dwight, I must never, never make him jealous. Hey! you look ready. Wait a minute and I'll be with you.' She rushed to her wardrobe and quickly changed into uniform. 'What now? More buzz bombs?'

'V bombs? They are everywhere,' said Emma. 'Even Aunt Emily admits that she ducks whenever she hears the engine cut out and knows that one is about to land, but she says that if it's overhead when the engine cuts, it will fall a long distance away, as it coasts on for a while and comes down in an arc. It's strange how we are so busy here but at Heath Cross they are slack again. They aren't taking our patients even when they have empty wards, and some theatres are on alert but not working. Margaret says she's bored to tears down there.'

'It's been a good winter on the whole,' said Bea. 'Cold but exciting. I hate an empty ward and the men on orthopaedics are fun. Most of them aren't really ill, just strung up on pulleys and getting more bored each day. I could fall for Charlie, the man who owns the barrow down in the market. He's so blatantly sexy and really quite bright. He has the other men in fits and Sister has to pretend she doesn't understand his double entendres. She handles them all very well, I must say.'

'Perhaps they'll bring back our staff to London if they are so slack. It was only to have been a temporary arrangement and they've had no time to erase the image of that place, except to clean it up a bit. I went down to see Ruth, the girl from Tommies who was so nice and she says they still have those terrible bathrooms.'

'I remember them,' shuddered Bea. 'We had some made respectable for our use with a little fresh distemper on the walls, but there was one in the main block that had a notice on the wall that said no more than three patients must be undressed and waiting for a bath while three others were being bathed.' She snorted her disgust. 'How Dickensian! It conjured up pictures of lines of naked men and women waiting in those chilly bathrooms until they were dunked in the water, like sheep running through a sheep-dip trough.'

'See you later,' said Emma. 'I have to fetch something for Sister. I wonder where we'll go next. We're both due for a move again.'

She went upstairs to the semi-private patients' wing where six paying patients shared a six-bedded room and received exactly the same treatment as the non-paying, and a few people had private rooms in which they were far more lonely than if they had been in the six-bedded ward, but they could have more frequent visitors. The food was the same but on better crockery, the nursing was certainly the same but they had the privilege of paying for each X-ray and blood test, all their drugs, dressings and physiotherapy.

There were some who thought they were getting extra care but as Sister said, dryly, 'How can we give better than our best, which we give to everyone?'

The diabetic wife of a Wing Commander lately back from South Africa, who was in a single room, was ringing her bell. Emma went in and reassured her that the evening dose of insulin wasn't due for another half hour and she hadn't been forgotten. She reminded Emma of Miss Styles at the Home in Bristol, centuries ago. She had the same spoiled – child expression of loneliness and the same desire to hold on to anyone passing who could give her words of comfort or entertainment.

'I'll be back,' said Emma crisply. 'Read some of those lovely American magazines, and I'll give you your injection at six.' She changed two dressings, went with a consultant on his evening round and gave out drugs and injections which had been supervised by Sister, and checked that the right suppers were given to the right patients. She made sure that Mrs Dane, the diabetic, ate all her carbohydrates as she needed stabilising after what her doctor suspected was a binge on the boat bringing her back to the UK.

At report, she found a note for her on the office desk. It was a card from Matron's office asking her to go there on her way back from first supper. She showed it to Sister, who sighed and gave her consent to be back late from supper if Matron kept her for longer than the customary five minutes. What now? Emma couldn't recall a misdemeanour. I haven't been out later than a late pass for ages, haven't killed any patients or broken up the ward so why does she want to see me now? She shuffled her feet outside the office door and was joined by Bea and two others in their set.

'What have we here?' asked Bea in a stage whisper. 'Not all of us bad girls, I hope?' The red light appeared above the door and showed *Enter* and Bea gave Emma a push. 'Go on, you are the blue-eyed baby around here, so you take the rap, and say I didn't do it, whatever it is. Soften her up for the rest of us.'

Matron looked up from a folder. 'Ah, yes, Nurse Dewar. I see you have had a recent medical examination and your BCG injections.'

'Yes Matron.'

'Good. I'm glad your set is up to date, and will need no further injections that might upset you and keep you off-duty.' She makes it sound as if we are going up the Amazon, thought Emma. 'I want you to go down to Heath Cross, Nurse. You have . . .' She consulted the document again. 'Ah, yes. You have done three months in Casualty and three months as a junior in ENT theatre. I heard good reports from all Sisters concerned and you are suitable for more theatre training. Did you enjoy the work, Nurse?'

Emma smiled. 'I loved it, Matron. It's what I'd like to do when I finish my training.'

Matron regarded her reflectively. 'I hope you keep that enthusiasm, Nurse. I have reason to believe that Heath Cross may be very busy during the next few months.' She listened as an ambulance bell rang below the windows. It was followed by another. 'On your way back, ask Sister in Casualty to let me know the numbers of the casualties now arriving and if they need admission.'

'It doesn't make sense,' said Bea later. 'We're all going to Heath Cross having been working our guts out here where they really need us. We need more staff here, not less, while Heath Cross has spare bods all sitting drinking coffee all day.'

'Do you know which ward you'll be on?'

'That's fine. I have men's surgical. Even Matron admits that I get on well with men and, surprise! I stand for no nonsense. I think I learned a lot the first time I nursed men. There was that boy Paul I rather went overboard for and since then

I've never let myself be so vulnerable.' She looked away. 'He died, you know. I did check.' She closed her physiology book as if that closed a chapter of another kind. 'If we're not busy, at least we can swot for our exams.'

It was strange to be back at Heath Cross. The forbidding walls and high gates were the same but a rash of Nissen huts had grown in the extensive grounds, forming a grey compound of stores and temporary quarters for staff and the many doctors and Army personnel who visited the hospital. A new theatre was being fitted out with blackout shutters and emergency lights as Bea and Emma explored the fresh developments.

'They can't be closing the place if they bother to set up new departments,' said Emma. 'The theatre might be just another hut but it's got everything needed for major surgery and all the necessary annexes. They make the excuse that each hospital must have its own theatre so that training can be uninterrupted but they managed well enough at the height of the buzz bombs.'

The corridors were quiet and the wards filled with neat beds covered with red or blue army blankets. Knots of nurses and students talked in the lounges outside the wards and there was no sense of urgency. Emma reported to Theatre B and was obviously an embarrassment to the Theatre Sister. 'I'll show you round, Nurse. We have no list today and it will give you some idea where to find everything.' The equipment was spotless, the lights brilliantly-polished and the floors shining from a recent mopping. Sister Blane took her into the linen room, the duty room and the surgeons' room and Emma tried to look intelligent when confronted with a long row of theatre boots in graduated sizes.

The anaesthetic room had two Boyle's machines with masks ready, tubes of lubricant and swabs in a dish, with the keys of the various cylinders marked with coloured discs and neatly placed on a clean cloth on a glass shelf.

'You will be dirty nurse in the theatre, Nurse. The junior is anaesthetics and you are responsible for checking swab counts and making sure that sterile gowns and gloves and dressing drums and packs are available at all times, and later you may scrub for minor cases.'

'Yes, Sister.'

'Oh, is that the time? Good. You can go over for coffee in the main refectory. There is no need to change aprons when we are not working on a list and you may take half an hour for this break.'

'She just had no idea what to do with me,' said Emma. 'I went on duty and she showed me around and then sent me for coffee.'

'Same here! No dressings to do and only five patients with six nurses. They get more attention than the PP wing, with very individual treatment. Off-duty is the best joke I've heard. I have a half-day off today and day off tomorrow.'

'So have I, but Sister did say that we must stay within walking distance of the hospital unless we have a sleeping-out pass. It does mean we can walk into Epsom or go on the Heath. This is going to be a rest cure. Poor old Beatties. They must be frantic just now. Did you hear the V bombs buzzing over last night, and the ambulances were driving in as our bus left.'

A keen wind blew over the frozen bracken and Emma wound her scarf high over her face. Bea suggested walking near the road to avoid the exposed and treeless path, and after ten minutes they abandoned the Heath and walked along the road, ignoring the wolf-whistles from the back of a convoy of

Army lorries going south. 'There *is* something up, Emma. I saw at least twenty lorries pass the hospital earlier, and now these. Is there anything in the paper? Have you heard any news on the wireless?'

'We'll buy a paper in Epsom, and look while we have tea. I hope that Fuller's is still there. It's the only place where the cakes are anything like pre-war.'

They poured tea from a pretty china tea pot into thin china cups, some of which didn't match the saucers but were much prettier than any they were likely to see in hospital. The lemon meringue pie was still delicious and the chocolate cake to which they treated themselves rather guiltily was ambrosia to their sugar-starved palates. 'I don't know how they do it,' said Bea. 'Blackmail, do you think? They know something bad about some high-up brass and get supplies of chocolate and egg?'

'We are lucky. They serve these on two days a week now to keep up the quality with reduced supplies,' said Emma who had been studying the menu. 'So there's no blackmail, just good organisation.'

'Nothing in the news,' said Bea. 'In fact, less than usual as if there is a clamp-down on anything that might start rumours.'

'Aunt Emily says that they are building something behind all those barricades round parts of the Island coast. Some of the locals say it is like bridges or parts of bridges, and I suppose that bridges need spare parts if they are bombed, but everyone knows about Bailey bridges. Surely they make them anywhere and don't need to hide them? They aren't new and every country knows about them and uses something like that.' She sounded doubtful. 'It must be something more. It's almost impossible for outsiders to cross to the Island now. Even the ones with passes have to report unless their passes are certain grades and there have been a few arrests of people carrying cameras in places where there are barricades and no pretty views to take.'

'I suppose there must be spies about. Makes me go cold to think of it,' said Bea.

'There are more troops on the Island than she remembers even in the last war – parachute troops, artillery and tanks. She says that Saturday night in Cowes usually means a punch-up. There are too many servicemen for comfort and they have nothing better to do than make trouble between the various units.'

'Well, they train them to fight and the best fighters are just that – aggressive by nature. They need outlets for their energy. Don't we all! I bet the girls have a wonderful time fighting for their virtue. That is, if there is such a thing left on that sanctified Island of yours.'

'Less of that goes on than you'd imagine. We're an insular lot and are used to the influx of summer visitors. We look on "overners" as strange specimens sent to entertain us but with whom we need have no contact unless we want it.'

'That explains an awful lot about you! But you can't tell me that there's no fraternising?'

'I went to a dance at Parkhurst Barracks when the Parachute Regiment were there last year. I made sure it wasn't Eddie's lot first! It was very well done, with the main hall hung with every colour of silk parachute, making it more like a sultan's palace than an Army base.'

'Before or after Phil?'

'The same week. He knew one of the officers and so thought I'd like to go there. He said I'd be doing them a favour. We didn't stay long but they could have done with many more girls. I was danced off my feet while Phil sat by the bar. Because we have had a garrison ever since most people's grandparents can recall, local girls are brought up with an in-built suspicion of men in uniform and so they find it difficult to get the right kind of girl to go to these shindigs. Any girl seen there in peacetime in the "other ranks" dances would be labelled a tart.'

'And do you all wear deep white collars and tall black hats and go to church four times on a Sunday?' Bea laughed. 'What about Phil?'

'Phil? Oh, I had a letter last week saying he was a bit depressed, although he tried to dazzle me with his rank, status and social life. He still thinks we should have married and tries to show me what I've missed.' She laughed. 'He has shown me! I know now that Aunt Emily was right. He will develop into a nice but uninspiring husband for some girl who thinks he is wonderful, but he does lack imagination.'

'Well, now you've finished with him for good, you can come hunting with me. That is, until Dwight gets back.'

'I don't hunt.'

'Well, at least stay in one place long enough for the hounds to sniff the rabbit. You never give them a chance.'

'You can talk! How many badges have you on your belts and how many broken hearts litter the airfields and camps? But maybe that's not quite the same, and I wish I could take life more lightly as you do, Bea. I think I've loosened up a lot since I started nursing but my family had such a stultifying influence on me that I'm still an inhibited schoolgirl when I meet someone really dynamic. The men I have kissed are usually ones I know I can control, and where's the fun in that?'

'I've seen that cool, "you may look but not touch" expression and they end up scared stiff of you. I've noticed some very puzzled and disappointed looks even among the medics here.'

'You imagine that,' said Emma uneasily. 'I get on well with the doctors.'

'In that virginal uniform, yes, and then you appear at the dances with your hair down and they think there is more to explore, but the lady gives them the frozen mitt, as Dwight would say. Talking of doctors, who do you think I saw?'

'The spotty new HS on your ward?'

'No, much better. I saw the one we met at the theatre the night we all went out with Dwight and Frankie and the other RAF boy.'

'Not Guy Franklin?' Emma said quickly.

'No, only David who has just finished a stint in Scotland and is coming south for posting. He said that Frankie sent his regards.'

'Is he coming south, too?'

'He didn't say. Why, are you interested? I thought you two tolerated each other because we made up a party. Pity. I like Frankie and thought you two might hit it off.'

'I think he dislikes me and I found him rather abrasive,' said Emma.

'Ah, well there are enough men about here, doing damn-all with time on their hands for a little harmless dalliance and I'm not going to waste my time,' said Bea. 'Look on it as your share of the War Effort, making men laugh and dancing with them, and maybe giving them the occasional non-sisterly kiss. You needn't do anything more.' She picked up her purse. 'Let's see what high fashion has hit Epsom High Street. What a thrill. They actually still have a dress shop.'

'Sister Blane said that they have dances three times a week now. Just a hop with a gramophone or piano but a desperate attempt to keep everyone happy.'

'Is there one tonight?'

'Yes, and tomorrow they have a recital of music

on records given by the Music Society which I believe flourishes.'

'Culture, too? This is exciting. Do let me know when they start a sewing circle and I'll do a sampler with my age and alphabet in different colours. I shall take *Weeks* to choose the colours.'

'You are an ass. I thought I might go to the music thing. It's all very well for you to look down your nose, but I have heard very little good music, and understand even less. I shall sit and absorb it.'

'All right, if it's Chopin.'

'Beethoven, tomorrow.'

'Well, I'll come and read. I like a little background to the thrilling story of mankind as portrayed in my physiology textbook.'

'Let's get back. I haven't unpacked yet, and I must look out something to wear after supper. Do you think anyone here can dance without ruining my shoes and laddering my stockings?'

'I'm glad we aren't living in the Villa this time. They've done wonders to the nurses' home and it's not as cold as the Villa, or wasn't, but I hear that Villa C has had a face lift and is empty as if waiting for an influx of special VIPs. The hall alone there could take mountains of luggage and equipment, but now its empty and the old cubicles have gone so it is destined for better things than we poor mortals, separated by walls of thin hardboard.'

Emma found the ironing room and pressed a skirt and the silk blouse that she hadn't worn since the night of the theatre when Guy Franklin sat behind her and laughed at the antics of the actors and made her want to share in his humour and warmth.

'I remember that blouse. Why haven't you worn it?'

'As it was a gift from Phil, I couldn't, but now I feel released and free to wear it again, Bea.' She watched with amusement as Bea turned to show off the circular skirt with three petticoats. 'Just as well you haven't a bus to catch. I'd feel as if I wore a teacosy with all that stuff, but it looks marvellous on you. If all else fails, you can do a cancan.'

'I need a parachute if I'm to stay upright after that stodge we had for supper. The food here hasn't improved and I shall have to visit Mama again. Pity the black market boy has gone but I think she does well out of the fat American Colonel and might spare a few tins, or should I say cans?'

'Not more Spam? Do they live on it?'

'Pity none of my family like peanut butter or maple syrup. We could swim in it. Why are you smiling?'

'Nothing. It's just that Aunt Emily said that if I fell in love I would know because it was like all the angels in Heaven pouring warm treacle down my back.'

Bea didn't laugh. 'Not *warm* treacle, duckie. Hot, scalding, blistering and sweet, and all enveloping until you drown.' She shrugged and ran down the corridor. 'Come on, we'll be first wallflowers.'

The Common Room smelled of stale beer and cigarette smoke but it was clean and the small stage was decked with potted plants. An upright piano stood at the front of the stage, with sheet music on a table beside it and wind-up gramophone was ready with a pile of 78's. Two students were looking through the selection with disgust. 'Got anything new?' they asked.

Bea nodded. 'I have some Joe Loss and some Edmundo Ross in my room, if you like to get them.' She gave one the keys to her room and told him in which block she lived. At Beatties, no male was allowed in the Virgins' retreat, but although the rules were the same, at Heath Cross they could be bent at times. Two nurses, passed wearing blouses made of parachute silk.

One asked if Emma had any clothing coupons to sell as she was hoping to buy a suit for her wedding. Emma thought of the ones that Aunt Emily had given her on condition that she used them for herself, so she shook her head. The girl was a Nursing Auxiliary with enough service stars on her uniform to show that if she had done SRN training she could have been qualified by now. 'I might as well get married,' she said. 'I missed my training and I can't stand any more scrubbing lockers and bedpans with no hope of doing anything more interesting, unless I have the good luck to be with a nice Sister. If I get married and have a baby, I can go back to the bank and have a cushy job eventually. If I do have a baby, my Mum will look after it rather than work in a factory.'

The girl looked sad. 'She wants grandchildren as most of her relatives have disappeared from their homes in Germany. She hasn't been there for years and she's married to my father who is British, but she had brothers there who were Jews and just disappeared in one of the pogroms.'

The first record went on the turntable and Emma smiled. How many times she had heard that tune at the sports club at home, dancing with the brothers and husbands of the organisers. '*An Apple for the Teacher*' had been the favourite for showing the steps of the quick step, but when Bea's records arrived, the scene brightened and some students who had been lolling in the doorway now came into the room and drifted to the bar, with feet tapping to the rhythm.

More and more filled the floor and Emma danced happily with a house physician with a nice turn of speed in the Latin American dances. 'Reminds me of the Bagatelle club,' said Bea. 'The music, I mean, not the décor! I wanted to make up a party with you and Dwight and someone, but we never managed it. It gets quite exclusive there and one can't always get a booking on the night it's wanted. HRH goes there a lot. I've been on the fringes of that set but I prefer to make my own fun and not to bother with protocol.' She was whisked off by a tall Canadian doctor, and Emma gathered round the gramophone, breathless, with two of the partners she had danced with and who now plied her with bright orange fruit squash from an indeterminate source of fruit and colouring.

A dark-haired man with a bright, friendly face sat near her, making her laugh. 'I don't believe a word, Tony,' she said, as he finished another tall story. 'You are quite the worst liar I've met in a long time!'

He looked delighted. 'You should believe me,' he said. His humour was sharp and deep with an edge of sadness, and it was the first time that Emma had heard Jewish humour. They danced together until a student called that this was an excuse-me dance. Tony clasped her tightly and vowed dramatically that he didn't want to lose her ever again and they laughed, content to go on dancing together. 'I like dancing with you, Emma, and you laugh at my jokes,' he said.

He really needs to be liked, she decided. 'We dance divinely together,' she agreed.

'What's your other name?' he asked, steering her away from the men who stood waiting to steal a partner.

'Dewar,' she said.

'Then we are both drinks. You are whisky. I'm Tony Goldwater. We were called Giltwasser but for obvious reasons we changed it when my parents came over from Poland, just before the war ... in time.' He grinned cheerfully. 'We have much to be grateful for. Giltwasser is a spirit with flecks of real gold in it, so I am gold, pure gold.' He turned to a tap on the shoulder and shrugged. 'Can't you push off? We are having an intellectual conversation,' he said. He was smiling but the tall man with fair hair and pale blue eyes was not. He just stared and waited. Tony laughed and gave Emma's hand into the one held out and bowed.

He's like Eddie, thought Emma. The same cool eyes, the same sensual mouth and the same arrogance. She sensed that under the correct and rather austere facade lay the same passion, the same violence. She danced stiffly and made no conversation and when Tony came back as the music was slowing, to claim her again and talk when the dancing stopped, she smiled at him.

The blonde man looked at Tony as if he was a worm. The music stopped and in the brief silence his voice came clearly and deliberately, with a depth of insult that made everyone within earshot stare and stop laughing. 'Why don't you put on a yellow star and take a walk round Prague,' he said.

Tony looked as if someone had kicked him in the stomach. Emma seized his arm and pushed him towards the bar, ignoring her partner, and people turned away and made loud conversation.

'What was all that about?' whispered Bea when Tony was talking to another student. Emma told her. 'Swine,' said Bea mildly. 'But Tony must be used to that by now. They are a brave and resilient race and very clever. That's probably the reason for all the hatred in Germany. The Jews are clever and can make a good living even during a period of depression and were the perfect targets for Hitler to use to deflect the anger of the Germans from the economic situation.'

'You seem to know a lot about it!'

'Dwight comes from a Jewish background. It's

fifth generation and on one side only, but certainly with roots in Lithuania, way back.' She glanced at Emma's troubled face. 'Don't take it personally, and for heaven's sake don't make a mission out of Tony. He'll make the grade with quite another kind of girl, I think. Jewish men tend to stick to their own race for marriage.'

'So you prefer the Eddie type for me?'

'He is a bit like him. No, not him either. Look over there.'

'David! How nice to see you.' Emma looked beyond him as if he might not be alone. 'Why are you here? Isn't London busy enough for you?'

'I've been sent to open the new theatre and the new block. I shall be living in Villa C with a lot of other bods from various hospitals and Services.'

'So Villa C is now an officers' mess,' said Bea. 'That means business. When does the balloon go up, David?'

'I know nothing but it's evident that something is in the wind. Villa C is exclusively for surgeons and anaesthetists and their teams, with room for more if we have visitors. I'm out of the RAF now and so is Guy Franklin, but remain on the reserve and could be called back at any time. By the way, have you seen him? I asked him to meet me here but he does what he wants to do and isn't very sociable.'

'Pining after a lady love?' asked Bea.

'No, studying. He is certain that sooner or later, he will have to do surgery that he has never attempted and he's genning up on it.'

'When did you arrive?'

'Today. Guy will work in Theatre C, doing civilian ops and will wander into other theatres if he's needed until they say what teams are to be formed. Did you know he passed his Fellowship and is now Mr Guy Franklin, FRCS? Not Frankie any more, at least not on duty, so you must treat him with respect, Bea!'

'Well, you got yours, too! But you won't get any added grovelling from me, so don't expect it.'

'I shall expect the right size theatre boots, and gloves that have no more than three patches.'

'That lets me out. Theatre is Emma's department. Remind her to order a larger size in caps! Why aren't you studying, too?'

He shrugged. 'I am, but I find the prospect of wounded men very depressing and I need a little light relief.' His eyes brightened as he saw one of the auxiliary nurses walking past, her face a mask of pancake make-up and her lips dewy and full in a shape that nature had never intended. Her tight black skirt was slit at the sides and her bosom was high and pointed under the thin rayon blouse. Emma could see the concentric rings of the padded bra that aped the bosoms of all the popular female film stars. David winked. 'I've had enough work and intellectual conversation for one day. Excuse me, ladies.'

Emma watched him dancing with the girl and he was laughing, the lines of strain disappearing fast.

'Good therapy,' said Bea dryly, 'but Matron would go mad if we appeared in that sort of get-up, even if we wanted to look like tarts. My dear father liked them like that and said it did a lot to soothe the frayed nerves as they never said anything to make him think about work. She's called Belinda, and works on eyes and orthopaedics.'

Perhaps Guy enjoys classical music, thought Emma as she glanced at Villa C when they went back to the nurses' home.

2

The sun shone with dazzling brilliance and the nurses in the duty room looked longingly across the green grass to the softly waving trees. 'It would be lovely on the Heath today,' said Nurse Osborne, the junior nurse who had the job of tying ten swabs together with thick cotton thread, ready for checking by the Junior Staff Nurse before they were packed into the huge circular drums ready for sterilising in the autoclave at fifteen pounds pressure.

'You can't grumble that you get no off-duty,' said Emma Dewar. 'This does get boring, but Sister says that soon we may have to use every swab and towel we can lay hands on, so get down to it.' She crammed a few more packets of counted swabs into a linen bag and put them with the other spares in a huge new cupboard that filled half the duty room.

Sister Blane was talking to a doctor who had come down from London for the day and set tongues wagging as he hardly left her side. Bets were being taken as to their relationship and whether this was the man to whom Sister wrote reams of letters when sitting in her office with the duty book open before her. The inaction made the perfect hotbed for gossip and conjecture and now rumour had it that David was going about with the fluffy little nursing auxiliary, who had more sex that sense and was given nothing too difficult or mind-bending to do on the ward where she worked.

In this atmosphere of boredom and edgy strain, after more insults, Tony had at last lashed out at Douglas Couts who now had to explain away a nasty graze where Tony's wide gold ring had caught his cheek. He now avoided Tony and never talked about him.

But even Bea, who could usually winkle out any news before it happened, failed to find anything to report about Guy Franklin. He kept very much to his quarters and appeared at only one Chopin-Mozart concert, bringing with him a huge book on surgery behind which he hid for the whole evening. He waved to Bea and Emma, but when the trolley of tea and biscuits arrived after the music, he had gone.

'I can't think what's eating him,' Bea said. 'I asked David if he thought we smelled, but he just shrugged and said that Guy was taking his work very seriously.' She frowned. 'Even David now calls him Guy, which sounds much more formal than Frankie. If I'd just passed a major exam, I'd want to freewheel for a bit.'

'What does he do?' asked Emma. 'Has he mentioned surgery . . . eyes or general or what?'

'He once said that he wanted to be an eye surgeon but they all do some general first before they specialise, and we don't have a specialist eye unit here as we do at Beatties. Some of the beds in my ward are eye beds and there are a few in the ward near theatre.'

The junior nurse yawned. 'Put the coffee on,' said Emma. 'Our insides must be dark brown with all this caffeine but it seems to keep us going.'

The porter came in with the basket of stores. 'What is it today? Dead fly cake?'

'No, Nurse. Sawdust cake again.' He tipped the slab of yellow cake down on to a plate and put out the tea and coffee, sugar and biscuits allowed to each theatre for use between operations. The junior nurse cut through the still fresh slab and handed it round. It wasn't too bad the first day it was cut, but on day two, it needed plum jam to help it down and by the third day even the birds turned up their beaks. There was tea at nine in the morning, coffee at twelve, and again after lunch and a brew of tea at three, and for a treat, coffee before going off-duty at night.

'I make very good coffee, now, but I forget what a patient looks like,' said Nurse Osborne. The telephone rang and Emma went to answer it.

'You must have wished this on us,' said Emma. 'Nurse Osborne, you will go to Ward 6 to help them. There's a convoy on its way with casualties from a buzz bomb. I thought I heard two go over this morning and they came down across the Downs, so we are the nearest to take in the casualties.' She rolled up her sleeves. 'I shall come to help admit them and Nurse Brown can stay to take any messages and report to Sister when she comes back on duty, then she can tell you what to do.' Emma put on her apron. It wasn't theatre work but it was better than nothing to kill the boredom and she could be useful.

'Do we lay up anything in theatre, Nurse?'

'Admin said no. We have to keep ticking over as we are, but help out in the wards if necessary.'

Ward 6 was busy. Nurses skimmed through the long ward, carrying chart holders, and one was laying up a dressing trolley. The Sister on duty gave Emma a brief smile and asked her to stand by and make a note of the name and position of any injury as each casualty was admitted, leaving the chart on the end of the bed as she progressed to the next one. 'The House Surgeon will be with you and he'll let Theatre A know what cases will need immediate surgery and the nature of the wound. I have no idea what is coming in,' she added. 'It may not be many but we have to be prepared.

I've alerted the blood bank and we have a store of plasma ready.'

Emma stood by the door as the first stretcher arrived. The man had blood on his sleeve, his face was dirty and his eyes reddened as if he had been in a very smoky atmosphere, and Emma was reminded of the night when she had looked like that except that her eyebrows were white with spent magnesium instead of dirty brown. Gently, she removed the jacket from the good shoulder so that she need not move the injured arm too much as she slid the other sleeve down. The bleeding had stopped and it looked a fairly superficial flesh wound. She made a note that he had recently had anti-tetanus injections and told the porter to take him to the far end of the ward to await the dressing trolley.

The next one had blood on his face and his hair was matted with it. He was in pain and the bleeding was getting worse. His scalp wound was deep and his eyes showed signs of pressure. He was put near the door, ready for transfer to the operating theatre and the HS wrote him up for premedication.

'No, leave him as he is until he gets to theatre,' Sister told the nurse with the dressing trolley. 'Do the ones who aren't bad and might be able to go home after treatment.'

Twelve patients were admitted, and seven of them had at least a small operation. It took all Emma's time to sort out who could have a meal and who must not have anything by mouth, and to make sure the notes were complete and could lead to no mistakes in the theatre.

One man sat moaning and rocking, one eye covered with a blood-soaked dressing. His other eye was covered with a grubby scarf, the only thing available at the time of the accident to keep the good eye from being affected, in sympathy with the injured one. He moved from side to side, trying to find rest and his moans became louder until the HS ordered an injection of morphine and wrote up his premedication after alerting the theatre to this urgent case. The ward eventually became calm again.

'You can go now, Nurse,' said Sister. 'We can manage.'

'Would you like me to come back to settle them when the night staff come on duty, Sister? I have been off-duty and it's good to have work to do.'

Sister hesitated then smiled. 'Thank you, Nurse Dewar. Not a very happy bunch, but as you say, it's good to be of use. If you could come back about nine o'clock just to help with the post-ops, that should give the night staff time to get organised. I shall look in, too. They have only two nursing auxiliaries and a first year nurse on night duty with a Staff Nurse.'

At last there was another topic of conversation at supper, and an air of importance surrounded the staff of Ward 6. 'You'll see David's popsie in action,' said Bea. 'She's on nights on Ward 6 – "Our Lindy", or Belinda Sykes to her enemies. I have never seen her in action, that is, work action on duty, but do tell me if she wears as much make-up on the wards? I should think she was as much use as a piece of soap as a nail file!'

'Maybe she has a heart of gold,' said Emma. 'I'm curious to watch her at close quarters and find out what David sees in her.'

Bea reached for more potatoes. 'That was awkward. Dwight called from Scotland. He's coming down here on a forty-eight hour pass, bumming a lift with the RAF and he wants you to come with us to a party in Epsom. He suggested you and David but David would want to bring Lindy and I just can't see it. Dwight specially mentioned you and I wondered if Guy would leave his ivory tower for five minutes and come too?'

'You could ask him. He does know Dwight and I could bear it,' said Emma, trying not to sound elated. She walked through the grounds of the hospital under a sky that was pale turquoise with pink flecked clouds, disinclined to leave the fresh air and the beauty of the poplar avenue. It was nearly nine o'clock. At least three of the cases would be back from the theatre and probably all of them if Casualty theatre dealt with the minor ones. Her own theatre was in darkness and she wondered why it wasn't in use as it was close to Ward 6. She swung open the ward door and the smell of ether told her that some cases had returned to the ward.

Four beds by the door held sleeping men, each neatly bandaged, but in a bed by the central desk where whoever was on duty would be able to keep an eye on him, as they wrote notes or gave report, was the man with bandaged eyes. He was moving restlessly as he recovered from the anaesthetic.

Emma ran forward as he turned to grope for a dish. She held his head from the sides, aware that under the heavy bandages, he might have further injuries. He vomited into the bowl and she wiped his mouth and tried to put him back on to the pillow. He grabbed at her dress and his hand pinched her breast, painfully. Emma drew back instinctively, and his hand desperately groped the air. 'Nurse!' he cried in a hoarse whisper. 'Someone! Nurse, Mother . . . Christ!' He sat up and began to swing his legs over the side of the bed. Emma put them back and tried to tuck in the bedclothes firmly. She looked about her for help. His chart wasn't at the end of the bed and she didn't even know his name. Screens at the other end of the ward showed where the night staff were tending another patient and noises of bedpans rattling came from the sluice.

'What the hell are you doing?' The icy voice cut across her panic.

'Trying to get this patient back in bed,' she gasped.

'Nurse Dewar, can't you see what he needs?'

'He needs a sedative before he does himself some damage,' she said. 'If you are in charge of his case, why not help your own patient, Mr Franklin?' The patient lay back too weak to struggle, but he still called for help and asked why he couldn't see.

'Nurse is getting some morphine,' said Guy Franklin, 'but before that, he needs something that I can't give him.' Emma stared. 'Don't you know when a man needs a woman to comfort him?' he said. He looked angrily round the ward and saw a uniformed girl in the doorway to the sluice. 'Nurse Sykes!'

Belinda Sykes came running. She saw the man threshing about and heard his cries of despair and went to him. Gently, she sat on the bed and drew his head slowly to her breast. 'There now, darling,' she said. 'Come to Lindy, then.' She rocked him to and fro and the Staff Nurse gave him morphine and Lindy stayed with him until he sank into a natural sleep, his dressing smudged with the pancake make-up that nobody bothered to notice.

Emma stood by, helplessly. 'Fear, not pain,' said Guy. 'He's young and he's lost an eye. The other has to be bandaged for a time, as you must know. He needs to have this explained as soon as he can listen coherently, but until then, he needs comforting, a little tenderness, something they don't teach in class, I suppose, so you think it can't be needed.'

Emma saw the pretty, painted face and knew why David, who had seen the slain at Dunkirk, wanted her animal warmth and love, 'I'm sorry,' she said, and fled from the ward, tears of utter misery and humiliation dimming her eyes.

'Nurse Dewar!' She heard his voice, less sure and more gentle, but she ran out of the building back to her room where she could fling herself on the bed and cry out her loneliness.

The next morning, ambulances came to take the cases further north, ostensibly to send them to safety away from more V bombs, but really to clear the wards again. Emma went on duty to the theatre, and everything looked the same as it had been before the convoy arrived and upset the peace and quiet.

The nurses were given the job of embroidering the initials of the theatre on masses of new gowns and masks and theatre caps, using red thread and sewing chain stitch, in spite of grumbles that marking ink would do the job much faster.

'If I have to see a single gown marked OTB when I leave here, I'll throw up,' said Nurse Osborne, who was trying to sew an O that wasn't square, and pricked her finger. 'We've hundreds of these things in the cupboard and the drums are overflowing and yet we do more! I thought I had come here to learn something.'

'Don't you know there's a war on?' asked the porter who brought in the only other kind of cake, dark with small currants and smelling of caraway.

Sister Blane seemed to share her views, however, and began to give classes on the laying-up of basic sets for different kinds of surgery, like appendicectomy, laparotomy and inguinal hernia. She showed Emma the technique of scrubbing up to assist at operations, in case she was needed in an emergency.

Emma was flushed with pride but slightly apprehensive. 'I'm not really ready for that yet, Sister.

I've scrubbed for tonsils in one ENT list, but I thought I'd have to be much more senior to scrub for abdominals.'

'It's good experience and if you know what's expected, you will have confidence. You wouldn't be scared, Nurse?' she said as if her reactions might be tested soon, and went on to show her the ENT instruments and the urological sets, as Theatre B was usually involved in these operations and might return to normal work some day.

'If we did get busy and two tables were in use, Sister what would we do for sterile dishes? Would we run out?'

'No, that would never do. We have to consider a purely hypothetical situation where there is a queue of cases and we are working flat out to cope, for say, twelve hours at a stretch.'

Emma gasped. 'We couldn't, could we?'

'I hope not, but it might happen. Now, this is what we do.' She swabbed a large low square table in the sterilising room with strong Phenol solution, which she explained to Nurse Osborne was another name for carbolic. She then took a rolled-up towel from a bin where towels were soaking in carbolic solution, rung it out skilfully by means of two long pairs of Cheatle forceps, and spread the towel evenly over the swabbed table, taking care that it touched nothing but the disinfected surface. She then took sterile dishes that had cooled in the main steriliser and put them neatly in sequence on the towel, took another wet towel and covered the dishes and the whole of the table surface with it. She returned the forceps to the jar of disinfectant in which they were kept.

'How long does that stay sterile?'

'Quite a long time, but of course, it must be laid up just before the cases come to Theatre and changed whenever possible, but it does give a good supply of sterile dishes if all the sterilisers are in use. As more dishes become available, empty them on to the wet set and fill the steriliser with the clean, unsterile ones, putting the label above at "Unsterile" until they have boiled for half an hour.'

'Do you use this just for emergencies, Sister?'

'No, when we have a long list of tonsils and adenoids, there is a very quick turn-around and the surgeon expects to leave one patient for us to clean up, while he scrubs and finds a fresh patient on the table and a fresh trolley waiting. It gives us very little time and of course, the preparation for each trolley must be as scrupulously sterile as the last.'

She watched as the nurses practised with unsterile forceps and towels soaked in water. The Senior Staff Nurse came back from convoy duty and gave other hints on theatre procedure including a pep talk to the junior on keeping the anaesthetic room tidy and the trolleys equipped at all times. She stressed the importance of testing the cylinders before and after each case, making sure that there was a spare cylinder of each gas used. Staff Nurse Seymour was efficient and very attractive, a fact that emerged when more and more doctors and students found excuses for visiting the theatre when she was on duty and Sister was off.

'Always make the students work,' said Nurse Seymour. 'They aren't all that important yet and ought to know what goes on behind the scenes. They come in handy for shifting heavy equipment and gas cylinders and they do pass the time.' She laughed. 'I'm trying to make this batch into human beings who will not think they are God as soon as they qualify. Aren't you bored? I wish we were really busy or back at Beatties.'

'What do you think is going to happen, Nurse?'

'Search me, Nurse Dewar. Nobody tells me anything until it happens,' she replied. 'But when I was with the convoy, I saw an awful lot of troop movements and some very heavy guns camouflaged on the backs of lorries. We passed an air base where I once had a boyfriend, and it was heavily guarded, and the convoy had to make a detour through quite narrow lanes, hardly wide enough to take the ambulances safely, as if they must keep all main roads clear for other traffic. Motor cyclists were patrolling the roads to make sure that no unauthorised car parked anywhere near a barbed wire fence or anywhere with a view of the air base.'

'The new block is swarming with doctors from Canada, America and other English hospitals. A professor from Edinburgh is there, looking as if he wishes he was behind a solid mahogany desk with a bevvy of fluttering staff round him, which he won't get here, and they are all looking a bit tense,' Sister Blane remarked cheerfully. 'At least you will have some fresh dancing partners.'

'If they are all consultants, what do they do?' asked Emma.

'Don't they stick to their own specialist work as they do at Beatties? If we have casualties, will they send them to definite theatres?' She thought of Mr Horrocks, who was only concerned with ear, nose and throat operations. Not many casualties from buzz bombs or mortar fire would need mastoid ops or to have their tonsils removed!

Sister Blane consulted a folder. 'They are divided into teams. We have four teams for this theatre, two for each table so that two shifts can operate.'

'Do we know who they are?' asked Nurse Seymour.

'I know two teams. We have Mr Samson and Tony Goldwater as his anaesthetist, with the usual gaggle of House Surgeons and students to assist.

The other team is Guy Franklin and Dr Michael Best.'

Emma looked startled. 'I thought that Mr Franklin had only just passed his Fellowship,' she said. 'Can he do every operation now – a full list?'

'He can do most things, and I'd rather have him do my gall bladder if I needed it done than most men behind a scalpel,' said Sister Blane. 'Having two tables going means that a senior man like Mr Samson can keep an eye on the less experienced surgeon without interfering, and be there to give advice and get him out of trouble if necessary. I don't know the other two teams. I have their names but they aren't ones I've worked with, and two of the doctors are not Beatties men.' She wandered off-duty as if she had all the time in the world.

Nurse Seymour was eyeing Emma with curiosity. 'Don't you like our Frankie? Or have you doubts as to his surgical skill? Most of the nurses are drooling over him and wondering where he has his love nest.'

'Love nest?' Emma felt empty. 'I didn't know he was married or engaged, or anything.'

'Nor do any of us, but he's too good-looking and nice not to have someone tucked away. I can spot a queer or a monk at ten paces and he's neither.'

'I didn't say I disliked him. I hardly know him,' said Emma, 'And I'm sure he's good at his job.' But the thought of working beside him in the theatre was frightening. She recalled every harsh word he had ever said, all the more because they had been uttered deliberately and not under a sudden impulse of anger; once, when he had insisted that she either take Phillip and love him or finish with him kindly and firmly, and now, she tried to close her mind to Lindy and the scene in the ward, when Guy had once more accused her of having no feelings, no womanly instincts to give love and tenderness, even in a professional situation.

'You must be the only girl here who doesn't think he's a bit of all right!'

'They may be right.' Emma shrugged, 'We just don't seem to be on the same wave-length.'

'Talk of the devil!' Nurse Seymour undulated towards the door. She spoke to Guy Franklin who smiled, made her laugh and then looked past her. Emma pretended to be very busy polishing a glass shelf before putting back the instruments in neat rows. She took up a cystoscope and then saw him approaching. She took a deep breath and became fascinated by the view through the lens, making sure it was clear.

'You look fierce,' he said easily. 'You aren't about to attack me with that?'

Nurse Seymour, who had decided not to leave the theatre, giggled. Emma put the cystoscope back in the cupboard as if it was hot. 'Just making sure that everything is in working order,' she said stiffly. 'Sister likes to know that everything is ready for any emergency.'

'Cup of tea?' Seymour asked sweetly, enjoying the tension. Guy Franklin smiled. 'I think I hear the kettle whistling. I'll make it,' said Seymour, grandly. She peeped back from the doorway but they were standing where she had left them, and from their faces she could read nothing, except that Nurse Dewar was slightly flushed and her hands twisted the polishing towel into a tight wad.

Emma shook out the cloth as if she was annoyed with whoever had crumpled it so badly. 'Can I do anything for you, Mr Franklin?' she asked.

'I just came to check. I believe we are going to a party,' he said lightly.

'Are we?' she countered, with studied hostility.

'Yes,' he said firmly. 'We are. Bea has been good

enough to invite me to make up a four and I was delighted to accept. Dwight will have a very short leave, which could mean he's to be sent to another base or be involved when the balloon goes up.'

Emma looked at him. 'There is something about to happen?' He nodded. 'Why can't we know?'

'It's been obvious for a long time that this hospital is expecting convoys of wounded, but they can't tell us when or it would be leaked to the enemy. This long wait means that nobody knows and that's good.'

'Dwight will want to have Bea all to himself,' she said. 'They might be relieved if we say we can't go to the party with them.'

'You're wrong. He wants you to go as chaperone.' Emma's eyebrows shot up. 'I know. I laughed when he told me, but he's got it badly and wants everyone to know he's on the level and not trying to use Bea. He wants her for keeps and not for a series of dirty weekends.'

'He's a very nice boy,' said Emma. 'And very good for Bea.'

'So, you'll forget how much you detest me and come and do your duty by your friend?'

'I can make the effort if you can,' she replied.

She expected him to go, but he touched two of the clamps in the cupboard and picked up a speculum. 'I'm sorry about last night,' he said. 'I was wrong, but I didn't realise that you had no idea of his name and what had been done in theatre. I was told that you had only just walked into the ward and had not been told anything.'

'I saw him on admission, but I had no idea that he would lose an eye. We didn't dare pull away the dressing before he went to theatre and a lot of the men had blood but no real injury under it.' She carefully folded her cloth corner to corner and again in a neat square. 'But you were right. I didn't know his name or any details but Nurse Sykes may not have known much about him either, as she has nothing to do with dressings and might not have had report. She was better than me in those circumstances. You are correct. I lack all the right emotions.'

He put the instruments back. 'Nevertheless, I apologise.'

'There's no need. When does Bea want us?'

He thrust his hands into the pockets of his white coat. 'I have a car. I'll pick you up at six-thirty.' He forced a smile. 'I hope we manage to get there without another emergency.'

'They might miss *you*, but what have I to offer in a crisis?' she said bitterly.

'Tea!' called Nurse Seymour and they walked to the surgeons' room as if there was a yard of electrified air between them. Emma sipped her tea while Nurse Seymour flirted mildly with the man who now seemed very quiet. He finished his tea and glanced at his watch, said thank you to Nurse Seymour and left without another glance at Emma.

'Have you two had a row?' Seymour asked.

'We don't know each other well enough for that,' said Emma.

'But you do know him? Or why did he come looking for you? He never chases the girls, as several have found to their sorrow.'

Emma sighed. The Staff Nurse would find out soon enough, so the right explanation might save a lot of inflated gossip. 'He had a message from a mutual friend. We've been invited to the same party and poor Mr Franklin is stuck with me all the evening. He isn't any more keen than me but we both like the other people and will have to put up with each other.'

'You lucky so-and-so. I'd change places with you. Have you a real boyfriend?'

'He's in South Africa,' said Emma, with the ease of repetition and felt guilty for using Phil even though he was far away and she had finished with him for ever. 'What does one wear for a very smart party in a huge house near Epsom?' she asked.

The afternoon went fairly quickly, with a steady stream of visitors attracted to the smell of coffee and Nurse Seymour's charms. Tony lounged outside the garden door on a theatre trolley, trying to get a sun-tan and teasing the junior nurses. He told Nurse Seymour she was the most beautiful thing he'd seen all day and then tried to ride the trolley down a slope meant only for the removal of bins and waste. He generally made a pleasant nuisance of himself but when he finally lay flat on the trolley, eyes closed, the juniors crept up and pinioned him with straps to the trolley and pushed him away under a tree where he cried for mercy and Nurse Seymour released him.

She told off the nurses, but with little conviction. 'It's your own fault,' she told Tony. 'You shouldn't encourage them. You are a qualified anaesthetist and should know better.'

'Don't be cross, darling,' he said and tried to kiss her apron. 'You really are cross with me.' He struck a theatrical pose. 'You hate me now and I shall go and kill myself.' He walked away, his head bent and his shoulders dejected.

'Silly ass,' said Seymour, but she looked as if she wanted to call him back. 'I never know when he's serious,' she said. 'I do know he had bad news about members of his family in Austria and feels very much alone.'

Emma went off-duty carrying her cloak. For May the weather was warm and the newly-opened leaves were a soft green. The tall poplars sighed along the avenue leading to the nurses' home and she pined for the Island. The countryside was fine and she was pleased to be back in the shabby, lovable, infuriating hospital but she knew that the sea wasn't just beyond the trees and it robbed the day of an essential quality. She took time over her bath knowing she had two hours in which to change, as evening off-duty was now earlier than ever.

She decided to wear a little black dress that she had made from fine woollen material that draped well. She was pleased with her efforts as a famous London store now had a service to help home dressmakers in war-time and would cut out any pattern to individual measurements, if the material and pattern were purchased at the store. Not only had the woman cut out the pattern but had taken Emma's measurements first and adapted the pattern so thac when sewn it fitted perfectly. She wore a slender chain and pendant that had belonged to her grandmother and carried a short fur jacket that Aunt Emily had passed on to her, saying she would never wear it again.

Guy Franklin inclined his head and smiled. 'On time. Have you seen Bea?' He glanced at her legs, smooth in gossamer fine black nylons and plain black court shoes. 'Black suits you,' he said and Emma blushed, remembering that he had seen her in black underwear long ago and he might now recall that meeting.

Dwight gave her a bear hug and was delighted to see them. Emma relaxed and kissed him. Dear old Dwight deserved to have a good evening. She saw the stars in Bea's eyes and was happy for her. Guy was watching her and they smiled at each other. 'We can't spoil it for them,' he said. 'Pax?'

'Pax,' she agreed and he kissed her cheek.

3

'Even my father doesn't give parties like this,' said Bea. 'The sunset looks as if it was made to order and a very expensive order at that.'

Emma stood with a fragile glass in her hand and looked across the famous Epsom Downs from a viewpoint that she had never imagined she would ever see. The huge house lay on a sweeping lawn that seemed to merge with the vast acres beyond, but with such careful landscaping that the effective fencing was completely hidden from the house. The whole place was immaculate, with fresh paintwork and expensive wall to wall carpeting and silk Chinese rugs dotted about as if carelessly, but in complete harmony with the décor.

The contrast with Heath Cross was painful and showed in a startling manner the contrast between wartime Britain and the world of wealth and plenty that existed in countries like America, which had not been physically shaken by bombs and shortages. Emma wondered how many aircraft had been given over to bringing all this from America for the benefit of the top brass of the US Army and other Services.

Dwight caught her arm. 'I want you to meet some friends,' he said. Emma was glad she had worn the little black dress and the simple but good ornament. It would have been too humiliating to have arrived in something cheap and obviously with a wartime Utility label. The gowns of the American wives were new and fashionable, making the wartime uniforms of the various forces the excuse to make fashion pseudo-military, by using silk and lace and fine barathea to achieve a slight resemblance, often exaggerating shoulder tabs, Sam Browne belts and tailored pockets in a mockery of their real purpose.

The host was a member of the White House Staff, seconded to the British War Office as America backed Britain more assiduously. He was genial and kind and as godfather to Dwight, very interested in seeing the girl whom Dwight wanted to marry and take home as his wife. It became obvious from conversation that he also had the job of ensuring that Bea was acceptable as a wife of an officer in the American Air Force, and to give official permission for them to marry.

'I was very, very pleased when I met Bea,' he told Emma confidentially. He laughed as if he was sure that Emma would share his views. 'We all thought, from some of the tales we heard back home, that our boys were being taken for a ride by unscrupulous gold diggers.'

'Really?' said Emma.

'Well, you know how it is. A boy sees a pretty face, she wants some nylons and he gets them for her . . .' He gave Emma the merest nudge with his elbow and Emma felt her temper rising.

'I hope you haven't been listening to Tokyo Rose or Lord Haw-Haw, Sir' said Guy, who appeared close to her side and touched her shoulder as if to reassure her. 'You hear tales about all sections of the community, even about your own boys, General. For the most part, American soldiers are welcome. Men like Dwight are accepted readily and we respect them as men and for what they are doing in the war.' He grinned. 'They pay us back for our hospitality by taking some of our prettiest and finest girls, *not* the ones that can be found in any country, even America, who sell their charms for what they can get. That type receive the most adverse publicity as they are easier to find and to exploit. Women like Bea and Emma are like Caesar's wife, above suspicion.'

'Quite so. You're right! My God, you're right and Dwight is damned lucky.' The General looked embarrassed. He tapped Guy on the shoulder. 'And so are you, my boy. She's a honey.'

'Well, you made the worthy General blush. Good for you. Any minute I expected him to ask me into his study to examine his war record,' said Emma dryly, trying to hide her pleasure in Guy's defence of her.

'They do try to take over a bit and then they are hurt and say we don't like them. They only have themselves to blame for the joke that will probably go down in wartime history.'

'What is that?' asked Emma, who had heard it several times in buses, taxis and in queues waiting for shoes and dress material, but thought that Guy deserved a punch line.

'There are three thing wrong with Americans. They are Overpaid, Oversexed and Over Here,' he chuckled.

'Not a word to Bea. She's forgotten that she ever felt like that and now thinks they are all wonderful.'

'And you, Emma?'

'I can take them or leave them. I've met some very nice Americans and some real nasties. Thanks, Guy. You said what I wanted to say, but much better.'

'It was only the truth, wasn't it?'

The question lay between them. He doesn't know what I'm like, she thought. It must be puzzling to think that I am either too free and easy, dating Air Force Officers while wearing black lacy underwear or I'm the girl with no sexuality and no real womanly feelings, heartlessly keeping Phil on a string and never giving anything to any man, even to a sick patient in pain.

She smiled enigmatically, and asked for another

glass of wine. The food was delicious, flown in from the States, and included delicacies like pâté and turkey and bananas. There were lobster claws and fresh tomatoes and salads; cream cakes that looked wonderful but were disappointing when tasted. 'All fluff and no flavour,' she said as she tasted Angel Cake. 'My Aunt Emily would have something very rude to say about this.'

'She's a very good cook?' Emma found herself sitting on a wide window seat with Guy Franklin, eating fairy-tale food and drinking white wine and telling him all about her aunt who was working hard with British Restaurants. 'She sounds wonderful,' he said. 'I'd like to meet her.'

'She'd like you, too,' Emma said, and knew it to be true. 'I mean . . .'

'You mean you forgot to dislike me for a whole hour and found we needn't fly at each other's throats each time we meet?' He fetched fruit and cheese and Bea joined them.

'I hope you're having a ball,' she said with a transatlantic drawl. She winked. 'Aren't they too, too wonderful? It's like watching an American movie. Can't you just see the General in a stetson? He's quite a pet and improves as I get to know him better. He seems to approve of me, which is a blessing or I might have had to kill him.' She bent lower and placed a hand on Guy's knee. The stones in the ring glowed with a fire that spelled out wealth and plenty.

'Bea! You're engaged!' Emma picked up the hand wearing the ring. 'When did he ask you? When did you give him an answer?'

'Just now, in the conservatory. Too, too old-fashioned. He made me go in the conservatory, locked the door and did all the right things.'

'He didn't go down on one knee?' Guy raised an incredulous eyebrow.

Bea dissolved into delighted giggles. 'He did!'

Guy stood up and took her in his arms. 'All happiness Bea,' he said and kissed her.

'Hey!' called Dwight. 'I saw that! Damned Limeys think they can get away with anything.' He smiled and sat with them, looking as if he could burst with pride and happiness. He turned to Emma. 'Now you have to congratulate me,' he said and kissed her firmly on the lips. 'My,' he said, 'you'd better behave, Bea. I might change my mind and take Emma.'

'Scratch her eyes out first,' said Bea calmly.

'Too late, Dwight. The General has already jumped to the conclusion that Emma and I are together.' Guy's laughter was almost convincing. 'Little does he know that we fight a running battle and are here on our very best behaviour for you tonight.'

Dwight looked puzzled. 'Take no notice, darling. It will take a long time to educate you into the tortuous workings of the British mind. Some of us,' Bea said with a meaning glance at Emma, 'never say what we think or feel and give the wrong impression. I must let you into our secrets gradually.'

'It'll take a lifetime,' said Dwight.

'That will do for a start,' said Bea sweetly.

'Would you like some more wine, Bea?' asked Guy. 'Or shall I order the man with the violin and the rose in his mouth?'

'Which means that we are being sentimental in public and it isn't done!' Bea caught at Dwight's hand and rested it on her cheek. 'Big strong men who fly those huge flying Fortresses can't be expected to understand mere mortals like us.'

Dwight grinned. 'C'mon, we have to tell the General and get his blessing.'

'He's a pet,' said Emma to break the uneasy silence when they were alone again.

'It's good to see you relax, Emma. Even if it is with someone's fiancé.' He regarded her quizzically but with humour. 'Do you feel safe only with men who have no sexual interest in you? Or with men you have known, or think you knew, since childhood?' He took two cups of coffee from a tray offered to them by a girl with a toothpaste smile and very tight skirt.

'I've plenty of men friends,' said Emma, 'but I prefer to keep them as just friends.' She sipped the coffee. 'This is the best coffee I've had since I stayed with Aunt Emily. 'Bea is very lucky. She is used to the best of everything and will get it when she marries Dwight. Most of this would be wasted on me, but I do like good coffee.'

'Bea is right for him,' said Guy. 'We were talking about your home. You were just going to tell me about the sailing there – or I hope you were.'

'I don't recall mentioning it. Do you sail?'

'Whenever I get the chance. I did some in France and Canada but the coast line here makes it impossible now, with restrictions, barbed wire and chunks of concrete everywhere to stop paratroops and beach landings. One day . . .' he said with a dreamy expression.

'One day?'

'I'll have small house with a boat-house attached and my own boat in which I can go off to unwind.'

'It used to be like that on the Island, but when I went back last time, I could hardly see the beach in certain areas. We walked to the top of Tennyson Down and saw the awful things they've done to the look-out over the Needles. It used to be one of my favourite places: when it was windy I could lean against the wind as if it held me back from the cliffs. It is the Western tip of the Island – you could look down at the rocks and surf on both sides of the Island. Now,' she said sadly, 'it's a mass of Nissen huts and brick gun turrets, barbed wire and wire fences to keep people out. I saw one of the rocks from the side but not the full line of the Needles. The bays were empty and sad, with concrete pillboxes and more metal fencing in the water. Even the gulls sounded upset.'

'Did you see all this with someone very close to you?'

Music came softly from the main room where the carpet was now rolled back to expose the parquet floor. 'I was brought up on the Island and it's a part of my life, so I do care about it,' she said, and avoided his eyes.

'That's not what I mean. You say you went back. Did you climb all that way on your own? I can hardly imagine your Aunt Emily having the energy after feeding a thousand hungry mouths.'

'Not alone. I went with a friend.'

'Come on, you two. Dancing has started and Dwight insists on showing me how to rock and roll.' Bea turned her eyes upwards in an expression of mock despair. 'My poor feet will never stand the strain.'

'You can't rock to that tune,' said Guy. He held out a hand to take Emma on to the smooth dance floor, under the soft pink suffused light reflected in mirrors and brassware. American Beauty roses, flown in that morning stood stiffly to attention in crystal vases, against velvet curtains drawn closely now as dusk fell and blackout regulations took over from the glorious sunset.

Emma found her steps followed Guy as if they had danced together for years. He held her close but with none of the suggestive pressures she had endured with many partners. The record player was good and the records new. Emma thought how much better the music sounded here than in the bare room at Heath Cross as the thick drapes and upholstery mellowed the sound. But we *do* have potted plants on the stage, she recalled, and laughed.

'Why are you laughing?' he asked.

'I was thinking of the dances at Heath Cross. These people would have a fit if we invited them to dance there.'

'I didn't know you danced. I haven't been to a hop at the hospital. I'll have to try it.'

'You don't even listen to music, do you?'

'I like music and I go to some of the concerts,' he said.

'And sit there with your head in a book all evening and leave before we have coffee.'

'You noticed! I do like music and have fairly catholic tastes. I like this one. Do you know it?' She shook her head and he waited until a certain bar was reached and sang, softly, *'Don't laugh at my jokes too much, People will say we're in love . . . Your eyes shouldn't glow like mine, People will say we're in love.'*

'I suppose Bea asked for that one.' Her gaze was fixed on the buttonhole of his lapel and his hand relaxed its grip on hers.

The music changed and the floor quickly emptied as the beat came fast. 'I can't do this,' said Emma.

Dwight took Bea into the middle of the room and two more American couples joined them. Emma watched, fascinated as the frenetic movements became wilder, and her foot tapped in time. 'Want to try?' An American Army Captain stood before her, smiling with a wide mouthful of very white teeth. She followed him and was glad that her skirt was full and free as she was whirled round, picked up and tossed like a leaf in the wind. It was exhilarating and fun and she was totally breathless when the music stopped and she hung her head for a moment, to recover.

'You should give exhibitions,' she gasped.

He clapped his hands. 'I'll dance for charity. Ten cents a dance. Any takers?'

'Do you want to try?' asked Emma.

Guy shooked his head. 'I know when the opposition is too great. I'll wait for something befitting my age and infirmity.' He watched the record being changed. 'Now that's good. It's difficult to get over here and must have come across with the lobster.' A few people danced to the slow beat of '*La Vie En Rose*', and Emma tried to make out the French words. 'Do you understand it?

'Not all, but even so, it's beautiful. Who is it?'

'Edith Piaf, a woman who knows how to live – to excess, some might say, but she takes all that life offers and sings about it: suffering, loving, hating, facing rejection – and passion.'

'The French are a passionate race,' suggested Emma.

'And we are not? We have so many inhibitions. It's too bad when we fall in love; *if* we fall in love.'

He looked at the glass-doomed clock on the Sheraton table. 'I wonder if Dwight is ready to leave yet. He's coming to sleep in the Villa tonight before returning to London.'

'Bea will miss him so much,' said Emma. 'I hope he'll be safe. Is it a good idea to be tied to someone for such an indefinite period if they are apart? They could be separated for months, even years!'

'I think they'll get married before he goes,' said Guy quietly. 'And I think they're right to do so. Why wait for Heaven if Heaven is now?'

Bea came to find her and took her to get their coats. 'We can't wait, Emma. Dwight got a special licence hoping I'd say yes.' Her eyes were bright as if she couldn't decide whether to laugh or cry. 'I adore that great hunk,' she said. 'We sleep at the hospital tonight, well-chaperoned! Tomorrow, we go to the apartment in St James' to pick up Father and get married in a Registry Office. Oh, Emma, I wish you could come!'

'I can't. You have a long weekend but I have to cover for Staff Nurse Seymour who is off for three days.' They hugged as if they were sisters. 'But I must give you something to wear. Something borrowed, something blue!'

'What are you plotting?' asked Guy.

Bea told him. 'And so we shall live happily ever after,' she said with a sob in her voice.

'I thought it was Cinderella who lived happily ever after once the slipper fitted,' he said and Emma blushed, remembering the time when he had placed her velvet mule on her foot in the hospital subway.

The drive back was quiet, with Dwight and Bea lost in a tight embrace in the back of the car. Guy kept his attention on the road, his face almost stern, and Emma sat deep in the folds of the fur jacket and tried to think of anything but love.

At the entrance to the nurses' home, Guy told Dwight to say goodnight and leave Bea with Emma. 'You don't want a pale bride,' he said. 'Emma, see that Bea gets some sleep.'

Dwight kissed his fiancée yet again. 'Thank you for coming tonight,' said Guy. He held Emma by the shoulders and kissed her lips. He smiled and glanced at the other couple who were still locked in each other's arms, and kissed Emma again with sudden tenderness, as if she was precious.

'Come on, Dwight,' he called. 'Beauty sleep!'

'Come on, Bea. I'll help you look out what you must take with you.' The pair giggled as they packed the suitcase with a new simple dressmaker suit that had cost enough to feed a family for a month, the nylons that Dwight had brought and some almost new underwear. 'What can I lend you? I know – my black velvet mules. They're still quite nice as I've hardly worn them.' Bea was delighted. 'But I have to give you something, too. What can I spare that I have two of?' Emma sighed. 'Nothing. Why get married in wartime?'

Bea laughed. 'Do you still have that gorgeous nightie?'

'The black one? Bea, you couldn't wear that!'

'Why not? I want Dwight to remember this terribly short time.' Her voice shook. 'I want to be everything to him. Girl-wife, woman, mistress, femme fatale; all of them. We have so little time, Emma.'

'Then take it with my love,' said Emma. She ran to her own room to get it, still packed in the box, unworn. She fingered the silk and wondered how Bea could wear it in front of a man. But the man was Dwight and she was so in love that it hurt to look at her. They would make love with a passion that Emma could only touch in a dream. Passion hadn't had much to do with marriage as far as she could tell in her own family, but she had seen only her parents' unhappiness. How had her father and mother come to conceive her?

Bea shook out the folds, and held the gossamer silk against her body. 'Won't you feel a bit self-conscious in that?' asked Emma. She laughed. 'If my mother saw it she'd make you wear a vest!'

'You are daft!' said Bea. It's going to be wonderful fun. It's just right and Dwight is going to be completely shattered. He'll never believe it was once yours!'

'Don't you dare tell him! I've never worn it and I'm glad to give it away in such a worthy cause. You won't mind that it is one that Phil gave me?'

'Not if it's as exclusive as this, duckie. I wouldn't care if Frau Hitler gave it to me, if there is such a person.'

'Do the people here know?'

'I'm not saying anything until I have that ring on my finger. They could forbid me to take my days off to get married, but once it's done, they can tut-tut all they like and even sling me out, but I'll be married. I hope I don't get pregnant!'

'Bea!'

'Well, I might if I'm not careful. I am going to be married and I am going to sleep with a man, duckie, or haven't you read your gynae books lately? Sometimes I wonder about you, Emma.' Bea sat on the bed, teasing and enjoying Emma's discomfiture. 'If you'd slept with Phil would he have had to ask your permission first?'

'Not from his last try,' said Emma. 'I envy you the ease with which you accept this. You seem so calm under that giggling face.'

'I am calm, deep down. I thought I was a butterfly like my mother but this is for real. I want Dwight more than any man I've known and I've fallen for a few, as you know. I wish you could get married at the same time. Go off sick and come with us. Make it a double wedding.'

'This has obviously turned your brain, Bea. I haven't noticed many proposals this week, I'm not in love and I'm not even engaged to Phil.'

'I hope I'm around when you really fall in love, Emma. I'd laugh if I saw you go all limp over a man.'

'You'll have to wait a long time,' said Emma. 'Now take this sleeping pill. Guy insisted that you have it.' But Emma had no sleeping pills and lay in darkness until she could rest no longer. She opened the curtains and looked at the pale sky behind the dark poplars.

Thoughts that she had thrust down in her memory for years now surfaced. She heard her parents arguing and the sound of reluctant agreement, the bedroom closing and a murmur of sound through the closed door. She remembered her mother's sulky face the morning after and knew that her father had got his infrequent way because breakfast was burned and she was hustled out to school as if she was the living proof of man's filthy needs. And yet her mother made such a fuss about weddings and babies as if it had nothing to do with sex, and marriage to Phil would have put the seal on respectability.

Emma held the fringes of knowledge, the onslaught of Eddie that left her repelled but not completely disgusted. Phil's attempt at seduction with wine and promises and the Americans she met at parties, who were easy to handle once they realised that the tall stories they'd heard of the easy girls they'd find in England were not always true, gave her a certain physical thrill which was gone as soon as they went away.

There were girls at Heath Cross, mostly auxiliaries who were not under such discipline as the nurses from the teaching hospitals, who would spend half an hour behind the tennis courts with a student or one of the visiting doctors and military medics from other countries, for six clothing coupons or a really good pair of nylons. It was confusing. For some, sex was beautiful and fine, for others a degradation to be endured in marriage, and for even more, just the enjoyable satisfying of a need, like a good meal or a warm bath.

There was no point in going back to bed, so she washed her hair and bathed and walked round the hospital grounds. She glanced in her pigeonhole although she didn't expect any mail and saw a package addressed to her. A slip of paper fell out. '*I want you to read this, Emma. Take care of it as I can't get another until after the war. I have a feeling that you have really finished with Scantal and I'd like to know.*'

Emma sat on a stone seat, under a badly overgrown lilac tree with fading purple flowers. Other shrubs were bursting their flower buds and the yellow chain of laburnum swayed in the breeze. In a little while, the mock orange would flower and scent the air . . . syringa, as she had called it since childhood, but someone had spoiled it by saying that it had some other, peculiar name, and that lilac was the real syringa. Mock orange blossom, but Bea would have real orange blossom today, if she did have flowers that were not the stiff roses beloved of the American hotels. At home, some brides had a sprig of myrtle in their posies, picked from the plant at Osborne House, from which Queen Victoria had taken a spray and which had supplied sprigs for the wedding bouquets of many royal brides since that time.

She opened the slim book. It was well-worn and not one that Emma recognised. It was a set of talks, sermons really, from a Prophet to the people of the town he was leaving. What a strange book! She had never heard of the author, Khalil Gibran, but as she riffled through the pages, she caught her breath and felt a softening of her lips as if she touched something beautiful, or received a message, not from the poet but from the man who had given the book to her to read.

It spoke of love. '*To know the pain of too much tenderness.*' She read more. '*When love beckons to you, follow him . . . though his voice may shatter your dreams as the North wind lays waste the garden.*' She took the book to her room before calling Bea, who wanted to be ready before the car arrived to take her to St James' with Dwight. Bea accepted that love would make demands, taking her away from her country and friends, and work she did so well. She showed her love and had no shame in her desire, only a deep pride and joy. Emma smiled when she saw her. 'It's as well you aren't going to the dining room for breakfast. They could read it all in your face,' she said. 'It's so obvious that you are getting married today.

She waved Bea away to the Villa, where Dwight was waiting for the car, and as she dried her own eyes, she knew why people wept at weddings.

4

'You missed all the excitement,' said Senior Staff Nurse Seymour.

'You mean something happened in Theatre B other than a steriliser boiling over?'

'As you will recall, Dewar, Sister Blane was off at the same time as you and I had Nurse Osborne and the new nurse. You know how scared she is of Theatre even though we haven't had a single case since she came here, and of course, it had to be her who found him!'

'Who was it?' Emma looked alarmed.

'Nurse Spence didn't even know him, and there he was, lying on the floor.' She paused for effect.

'*Who* was there? Tell me, for heaven's sake!' said Emma.

'We came on duty first thing and I thought it was strange that the light was on in the anaesthetic room. I sent Nurse to turn it off as we all know the rules. Can't miss those posters telling us to switch off every light not needed. Well,' she went on quickly as Emma tried to say something. 'She screamed and we came running. You can imagine! There was a leg sticking out of the doorway; a leg in a surgeon's boot and operating pyjamas! There was a body on the floor and one of the Boyle's machines had a bubble going through the column for nitrous oxide and there was an empty syringe on the trolley by its side.'

'WHO?'

'The worst thing was the rubber face mask on the end of the long jumbo tubing from the gas. It was swinging as if he had only just fallen and the mask had slipped away.' She saw the real horror in Emma's eyes. 'Don't worry, no one is dead. It was that fool Tony, assing around. You remember when the juniors tied him to the trolley? We'd all got a bit fed-up with his practical jokes and had been fairly nasty to him that day.'

'He went away saying he was going to kill himself because nobody loved him.'

'Yes, you heard that, too. Well, that night he had a small gas to give in one of the minor theatres and decided to get in here before we all came on duty. He was behind the door laughing his silly head off when we turned over the body. It was stuffed with clean linen, which didn't endear him any more and I was so upset I thought my pulse would never come down, and Nurse Spence had minor hysterics all the morning.' Seymour laughed. 'When it came to the point, I think he was more upset than we were. Imagine having three furious and hysterical females on your hands at seven am.'

'Is he still alive?' asked Emma, with feeling.

'We nearly killed him, but decided that it was too good for him so we just debagged him.' She giggled. 'It's true what they say about Jews!'

'You didn't!'

'We did – and made him go back through the grounds to the Villa in his underpants. We let him have those,' she added generously. 'It was a bit early and not a lot of people saw him, worse luck.'

'Does Sister know?'

'Not officially, but by now I think that everyone in the hospital has heard a version of what happened. Some are a bit more colourful than what actually did happen, but we aren't telling.' She looked round the empty clinical room. 'It shows how idle we all are. We're so fed-up with doing nothing that we get up to things we wouldn't even consider in normal times. Imagine debagging a doctor at Beatties!' She frowned. 'The medical students need more to do. They spend their time pursuing the nurses round the grounds, drinking anything that will fill a glass and keeping very late hours, so that if we had a real emergency they'd be fit for nothing.'

Emma stifled a yawn. She felt half-dead too, after a bad night. 'Sister said you wanted to go off early, Nurse Seymour. When does she come back on duty?'

'She said that I could go when I've given you report, not that there's anything to say except that we had a delivery of new gallipots and some more hypodermic needles.' They checked the drug keys and Emma pinned them inside the top pocket of her dress, and sat down in the duty room.

It was impossible to pretend to be busy. The nurses took the last of the gowns to be marked into the sun, but the pile didn't seem to grow smaller as they hardly touched the work. They had learned a lot about the theatre, practised trolley settings and wet sets until they were all expert and the floor of the theatre had been mopped so many times that Nurse Seymour said it would be worn out before it was used. A few students drifted by, hoping to chat to Nurse Seymour over coffee, but saw Sister on duty and went away again, and Emma dreamed, her textbook idle on her lap.

Bea would be a married woman by now. She would have lunch with her father and Dwight and Guy who was Best Man, and the General, who had promised to meet them all after the ceremony. After that? Emma closed her book and put it away. They would stay in the apartment in St James' while Bea's father went to his club. A day and a night with Dwight, her new husband, was such a little while, and even the General might not be able to pull strings to make it any more.

She smiled. It would take the threat of the Tower of London at least to make Bea come back to Heath Cross before she need and she would probably not return for another day after her time off, and be very late on duty. So, Emma was surprised when Bea came back late the next day, driven in an American Staff car with a chauffeuse who Bea said looked lemon cool and as if she was moulded from cream and plastic.

Bea looked tired, with dark rings under her eyes, and when she waved the car away, she smiled ruefully as if aware that the driver made her look like a wilted daisy. 'Emma?' she called when she reached her room.

'Bea! I was so sure that Dwight would manage extra leave! Are you all right? You look dead tired. Have a bath and I'll make some tea and bring it to your room.' She saw that Bea hadn't heard a word, so she shook her gently. 'Bea! Bath now and then tea in bed! If you want to be alone, I'll just leave it but you must have something.' She wondered if she had bothered to eat, and made toast. When she took in the tray, Bea was sitting up in bed with her knees drawn up to her chin. She had washed her hair and looked like a sleek rabbit.

'Thanks, Emma, what would we do without our cuppa?' She ate two pieces of toast as if starving and drank three cups of tea. Emma sat and watched the sparkle return and said nothing. Bea wiped the last of the Marmite from the plate with a crust and pushed away the tray. 'It was wonderful,' she said. 'I knew I loved that man but now . . .' She hugged her knees again. 'He's my husband, till death us do part.' Her radiance was almost too much to bear.

'Get some sleep,' said Emma gently.

'Don't go! Talk for a while. I need you, Emma.' Her voice trembled. 'He had to go. Even the General couldn't swing it as I know it will be a big raid.

They have to go tonight, to soften up the enemy, to use the General's expression. He laughed and said he knew I wasn't a security risk but I have to tell someone, Emma, and it has to be you! They've been sending wave after wave of Flying Fortresses over, bombing and bombing in preparation for what we've waited for here. Our lot sent Lancasters and everything that can fly and our Pathfinders are busy pinpointing targets and leading the squadrons. It's going to happen soon, Emma, and we have to be ready.'

'They say the weather is bad at sea. I had a letter from Aunt Emily and she says that even in bright sunshine, the boats at Yarmouth haven't put out for several days and the fishing boats are idle. If we are to make a landing, it can't be now. Everyone down there on the coast says we are poised to invade France and they will take those strange bridges with them. They check passes now if someone is found alone walking at night or too near the barracks or the defences. The locals know more than the Government think but we are a cagey lot when strangers ask questions.' She felt a new bond with Bea, able to talk about such matters and know that they could keep their own counsel.

'It will stop soon. June is a good month, isn't it?' A distant rumble of thunder gave her words the lie. 'The water will flatten out soon,' said Bea. She sighed. 'Bed, now, but alone. I'll have to hug my pillow.'

'Sleep well.'

'I shall say my prayers for the first time since I left school. I shall pray for all of them.'

The rain came down in big warm drops against the billowing curtains as Emma went to her room. She put out the light and drew back the blackout. Over the poplars, now bent slightly to the storm, a dark sky was seared by sharp streaks of pain until the catharsis of thunder cooled the air and the clouds hid the wounded sky.

The book that Guy had left for her lay closed on the bed. There was no need to read any more, as she knew so much by heart. Bea was suffering and yet she was far happier than Emma had been in her entire life. She knew love without fear. The words in the book accused her: *'If in your fear, you seek only love's pleasure and peace ... pass out of love's threshing floor into the seasonless world where you shall laugh, but not all of your laughter, and weep, but not all of your tears.'*

Who is he to lecture me? she thought angrily. Let him waste all his big brotherly compassion on Bea. I can't help my nature and my upbringing. She put the book in a neat parcel and tied it with string, but she wished she had read it once more, and as she put it on the dressing table ready to take to the lodge to go with the rest of the mail, she tried not to think of Guy and his warm lips, even if the kisses had been only the expected tribute after a date with friends.

In bed, she hugged her pillow as Bea would be now and fell asleep to dream of Guy with his arms round her and her body stirring to life beneath his touch. 'So little time,' she murmured. She slept deeply and woke to clear skies from which all cloud had vanished. The poplar leaves shook off all dampness and moved like polished feathers in the breeze. She dressed and took the book to the lodge, then went on duty.

The sterilising room had a leak in the roof and the junior spent an hour mopping up the puddle while the two grossly underworked maintenance men grumbled and repaired the roof.

Bea looked as if she had never been away, but the news had leaked out. The American Staff car had taken a little explaining, and she was forced to tell the powers-that-be of her altered status. 'There was a bit of a row at first,' she admitted to Emma. 'But when I told Matron that Dwight had to go away on urgent business, she was sweet. I had a strong feeling that she knows something that we don't.' She looked sad. 'That made it worse. I could see pity in her eyes as if she thought that Dwight might not come back.'

'You are imagining it. The bombing is nearly over now and we haven't had raids for ages.'

'In this country, perhaps. What of the pilots and navigators who bomb Germany? The anti-aircraft batteries are strong and the German fighters aren't exactly amateurs. Dwight said it was getting hotted-up.'

'He'll come back,' said Emma firmly. 'You must believe that he will.'

'If he doesn't, I know I'll die too,' said Bea. 'I mean it. I just can't live without him now.'

'At least you are married. You know what it's all about now; not just the sex, but being together and exchanging vows.'

'You aren't regretting Phil, are you? If you'd been lovers you might feel as I do.' Bea laughed. 'No, he's not the one to thaw you out, and you've been so blind that I wonder if you'll ever see who is there, waiting.'

Emma turned away. 'I hope I don't leave it too late, as my aunt did. She waited and had nothing when her Arnold died, but I have a sneaking feeling that they did make love, at least once. The others swanned off and married early and it was taken for granted that she would stay to look after my grandparents, and so she did that.'

'Self-sacrifice runs in the family! Be warned and be ready!' Bea giggled. 'My mother doesn't yet know I'm married. We tried to get in touch but she was away and she'll get my telegram later. What will really make her furious is the fact that my father knows about it and she doesn't. She'll never forgive me, but I don't think I can take much more from her. She dresses like a girl of eighteen and makes up far too much. The men get younger and more precious and she hates having a grown woman as a daughter. Having a *married* daughter will kill her! I ought to make her a grandmother. That would really be fun!'

'How do you know you haven't?' Emma thought of the unromantic sheath that Phil had tried to use. 'Birth control must be very unromantic.'

'Some can, but I got fixed up with a diaphragm. Knowing my family's tendency to fall into bed with people easily, I was afraid I might be tempted. I went for a medical and asked for a cap and they gave me one without any questions. I didn't ever use it, thank goodness, and was able to take it on my honeymoon. Don't shake your head at me, Emma Dewar. It was inevitable and I'd rather be safe. We may not have much time.' That phrase again, with its desperate undertones. 'Dwight was very relieved that he didn't have to take responsibility.' Bea smiled wickedly. 'I bought two size seventy which seems about right and you can have the other one.'

'I'm not Belinda!'

'You'd rather pretend that he forced his evil way on you? If it's who I think, you'd be insulting him, and you know the rules here, so it's a lover or nothing unless you are lucky like me to marry someone who has nothing to do with medicine. Marriage between staff is forbidden and you'd have to leave Beatties if you got married.'

Emma's face was scarlet. 'Stop it! I haven't even been asked,' she said. 'Do you think he does love me, Bea?' she said, in a low voice.

'Idiot,' said Bea. 'He knows that you have finally

told Phil to forget you and if you lose Guy now you've only yourself to blame.'

'I know so little about him,' said Emma.

'I didn't even know Dwight this time last year and have seen only photographs of his family and yet I know him better than I know myself. There were snaps of two gorgeous horses, so even if I hate the family, I'll be in love with them. It happens all of a sudden, duckie,' she said. 'You don't need it all spelled out.'

'Want some more tea? Or could you eat a dried egg omelette? You seem almost back to normal.'

'Aunt Emily sending more food?' Emma nodded. 'Bless her. You will tell her that she saved my life?'

'She hasn't forgotten the tin of Swiss biscuits,' Emma reminded her. She picked up the tray and took it down to the kitchen. Even Bea could be shy of meeting everyone in the dining room just yet. The small kitchen was empty but there was bread and milk on the table. Emma reconstituted the dried egg, whipped it up with milk and seasoning and fried it quickly, flowing the yellow liquid over the hot pan to get to the heat, then folded it over and slid it on to a warm plate.

'That looks like the real thing,' said Bea as if she was still very hungry.

'It's easy enough. I can't think why more people don't use it but some say they can't make a good omelette so Aunt Emily collects a lot that is going spare. It's still rationed but she gets plenty to make lots of biscuits and cakes and has some over to send to me.'

Bea ate with relish. 'Love makes me hungry,' she said. 'I shall have to watch my weight or they'll all say I'm pregnant!'

'You'll lose it when we get busy,' said Emma. 'Listen!' In the distance, the heavy roar of aircraft told of more waves of bombers destined for French and

German targets. 'It's much warmer.' They listened to the planes and looked out at the clear sky. 'If the wind settles, the sea will calm down quickly,' said Emma.

'I think you are as restless as I am. Let's walk in the garden. Everyone is either in their rooms or at the concert. Had you forgotten there is one? I saw Tony and he asked me if we were going, but I was in no state to take in what he said at the time.' They washed the dirty plates and went out in to the still, warm dark. A single bat flickered across the path but Emma took no notice of it. The shadowy trees cast strange shapes on the bushes beneath them and the leaves stirred slowly, making little sound above a sigh.

'It's much calmer,' said Emma. A shriek of mock alarm and some laughter came from behind the pavilion. 'Warmer for outdoor sports, too,' she added dryly.

'Our Lindy working overtime, do you think?'

'Don't!' said Emma. 'I am ashamed of all I've said about her. When it comes to real values, I fall short of girls like her. She did everything I should have done and Guy was furious with me.' She shrugged. 'So what chance have I of making him love me? I was useless.'

'Don't you know why he was so upset? He did the operation! He was Eye Registrar back at Beatties and he was called to the theatre. He had to tell the man that unless he lost that eye, the other might react in sympathy and he could go blind. There was some doubt about it until the dressings were off and the patient had to be kept still.'

'It doesn't excuse me, although I can't think what Sister Tutor at Beatties would say if she saw her nurses hugging the patients for whatever purpose! But perhaps that night she might have ordered it.'

'She'd have to get it written up as a prescription.

Can you imagine the house surgeon signing for one good hug and cuddle, PRN?' Emma smiled, reluctantly. 'Forget it duckie. I'm sure that Guy has. He was full of the joys of spring at the wedding and sorry you couldn't make it. Dwight sent his love, by the way. Not too much, I'm glad to say.'

They walked down to the main gate, now locked for the night, then back through the corridors, past the silent, empty wards, and the black triangles of gardens seen through the open-sided walls of the corridors. 'What a strange place this is,' said Emma. 'Nobody outside would believe that we eat our meals with blunt knives with half an inch of bad cutting edge. Even the original staff here must have used them all the time to prevent patients from taking them from the staff refectory.' She put a hand out to pick a few buds from a bush growing outside the corridor. She crushed the buds and sniffed. 'Not much scent yet. You could have taken some for your wedding if it had been ready, Bea. Orange blossom, or at least mock orange. The gardens look neglected but the bushes seem to flourish.'

'The patients did most of the gardening. I saw some who still live in D-Block and work in the laundry. They file past the ward window each morning, slowly in a crocodile, with an orderly. They carry paper carriers containing their personal treasures. I was going down the same path one morning and one old lady with a sweet face and silver paper curlers in her hair asked it I'd been to America.'

'What did you say?'

'I said yes, and she said that in that case, I would have met her daughter. Emma, she sounded so convinced! She showed me a photograph of a film star and said that as soon as she could get to New York, a car would be sent to fetch her and take her to the luxurious apartment where her daughter lives. I began to wonder which of us was sane and which had lost her marbles! I could never do that kind of nursing. I'd be in tears all day. I wonder . . . what if her daughter *is* a film star? It could happen.'

'It's a crazy place. If we stay here for much longer with nothing to do, we could become patients, too.' Music from the Common Room came through the closed curtains over open windows. A Chopin Valse soothed the night and seemed silver-bright in the stillness. They went in and sat at the back of the room. Figures sprawled on sagging settees and deep armchairs and Emma thought of the figures in the National Gallery exhibition war artists' work. Guy reclined on a frayed chaise longue, his eyes shut and his body released from tension as if in sleep, but even in repose, his face was strong, his mouth firm and he seemed endearingly young.

Emma shivered. Suddenly she knew that men would die and soon. Why think of the other poet, from the First World War? Siegfried Sassoon, writing:'*You are too young to fall asleep for ever; And when you sleep, you remind me of the dead.*'

Guy looked back as if conscious of someone watching him. He smiled and patted the seat beside him. Bea hung back and Emma went forward and whispered, 'Bea's very tired. I must get her to bed.'

He took her hand, briefly, and kissed it. 'Good. She needs time to unwind. Emma?' She came back. 'She's lucky to have you. You can be very . . . caring when you allow yourself such luxury.' Emma followed Bea and heard the *Polonaise* that followed them as they went to their bedrooms. Nothing soothing in that work, but a beautiful, heartrending futile defiance.

5

'It was almost too hot on the Heath,' said Bea. 'I tried to walk across and was halfway when they sounded that awful siren. I had to run to get back on duty. What's the panic?'

'Nothing,' said Tony Goldwater. 'False alarm or as they so kindly put it, a test to see how soon we get back on duty. It wouldn't do for us to be caught on the Heath by the naughty enemy.'

'I believe you did it. We all know that you are quite insane and play sick jokes on unsuspecting staff.'

'You heard about my best one?'

'I think everyone in the hospital, including the GPI's in B-Block must have heard. You are suspected of being the next admission there. They have a bed ready.'

'I'm not that bad, Bea. It was only a joke. I had no idea it would look so realistic.' He shrugged. 'I had a rocket from my boss about it. Saw his point, actually. We must have the apparatus ready for use at all times.'

The siren sounded twice again that day and again the next morning. Games of tennis were abandoned, people streamed in from the garden and the Heath and some panted along on bicycles from Epsom and the park. It became unprofitable to go far from the high walls and nurses sun-bathed in corridor lounges, hoping to absorb a tan through the vita glass windows.

Bea had been off-duty all morning and Emma was washing her hair, trying to get used to night duty. Most of the night staff with so little to do, slept on theatre trolleys, on folded blankets in ward kitchens and even in the empty studies by the side-wards that students used during the day, although this was forbidden. Emma hadn't been on night duty long enough to absorb the bad habits, but spent the quiet hours swotting, and Guy came to talk late in the evenings, but could say little when the other nurses were there.

Coffee was the main drink of the night, simmering gently in jugs resting in the small sterilisers and attracting a steady flow of consultants, registrars and house surgeons on their night rounds. New faces appeared every day, including a team from a famous London hospital which had worked with Fleming and had the latest details of the new drug, Penicillin.

'I couldn't sleep today. A pair of damned pigeons were cooing outside my window and I hate the things, but I suppose I slept for longer than I thought I did, and after washing my hair I feel a bit better,' Emma said. She yawned. 'Another dull night. If you feel like it, slip along about ten after Sister has done her duty visit. Tony and Guy said they might come along and it passes the time to chat.'

'Try to sleep for another hour or two. I have to get back on duty. Sure you don't want any lunch?'

'I made some cocoa and ate some biscuits, but I haven't got used to eating dinner when we come off-duty in the morning and I may enjoy breakfast tonight if I'm hungry.' She dozed and woke and dozed again, flinging off the bedclothes as it grew hotter and hotter. It was a relief to dress and to walk across to the dining room. A light-headed detachment from her surroundings made her seem enclosed in a brittle glass case from which she had only a tenuous link with reality. Heavy wheels from the road outside made no impression on her, and she sat in near silence eating half-cold fish cakes and drinking tea. She pushed aside the toast and jam. 'I think I'll get along,' she said to the nurse at her side. 'I want to read a few chapters before the doctors come demanding coffee.'

Emma walked along the corridor through the slanting rays of evening sun which made golden shafts in the dust. She stood aside to let a trolley go by. Four soldiers walked up from the main reception entrance followed by six more. Emma registered the fact that they were in uniform and were dusty; very dusty. The first two looked tired and the next man had dried blood on his face. Emma stared and ran. She arrived out of breath in the theatre to find every steriliser bubbling madly, two trolleys laid up and covered, and the theatre staff flitting about arranging the tables, testing emergency lights and making all the preparations necessary to enable two surgical teams to swing into action.

'Nurse Dewar, report to Ward Sister across the way to help with admissions. We don't know when we'll be needed, but we have everything ready, tell her. I shall stay on duty and if nothing much happens, some of the day staff must go to bed or they'll be fit for nothing tomorrow.'

'Yes, Sister.' Emma fled to the ward where the red and blue blankets had been folded back from the clean linen. Bea raised her eyebrows then went quickly into the clinical room to lay up dressing trolleys.

'I saw soldiers in the corridor, Sister.'

'Yes, isn't it a relief. The balloon's finally gone up.' It was like the bursting of an abscess, giving relief even when knowing that the relief would bring pain and prolonged anguish to so many. Emma stood by the ward door, watching the stretchers bring in wounded men, still in filthy battledress. She looked at the beds and covered them again with the protective blankets. There was no time to undress anyone and they were put on the beds fully-clothed. There was no time to ask questions either, as they came in so fast, filling the thirty-two beds and spilling over to the next ward.

An orderly procession formed, with Sister at the head with the house surgeon, and two students in white coats, looking scared out of their wits. A gowned and masked nurse followed with another nurse, ready to dress wounds that the first examination revealed. Nobody knew what lay under the blood-caked uniforms and Emma took a large pair of scissors to cut away any garment that couldn't be removed normally without hurting the man.

Three men had a big letter T written on their foreheads and the time the tourniquet had been applied was written on a note pinned to the front of the tunic. Sister ordered one of the students to release one that had been in position for more than twenty minutes. 'Release just enough to establish the blood flow,' she said, 'then tighten it again and make a fresh note of the new time. Not like that, you fool! Do you want him to bleed to death?' She stemmed the arterial spurt and made a note of the new application. 'Haemorrhage and crushes first,' she said firmly. 'No good undressing them. That one is a femoral. Have to cut away his trousers, Nurse. Do him first and alert the theatre. He will go straight away. What are we doing about premedication?' she asked the house surgeon. 'Tell Theatre Sister, two thigh wounds from mortar fire, I think, and two shrapnel but with good pulse rates so they can wait, but we may find something needing more urgent surgery if the noise from the other end of the ward is any indication. Go and see what he wants,' she told the other student.

The team got into a smooth routine and the

notes attached to each chart holder became complete, presenting a rough but clear picture of each man and his condition. Several of them were able to have wounds dressed in the ward and Bea emerged from behind a screen reeking of antiseptic and wearing a gown that she had no time to change between cases.

Sister smiled, briefly. 'Don't worry, Nurse. Clean them up and clear away any debris in the wounds. If you use sterile forceps, you won't contaminate the next one and at present they aren't infected.' Bea picked particles of battledress from a gaping wound in an arm, sluiced the area with flavine and applied Tulle Gras, the antiseptic jellied gauze that would stick less than an ordinary dressing.

Another staff nurse went along the line of beds checking drugs ordered by the house surgeon and giving the injections needed for premedication and the relief of pain. At least three men were losing blood and had to go to the theatre before the premeds had time to take effect.

In the corridor outside the anaesthetic room, a doctor took blood for cross-matching and the trolley from the blood bank arrived with supplies of intravenous saline and glucose, plasma, and whole cross-matched blood for the first of the wounded.

'You can go now, Nurse,' said Sister. 'You can't do more here. Tell Sister, thank you and good luck.'

Emma went back and changed into a theatre gown. She was asked to undress the men and try to get each one into the theatre covered with a clean sheet if it was impossible to gown him. A pile of large cotton swabs was put in the anaesthetic room for swabbing away dried blood and dirt once the patient was unconscious and more vigorous measures could be taken to clean him up.

The two operating tables were in use, two small rooms held anaesthetised men and in the sterilising room clouds of steam emitted from every crevice. A wet set was prepared and trolleys for the next cases were ready laid up with general sets of instruments, ligatures and sutures and needle holders, packing gauze and swabs, and drums were ready with anything more that could be wanted.

Soiled gowns piled up, gloves were discarded, ripped or dropped and the swab drums lost their full fatness. Drip stands were brought in and got in the way, but everyone was on his or her best behaviour and performed the duties for which they had been trained.

'Nurse Dewar, take over trolley laying. I want a general set for Mr Samson, with stomach clamps and a Paul's tube.' Sister smiled over her mask. 'He doesn't know what he wants but he expects me to know, bless him! I think it's almost certain to be a perforated gut, but keep the clamps separate on the wet set in case he doesn't use them as we may need them for another internal bleeding that Sister sent a message about.' Sister went back into the theatre and called the day staff. 'Off you go,' she said firmly. 'Go straight to bed and no argument. You'll be needed in the morning. I want you back here at seven. No, Nurse, you can't stay! Someone must be fit for the next convoy and you can't work all the hours God sends.'

Dimly, Emma was aware of comings and goings as she laid trolleys, pushed them into the theatre and cleared dirty bowls and bloody swabs and thrust soiled towels into linen bags. There was satisfaction and an almost soothing therapy in the smooth exchange of clean sterile trolley for dirty, the hiss of the steriliser which was ready for use and the knowledge that she had enough sterile and cool dishes ready for any sudden call. Cool dishes were important as bowls from the boiling water held the heat and were dangerous to hand to an unsuspecting surgeon or a scrubbed nurse. Jugs of lotion were re-filled, empty bottles put neatly for return to the dispensary in huge baskets and buckets of dirty dressings, torn battledress remnants and gore were taken by the students to the incinerator for burning.

Mr Samson stretched and handed the needle holder to his house surgeon. 'You stitch this one.' He examined three pieces of shrapnel taken from the man's back. 'Put them with his notes, Nurse. He'll want them as souvenirs. I think I did a good job there, Sister. The big piece nearly got his spine but he's going to be lucky.'

Sister smiled. 'You're all doing very well,' she said. She glanced across at the other table where Guy Franklin was suturing a crooked hole in an abdomen. 'Are you draining him, Mr Franklin? Have you the right size tube?'

Guy nodded and his eyes above the mask were bright with the interest and excitement that was throbbing through the department, now that the long weeks of inaction were over. The tension flowed away as the more urgent cases were sent back to the ward.

'We had a few bad moments when we were told we must be ready for anything, Sister,' Mr Samson laughed. 'They said that in Theatre D they had one ENT surgeon, and one gynaecologist and wondered what would happen in between in the upper abdomen! I had to read up about amputations and practise on a cadaver as I haven't done one since I was a Registrar.'

Guy Franklin peeled off his gloves and for the first time that night, both operating tables were empty. Nurses swabbed the floor and the smell of fresh Dettol filled the room. Emma seized bowls of soiled instruments and scrubbed each one furiously before putting it with its fellows, the artery forceps on long pins and the clamps in sets. She filled another steriliser with the perforated trays that each held a general set of instruments, made sure the water was really boiling and turned the switch to time it. She cleared the rest of the used material and looked into theatre to make sure that the runners had cleared it all.

It was strangely silent. The floor gleamed wetly and the Boyle's apparatus from the last anaesthetic was being wheeled from the theatre. The surgical teams had gone. 'Get a cup of coffee, Nurse,' Sister said. 'Mrs Samson and some of the other wives have set up a canteen for staff in the first ward lounge along the corridor.'

'But Sister, I have only one trolley laid.'

'Mr Samson said that everyone must have a break of fifteen minutes. I shall leave when the next two are on the tables so you'd better go now.' She glanced at the full wet set. 'I see you've got plenty in reserve and if there's a sudden scare I'll lay up the next trolley. I might get two hours' sleep or more if the cases thin out. I'll leave a message to call me when necessary.' Suddenly, she looked very tired.

'I'm sure we'll manage, Sister. You taught us well.'

'I can see that,' she said dryly. 'I feel almost superfluous.'

Emma peeled off her damp gown and ran a comb through her hair. She put the theatre cap back on again and went out into the dark corridor. The lights from the ward glowed through the porthole windows in the double doors and the corridor was strewn with piles of linen bags sluiced almost free of blood but leaking dirty water through on to the tiled floor. She walked slowly in the direction of the canteen, wondering if she could face talking to people who were eating and drinking, relaxing and laughing, which she knew would be the normal outlet of every surgical team after tension.

In the darkness came a glow of cream flowers against dark green leaves. The air was warm and humid, the sky empty of stars or moon but the flowers shone star-like in the dull blue light of the corridor. She went across and took a deep breath, inhaling the heady scent of the mock orange blossom and let the cool petals soothe her mind. I shall remember this scent and this night for the rest of my life, she thought. She picked a large spray and took it with her into the canteen. Tony was telling dirty jokes and Guy was slumped in a chair staring into space until he saw her. He raised a hand but didn't get up and Emma went to find some coffee.

One of the wives handed her a cup of very good coffee and biscuits that had never seen a ration book, and Emma sensed a reluctant envy that the coffee-makers could not be more deeply involved in the true nature of the night's work. 'Syringa doesn't keep in water,' said Mrs Samson.

'Never mind,' said Emma. She drank her coffee and went back to the theatre, still holding the spray of flowers.

There was no time for thinking. Mr Samson was already scrubbed and the students were hovering over the sterile trolley hoping that a nurse would tell them what *not* to do. The Senior Nurse came out of the scrubbing bay, pulling on her rubber gloves and Emma whisked off the covering towel and checked that everything was there for the third perforated gut that night. She set another trolley for Guy whom she could hear scrubbing and then she looked at the list. As each case was ticked off, the details of the operation were added, both to the list and to the notes by a student whose main concern was to keep the record straight. Each man, if conscious, was asked his name when he came into the anesthetic room to make sure the diagnosis matched with the notes. His name and diagnosis was read out before the surgeon took up a scalpel and he made comments to be noted while he worked.

It all worked smoothly, except when another wound was noticed just as one man was being lifted on to the trolley to take him back to the ward. Shrapnel was difficult to see if deeply embedded, as it seemed to burn a way under the tissues and the skin closed over it. A person in pain is often unaware of the source of all the pain but feels one ache all over.

Five pieces of metal were found in one chest wound and Mr Samson suspected there were more but he dared not probe again as Tony was making perturbed mutterings, so he stitched in five drainage tubes and a pack of gauze and sent him back to the ward. A trolley rattled into the sterilising room with drums still warm from the autoclave, and the pile of swabs that would last for ever had dwindled alarmingly in one night. Empty drums faced nurses each time they went for more dressings and there was no time to fill them. Emma saw a student looking slightly green when Mr Samson plunged a hand into a bloody mass that had once been a good functioning kidney so she beckoned him and asked if he'd mind filling some drums and taking them to the sterilising unit.

His relief was overwhelming, his help considerable and work went on through the long night, through a rosy dawn, with each surgeon taking any case that presented at his table, even if it had nothing to do with his special branch of surgery. There was time for nothing but trolleys, and instruments, shouted requests over the noise of the temperamental diathermy machine and an ever-present need for more swabs, more gloves, more gowns. The day staff came on with two fresh surgical teams, the wet set was stripped and reconstructed, the theatre washed down in half an hour and the new teams were in business.

Emma felt as if she had been boiled in her own steriliser. She caught up her books and went wearily into the corridor. I need a bath more than food, she thought, but she was hungry, too. She passed the bush of mock orange and picked three fine sprays. In the dining room she saw the night staff from the other theatres, staffed by other hospitals. We all look the same today: tired, drained and unattractive. What a lot of wrecks! They sat limply drinking tea and waiting for the meal to be ready.

'Don't you know there's a war on?' asked one of the kitchen staff who was late on duty and bad-tempered.

'We guessed,' said a normally sultry blonde from a very aristocratic family who now looked like the model for a 'before beauty treatment' advert. 'We have been up all night,' she added with commendable reticence.

Another Senior Nurse pushed greasy hair back from her face and gave up the struggle to pin on a cap. 'This is only the beginning,' she said. 'Our troops landed in France and this lot were the ones they thought could travel. They kept the really badly wounded in base camps and another convoy came in just as I passed reception.'

Emma ate cottage pie and cabbage, enjoying nothing but becoming less hungry. The square of jam sponge was better and she had two helpings, her body greedily absorbing the sugar energy. In the nurses' home the open windows let in clean sunshine and the birds sang as if the summer was full of peace and promise. Emma closed the curtains to shut it out and sank into a deep sleep edged with a mourning crëpe of dread.

The men with half their leg muscles shot away . . . what would they do? The ones with pieces of metal lodged so dangerously close to vital centres that they couldn't be moved, how would they live? 'At least nobody died on the table,' she murmured as she closed her eyes again.

6

'I could do wound dressings with my eyes shut.' said Bea. 'I seem to do nothing but scrub my hands, soak them in sublimate and swab away bits of uniform.'

'At least you know what you are going to see,' said Emma. 'The last convoy came straight from the boats and aircraft.'

The swinging efficiency of the first two nights and days had swayed under the impact of the next convoy. Emma heard trolley wheels while Mr Samson was tidying up some lacerations and the last of the daytime convoy had been tucked up in bed after surgery. They all hoped for a slack night, and the trolley wheels had as much comfort as the wheels of the tumbrils going to the guillotine.

The first case came in at once, straight from the ambulance, with saline drip swinging from an orderly's hand. The instrument trolleys were ready and Emma went into the annexe to help prepare the patient as he was restless and in obvious pain. The junior nurse looked helplessly at the blood-soaked trousers revealed as she pulled down the blanket. His pulse was fast and thready, he was very shocked and his eyes had the lacklustre of a rabbit caught in a snare. He's quite beautiful, thought Emma. 'No, Nurse, don't attempt to undress him. He's bleeding and they are rushing blood along as quickly as they can. We'll cut away his clothes when he's under.' He lay like a young Greek, not the dark Greeks of modern Athens, but a classical, curly-haired Adonis of myth and legend.

The anaesthetist drew up the thiopentone into a

syringe and the junior nurse stood back, hoping that Dewar would cope. The man looked up and winced. 'I'm scared,' he whispered. Emma took his hand and held it tightly. 'That's better. Don't leave me, will you?' She smoothed the damp hair from his brow and knelt by the trolley, her face close to his. He half-smiled as she watched his face, and the fear dissolved into dimness and oblivion as the drug took effect. Emma told the nurse to hold his jaw and took out the scissors. The anaesthetist nodded when she looked at him for permission to continue, and she neatly cut the side seams of the trousers. The shirt was stuck down too and she reached for a swab of warm saline to sponge it free. As she gently prised the shirt away, she felt something give and the bleeding began again.

'He's bleeding,' she said. 'We ought to have the surgeon in here.'

'I'm setting up blood now,' said the anaesthetist. 'Carry on. He might be all right. It has to come off if they are to do anything.' Already, blood seeped over the edge of the trolley. The wet shirt came away, and she saw what lay under it. 'Get the surgeon!' she called, not daring to look away from the swab that now controlled the bleeding.

'I'm here,' said Guy. She had sensed a figure in the doorway and now knew he had been there all the time. She held the emergency dressing in place until the man was on the table and called for the instrument trolley to be brought in and the diathermy to be ready with a sealing probe. The Senior Nurse came quickly, shaking antiseptic fluid from her gloves and took over. Emma went back to check that all was ready for the next case and then watched as Guy swabbed and cut and tied off bleeding points or seared them with the diathermy. Only then did anyone realise the extent of the damage. The handsome boy lay under the face mask and his shoulders and body were untouched above the line of blood.

'What is it, Guy? It looks a bloody mess from here,' called Mr Samson.

'They shot off his balls,' said Guy. 'And took off the tops of his thighs.' His face was hidden by his mask but his eyes were angry. 'Tie, Nurse! Not that, you idiot! Thin catgut and then the diathermy again.' He threw one sodden swab on the floor and the smoke from the coagulating needle smelled like the searing of a horse's hoof by a red-hot shoe.

Emma went back to lay another trolley. She dropped a bowl on the stone floor and sensed rather than heard the expletives of the men intent on their work. She controlled her shaking hands and completed the trolley. Oh, God! This is getting worse. How can we cope? What if one of the surgeons lost his nerve as she had nearly done? She had no responsibility for the men's recovery. She could only serve and comfort. Now, she could comfort. She had smiled at the motto of the Home on the Downs in Bristol, *Loves Serves* but it was still viable here.

The blackout curtains were dull with steam. There had been no timber for good shutters and the heavy black material was losing its colour. The floors were sound but basic and the outlet fans did little to take away excess steam. She reached up to an inconvenient shelf for a jar of mercurochrome. It was a bad theatre if one looked at the planning; badly sited, badly built and inadequately finished. And I love it, she decided. I love everything about it. The staff, the work, and the feeling that I am able to give something back to these men.

She brought the used trolley out and cleared the instruments. The anaesthetic nurse asked for more sterile canulae as the vein had collapsed in the next patient and Tony Goldwater had to cut down and stitch in a fresh one. 'What is he?' asked Emma.

'Internal haemorrhage, Dr Goldwater said.'

'Clamps,' muttered Emma. 'Whose table?'

'Mr Franklin.'

Emma looked into the theatre. The boy lay peacefully on the trolley, ready to be taken to the ward. Guy was writing on the chart and the porter held the blood bottle aloft. The sleeping face gave no hint of the agony to come when he learned what had happened. Emma drew the blanket higher and when Guy glanced up he saw tears soaking her mask.

'I'll need clamps next,' he said briskly. 'Put in some long intestinal forceps, Nurse.'

'It's all on the trolley, Mr Franklin,' she said clearly. She checked that the floor was clean and that no used swabs lurked to upset the swab count if this was to be deep surgery, and at half-past four Mr Samson stopped the anaesthetist from inducing another patient.

'If we don't have a break, we'll do more harm than good,' he said. 'This lot has been a bugger.' He sent a message along to the canteen to make sure that food was ready, and dismissed the nurses first with the other surgical team. 'Tell my wife I'm almost ready,' he said, then sank into a chair in the surgeons' room.

He took off his cap and boots and Emma handed him a large clean towel. 'Thank you, Nurse. A shower will do me more good than food.'

'But you will eat, sir?'

'Yes, I'll be along or my wife will be on my tail. Tell her ten minutes, Nurse. There's nothing that can't wait for three quarters of an hour. Can you be ready by then without busting a gut?' Emma nodded and smiled. He was bone weary but even the conviction that he hadn't saved the life of his last patient did nothing to stop him considering his staff. 'Take her away, Guy, and make her have some food. She's had some nasty shocks tonight, too.'

She saw that Guy was waiting for her and she slipped off her theatre shoes and gown. The corridors were teeming with people. 'Oh, not another convoy!' she said.

'No, this is the lot we patched up yesterday, going north, but it means more coming in tomorrow. What am I saying? It *is* tomorrow.' The scent of mock orange filled the air. 'That's good.' He paused to breathe in the perfume and Emma picked another sprig. 'It seems impossible that something as white and pure as this could be here after all that carnage,' Guy said, and his voice was softer. He pulled her into his arms and rested his face against her hair, and she knew that he was even more tired than she had suspected.

'You were wonderful,' she said. 'It must have been terrible. Eye surgery is so much more refined than this . . .'

'Butchery? Is that how it seemed?'

'Anything but that,' she said. 'Guy, I'm sorry.'

'Sorry?'

'I know how you must have felt the night I couldn't give any comfort to the man who lost an eye.' She made to walk on, twisting the spray between her fingers, but he pulled her towards the dark shadow by the bush and his mouth was hard on hers. It held a fierce need, a desperation that cried for understanding and a wanting that went beyond physical contact, and she held him close and gave kiss for kiss until he as suddenly pushed her away and bent to pick up the crushed flowers.

'Such beauty, gone so soon,' he said, and she knew that it had nothing to do with the flowers, but was a requiem for the lost manhood of a soldier.

The canteen was nearly empty. They were the last teams to be served and the women behind the heated trolleys were clearing up after the last batch. Guy collected bowls of soup and hunks of National bread and they sandwiched Spam fritters in the bread, surprised that they were hungry. The tea was only slightly stewed and when Mr Samson arrived, he joined them, looking as fresh as a man starting an early morning list. A pile of magazines lay on the table. 'My wife brings them in. I don't know when she thinks we might read them but they could fill five minutes when we pause for breath.' He watched Guy open one and added hastily, 'They aren't mine; we have droves of Americans through the house and they leave them.' Guy grinned and Mr Samson laughed. 'All right, I do look at the pictures.'

The middle page fell open. A girl sprawled across a fur rug wearing a filmy black garment, black stockings and shoes. She lay on her front with the curve of her breast showing full and inviting through the thin fabric. 'Varga Girls, sir?' said Guy. He chuckled. 'I see the artist has a curious and novel slant on anatomy.' He looked at Emma, who was blushing. 'Ah, do you see a resemblance to someone we know? Now where did I last see a girl in black? It was so long ago. At least a hundred years.'

'I have to go back and get trolleys laid up for you,' she said, but her lips twitched and her eyes held the message that he seemed to need. She peeped into the ward to see if Bea was there but saw her scurrying down the ward pushing a dressing trolley. The ward was full to bursting and it looked as if the very ill men had stayed there for nursing instead of being sent north to make room for more casualties. The white bandages were stark against red blankets. Some lay flat with drip needles in their arms, and one bed was surrounded by screens from which shone a bright light. Bea pushed the screens apart and pushed the trolley through. Emma caught sight of blood on the sheets and turned away. It was no time for a social call.

The theatre was clean and the nurses were busy filling drums to make a full load for the autoclave. Emma laid up two trolleys and went to the anaesthetic room to see the notes. The Senior Staff Nurse sighed and went to scrub yet again, wondering if her hands would ever recover and be soft again.

One case after another seemed to become one huge long operation with no further dramatic moments, and it was a shock to be hustled off-duty by the day staff. Work had become obsessional; an indispensable part of existence with any life outside the steamy department an illusion.

'Are you going to bed after breakfast . . . dinner or whatever it is at half-past eight or nine in the morning?' asked Guy.

'I know how you feel,' said Emma. She lifted drooping eyelids to his tired face.' I feel like death, too, but if I go to bed too soon, I'll wake early and be tired tonight.'

'Come for a walk and we'll find a peaceful spot on the common,' he said. 'I need you, Emma.' He looked uncertain but the raw grief was still there, wanting solace.

Emma took a deep breath. 'Give me an hour to eat and have a bath and I'll meet you by the gate.'

At least she felt clean again and Guy was already waiting at the gate. Emma walked faster. The sun was hot even at this hour and early bees explored the opening flowers, unmoved by wars or human incompetence. Guy glanced with approval at the spotless cotton dress and she smiled. They walked along the road and on the Heath through gates open to receive more Army ambulances, and lorries full of stores. 'Not us,' said Emma. 'All our wards are full. I checked.'

'How is Bea?'

'I haven't seen her to exchange more than a few words. She seems to be Queen Bee of dressings. She was up to her elbows in gore.'

'Weren't we all?'

Emma didn't reply. There was no need for words, no energy for talking. They had shared last night, shared the same despair, the same elation, the same strain. Talking could come later. She looked at his profile. After this they might stay together or move on and meet maybe in the future; that is, if they had a future to which the other came briefly when old friends gathered and old times were discussed. They might never talk about any of the drama through which they were living. It went too deep. Maybe too deep to bond them together after it was all over?

'I love the smell of bracken in all its stages,' said Guy.

'So do I.' Emma picked a light green frond from the top of a new spring shoot. It curled back over her finger. 'It reminds me of a sea horse,' she said. 'I used to imagine that they were fairy sea horses riding on the Downs at home, and when they grew bigger, they came over my head and we played hide and seek among them.'

'Do you always pick things? You picked those flowers last night.' He glanced at her. 'And we dropped them.'

'I always pick flowers,' she said. She bent to pick a few yellow, daisy-like flowers that grew like a weed on the Heath. 'Ragwort. At home they are covered with stripy caterpillars in summer.'

'I don't believe you.'

'It's true!' She looked up, startled. Who was he to

say it wasn't so? He was quietly laughing. ' I don't suppose you've ever noticed, but that's no excuse for calling me a liar,' she said. She was smiling, too.

He kissed her gently. 'I'm sure that even the sea horses are real to little girls wandering free on the Downs among the harebells and the gorse.'

'You know about harebells?'

'I know about many things, "about the wind on the Heath, brother, all good things", as the gypsy said.'

'We have gypsies, too. They have a settlement by the river. Not tinkers; the real ones, the Romany. They sell flowers and pegs and trade with horses. My grandfather used to trade with them. He liked gypsies.'

They sat by the pond made from a gravel pit and watched the dragon-flies under a willow. A few water-lilies lay on the surface of the water looking like pale hands, pleading. 'You aren't thinking of picking those, are you?'

'I was hoping you'd be a gentleman and go and fetch them,' she said.

'You haven't seen films with leeches in?'

'What's that got to do with it?'

'Leeches! I saw enough blood last night. I don't want to watch my own being drained away. I thought you knew everything. You must have leeches in the stew ponds at home?'

'You know about stew ponds? How they freeze in winter and have tadpoles in spring?'

'We have them at home too, but you'll see them in time.'

'I know nothing about you, Mr Franklin,' she said lightly.

'I live in a Dorset town with my parents. My father is a local GP and my mother paints.'

'You sound as if you like them.'

'I do. I think you will, too.'

'I hate mine. I had a letter this morning saying that my mother wants me to give up nursing and take a boring job in Bristol, where she can keep me under her thumb and grumble without stopping.'

He held her tight. 'You can't. I love you, Emma. I can't lose you now.'

'I've fought all the battles that I shall ever fight with her and I doubt if I shall visit them often again. My real home has always been the Island.'

'Would you come away with me, Emma? Leave even your Island? Marry me?'

'Yes,' she said, and her eyes filled with tears. 'Oh, yes, Guy, if you want me.'

'But you'd like to be married there?' She nodded. 'Could your aunt arrange it when we have some leave?'

'I'm sure she would.' Emma caught her breath. His lips made her feel as light as the breeze and she looked into the face of the man she knew she loved beyond life. 'But we can't marry yet. They'd turn me out if I married someone from the same unit. You know the rule and I want to finish my training.'

'Bea got married.'

'Not to a medic in the same hospital.'

'We'll keep it a secret, but I want to marry you.'

'It will take time to arrange,' said Emma. The last of her inhibitions made her blush and he lifted her face to look at her expression. 'We can't wait, can we Guy? Everything is so uncertain that we may not have much time.' She was amazed at her own calm and the wonderful tenderness in his eyes told her that she was right. This would last for ever but it must begin now. She took his head in her hands and brought it to her breast. 'I'll be here when it's all over, if we last that long, and before we can marry, there is now.'

He kissed her fiercely and they clung together,

their desire tinged with sadness at what had gone before that night, but the tide of love softened their pain and engulfed all Emma's fear.

They held each other in love and exhaustion. 'I thought you had doubts about being tied,' he said at last. He grinned. 'You'll have to marry me now.'

'That was before,' she said. 'Now, I am completely happy.'

'Completely?' He traced her lips with a finger as if to etch her face in his memory, with every detail correct. 'We have each other now, for ever, so smile, my darling. There is still a trace of sadness there under that happiness. It's the same expression I saw when you picked that spray of flowers. Do you regret this?'

'No, I love you more than I dreamed possible, and we have some things to share that other people will never understand. It's all wrapped up in our love. I shall pick a spray of syringa every year at this time even when everyone says it fades quickly in water and isn't worth the effort. It will remind me of the night I grew up and you will remember the boy last night.'

'What will your Aunt Emily say? Will she approve?'

Emma laughed. 'She'll ask about the treacle and get on with a huge piece of crochet she's making for my bottom drawer.' She brushed the leaves from her skirt and tried to smooth out the crumpled cotton.

'Treacle?'

'You'll have to ask her about that. Just tell her she was right.'

He took her in his arms again and they stood kissing among the high fronds of bracken until a wolf-whistle from the back of an Army truck told them that they were no longer hidden from the road. 'Back to sleep,' Guy said, 'and tonight,